GUNS N' BOYS

Swamp Blood - Book 4

Love is so...

K.A. Merikan

Acerbi & Villani Ltd.

Editing by Kelly Hartigan (Xterra Web)
http://editing.xterraweb.com/

Cover Design by
Natasha Snow
http://natashasnow.com

Table of Contents

Chapter 1 - Mark

If Mark were asked for the definition of 'dive bar' he'd just describe Chuck's Bar & Grill. He'd try to go in later, but it got so loud whenever someone opened the door that he preferred to stay outside for now, even if the air made him sweat from the heat.

At least he had a bit of entertainment, courtesy of Fred, the knight in shining armor Mark had been waiting for all along. Handsome, helpful, smart, with his own business, Fred was just the kind of reliable older guy who could give him a new start in life. Even if he was a bit boring. And twenty years older than Mark.

How long 'til you make it here? Fred asked in a short text message, complete with a smiling emoticon. Mark was ashamed that some days he made so little progress in his journey, but it was a long way from north to south, and not everyone was keen on taking a teenage hitchhiker.

Mark's last ride left him in this middle of nowhere, as the guy was going back to his wife.

I'm in the area. Probably a few more days. Saying good-bye to my life of no-good ;). Mark lit himself a cigarette

and sat down on a wooden bench just outside the bar. Even the smoke couldn't kill the stench of stale water coming from somewhere close. The air was so humid his lungs felt heavy.

Bummer... I hoped to invite you for a nice dinner with friends this weekend, answered Fred.

Oh yeah? Gonna have some nice grilled sausage? Mark snorted and pulled out his earphones when the roar of a bike drowned out his music.

He looked up from his beat-up phone to see a tall, muscled man dismount a beastly-looking sport bike. He was far too good-looking for the dirty, smelly dump behind Mark's back. It was almost as if the guy drove here all the way from the set of a music video to pull Mark away from his new life at Fred's side.

The phone beeped again, but Mark was too preoccupied to care about the reply as the biker god moved his way. He took off his helmet, revealing a shaggy bush of dark blond hair, and as he got closer, Mark also noticed stubble that he'd love to rub his hands all over. His muscular arms were tattooed and dusted with blond hairs, and he had several inches on Mark. When their eyes met for a short glance, Mark's heart skipped a beat. Would he stand a chance? Even straight-ish guys rarely refused a BJ.

The biker missed a step, and his eyes darted away, only to return to Mark's face a second later. "What?" he muttered in a thick Southern accent.

Mark slipped his tongue from between his lips as his breathing grew shallow from the proximity of that strong body. Even the Louisiana heat wasn't too much anymore. Not many of the guys Mark had scored on the way here were this attractive. "You alone?" he eventually asked, stuffing his phone deep into his pocket, along with Fred's words. The boring life could wait a few more days.

The blond frowned, and even in the faint light from the bar, Mark could see his eyes were as blue as the sky over a tropical island. Fuck, he loved blonds.

"What's it to you?" the biker grumbled and glanced at the bar, but Mark could swear that when he turned back his head, he took half a second to check Mark out.

The air in Mark's throat was so hot it burned him on the inside, but he couldn't stop himself from going for his prize. "I'd suck you off, if you want. It's fifty dollars, but I'd take thirty from *you*."

Mark watched the pretty piece of man with his eyes wide open, but a part of him was ready to run if needed. It wouldn't be the first time, but this guy was too good to miss out on. It was always better to regret doing something than not going for it at all.

The biker took a deep breath that made his chest look wider under the white T-shirt he was wearing. Mark could swear even the guy's nipples got more visible.

"Do you live here?" he asked in the end, not moving by an inch.

Mark exhaled, his whole body softening with relief. The biker had taken the bait. He was afraid someone might know, but Mark wouldn't tell anyone. He prided himself with how discreet he could be when he wanted. "No. Just passing through," he whispered, and it seemed that even with the background of loud music coming from the bar, the biker could understand him easily.

"Let's go somewhere else," the man said and turned toward his bike.

Mark had to bite his lips not to grin too hard at the outline of Blondie's wide shoulders. Truth be told, he'd suck a guy like him for free, but every opportunity to make an extra few bucks was good. He now had less than ten dollars in his wallet, and if he wanted to reach Fred's home within the week and start sleeping in a normal bed, he'd have to step up his game.

He nodded, even though the biker couldn't see him anymore, and followed, throwing his backpack over his shoulder.

The guy put on a helmet and pointed at the back of his bike. "Hop on." The tension between them was getting thicker than the damp air, and right now, it was Mark who would spend his last ten bucks on fucking this guy. Maybe they'd go to his home, and Mark would get to experience that whole amazing body on his naked skin? It would be the perfect ending to a really shitty day.

He grinned when his knees brushed the backs of the man's thighs, and he stole a moment to sniff the leather vest with a picture of a coffin and a monstrous hand sticking out of it on the back. The patches read Coffin Nails MC Louisiana, and it only made Mark hornier. This guy was a member of a real outlaw club that recently made the news in connection to a drug war on the West Coast. A real man.

"Hold on tight," the biker mumbled from behind the helmet and revved the engine before driving off the gravel so fast that little rocks hit the back of Mark's legs. He grabbed the rear of the seat and took a big gulp of air as the metal beast between his legs awakened and rushed down the empty road, straight into the darkness beneath the trees. Mark closed his eyes for a moment, his heart beating like crazy when he dared to look ahead again past the muscular arm and at the faint ray of light ahead.

He had to remind himself that his clients were rarely like the guy in front of him and more often like the creepy uncle wanting you to sit on their knee on Christmas Day. He couldn't have any hot guy sway him from his long-term goal, no matter how blond his hair or how blue his eyes. None of that would matter tomorrow when Mark had no money to buy breakfast.

They drove for a good twenty minutes, and Mark's dick was at half mast by the time they stopped off the road

in the middle of nowhere. He swallowed hard and pushed his cheek against the stranger's shoulder, brushing it against the hot leather of his vest.

"And what will you do to me now?" he teased, even hornier with no one around.

"You know what we'll do," the biker grumbled as he took off his helmet and dismounted, propping his bike behind some bushes so that it wouldn't be visible from the road. He was still just as handsome as Mark thought at first glance. "Come on, we'll be alone here." He took a deep breath and went down a narrow path to a white, boxy building that looked like roadside restrooms.

Mark bit his lip and followed him with a broad smile, inhaling the warm air as they moved through a patch of tall grass. "You are insanely hot," he whimpered, following the biker like a hungry puppy. His mouth was already watering at the thought of opening those worn jeans and accepting whatever monster was hiding inside.

The biker looked over his shoulder with a surprised expression that quickly turned into a cocky grin that made Mark melt. "I work out."

Mark ran up to him and made a point of squeezing the biker's bicep. It was so thick and hard. "I can feel that. I imagine there's a lot of steam to release with a body like this."

The guy took a deep breath and pulled Mark into the little building smelling of stale urine and concrete. "You wouldn't believe how horny I am."

Mark sank to his knees right there into the grime that hurt him even through the denim of his jeans, but he didn't care. He hooked his fingers through the belt loops of the man's jeans and pulled him closer. "Show me."

The guy leaned against the wall. "You are over eighteen, right?" he rasped, and once Mark's eyes adjusted to the darkness, the biker made the prettiest picture with his hair wild around his face when he looked down.

Mark could barely look away. Unable to speak, he just nodded, like he always did whenever someone cared to ask. These were the good guys, and he didn't want it to weigh on their conscience that they screwed a sixteen-year-old. It wasn't as if anyone would know.

The biker's dick was already tenting his pants when he pulled out his phone. The way his stomach moved under the tight T-shirt made Mark want to stick his head under the fabric and kiss the hard abs. He wanted to do so many things to this guy that he couldn't focus anymore.

The biker unbuckled his belt and slid his fingers into Mark's curly hair, pulling him closer to his crotch and closer to that hot, masculine scent Mark just wanted to rub all over himself.

He pulled the jeans lower and looked up into the faint light of the cell phone looming over him. His stomach turned. "Are you filming this?"

"Yeah, I'm gonna jerk off to this so many times. So fucking hot." The flush on the biker's face and the dimples hidden in his stubble made him look almost cute, but there was nothing sweet about his words.

Mark groaned and reached up to try to push the phone away. "You're paying for a BJ, not copyrights."

The biker's grip on Mark's hair got stronger. "Just suck my fucking dick."

Mark's lips pressed tightly together. That was a line he wouldn't cross. There was always a chance he'd land a modeling job through Fred's business, and then what? Suddenly this recording emerges and destroys his career?

"So put the phone away. I'm not doing it otherwise."

"You don't fucking tell me what to do," the guy snarled, becoming less hot and more menacing by the second.

Mark wouldn't take this bullshit. "Let go, or I'll fucking bite you!"

The biker painfully twisted his grip in Mark's hair. "You'll get what you wanted, and it goes both ways, so open the fuck up and stop complaining, you little whiny shit!"

Mark shuddered, looking around for some kind of weapon, but he could hardly see anything in the thick darkness illuminated only by the faint blue light of the phone. His mind went blank, only to suddenly rush forward when he heard voices outside.

A laugh. Words in a soft, unknown language. Without thinking, Mark screamed. Even if the people outside ran away, not wanting to get involved, at least he could hope to distract the hot-as-hell asshole.

"Help! Let go of me!" Mark screamed as loud as he could. "Please! Help!"

The biker pulled him up with so much strength it almost broke Mark's neck. He put his hand over Mark's mouth and hissed. "Shut up."

But the sound of footsteps only grew louder, and just as Mark's skin broke out in goose bumps, a tall, broad-shouldered shadow stepped inside.

"The fuck you think you're doing, huh?" he asked with a clearly foreign accent, spreading his big arms to the sides. Another person's hand pulled at his shoulder, but the man wouldn't have it and shrugged it off.

"Piss off!" the biker yelled and dropped his phone, too focused on pulling up his pants.

Beardie came closer, even taller than the blond, but not nearly as menacing with soft lines on his body and large eyes that Mark already knew as smiley. Only as he walked, Mark noticed he was swaying a bit too much, as if he had just had a few shots.

The other stranger shook his head and combed back his long black hair. "What are you doing?" he asked his friend, even though Mark could distinctly feel the burn of the man's dark gaze on his own skin. It was the same guy who had bought him a pack of condoms a few hours ago.

But Mark was too busy with the fallen phone to care. Anger bubbled up in his chest as he thought of the biker recording him without permission. What a freaking douchebag. And for that phone, Mark could eat in diners for a week. He snatched it before anyone noticed, especially the biker, who was too busy eyeing the new arrivals.

Beardie pointed at Mark. "We have to help him," he said with a slur to his words.

Just as Mark was about to sneak away on his hands and knees, the biker grabbed his hair again and pulled him back into the darkness. "He's not going anywhere. This is none of your business!"

Mark looked at the two strangers again and tried to get away from the biker's clutches. He didn't deserve this! Hadn't he been nice all along? "Fuck off, you pig!"

The longhaired foreigner shook his head and spoke with a voice as smooth as steel. "Let him go."

"Who the fuck do you think you are?" the biker hissed.

"I can deal with this, Dom, step back," Beardie said drunkenly and took another uncertain step toward Mark. "You better let him go, or... else."

Dom put his palm over his face and let it slide down as a pained groan escaped his lips.

The biker grabbed Mark around the neck and pulled him back so hard it yanked the ground from beneath Mark's feet. "Or else what? I'm taking him, so fuck off!"

Mark yelped when a gun flashed in the darkness. Beardie pulled it out from a holster by his belt and pointed it at the biker, but in the state he was in, anyone present was a possible target. "Or I'll shoot your brains out!"

The biker instantly let go, just to pull out a gun of his own and point it back at Beardie.

It didn't even take a second for the third man to pull out a black beast of a gun and shove Beardie behind his back with a stern expression.

"This ends. Now," he growled.

Chapter 2 - Domenico

A few hours before

Blood stung Domenico's eyes as he blinked away the red film that clouded his vision. Seth's feet were dangling inches above the crimson puddle, his arms tense and his joints unnaturally stretched. He was like a broken bird, laid open, with skin crisscrossed by open wounds. His chest was barely moving at this point, but the dark, beautiful eyes stubbornly refused to cloud over. He kept looking straight at Domenico, begging for help when his tongueless mouth couldn't anymore. But Domenico was powerless.

"You really thought you could just piss away all that I have taught you?" Luigi Tassa hissed, circling Seth's body and sending Domenico glares of pure disappointment. "That you can choose this piece of meat over your own father?"

Seth's skin erupted with goose bumps the moment Luigi put his blade against the body.

Domenico spat a yell, but it came out muffled through the thick gag of cloth. He yanked at the cuffs, hands numb from constantly pulling. His thumbs were out of their

joints, radiating with pain, and yet he still couldn't pull them through the tightly closed metal rings. The pipes he was cuffed to were too thick to break, but Domenico smashed the back of his head against them so hard his brain rattled. He wanted to die first. Luigi wouldn't see any reason to hurt Seth anymore once he'd be gone.

"Oh, no you don't," came a raspy voice from behind. It took Domenico a moment to recognize it. Vincente grabbed Dom's hair and held his head in place.

Luigi drove the blade into Seth's skin, yet not deep enough to really quicken Seth's death. The muffled cry Seth let out shattered Dom's heart more efficiently than any bullet could.

"I knew you'd be weak," Luigi went on. "That's why I never told you that you were mine."

Domenico cried out, stabbed in the chest by the two blades that could hurt him most. He wheezed, flinched, but kept struggling against the cuffs until they cut into his flesh. He would hack away skin and muscle if that was what it took to free himself. Seth was still alive. Even badly hurt, he could be taken care of. Domenico wouldn't let anyone take him away. They would flee, and with that firm belief ingrained in the center of his brain, he pulled through the agony of the metal destroying his hands.

Luigi squinted at him. "This is a lesson for you, Domenico. A man like you cannot have love, or it will be used against him." He threw away the knife and pulled out a gun. Not just any gun, Dom's Beretta.

Domenico stopped breathing, completely frozen, his eyes fixed on Seth's painfully neutral face. All traces of hope were gone from it at this point, and through the layer of sweat and blood, it almost looked serene, as if Seth had finally moved on, leaving Dom all alone with the horror of what was happening.

The bullet went straight into Seth's temple, and like in the most disgusting of cartoons, his brown eyes popped

out of his skull, tearing up with blood, as brain and bone exploded from the other temple.

Domenico screamed, grabbing at nothing as thick air, drenched with the coppery scent of blood, poured into his lungs. It was dark. Something was holding him down, and he fought it until he managed to get his numb hands free. Only now, his senses were fully kicking in, and he realized the air wasn't thick with a metallic aroma. All he sensed now was the damp smell of cotton, mold, cologne…

Seth's hot, beloved body was alive next to him, sleeping soundly in a T-shirt despite the heat of Louisiana in July.

"Dom? What is it?" Seth muttered groggily and slowly turned his face to Dom, but kept his eyes closed. Even with the messy beard he had grown in the past months, he was still the sweetest image Dom wanted to always wake up to.

Domenico took a deep, hollow breath and dropped back down to the bed, straight into the permanent dip the previous occupant of their apartment had left in the mattress. He slid his arms around Seth and pushed his face against his furry neck. He was barely suppressing the shaking in his limbs as he traced his lover's warm skin with his fingertips. He slowly calmed down, recognizing its softness, the familiar scent of fresh sweat, and the sea that somehow always clung to Seth's skin at night.

"Must be a dog outside," he lied, not daring to look up, like a little boy afraid of staring death in the face. As if this all turned out to be a dream, and he'd wake up holding a lifeless corpse.

Seth groaned and turned his back on Dom again. "I'm barely sleeping in this heat."

Domenico gritted his teeth as Seth twisted out of his tight embrace, leaving him with just the image of a warm, wide-shouldered body. It was just another rejection shoved into Dom's face, but he shook his head and slipped out of bed, grateful for how cool the wooden floor felt under his bare feet. There was faint light coming from underneath the blinds. He could as well let off some steam if Seth was still tired.

As his eyes adjusted to the change of brightness, he took in the narrow bed, the white wardrobe they got at Target, and the two chairs they used as nightstands. There was hardly any space left to walk in the bedroom, not enough for him to exercise without yanking Seth completely out of the sleep that was slowly aiding his recovery from that horrible night three months ago, the same one that invaded Dom's dreams and choked him in his sleep for at least one night each week.

Despite Seth's injuries healing, nothing had been the same since then. His broken ribs should be fine now, yet Seth still complained about pain and problems with breathing. His right hand, where Vincente's knife had pierced it was still weak, and any time Seth dropped something, he'd get so agitated Dom found it hard to watch. The cut in his cheek had been one of the reasons for him to grow a beard, and to Dom's utter frustration, Seth wouldn't let him touch or see the scars where his cut-off nipples had been. Even though Vincente was as dead as the alligator skull hanging in their living room, the pain he'd inflicted was a continuous presence in Dom and Seth's relationship. All Domenico wanted was to have his happy, sexy boyfriend back. It almost seemed that the more Seth healed, the more frequent and intense Domenico's nightmares got, and each one chipped at his soul. Piece by piece.

Moving quickly warmed his body despite the morning chill, and the rays of bright sunshine caressed his skin in a way so pleasant he considered staying on the road. But as much as he wanted to, the locals were already snooping too much around the foreigners living with a beautiful blonde woman, even without seeing the regime Domenico put himself and Dana through every single day.

Dana kept one step behind, even when he silently challenged her to a faster pace. She was efficient like a gun, but not yet precise enough to be considered flawless. Her life was still a bit of a mystery, as Dom was pretty sure parts of her story must have been lies. But was it the piloting a helicopter in South America or that she went all the way to Vienna trying to find him when she was just eighteen? He had no idea, as her face was devoid of true emotion, and he was pretty sure she was far on the sociopath spectrum. What he did know was that Dana had a minor obsession with him and was eager to soak up any information she could get. As long as she didn't try to flay his face and wear the skin as a mask, he didn't mind the worship in her eyes. Having her around was a bit like owning a watchdog, so Domenico couldn't complain too much.

"Are we going to be out long?" Dana asked after about half an hour.

"Yes," was all he could force out without gritting his teeth. Even despite running at full speed through the park grounds now, he was getting increasingly agitated. He didn't need those dreams on top of all the problems he already had. He'd been so patient, and yet even with the best intentions, his patience was slowly running out.

Why wouldn't Seth talk to him anymore? Sure, they'd exchange sentences about each other's days, Domenico complimented the food Seth managed to prepare, but as Seth's body was still healing, he refused to participate in any exercise, and every time Domenico tried

to get closer to him, it just wouldn't happen. How long was Domenico to sleep in the same bed with his own fiancé but be banned from touching him? He did masturbate, which helped, but at the same time, each *no* sounded more and more like genuine lack of interest. Did Seth despise Domenico for what he did to Vincente? Seth's ribs should have healed by now, and there were no blow jobs either, as Seth said the scar in his cheek was still tender. And even though Domenico greedily watched each smile on Seth's face, he could almost touch the wall between them, and it was driving him mad. He was not a fucking *castrato.*

It took a good three hours to wear out Dana, and physical activity always helped Dom let off some steam as well, so as they were heading back home in the morning sunshine, Domenico tried to keep his mind clear. Another day. A clean slate. Soon enough they would be heading to Mexico anyway, and maybe the trip would give Seth a push into expressing himself better.

They were approaching the house when Dom got a text message from Seth. *Don't come in yet. Wait on the porch.*

He stopped and looked back at Dana before stripping off his shirt. He used it to wipe sweat off his skin and shrugged. "Did he break something?" he muttered, slowly sinking into a crouch.

"Why? What is it?" Dana frowned and instantly looked around, as if they were to be invaded any moment now. Her face was red from exhaustion, and it spilled over her tan.

"He asks us not to come in. I could use some water," said Dom as he gave up and sat on the asphalt in front of the tiny home in a row of mismatched but equally gray buildings. As much as he tried to keep up appearances, fatigue was getting to him.

A few minutes later, Seth opened the door and came out in a simple T-shirt and jogging bottoms, with a

cardboard box in his hands. Dom's gaze instantly darted to his lover's injured hand and saw the fingers trembling slightly.

He swallowed hard but his heart thumped in his chest, and he got up, approaching Seth. "What is it?" he asked.

"What day is it today?" Seth smiled, catching Dom's gaze.

Domenico frowned and shook his head. Was it Tuesday? Without a reason to keep tabs on the calendar, it fled his mind.

Dana pointed at the door and went inside when Seth nodded at her.

"It's your birthday." Seth leaned closer and placed a chaste kiss on Domenico's lips. It felt like the first one in forever.

Domenico drew in a sharp breath and pulled Seth closer, deepening the kiss, with his tongue sliding against the roof of Seth's mouth as their chests touched. Seth's breath tickled Dom's skin along with the hairs of Seth's beard. And for once, Seth didn't pull away right away, but opened his mouth wider. How much Dom would give for that invitation to be extended to his dick.

He nipped Seth's lip and brushed their foreheads together, holding on to Seth's warm nape. "Maybe we should hide in the bedroom for a little while then?"

Seth chuckled. "I thought you'd prefer to take a look at your gift." It seemed as if he wanted to take a step back, but Dom held on to his nape and wouldn't let him.

"Good, let's go there, and Dana can show herself out. Since it's my birthday," he muttered, giving her a low glance through the window.

Seth licked his lips and nodded. "I made a reservation for us at Chuck's later. I also thought we could go shopping. I wanted to pick up a few more things for the alligator hunt."

Domenico pulled away and threw his tank top to the ground. "Alligator, huh? That's pretty important."

"Yeah." Seth nodded as if he didn't notice the sarcasm and went inside, passing Dana on the way. "I wanted to make a birthday feast for you today, but I don't have all the equipment to catch the thing just yet, and I thought it would be half-assed to just buy the meat."

Domenico exhaled and shook his head, stepping away from the house. His veins were burning with the need to kill something. He could wrestle the fucking alligator if Seth wanted it so much. Would that make him lovable again?

Seth looked over his shoulder. "You don't want to see what I have for you?"

Domenico put his hands on his hips, taking three breaths, but eventually followed Seth, feeling grimmer by the second. "How did you know anyway?"

Even with the fucking beard and the size of a lumberjack, Seth looked as shy as the first time they had fucked, when he glanced down to the box with a half smile. "It's engraved inside the ring. The one that your mom gave you."

Domenico sighed and stepped closer, grabbing Seth's hand. His fingers sought the signet, which was still on the familiar, warm hand that now too frequently strayed away from Dom's. "Yeah, I remember."

Seth led him inside and they sat on the couch. He passed Dom the box and ran his hand through his slightly longish hair. Domenico thought it needed some grooming, but antagonizing his already withdrawn lover was the last thing he wanted. "It's nothing special, but it's what I could manage with the microwave..."

Domenico blinked. "Food? Did you make me a chocolate dick?" he asked with a small smile as he opened the box.

The cake inside looked a bit crude, topped off with sliced Snickers bars and bits of brownie, but the smell of chocolate was nice. Next to it stood a can of whipped cream and paper plates.

Seth snorted. "I should have thought about that, sorry. I know it's nothing like the ones I used to make, but I know you like sweets, and the store-bought stuff is mostly shit... Though I'm not sure how this turned out anyway..."

Domenico put his arm across Seth's shoulders and nuzzled his cheek, sniffing their cheap bath gel, which on Seth's skin somehow managed to smell sophisticated. "It's Snickers. Bound to be good."

Seth reached inside for a knife, and Dom's senses instantly sharpened, like they did every time Seth would hold anything deadly in his recovering hand. Slowly but steadily, Seth cut each of them a piece. The cake was a bit messy inside, with bits of meringue crumbling out, but at least it wasn't a fucking fried alligator, caught without a license.

Domenico wouldn't want any of *that* shit on his plate. "Looks good," he lied, still petting Seth's shoulder. Should he take a bath now, before Seth got grossed out by his sweaty body? It had been months of celibacy. No man could be that patient.

Seth smiled a bit wider and sprayed lots of whipped cream on both their plates. "I will make something better once I have a proper kitchen. It's not like we are going to stay here forever."

Dom could swear there was a hint of question in that last sentence. "I know, I hate it too," he said, digging in. The cake was gooey with caramel and chocolate, but he managed to scoop some on his fingers.

"I'm sorry we had to stay here because of me. I promise I'll be better in no time," Seth said before filling his mouth with cake.

Domenico pushed some into his own mouth as well, but even with the sweetness spreading in his mouth, his mind settled on Seth. "We should get you to a better doctor. You're young. You should be fine by now."

"I know. It's the ribs, but I'm sure I'll be fit to travel. You're probably sick of the beard as well, but we have to stay under the radar." Seth put the plate away after eating just one bite.

Domenico brushed his fingers through the soft, bushy hair on Seth's face. "Let's go to a doctor tomorrow. I'll arrange something."

"Can't we wait till next week or something?" Seth looked away but cuddled up closer.

Domenico picked up more of the cake, and he could swear it tasted better with each bite. "Why? You can't do all the things we used to do together."

"'Cause I know it will get better with time. I think the mind can influence the body a lot, and I just need to keep trying." He clenched and unclenched his fist over Dom's chest.

"But I had my ribs broken, and it shouldn't be a problem anymore. Why don't you let me feel them?"

"It's not like you're gonna feel much through the layer of fat." Seth laughed and trailed his fingers over Dom's ribs.

Domenico snorted. "Yeah, right—" He wanted to say something more, but the way Seth's touch made his skin explode with sensation stopped all and any further words from coming out of his mouth.

"Did you and Dana have fun?" Seth asked, and the question jarred with the way his fingers slid to Dom's stomach. Dana was the last thing on Domenico's mind right now.

"Fuck Dana. I'm more interested in you," he muttered, pushing away the cake. All his senses were

focused on the rough, warm touch of fingertips lazily dancing over his flesh.

"Maybe we could go on that alligator hunt together then? Would you like that?" Seth leaned closer and kissed Dom's ear.

Domenico scowled, but leaned into the touch, sighing with approval. "You want that?"

"Only if you promise to leave the killing to me this time." The heat of Seth's breath was like an additional set of fingers caressing his skin, and Dom's heart began pounding. How long had it been since they'd been close like this? Two weeks? Three?

Domenico groaned and pulled Seth's hand lower, to his cock that was filling at a rapid speed. He needed the touch, at least some skin against skin, if he couldn't have Seth the way he wanted to.

Seth sucked on Dom's earlobe and struggled with the button of Dom's shorts. "Is that a yes?"

Domenico rasped in agreement and ground his hips against Seth's hand, already overcome with red-hot need. He wanted to come down Seth's throat, lay down on him, hold on to his hair, and lick his sweat.

When Seth managed to slide his hand into Dom's pants and his thick fingers curled around Dom's dick, he knew he'd even promise to eat the fucking alligator. Raw if necessary. Seth left kisses down Dom's neck and pushed Dom's pants lower for better access, leaving any exposed skin on fire.

"Fuck..." Domenico closed his eyes and turned his body toward Seth's, sliding his arms around the big, cuddly chest. Just smelling him up close was enough to send Dom's mind up into the air.

Seth's hand started a slow and steady rhythm, and Dom wanted to fuck his fist just to make it faster. His imagination combined with the scent, dreaming up a concoction of the dirtiest imagery. Dom needed to fuck

Seth's tight ass so bad. There was a closeness to their sex, even at times when it was all about a quick raw fuck. The way Seth opened up to him, the way he moaned and whimpered when Dom pushed his dick inside was something Dom needed more than oxygen.

"I wanna do it," he whispered, slowly massaging the flesh of Seth's back through the T-shirt that seemed a permanent fixture on his lover's body. "How about that?"

"About what? About fucking?" Seth whispered and the moves of his hand quickened, even though he wasn't gripping as steadily as he used to.

Dom couldn't care less. He nodded fervently and squeezed Seth through his sweats, happy to find him just as hard as Dom himself was. "Yeah. I'd flip you over and rim you for half an hour. I'd eat your round, beautiful ass until you'd be begging me to push my cock in."

Seth groaned, and Dom knew that sound of arousal by heart. "Oh, fuck... You'd push it in hard, all sweaty and strong. I love you like that." Seth was losing his breath, and the way the usual wall around him slowly crumbled had Dom as horny as ever and on the verge of orgasm already.

"Yeah?" rasped Dom as he pulled out Seth's cock and pumped it gently. "I'll fuck you until I come inside, and then I'll fuck you again, because you're mine. I want this so bad..."

Even just holding Seth's cock in his hand, feeling it throb with heat, was as close to fucking as ever. "Yeah, bareback," Seth rasped, jerking Dom off at a furious pace.

Domenico hissed and shuddered as Seth dragged his fingers over the sensitive flesh below the head of his cock. He was sweating. He was coming with the image of Seth's ass trembling each time Dom slammed into him.

Seth murmured into Dom's neck, holding his other hand on Dom's tense stomach. "You're so ridiculously hot," he whispered, giving Dom that sense of validation that could string him along forever.

"Oh, fuck... so are you... I just..." Domenico leaned in and captured Seth's lips in a hard, demanding kiss. His head was pulsing with the waves of the recent orgasm, but even after coming, he was still as hungry for Seth as ever. He pulled up Seth's hand and lapped at the center of the palm while holding Seth's gaze.

"I know, I'm working on the grip," Seth whispered and half-closed his eyes, while slowly rocking his hips into the touch.

"Your grip's fine," rasped Domenico, swallowing down two of Seth's fingers and sucking up all of his own seed. The salty aroma bit at his tongue but was just too delicious to stop until Seth's hand was pristinely clean. "How about your hips? Are those fine, too?"

Seth swallowed, and his lips parted. "I... I mean—how?"

Domenico rolled off the sofa and pushed Seth's knees far apart before diving in toward the red, throbbing length of Seth's cock. It smelled of soap and arousal, which Dom could swear was the most beautiful scent on earth. "Fuck my mouth."

Seth stilled for a bubble-bursting moment, but his fingers slipped into Dom's hair, and he pulled Dom's head closer. His chest heaved and even though different from the way Seth used to be, he still presented the hottest picture with his cheeks reddened and tongue trailing his upper lip.

"You like that. You want to come down my throat and hold me down," whispered Domenico opened his lips, only to trace them with his tongue as obscenely as he could. He was still on fire. In need of more than a simple hand job.

"Yeah, I want you to swallow my load," Seth said, but it came out quiet, as if he were shy about it. He pulled Dom's head closer by the hair, the force sending tingles of arousal down Dom's body even after the orgasm.

Domenico moaned and brushed his teeth lightly up the length of Seth's cock, lapping at the thick vein on the underside. His mouth was watering. His throat relaxed, and all he wanted was that thick, lovely cock ramming in and stealing his breath. "Then make me swallow."

There it was. A familiar glint in Seth's dark eyes. It had been missing so often lately, yet Dom would never forget how it looked. Seth yanked Dom's head closer, making him swallow half his cock in one go, and didn't let go. Holding Dom's head in place, he rocked his hips up, pushing in farther and demanding entrance.

Domenico howled with pleasure, or at least tried, because it came out muffled, and judging from Seth's reaction, it sent vibrations all over his cock. He relaxed his throat further, and two thrusts later, the head finally invaded his throat, pushing its way through into his neck. He could almost cry with how good it felt.

"Fuck, yes!" Seth hissed, and fucked Dom's mouth so hard his balls slapped against Dom's chin. "Swallow it all…" The grip on Dom's hair tightened when Seth came, his cock throbbing between Dom's lips.

Domenico grabbed Seth's thighs, out of breath but holding on, not wanting to let a single drop of cum escape him. It was only after several seconds that he slowly withdrew, delighting in the way the fat dick retracted out of his mouth. Still, he kissed the tip and nuzzled the middle of his cock before burying his face in Seth's balls. He loved how they felt, smooth in their fleshy sheath, even with the fluff of pubic hair.

"You could get a better boyfriend than me with those skills," Seth said, gently petting Dom's hair.

Domenico grinned, relaxed and happy with his head resting on Seth's thigh, with cum in his stomach and the scent of Seth's arousal clinging to his skin. "Maybe. But I'd rather have you."

Seth bit his lips and pulled up his pants. "I can't even cook for you properly now."

Domenico grinned. "If I wanted a cook, I'd hire one." He pressed a soft kiss to the flesh still visible between shirt and pants and slipped his arms around Seth's midsection, eagerly resting after the most satisfying moment in three months.

"I was planning my first hunt in a few days. I even got a recipe for batter with local spices." Seth stroked Dom's hair, looking down at him.

Domenico scowled. "Why are you so determined? Nobody actually *wants* to eat those things. I'm sure people don't have a choice..."

Seth raised an eyebrow. "What? Of course they do. Apparently, it tastes like chicken."

Domenico rolled his eyes and nuzzled Seth's pec through the thin shirt. "That's what people say when they think something doesn't taste like anything."

Seth groaned and weaseled out of Dom's grip. "Why do you have to make it so difficult? I just wanna try doing something new."

Domenico backed away and sat on his heels. "You keep complaining about your ribs and hand. That's what you should deal with, not with an animal that could make you even worse."

Seth frowned and opened his mouth but didn't say anything in the end, which was even worse than listening to him moan about the alligator issue. He walked off to their bedroom, leaving Dom on his knees, with happiness oozing out of him as if there were a wound he couldn't sew up.

He got up, staring at the cake, which now suddenly seemed bitter and unappealing. Not so long ago, he'd call it a sweet gesture, but in the light of Seth's recent behavior, the cake was more like a half-assed try to stop him from going crazy.

Domenico slid onto the sofa and pinched the bridge of his nose. His whole life was slowly revealing its thin, breakable legs.

Chapter 3 - Domenico

Domenico's mood was steadily deteriorating. The shower felt more draining than the long morning training, and instead of sweat and worries, it was all traces of good humor that were going down the drain along with the dirty water. Dana's eyes drilled into him with a curiosity he didn't want to address. She had no idea what he was going through. In fact, once, she even told him she didn't understand why people would make their lives so complicated with sex, but he had neither a way nor a desire to explain his position to someone who couldn't possibly get it.

He was Domenico Acerbi, and throughout his life, sex had not been a complicated issue. While not always desired or particularly good, there was always relief to be had. A warm body. An escort to spoil over the weekend and woo into bed despite the agency saying it wouldn't be part of the package. With Seth, stuff had stopped being straightforward, but contrary to what Dom believed about himself, the cold shoulder he kept getting didn't only spur anger. With each week, the horrid nightmares were longer

and more detailed, and he kept losing Seth in every single one of them. The worst thing was that despite the boring nature of their everyday life, the dreams felt all too close to reality.

They stopped at the same Walmart they had shopped at for the past months, and Dom was pretty sure this trip would be just as uneventful as all the others. Seth didn't seem particularly excited about the day either as he strolled between the shelves, stocking up on tuna, rice, and some vegetables. He even scowled at a can of processed beef.

"We don't have to buy that," said Dom as they walked through the narrow aisles with generic white tiles on the floor. "It stinks worse than canned salmon."

"At least the alligator would be fresh," Seth grumbled, pushing his cart into an aisle with hunting equipment.

Domenico snorted. "Might as well buy a goat. At least it wouldn't kill you."

"I don't want a goat. Anyone can have a goat." Seth frowned, but at least turned to face Dom. "I could have a fucking goat in Mexico. This is *the* place to try alligators."

"There are other things you haven't tried in a while," snarked Domenico, walking on with his gaze fixed on a wall of canned soups. He'd had far too much of that abomination recently.

Seth threw a set of knives into the basket. "Yeah, 'cause there isn't much to do in this shithole. We're in hiding. I can't even run a blog or anything."

"Oh, so you need Internet now to be entertained? I must be getting fucking old," growled Domenico, more agitated by the second. He hated the way Seth kept pretending he didn't understand what the conversation was about.

Seth pouted and slouched over the shopping cart. "You *are* one year older today. But it doesn't matter if you spend all your time with Dana anyway."

Domenico turned around and poked Seth's chest with his index finger. "I'm *not* fucking her!"

"I know that. You're afraid to even look at pussy." Seth backed away by a step.

"And no one's stopping you from coming with us. I told you it might be good for you to keep moving, and you still sit on your ass all day and sulk!"

"Yeah, right," Seth hissed at him. "I'm gonna go running with my ribs still healing? At the pace of a fucking turtle behind the two of you with your fucking... lung capacity." He turned away from Dom and pushed the cart into another aisle.

Heat rose in Domenico's chest, and he followed Seth, quickly grabbing him by the shoulder. "I would have run with you. I always did. It's you who chooses not to engage in anything we used to do together!"

Seth pushed him away. "Oh, so now you've *always* slowed down for me? I remember being pretty good at running."

Domenico snorted and shook his head. "Yeah. You used to be pretty good."

Seth gave him a glare and pushed the cart toward the cash registers without a word. Dom was pretty sure not stopping by the sweets and chocolates was an expression of spite, so he took matters in his own hands and stocked up on as many chocolate bars as he could carry without a basket. He might have looked a bit ridiculous, but he was in a place where people ate reptiles and shopped in their pajamas. He'd seen it with his own eyes. He joined Seth at the register and poured all the sweets into the basket, topping off the pre-existing landscape of cans.

"Oh, great, I wouldn't have expected that." Seth rolled his eyes. "But I suppose you need them with all the training you do with Dana."

Domenico shrugged. "No. I just figured the sooner I die of a stroke or hypertension, the happier you'll be. And that's what I do all the fucking time: try to make you happy."

Seth grabbed a few chocolates from the shelf next to the register and added them to the pile. "There. Let me help you."

Any hints of a smile dropped from Domenico's lips, and he shook his head, staring straight into Seth's eyes. "Wouldn't it be easier to just dump me?"

"Is that where this is going?" Seth bared his teeth. "You're trying to provoke me into dumping you? You're gonna have to try harder than this bullshit." He pointed at the chocolates.

Domenico leaned closer and lowered his voice, though with the way his throat clenched, he wasn't sure how much of the sound was his own will. "Do you even love me anymore?"

"Really? Here? In fucking Walmart?" Seth spread his arms and looked away toward the register. "Why isn't this fucking line moving?"

Domenico swallowed hard and shook his head at this obvious way to avoid a difficult question. He combed his hair with his fingers and looked at the young guy who blocked the line by arguing with the cashier over a pack of ribbed condoms and a large bag of Milky Ways. His head was a nest of curly dark hair, and Dom couldn't quite pinpoint his ethnicity with his skin dusky, but more olive-tinted than brown. A part of Dom instantly tensed up over this boy possibly being Sicilian, but he didn't seem like a threat with his slim limbs and tight skinny jeans. He probably wasn't even eighteen, judging by his boyish features: big eyes, pouty lips, and slightly rounded face.

"Don't sell them to a kid, Gina," screeched a woman standing next to the boy.

"Seriously! All I want is some rubbers. Big deal. It's not illegal to buy them, you know?" The guy spread his lips in a brilliant toothy smile and picked up another pack from the shelf. "I'll have these extra strong ones as well. You know, for *anal*."

Domenico couldn't help but smile, even with the invisible weight holding his chest down.

The female customer made a low, unhappy sound and covered her mouth. "That is disgusting. You should call security, Gina!"

The cashier looked between the guy and the woman she obviously knew, going from pale to red-faced. "I-I think I will need to consult with the manager."

"I'm gonna use some of them as balloons, if that helps your bigoted brain," said the guy.

Seth groaned. "Oh, come on! How long is this gonna take? Sell him the rubbers and let's get on with this."

A few other customers in the line nodded and murmured their approval.

The agitated lady turned toward him and got even redder than she had been, shaking her backcombed hair. "You're one to talk! I know you! You both live with a woman, and there is only one bedroom in that house. God will judge you!"

Domenico bit his lip. "The last time I checked, God didn't take kindly to old poodles who stick their noses in shit that isn't theirs."

"There are no rules on looking out for your neighbors. There are on the other hand rules about fornicating!" She grabbed the boy's T-shirt, and he opened his big eyes wider.

"Let go of me, you crazy woman!"

Domenico snorted. "God knows his *true* child from some wannabe, who mindlessly listens to what their pastor says."

Seth groaned and put his hand over his face, but the woman wouldn't let go of the ridiculous argument.

"I haven't seen *you* at church!"

"That's because it's not a church. It's a gym hall with stained glass windows."

The boy pulled out of her grip. "Fuck this bullshit!" He put a dollar note on the counter and took his bag of Milky Ways, leaving the condoms behind.

Seth peeked out from behind his fingers. "See what you've done? Now he's gonna go off and have unsafe sex."

"It's for the better for him to not fornicate at all," the woman said. "Even those satanists from the woods know that much!"

Domenico frowned, but he had no idea what she was talking about. Did she mean some swamp people? "And it would be better for you to have sex for once and stop bitching, you jealous cunt," growled Domenico, taking the two packs of condoms and putting them on his pile of chocolate. "Didn't God tell you to multiply? Take that advice seriously. We're running out of people. It's pretty tragic." Domenico smiled to himself. Were he straight, he'd multiply with the best women. The world was missing out on his genes.

The woman huffed and pushed out of the line. "I've had enough of this lack of respect! Henry will hear of this." She pointed her finger at the cashier who looked flustered by the whole exchange.

"I'm sorry," she muttered as she begun quickly scanning the items for the next person.

"And who's that important Henry person? The postman?" asked Domenico, pushing his hands down his pockets, even as he looked sideways at Seth. Did he notice the condoms?

If he did, he didn't mention it, and as they bagged their shopping, he made a point of ignoring all the chocolates and only dealing with the things he'd gotten off the shelves. As if not wanting to have Domenico see how upset he was, he spoke to the cashier.

"Who did this lady call satanist again?"

The cashier shook her head, seemingly happy about the change of subject. "There is this pagan cult living in a former military base an hour away from here. But they don't ever mingle with anyone else and stay on their own land, so most of us don't really care about their beliefs. Live and let live, right?"

Seth gave her a stiff smile and continued with the topic.

Domenico shook his head and, for the first time during their time together, paid for his stuff separately. It seemed that the wall between him and Seth was steadily thickening, as if an invisible hand made sure to layer plaster over all the cracks Dom managed to make. He'd hoped he made a big indent in the morning, but it looked like that one was sealed now as well.

Seth walked out first, heading for the car with his bag. They passed the boy who'd caused the fuss. He sat on the sidewalk eating the bite-sized Milky Ways, hunched over in demonstration of his unhappiness.

Domenico stopped next to him and dropped the two packs of condoms into his lap. "Share?"

The boy looked up with a smile stained by chocolate. "Hey, thanks!" He held out the pack of sweets and put the condoms into his pocket.

Domenico took one bar and winked. "Don't get a girl pregnant."

The boy chuckled. "Not gonna happen."

"Dom! Come on!" Seth yelled from the car.

Domenico looked at him and sighed before slowly making his way to the ugly old pickup they had bought

after a few days in hiding following Vincente's death. He still wanted Seth to answer his question, but the moment had passed, and he didn't want to repeat himself.

Chapter 4 - Domenico

The way to the bar passed in silence even louder than the radio playing annoying pop songs. Dom had no idea how they were to spend two hours having dinner in this atmosphere. He didn't really want to. Any and all romantic gestures seemed fake. He'd much rather be alone. Or drink himself to sleep in a real church.

Chuck's Bar & Grill wasn't impressive, but the food was better than fucking tuna sandwiches. And judging by Seth's choice of drink, he was planning to get smashed. He'd gone to the bar and, frustrated by the bartender's inability to make a proper Bloody Mary, he improvised and made himself a whole pitcher of the drink with a generous amount of vodka. He'd spent a good twenty minutes chatting to the bartender about drinks and even left the guy a recipe, as Domenico sat alone at the table. On his birthday.

"Do you know what you want to have?" Seth asked once he got back, not even looking from behind the menu. It was the most bullshit kind of small talk Dom could think of. It fit the grim, old bar with lots of nutshells on the floor.

"You. With an apple between the teeth," said Domenico, glancing at him from across the table.

That got Seth's attention. He raised his eyes with his lips parted and downed his glass of Bloody Mary before speaking. "What is that supposed to imply?"

Domenico shrugged. "What do you think?" Slowly, he looked up at his lover, playing with the neck of his Coke bottle. He was tired of all this. It was almost as if all his life choices decided to backfire on him.

"I don't know. Maybe that you just compared me to a pig." Seth refilled his glass.

Domenico frowned. "No. I said I want to stuff you. And eat you."

Seth buried his nose in the menu again. "That your thing now? Cannibalism?"

"And guns," said Dom, looking straight into Seth's eyes over the open menu he didn't care much about.

"What do you mean by guns?" Seth held his gaze with that defiant expression. It felt as though they were butting heads without even touching. Dom would fuck that attitude out of him in a minute if he got the chance.

He leaned back in the chair. If Seth could bullshit him all the time, two could play this game. "I used to do that a lot before we met. I'd have the guy suck on my loaded gun. With the safety off. I came so fast every time."

The way Seth's pursed lips parted told Dom he was eating it up. "Y-you for real?" Seth asked and had more of his drink. As gullible as always. Dom kind of missed that.

A sense of warmth spread through his chest, and he almost wanted to grab Seth's hand under the table. "Yeah. It's fucking hot."

Seth took his elbows off the table and backed into his chair with his eyes widened. Sure, it was mean to tease him like that, but it felt great to have all of his attention for once.

"And... um... is that something you want to do?"

Domenico bit his lip. "What if I do?" he asked, leaning forward and touching the edge of the table very gently, the same way he sometimes teased Seth's skin with the briefest sensations.

"I-I mean... They say, always try something once, right?" Seth laughed nervously, shying away from Dom's gaze. "And... maybe it'd be better if it was with the safety on?"

Domenico stopped himself from frowning. Seth obviously did *not* want to be put in that position. Why would he go with it? "No. It must be with the safety off. Deep down your throat."

"Maybe just for your birthday?" Seth whispered, slouching over his glass.

Domenico stared at him, unsure what to say. He didn't know what he hated more—the lack of any sexual gestures coming from Seth, the way he walked out on Dom after an amazing blow job, or the fact that he was clearly ready to go against his instincts and put up with as crazy a demand as this.

"Can I wear lingerie while you suck it?"

Seth blinked and looked up at him. "You bastard! You think this is fucking funny?" He slammed his fist on the table so hard the cutlery rattled, and other customers looked their way. "I can't believe this shit!" He got up and headed for the back door of the bar, tense like a bull on steroids.

Domenico got to his feet right away and stormed after him. "We'll be right back," he told the waitress before rushing outside into the backyard of the bar. He had to squint to shield his eyes from the setting sun, but Seth's huge frame was hard to miss.

"Joke for a joke."

"How was that a joke, you asshole? Gun sucking? Seriously?" His face was red and he barely breathed leaning against the huge metal barrels stacked there.

Domenico walked up to him and grabbed his arm. "I thought you'd tell me to fuck off. You do it all the time anyway. And you agree to something this fucking stupid? What's wrong with you? One stray move, and I could've killed you if we went through with it!!"

Seth put his fingers into his beard. "I don't know! I panicked!"

"What do you mean you *panicked*? What the fuck? It's like I don't know you anymore!"

Seth's lips trembled. "What if this was some deal breaker? I didn't know what to say! I wanted to compromise."

"Deal breaker?" Domenico drew in a sharp breath and yanked harder at Seth's arm. His heart was beating so fast it was making him lightheaded. "I don't need God-fucking-knows what. I just want you with me. I don't fucking know what's going on with you!"

"Nothing's going on. I'm working through stuff. I'm fine. It's not my fault my body's messed up."

"Yeah? It's my birthday. Let's go to the fucking doctor," hissed Domenico. "My idea of fun. Ha. Ha."

Seth frowned and rubbed his forehead. "I'm sorry. I wanted it to be nice tonight."

"Did you? All you ever talk to me about is alligators."

"You said you'll go hunt them with me…" Seth slowly reached out to Dom and put his finger in the belt loop of Dom's jeans.

Anger evaporated out of Domenico almost instantly. He looked up at Seth's hunched shoulders, the curve of his mouth, his dark eyes, and he found himself unable to look away. "I just want you to be with me. It's like you're there, without being there."

Seth stepped closer, and Dom exhaled when Seth's arms slid around his neck. "I'll try to be a better boyfriend. I promise."

Domenico held him tight, hoping no one would see them here. But even if he'd never trade this brief moment of simple relief for peace. They'd move if there was no other way, but now he wanted to feel Seth's arms all around him. He loved how big and tall Seth was, and his body, even though it had softened since the ordeal with Vincente, was just as pleasant and warm as it had always been. If only Seth would let him, he'd gladly fall asleep with his head on Seth's pec, soaking up his masculine scent.

Dom used to only go for the tight-bodied, chiseled types, but softness looked just as good on Seth. Even the beard was fine, always freshly washed and soft. "I love you," he whispered, stroking the broad back.

"I love you, too." Seth kissed the side of Dom's head. "I will never stop. It's just complicated sometimes. Let's go finish your birthday meal, huh?"

Domenico smiled and stroked his thumb down Seth's face. His heart thumped in agreement, light and warm. There was no trace of lies in Seth's voice, and Dom believed his every word.

They made their way back to the bar and ordered a ton of food, including two desserts for Dom, who couldn't decide between a banana cream pie and a chocolate malt. After the tension dropped, all of a sudden there was plenty to talk about, and two cocktails later, Seth even started nudging Domenico's leg under the table. It was almost as if someone had reprogrammed him to act like his old self again. Hours flew by like crazy, and Domenico didn't even mind the waitress butting in to ask who they were. He chose to go with the moment and told her all about Dana being the sister they only met recently, and seeing Seth's eyes flicker with amusement only spurred him on to continue with his tale. In Domenico's version of the world, Seth was a veteran of a bloody war in a post-soviet state, with a made-up name based on a word he spotted in the menu. Domenico was a professional chocolate and coffee

taster and only left the stress of his job to help out his big brother come back to health.

When the waitress heard that, she brought him a third dessert, their version of a tiramisu. Seth tried it and couldn't stop laughing at how bad he thought it was, though it wasn't actually *bad*. The problem was that it didn't taste much like tiramisu. Seth must have had five or six glasses of different alcohols, and despite his speech getting slightly slurred, Dom liked to see him so completely relaxed and smiley for once.

"Look to the bar," Seth whispered, leaning closer over the table. "But discreetly."

Domenico squinted at him, leaning back with grace. "I'm always discreet," he said, before slowly tipping his head to look where Seth indicated.

The boy they had met at Walmart was there, and he was being refused service yet again, this time over alcohol. Domenico's mother let him drink some table wine as far back as he could remember, and he thought it was a responsible way to go about it, but it looked like the kid wouldn't be getting anything here tonight.

"Not his lucky day, huh?" asked Dom. "I got him rubbers, but I will not be buying him stuff he doesn't need."

Seth sniggered. "I bet he's not gonna get a chance to use those rubbers any time soon."

Unfortunately, Seth wasn't as discreet as Dom, and the boy looked back at them with a smile. He caught Dom's gaze, and Dom's gaydar started ringing, but he got a confirmation of his suspicions seconds later. He could hardly believe the audacity of the kid when the boy conspicuously pointed at Seth, himself, and Dom. He then made a suggestive gesture, pushing his tongue against the inside of his cheek, and raised his thick dark eyebrows in question.

Domenico looked at Seth, with laughter bubbling up in his chest. "He wants to suck you off."

Seth turned around, completely losing any pretense of discretion. "What?" He snorted. "He's like half my size. Cocky little dick."

"Yeah, he's scrawny. Not my type either. And I'd rather focus on your cock and ass in bed tonight," whispered Domenico.

The way Seth bit back a grin had a pulse of electricity go down Dom's chest. "You seem eager..." Seth nudged his foot under the table.

Breath caught in Domenico's throat. That was it. The invitation to sex. He could almost hear the angel choirs in the background. "Are *you*?"

Seth looked away and finished his drink with a silly smile plastered over his face. "Yeah, I miss you," he whispered and put his hand over half of his face.

Domenico bit back a moan and quickly fumbled with his wallet. The boy from the bar must have lost hope and strolled all the way to the exit, but that wasn't Domenico's concern. He had something much better than a scrawny teenager who couldn't even buy a beer.

"Miss you too. Like hell. I just wanna push you into the mattress."

Seth's eyes glazed over, and he stretched as he got up. "Oh, so you have a plan..."

Domenico dumped some bills on the table and got up. "I always have a plan. It usually involves getting you naked."

Seth stumbled slightly on his way out, and Dom quickly put an arm under his. He couldn't help a smile, as it reminded him of that time when he took Seth home drunk in Berlin. Seth had been so pliant, so ready to fuck. It had gotten dark since they'd entered the bar, and yet it felt like less than an hour ago. This birthday would end on a high note.

"I thought a made man should have more on his mind," Seth whispered into Dom's ear as they descended

the few wooden stairs outside and walked into the improvised parking lot. There were some young men hanging out at the back of a pickup, so Dom didn't do the one thing he wanted—grab Seth's ass—and chose to save it for later.

"I'm not that anymore. You completely infested my brain."

Seth laughed. "I must have, because you forgot to eat your third dessert..."

Domenico scowled. "Fuck."

"Come on, Dom..." Seth opened the door and managed to get in after three attempts. "You had cake today, ice cream..."

"I still wanted that damn malt shake!" grumbled Domenico, getting into the driver's seat. It should really have been him to drink on such occasion, but now, when he looked into Seth's shining, happy eyes, he didn't feel one bit sorry about being the designated driver.

"You'll get a better dessert..." Seth leaned closer and put his arm over Dom's shoulders as he planted a kiss on Dom's jaw.

Domenico drew in a sharp breath and quickly started the engine. If this was to work, he needed to go fast, before the alcohol evaporated out of Seth's head, or before he got too sober to accept Dana in the other room. Then again, they could always have Dana spend the night elsewhere.

He rapidly drove out of the parking lot and started toward their house, which was almost half an hour drive away, in a different town. "What do I get?"

Seth looked around and grabbed a half-eaten pack of Oreos. "These?" He laughed and nipped at Dom's cheek, only reminding him just how desperately horny he'd been.

"Yeah, give me some of that," whispered Dom, driving into the dark with just the headlights to guide him.

Seth gave him two at once, and Dom was more than happy to eat them. "But Dom, you didn't put your seat belt on." Seth sighed and leaned more of his weight on Dom when trying to reach the other side of the seat.

Domenico shuddered, grasping the steering wheel harder as the scent of man and booze penetrated his nostrils. When Seth leaned even lower, Domenico couldn't suppress a laugh, even though the situation also made his blood flow quicker. "To someone outside, this would look like you're sucking me off."

"You bastard. I'm just worried about your safety," Seth snorted and leaned down, pushing his face against Dom's crotch.

Domenico let out a groan and raised his hips, already getting hard, already eager to push his cock into each willing hole, to kiss a trail down Seth's back, to eat his ass, to spread him open and ram in while he wailed in pleasure. He couldn't bear the thought of having to wait for half an hour.

And then the best thing happened. Seth unzipped Dom's pants. He hadn't given Dom a blow job in months because of the wound in his cheek. Could it have healed enough? Finally?

"Ohh, fuck... what if I crash?" whispered Domenico, but his hand slid into Seth's hair and kept him close, as if it were an entity with its own mind.

Seth chuckled, and his lips trailed over Dom's dick through his briefs. "It will be a test of focus."

Domenico bit his lip and took a deep breath. He was stuck between a rock and a hard place. "I won't be able to fuck you if you suck me off."

Seth looked up with a half-lidded gaze that made Dom feel the rope around his neck tug at him even harder. "But I'm so horny, and you're so hot..."

A moan left Domenico's mouth, and he gently brushed his finger across Seth's lips, pressing it inside their

warmth. Seth was horny, and it seemed like a now-or-never situation. Dom's mind was clouded with images of that large, strong body flexing under him, the round buttocks bouncing against Dom's hips as they fucked. There was no way this could wait until they get home.

"Kiss me now, and I'm gonna find a cozy little spot for us to stop."

Seth grinned and straightened up to place a kiss on Dom's cheek, but his large, hot hand found its way to Dom's crotch and squeezed his dick.

Dom grasped the steering wheel harder and bucked his hips, silently praying for his cock not to disobey. He just wanted to come inside Seth. Was that too much to ask?

"What about the cookies? Give me one," he offered to distract his drunken lover.

Seth held up an Oreo. "You think you deserve this cookie?"

Dom frowned. "If I don't get that cookie, I'm gonna stop on the side of the road, pull down your pants, and spank you for anyone to see."

For a split second, Seth looked more sober when his eyes widened. "Wow. But what will that earn you when... the cookie is gone?" Seth finished in a dramatic tone and put the Oreo between his open lips.

Domenico gasped. "The cookie!"

Seth squinted and put the Oreo in his mouth. Before Dom could act, he got the last one out of the packet as well and stuck it in his mouth. He spread his arms in challenge.

Domenic squinted at him and shook his head. "You will give me such good head for this. It's my birthday, and you eat my fucking Oreos?" he asked, though he wasn't *really* angry. In fact, the playfulness Seth showed now was something dearly missed.

"Sorry. Not sorry." Seth mumbled with his mouth full and a smile in his gaze.

Domenico rolled his eyes, but a small dirt road ahead made him press on the brake so suddenly, Seth fell forward, barely missing the windshield with his head. Domenico drove into the road without thinking, only to realize it led to what looked like an old rest stop with a small building looming in the faint light of the headlights. He licked his lips and opened the glove compartment, frantically looking for lube.

Seth unbuckled his seat belt and got out of the car, not bothering to look back at Dom. "Romantic." He snorted.

Domenico moaned. "I'll show you romantic once I get my hands on you," he said, drunk with lust as he jumped off the car and rushed to the other side. He grabbed Seth by the nape and pulled him down for a hot, hungry kiss that only made his arousal spike. As much as he preferred men clean-shaven or scruffy, the beard tickling his skin did feel nice.

"Will you fuck me hard?" Seth whispered into Dom's lips, sliding his hands up Dom's forearms in the darkness.

It was music to Domenico's ears.

He grabbed Seth's sides and nipped on his lip, pulling on the flesh. "As hard as you want. I'm gonna breed you and then lick it all off." He pulled Seth toward the small building, in hope to find shelter, in case someone decided to stop here as well. It was only when a loud cry tore the air that he stopped in his tracks and held Seth in place. A youngish, male voice was calling for help.

Seth turned his head that way, and when they heard another yell, he pulled out of Dom's grasp and rushed in.

"The fuck you think you're doing, huh?" Seth asked, spreading his arms to the sides.

Domenico blinked and rushed after him, but Seth was already inside the little building, standing on broken tiles of what looked like a public restroom. In the faint light

coming through the open door, a muscular man in a leather vest was pulling up his pants with the urgency of a teenager caught with his dick in his fist, but it became clear why when Dom noticed the person who he was with was male. It was the audacious boy Dom and Seth had met at the store and then at the bar, the same one whose threesome offer they refused.

"Piss off!" the man with a bush of blond hair yelled as soon as he zipped up his pants.

To Dom's frustration, Seth took a few steps forward. The boy watched him from the floor with his lips parted. Of course. There Dom was, trying to end his birthday with a good fuck, and instead, he was to play a fucking social justice crusader.

"What are you doing?" he asked Seth, who looked back at him with those big needy eyes.

"We have to help him," he said with a slur to his words and pointed at the boy, who was already trying to sneak out on hands and knees.

The blond grabbed the boy's hair and pulled so hard Dom felt the skin on his head twitch in sympathy. "He's not going anywhere. This is none of your business!"

Dom wanted to just leave, stop Seth from turning even more attention on them, but the moment his eyes met the teenager's, he knew it was a lost cause. He would not let some stupid kid get raped, just because he wanted to have a nice quiet evening.

"Fuck off, you pig!" the kid screamed, struggling against the tight hold the other man had on his hair.

"Let him go," said Domenico.

"Who the fuck do you think you are?" The blond hissed, looking up at Dom with bright eyes that held a surprising amount of menace.

"I can deal with this, Dom, step back," Seth said drunkenly and took another step forward before Dom could push in a word. "You better let him go, or... else."

Dom put his palm over his face and let it slide down with a groan. His senses were alert to anything that could put Seth's drunken ass in danger, but when the blond man grabbed the teen so hard he lifted him off the ground by the neck, it was high time to act.

"Or else what? I'm taking him, so fuck off!"

To Dom's annoyance, it was Seth who pulled out a gun first. He pointed it at the blond, but his hand was swaying from side to side like the head of a sleep-deprived puppy. Domenico made a mental note to always disarm him when he got drunk.

"Or I'll shoot your brains out!" Seth yelled and turned his gun sideways, as if he were in a crappy action movie.

The blond instantly let go of the kid, just to pull out a gun of his own and point it back at Seth. Domenico's world slowed down. His hand reached for his trusty Beretta before he could even consciously think about it. He aimed straight at the blond's hands, ready to shoot the gun out of them. "This ends. Now."

Seth nodded. "Yeah!"

The kid sniffed and made pleading eyes at them. "Please don't let him take me."

Domenico gritted his teeth and stepped in front of Seth. As expected, the blond immediately aimed the gun at him instead, but his body was tense. There was a slight shake to his hand. He was just a local thug. Domenico could handle this.

"Hand over the boy, and we'll leave."

The guy's lips were pursed, and he eyed them all, breathing hard. "You're not from here, are you?"

Domenico snarled. "Thank fuck for that."

Seth tried to slip out from behind Dom, but that was not an option, so Dom pushed him back. "Yeah, who'd want to live in this shithole!"

The blond took his time to assess them but gave the kid a kick, pushing him forward. He took a step back, and then another, to an exit on the other side.

Domenico kept him in his sight until the guy disappeared, and the sound of hurried footsteps was followed by the roar of an engine.

Domenico sighed and pulled the safety on before hiding the gun in the holster. His eyes trailed to Seth's hand, which was still clasped on the gun he shouldn't be holding in his drunken state. Dom grabbed its barrel and easily pulled it out of Seth's grip. "It's no time to play the hero."

The kid slowly got up, eyeing them both warily, but didn't say a word.

Seth pointed at him. "We showed him."

Domenico sighed and shook his head at the boy. His heart rate was slowly getting back to normal now that Seth wasn't in danger anymore. "Three times in a row we have seen you in trouble. Do you have a death wish?"

"I—He seemed all right at the bar," the kid muttered, and when he hugged himself, he looked much younger than he did when they saw him in town.

"He was twice your size, you dumbass. What were you thinking?" Domenico shook his head and stepped closer, grabbing the kid's face and tilting it upward to look into his big brown eyes. He purposefully pulled him closer to the door for the bright moonlight to disperse the darkness and see it properly.

The boy frowned and pulled away quickly. "It's none of your business, he was hot."

Domenico grabbed him by the neck and pushed the little shit against the nearest wall, not to really hurt him, but hard enough for the boy to feel the pain. "No? You asked for help, and we answered. Kinda makes it my business."

The boy whimpered, and Dom felt Seth approach by the scent of vodka close behind him. "Don't hurt him..."

Domenico smirked, pinning the kid to the wall with his eyes. "No? Why not? He'd be probably bleeding on the floor it weren't for me."

The kid grabbed Dom's wrist, but he didn't have much force to him. The blond could have done anything to his twig-limbs. "I'm sorry! I mean... thank you," he uttered.

Domenico nodded, slightly less agitated now that his help had been acknowledged. "That's better. What's your name?" he asked, wondering who this kid was. Was he on the run?

"Mark. Mark Copaescu." Their eyes met, and Dom was pretty sure he was telling the truth.

Seth stepped closer, into Dom's line of sight. "Do you need a ride somewhere, Mark? Are you hurt?"

Domenico sighed. "Clearly, he's not. He's also underage and so stupid it's painful. Where is your mommy, Mark?"

The boy swallowed so hard Dom felt the push of his Adam's apple against his palm. "I'm on my own..." Another stupid thing to admit to strangers with guns.

"Aww... That's so sad, Dom," Seth slurred, holding his forehead.

Domenico shrugged. "What does that mean, Mark?" asked Domenico, slowly letting go of his neck and stepping back to offer him just the right amount of personal space for the boy to be willing to talk.

Mark shot Seth a glance but then looked right back at Dom. "I don't need to tell you anything," he grumbled and crossed his arms on his chest.

"You do," said Domenico without even a second's hesitation, letting his real accent slip into the sentence and curl around the English words.

"Why?" moaned the boy, and Dom could sense the fear in the air. "And it's not like I'm totally alone anyway. People would be looking for me if I disappear."

Domenico snorted. "Would they? What are their names and addresses?"

"What? So you can send them a fake note from me? That I'm all right and they shouldn't worry? Sorry, not gonna happen." He took a step to the side, only to bump into Seth.

"He doesn't mean it that way. We just want to give you a ride home, right, Dom?"

Domenico sighed and looked at the front of Seth's pants, so out of reach. "I suppose."

"Just a ride?" Mark looked between them, and it was painful to watch. What kind of assurance would their word give him? They could say whatever they wanted and then butcher him in the woods anyway.

Seth nodded. "Just a ride."

"We're not up for a threesome," said Dom, just to get *that* out of the way.

Mark slowly nodded, and Dom could almost see the cogs frantically turning in his brain. "Okay..."

Seth gave Mark a wide smile and petted his hair, as if the boy were a puppy. He turned around and left the restroom. Maybe they could leave Mark in the car and have a quick fuck before the drive? No, that wasn't an option. Dom didn't want a quickie. He wanted to touch Seth all over and sate himself after months of celibacy. "So, where are you staying?" he asked the boy, gesturing for him to move first.

Mark swallowed and kept looking over his shoulder as they left. "In... the motel."

Domenico frowned. "They have a motel in town? Where?"

Mark put his hands down his pockets. "In... I mean, if you get me to town, I can get there on my own."

"Are you a runaway?" asked Domenico, following Seth, who was already climbing into the car as well as he could with all cells in his body soaked by liquor.

"Why are you so persistent? Jeez! Just get me to town and I'll be fine."

Seth looked back at them with a frown. "There's no motel in town. Where would you stay?"

"Oh, my God!" Mark raised his arms in frustration. "I don't know! Airbnb? Couchsurfing? The Hilton? I'll find something."

Seth looked into Dom's eyes with a tenderness he rarely displayed these days. "Aww, Dom, let's take him."

Domenico scowled and looked at Mark. "He's not a dog."

"I didn't say he was... but... you know. If he just needs a place to crash, he can stay the night. What if he gets into more trouble?"

"And what, you want to leave him at Dana's mercy?" Domenico rolled his eyes.

"I think there's a futon in the closet," Seth said once they were all in the car.

"I wouldn't be a bother... Just for the night... Oreos!" Mark grinned as he grabbed the cookie packet, but his face was the picture of disappointment when he realized it was empty.

Domenico groaned and pushed him inside. From the look on Seth's face, he assumed that Seth would definitely not forgive him if he left the kid here. "Hungry? When have you last eaten? The chocolates at the store?"

"I'm fine, I don't eat much." Mark shrugged, looking at Seth for a longer while.

Domenico squinted but didn't say anything and climbed into the driver's seat. Of course, the boy would end up between him and Seth. Like a fucking slutty wall.

"So who's the guy?" Seth wiggled his eyebrows at Mark as Dom started the car.

Mark shrugged. "Just a guy. Was gonna give him a discount, 'cause I like blonds."

"Great. He's a whore, and he's gonna be using our bathroom," grumbled Domenico, starting the car. He drove out of the rest stop and headed down the empty road. This night was going downhill fast.

"I mean, we took him, so he's our responsibility." Seth nodded.

"I'm not a whore! I have other things going." Mark crossed his arms on his chest and pouted like a little kid.

"Have you seen any weird rash or sores lately?" asked Domenico, without taking his eyes off the road. "We're healthy and staying that way."

"I'm fine!"

Seth grumbled. "It's not like you ever checked yourself for STDs."

Domenico snorted. "I'm fine. Strong as an ox."

Seth bit his lip with a smile. "I know... I love that..." Seth tried to reach him over Mark's head but ended up failing.

Domenico grinned anyway. Seth's words were like an injection of warmth straight into his bloodstream. "You're gonna get all you want tonight," he said, speeding up. He could only hope no deer would suddenly jump in front of the car.

"So... am I invited to that as well?" Mark grinned and looked between them like a kid in a candy store.

Seth started laughing, leaving Dom to answer.

"Of course not. How old are you? You can't buy a beer or condoms without an adult helping you out." Domenico shook his head at the boy's attitude. "You're selling yourself too cheaply."

"You don't know how much I charge." Mark raised his eyebrows and nose, making himself look like even more of a brat. "And for the record, I'm nineteen."

Domenico laughed out loud. "Sure you are. You heard him, Seth? He says those bright big doll eyes are nineteen."

Seth grinned back at him. "Yeah, right. And I'm fifty."

Mark pursed his lips. "You could be old. You have a beard."

"Idiot," said Dom. "Maybe if *you* were older, you wouldn't have gotten into the car with two strangers who carry guns. We could sacrifice you to the devil, use your skin for lampshades, and cook your flesh for dinner."

That shut Mark up, but Seth was quick to talk. "But we won't. 'Cause we're the good guys. You're a hero, Dom. You saved him tonight."

"And he saved me from a good fuck," grumbled Domenico. "I broke a business deal with his client. That's hardly heroic. In fact, it's much more of a heroic act to be in this car now without punching anyone."

"But you saw that guy. He was so violent..."

Mark nodded without looking up. "Fucker tried to film me giving him a BJ."

Domenico scowled, and his blood boiled. "Oh, that's vile. Should've broken his nose. You don't film anyone during fucking. That's blackmail material right there."

"I should have known a guy that hot going for me is some kind of psycho."

Domenico frowned. "Christ. Since when am I your therapist? Man up, and you'll have any guy you want."

"Even you?" Mark looked up at him with a stupid grin, and when Seth didn't protest, Dom realized his fiancé had dozed off with his head against the window.

Domenico shrugged. "You'd have to try harder. Right now, you're just a stray kid who I found on his knees in a public toilet."

Mark groaned and leaned against his seat. "Yeah, whatever," he muttered.

Domenico chuckled. "Not all is lost. Stop fucking idiots, get stronger, and you'll be a man of worth. That's how it works. If an adult wants to fuck a scrawny kid, there's something wrong with them."

Mark didn't answer, but the trace of thoughtfulness on his face made Dom optimistic that maybe at least something was sinking in through that mess of curls.

When they got to their house, he had to wake Seth up, which was a hard task with the state of drunkenness he was in. And if that weren't bad enough, as soon as Seth got out, he puked in their driveway, dropping to his hands and knees.

Domenico stepped back and watched, wide-eyed. Slowly, he looked at Mark and scratched his head, having completely lost hope for a birthday fuck. The full moon high up in the sky was laughing at him. "If you take the groceries to the kitchen, you can have food."

Mark quickly nodded and got the bags. At least he had enough of a brain to not comment on Seth.

"I'm sorry, Dom," Seth mumbled from the ground. "I feel so ill…"

Domenico kept behind him, not to fall victim to any stray vomit, but he approached the trembling back and gently petted Seth's head. He could only hope some wild animal would take care of the disgusting puddle at night. If not, Dana would have another way to make herself useful.

Domenico scratched Seth's head, showing him his… well, support. "You'll be so hungover tomorrow."

"I don't wanna…" Seth moaned, trying to get himself up and almost pulling Dom down with him in the process.

"Who is this?" Dana asked from the house.

"Someone who's sleeping with you tonight. The sofa, it unfolds into a bed, doesn't it?" Domenico patted Seth's back and asked him if he was okay to go inside.

"What?" she hissed. The last thing Dom needed now was an attitude from her. He groaned.

"The kid's gay. Your virtue's safe."

Seth moaned from the ground, and Domenico dragged him to his feet with resignation spreading through his chest.

"Thanks," Seth muttered, and Domenico cringed when he got a hug that surely got his hair dirty with vomit.

Dana huffed. "You pick up strays now? Are we getting a dog next?"

Domenico shoved Mark forward. "Don't drink anything she gives you," he said quietly, knowing Dana's professional love for rohypnol. "Other than that, you'll be fine." He stepped forward, trying to convince himself that he was still as clean and nice-smelling as when they were leaving the house.

"I've got food," Mark tried, but it only got him a glare from Dana as he passed her in the doorway.

"I'm sorry," Seth repeated as Dom helped him into the house, struggling with the weight put on his shoulder. He could barely believe that the second time he'd ever fucked him, he'd held Seth up against the wall. Then again, that memory gave him a tingle of satisfaction. Seth was the only fuck who had ever been his and his only. He wanted to claim him again, but not like this. Not drunk to the point of being sick. Domenico sighed and led Seth all the way to the bedroom. He turned on the light with his forehead and stepped into the cramped room, shutting the door behind them. He should have let Seth suck him off in the car.

Dealing with a man this drunk was tedious, but at least he had Mark out of his hair now. And on the topic of hair, Domenico needed to wash his. Not to mention that he needed to wash Seth's beard. Seth complained that all he wanted was to sleep, but Dom wasn't having any of it and pulled him into the small bathroom with mold in the

corner and a friendly spider that they'd named Santo, after Seth's cousin who had helped them fake their deaths.

Domenico closed the toilet lid and sat Seth down, quickly pulling up his shirt to reveal his massive chest with a patch of curly hair running down the center and the dark scars that were left after Vincente butchered Seth's nipples.

"Don't..." Seth grumbled and put his arm over his chest to hide his scars, but he kept swaying from side to side and couldn't even keep his eyes open.

"Don't be a baby," muttered Domenico and pulled away Seth's hand to take a look at the dark tissue. It suddenly hit him that he'd never seen them after the whole ordeal, and a sharp tingle went down his back when he brushed the new skin with his thumb. What a beast Vincente had been to do this to his only brother.

Seth managed to open one eye. "I said, don't. They're disgusting." He tried to push Dom away, but he didn't have much strength.

"No, they're not. They're scars. I have many scars," whispered Domenico, slowly tugging Seth to his feet. He couldn't stop himself from staring at the deliciously soft angles of Seth's chest, at the navel Dom wanted to lick, but with the state Seth was in, he didn't want to touch too much.

"Yours are pretty," Seth said in a way so mumbly Dom could barely understand him. When he tried to walk into the shower stall in his shoes and pants, Domenico rolled his eyes and pulled at the back of his jeans. Even slipping his finger under the waistband of Seth's pants made him feel like he was somehow *on the in*. Like he had permission to touch. But knowing Seth was drunk enough not to remember a thing tomorrow, he just pushed the denim down Seth's legs.

"Yeah, yeah. I'm pretty as a doll. You can braid my hair tomorrow."

Seth giggled, and for a moment Dom was afraid he would topple over when he stood on one leg while Dom took off his shoe. "I always wanted that. I can't braid though."

"Good, I'm not Rapunzel," said Domenico, methodically untangling Seth of his out clothes.

As soon as Seth was naked, Dom guided him into the shower stall, but Seth went strangely quiet, and his eyelids were drooping. He leaned against the wall and avoided the first rush of cold water when Dom turned it on.

"Are you falling asleep already?" Domenico quickly shed his own clothes, but his glance trailed slowly down the powerful body next to him. Seth's presence took up most of the space in their tiny bathroom, his scent penetrated Domenico's senses, and he couldn't help but feel cheated that he couldn't touch all that tan skin the way he wanted. He'd gladly let his lips and fingers roam in the thick bushes of dark hair that grew over the warm curves and plains.

Seth mumbled something that sounded like a *no*, but could have also been a *yeah*, and he shied away from Dom and the water when Domenico joined him inside the stall for a tight squeeze. Even seeing the curved side of Seth's ass was a better turn-on than any porn vid could ever be. Yet Dom was stuck making sure Seth had no vomit in his beard once he went to sleep. It was a job to be done. Dom had scrubbed brains out of tiles before, so he could deal with some puke.

Domenico tested the water on his own hand, which made him feel like he was taking care of a giant baby, then made Seth wet and cleaned him with liquid soap as efficiently as possible. At this rate, Seth would slide down in the shower, and it would then be up to Dom to somehow drag him out.

In the end though, he got so frustrated with Seth constantly tipping over during the quick drying with the

towel that Dom ended up throwing him over his shoulder, to the vocal protests of his spine, and took his personal man mountain to bed. He didn't bother dressing Seth in anything and just covered him with the sheet. Washing himself was a brief affair after that, and as Domenico slid into bed in a pair of Armani briefs, his only comfort was the fact that Seth somehow ended up curling up against him. So what that it made Domenico feel unbearably hot in the non-air-conditioned room? He at least got a scrap of willing touch from his reluctant lover.

Sleep wouldn't come for hours as Domenico lay in bed with Seth's thick, warm hand heating up his stomach and a head full of unwanted thoughts about all things lost. Much had changed since his last birthday. One year back, he was in Argentina on a job, and his mother had called him early in the morning to wish him well. Tassa had called as well, which was back before Domenico smashed his brains all over the floor. Domenico then had a solitary dinner and a whole coffee cake to spend the evening with. He hooked up with a guy in a bar. The guy had been fun.

Still, despite everything working out technically, Domenico wasn't sure which birthday was less satisfying.

He fell asleep to pale light falling through the blinds.

Chapter 5 - Mark

Mark wasn't sure where he was for the first few seconds after waking up. His shoulder hurt a bit, and he opened his eyes when he realized he lay on the floor.

He yelped and sat up when a pair of blue eyes squinted at him. It was the hot witch from yesterday. Right. She had made him sleep on the floor, and she wouldn't let him eat any food despite Domenico allowing him to. He was starving. Did she have no heart?

"You can go now. It's not like anybody would miss a stray," she said from the sofa, which was already free from her bedding, a perfect display for her athletic body in denim cutoffs and a tank top she wore without a bra. Mark tried not to stare at her perky nipples, but it was no use.

"You would." He gave her a silly grin and slowly got up.

Dana stood up so quickly it startled him into banging his head against the wall. "Dream on," she said in a low voice, and circled Mark in a way that uncomfortably reminded him of hyenas rounding up wounded prey.

"I mean, I got invited here. What's your deal?" Memories of the previous night were slowly flooding back in, and Mark patted his pocket to make sure he still had the biker's phone. Bingo.

"What are you looking for? I don't need to get my money off little kids in the playground," said Dana

Mark bit his lip, uselessly trying to fight off a silly grin. "Oh, yeah? You get it from them?" He pointed at the door of the bedroom where his saviors had disappeared yesterday. "Are they bi?"

Dana snorted. "I think Seth likes you. You should approach him only when Dom isn't looking."

Mark gave a slow nod. It had been Beardie, Seth, who had told Dom that they should take Mark in for the night. Maybe he was hoping to spice up their sex life, but didn't know how to communicate it to his partner? Then again, Mark could hardly believe there could be a boring sex life with a man who looked like Dom. Even the ugly, uneven scar that ran across his face didn't make him any less attractive. The guy radiated charisma. *Then again*, Domenico had claimed he was religious, back in the store. Maybe he was one of those religious gays who liked to fuck under the blanket, in the dark. Or just did blow jobs. Or not even that. Mark had met a priest on his way to Louisiana, who paid him just to cuddle for the night. The priest's hard-on had poked Mark's back through the night, but the guy had kept his promise.

As Mark's thoughts drifted, Seth emerged from the bedroom in just a T-shirt and boxer briefs, looking too hungover to speak.

"Hi," said Dana, without breaking the hard gaze she settled on Mark. "Are you alive?"

"Yeah, yeah." Seth waved his hand at her and turned around to put the kettle on.

Mark bit his lip. The guy was *big*. Tall, broad-shouldered. A bit pudgy, but his ass was so round Mark

couldn't take his eyes off it, even though Seth wasn't exactly his type. "Morning!"

Seth groaned and waved at him as well without turning around. "You don't have to yell."

"I can get you some painkillers. Always works on me," Dana said, even though her voice sounded strangely flat, as if there were a tiny alien in her head, communicating through an advanced version of text-to-speech.

"Dom already gave me some, thanks. I need coffee now, and I'll be fine. I haven't drunk this much for ages. It was good, but then it was bad. I guess Dom's birthday is as good an excuse as it gets. Anyone else wants coffee?"

"Me!" Mark quickly said, and almost froze on the spot under Dana's gaze.

Seth frowned and looked back at him, as if it were the first time he'd ever seen Mark, but before he could say anything, Domenico stormed out all fresh-faced, in a pair of black jeans and a tank top that revealed smooth, muscled arms. Nicely tanned, sandy with a cool olive undertone. Mark could lick them all over.

"Me." He walked up to Seth and slid his arm to his partner's back, kissing his cheek. In the position they were in, they seemed to merge seamlessly into one another by the kitchen counter.

"Decaf," Dana said flatly.

Seth turned around to Dom and gave him a kiss so intimate that Mark averted his eyes, feeling as if he were infringing on their privacy.

"I don't do decaf. You can make it after I'm done," Seth said.

Domenico grinned and slid both his arms around Seth's waist, resting his head on the big shoulder. Some of his smooth hair fell down Seth's bare arm, and Mark averted his eyes again.

Dana hissed. "It's in the jar. What's your problem? Just dissolve the packet in water."

"Blasphemy," chuckled Domenico and otherwise ignored her.

"It's against my principles," Seth mumbled as the kettle announced the water was ready. "Like vegetarians refusing to use a knife that touched meat."

"Even the kid drinks normal coffee," said Domenico, acknowledging Mark's presence for the first time.

Mark gave him his smile number five, but then looked out the window. Shit. He didn't even know where he was, or how far away from Fred's place. What if they'd gone the other way, and he was even farther from his destination now?

"Is there cake left? You know, from the birthday?" Mark asked.

Domenico frowned. "It's my cake. I told you to have other food. There are chocolate bars in the cupboard."

"Maybe you shouldn't encourage him," Dana said with a straight face. "He's not training as much as you and I."

Mark straightened up and took his shirt off to pat his stomach. "I might be young, but I do stuff." He wasn't as skinny as a year ago. He tried to eat meat and work out, so that Fred wouldn't be disappointed when they finally met.

Seth snorted and turned around to say something but was instantly distracted when he picked up the kettle and it tipped over in his hand, pouring some boiling water over the counter. Domenico's hand was on the kettle at lightning speed, and so the spill wasn't too great and didn't splash Seth.

"Karma," Dana muttered.

Domenico shot her a cool glance. "What was that? You want to sleep outside?"

She pressed her lips together. "I'll go jogging if you're busy."

"Do that."

Mark frowned, watching them. So they'd taken her in as well in some sense? Were they some kind of charity-fags? Maybe he could get more out of staying here then? He slowly rubbed his neck, remembering the tight hold Domenico had over his throat yesterday. The outburst could have been a one-time thing if the guy was a man of God and all that. Anyone would go a bit mental when having a gun pointed at them. And this was rural Louisiana. Many people carried guns, so it was no biggie.

As soon as Dana left, Mark went straight for the bags with groceries and pulled out a chocolate bar. He spoke when he noticed Seth open sliced bread. "Can I stay for breakfast? Please?"

Domenico shrugged. "You're having coffee, aren't you? You already invited yourself for breakfast," he said, massaging Seth's back.

Mark noticed Seth's hand tremble slightly, and it had a big scar on top, but he was still him who prepared sandwiches, which was a bit strange. Mark wasn't complaining. He munched the chocolate all too quickly, and his eyes went wide at the giant Snickers Dom pulled out of the bag.

"Dom, I'm making breakfast," Seth moaned.

"I know. I'm gonna eat breakfast. I'm hungry as a wolf," said Domenico, with a kiss to Seth's shoulder.

Mark grinned and nodded. "Yeah, I get like that after fucking too." He took a seat by the small table, eager to get some protein.

Domenico's eyes could freeze hell over. "You think you're funny, kid?"

Seth groaned and pulled away from his partner, which only made the atmosphere denser.

Mark swallowed. "No, I... I mean—Have you been together long?" Changing the topic was the best course of action. He was *not* walking out without breakfast! And the

fucking thing was a real cock-up if he was right about Dom being some white marriage sort of freak.

But Domenico's shoulders relaxed, and he leaned back against the counter as the scent of coffee slowly filled the room. "Almost a year now, right?" he asked, nudging Seth, who rubbed his eyes and smiled for the first time since he'd walked out of the bedroom.

"Yes. Almost a year." He reached out and ran his fingers through Dom's hair.

Mark laughed. "'Cause you act like an old married couple."

Domenico chuckled, and his eyes immediately lit up as he gathered Seth into his arms. In contrast to Seth, his body was all lean muscle, as if he was a personal trainer. Maybe he was into bears, or something?

"Nah, we're still only engaged."

"Oh! So you're gonna get gay-married, and all that? Get a dog, a white picket fence?" Mark snorted. He was *never* getting tied down!

Domenico grinned and nudged Seth's shoulder with his forehead. "Not sure about the dog, but it is gonna happen eventually."

Seth shook his head and slid out of Dom's hold. He carried all three plates to the table with his left hand, with the balancing skills of a waiter. "Oh, is it? You haven't asked me."

"Ouch. Buuurn!" Mark hissed, but was quick to tuck into a tuna and mayo sandwich.

Domenico frowned at him and crooked his head. "That's what happens after one gets engaged."

Seth raised his eyebrows and sat next to Mark. "I mean, the ring is a symbol of commitment, but it doesn't have to mean marriage and the whole shebang."

Domenico frowned, and the earlier smile faltered on his face. "Not where I'm from."

"You don't even have same-sex marriage *where we're from*. But we don't need that anyway." Seth bit into his sandwich.

Domenico shook his head and walked up to Seth. He put both his hands on the table and leaned forward. "Don't we? You wanna live together without God's blessing?" he asked, dead serious.

Mark bit back a laugh, because the guy didn't sound like he was joking.

Seth looked up at Dom, chewing for a longer moment. "I don't like weddings."

Domenico frowned at him. "Well, you're gonna have one."

Seth groaned and didn't say a word, which Dom must have taken for *I will*, because he sat down and began eating as well. Mark thought it was a good moment to change the topic slightly.

"Wouldn't you miss fucking other guys when you get married?" he asked.

Domenico laughed and banged his hand on the tabletop. "Why would any of us go for the second-best?"

Seth rolled his eyes.

Mark swallowed his food. "You know, to try different things. I've had a blond, a brunet, a redhead, a businessman... I could keep going."

Domenico shook his head. "We're adults. I'm pretty confident I had my share of experiments," he said and grabbed a Twix, which he then threw at Mark. Only when he grabbed the bar in midair did Mark realize he reacted like a dog.

Seth ran his finger over Domenico's forearm but then got himself a cigarette from a packet on the table. "Better tell us how old you are."

Mark groaned. "Eighteen. Legal since last month."

Seth let out a huff of smoke through his nose with a smirk.

"In your dreams, baby boy. You're fourteen," said Dom, squinting at Mark over the table.

Mark's lips parted in shock. "Am not! I could grow a beard if I wanted to!"

"Right. You just choose not to." Seth shook his head. "I'm gonna be more generous and guess fifteen."

Mark grumbled and chewed his Twix. "I'm sixteen. Almost seventeen. I am *not* fourteen. What the fuck?"

Domenico shrugged. "The fourteen made you tell us the truth. And since you're only sixteen, where are your parents? What are you doing fucking guys in public toilets?"

Mark pouted and slouched in his seat, consoled only by the taste of chocolate. "I just needed some cash. I thought he could give me a lift after as well."

"And why would he do that? Did he look like a nice guy to you, you little dumbass?" asked Domenico.

Mark couldn't help a smile. "He did look *nice*."

"Come on, Dom," Seth said and waved his hand. "It's most important that nothing happened."

"But it could have." Domenico rolled his eyes and looked at Seth. "Can't believe you're supporting him. Would you do what he did?"

"Hell no!" Seth leaned back in the seat with his cigarette. "I'd find a different way to make the cash."

Mark frowned. "Whatever."

"What was that, you little ungrateful fuck?" asked Domenico, leaning over the table, with his brows gathered into a deep frown that made him look both sexy and dangerous.

Seth put out his cigarette. "Jeez, Dom. Don't talk to him like that."

Domenico gestured at Mark. "Why not? Sixteen or not, a whore's a whore. Someone should tell him the truth before it's too late."

Mark felt his face heat up, and he put down the other Twix to make a point.

Seth slapped the back of Dom's shoulder. "Dom! He's a teenager, you can't say that!"

Domenico took a cigarette from the pack left on the table and lit it quickly. "I could take far worse when I was his age."

"You grew up in different circumstances. You must be able to see that," Seth said, but Mark wouldn't take his pity.

"I'm totally fine. It's not like I will be doing this forever. I've got better things coming my way."

"Oh, yeah? What's your plan for the future then? Working with *wieners*?"

"Much better." Mark crossed his arms on his chest. "There's this guy, Fred, I'm going to, and he will help me find a job. He's got *connections*."

"Oh, that's right. *Fred*." Domenico nodded, and for a few seconds, Mark almost believed Domenico knew his prince. "You will be making hot dogs for his friends as well."

"That is *so* rude! Fred's a good guy," Mark hissed.

Seth shrugged. "Give him a break, Dom. Even if he's to be some go-go boy or something, that's still better than street prostitution. This way, he wouldn't be in danger."

"I won't be a go-go boy!" Mark bristled up.

"Oh, you seem to have it all figured out," said Domenico. He leaned back in his chair, with smoke dancing around him in a patterned cloud. "You're a genius. You have a degree at sixteen."

Seth licked his lips. "It *can* all work out for him..."

Domenico glanced between Seth and Mark. "You think? He could have been rotting in some ditch by now for all we know."

Mark got up from the chair and spread his arms. "I didn't ask for your help! You can't talk this shit to me just because you're *old*."

Domenico dismissed that last comment with a gesture. "You screamed for help like a little girl."

Seth smirked. "Ouch. Buuuurn." He mimicked Mark's earlier comment.

"I've had enough of this bullshit! I'm out!" Mark grabbed the other Twix and his backpack and went for the door. He was not leaving chocolate behind just because they were dicks.

"And now he's throwing a tantrum," said Domenico as Mark was closing the door.

He went into the quiet street outside, suddenly overwhelmed by the little houses with dirty walls and the trees visible across the street. He had no idea where he was, and the thick air punched his lungs like a fist.

Mark was determined not to let them win, and he started walking to nowhere, increasingly anxious. At least he had the biker's phone to sell, so there was that. And he had sneaked a granola bar into his pocket before Dana could spot that.

But after walking on for ten minutes, he got to the end of the sidewalk, and there was nothing in front of him but forest and road.

He swore and sat down on a fallen tree, trying to forget Dom's words. Fucking saint. Just because he didn't fuck his boyfriend and gave street kids condoms didn't make him superior!

Mark pulled out the granola bar. He would need the energy before he started a long walk that would probably lead him into a swamp where a gator would eat him. He sniffed and rubbed his eyes. He'd never asked for a life like this.

As he sat there with the empty wrapper, he startled when a heavy arm covered his shoulders. Seth sat next to

him and passed him a packet of Oreos. Mark didn't know what to say, so he started eating and only spoke once he went through half of the cookies.

"I'm not stupid," he whispered and leaned his head against Seth's shoulder. "I know my life's messed up, but I'll manage…"

Seth petted his hair, and for a moment, Mark wanted to be his forever. "I'm not judging you. Sometimes, you're forced to do things that you don't want to do. We'll take you to Fred if that's what you want. But maybe give it a few days, okay? We're leaving soon anyway, and you could recuperate after the traveling you've done."

Mark swallowed, overwhelmed by the free kindness. "I don't think Dom would agree to me being there…"

Seth sighed and slouched his big, strong body. "He will. He's just hotheaded."

Mark flinched when something hit his shoulder, and he stared at the asphalt, stunned to see a chocolate candy. When he looked up, he saw Domenico walking over with a white plastic bag in hand. Wind blew into his hair, uncovering the handsome face hidden behind a pair of shades. The big scar running across his nose and cheek did nothing to make the freakishly symmetrical face any less appealing. "You two left me bored."

"We'll take Mark to this Fred guy in a few days," Seth said, and Mark liked the confidence in his voice.

Domenico stopped right next to them and reached into the bag, taking out another piece of candy. "Is that really necessary?"

Seth looked up at him and poked Dom's thigh. "We could see if the guy's not some psycho."

Domenico sat cross-legged in front of them. "So what about your family? You refuse to answer," he asked after several moments of contemplating the chocolate.

Mark groaned and looked away. "'Cause they're dead." He was not about to share his life story with strangers, no matter how nice they seemed. "They were originally from Romania, but I grew up in New Jersey. We had no family here, and I didn't want to go into foster care."

"And you've been on your own all this time?" Seth asked and pulled him a bit closer. Mark couldn't help but lean into the hug. Seth smelled good, even with the lingering aroma of cigarettes.

"You can't even protect yourself when something happens. For all we know, you could be dead within the year," said Domenico, pushing a piece of chocolate into his mouth.

Mark laughed nervously, as the truth behind that statement touched him briefly. "I can run pretty quickly."

Dom shrugged. "Wasn't good enough last time."

"This stuff really doesn't happen often. I try to be smart about it. I just saw all that hair, and I lost my mind." Mark sighed at the memory of the handsome asshole who refused to stop recording him. Served him right to lose the phone.

Domenico tossed a hard candy at Mark. It bounced off his fingers and rolled far enough that he had to crawl a bit to reach it.

"I could show you some moves," said Dom.

Mark blew air at the candy and ate it, smiling at the soothing caramel flavor. "And what kind of moves do you know?"

Seth nodded and pulled away to Mark's dismay. "He could teach you self-defense."

"And ballroom dancing," said Domenico.

Seth snorted. "What else are you gonna teach him in a week? Wine-tasting?"

Mark smiled wider. "Yes, please."

Domenico pulled out a cigarette out of a packet. "You're too young where we are now. And I never break the law."

Mark didn't like the way Seth broke into a laugh at those words, but something warm spread in his chest when Seth leaned over to Dom and kissed his cheek. "Never."

"You guys are so sweet," Mark said.

Domenico raised his hand. "Rule number one, kid— don't steal my food. Rule number two—never use the words 'sweet' or 'cute' when referring to men. Words and semantics matter. It's this kind of language that digs at the foundations of masculinity of the men today. All wimps and hippers."

Seth grinned and nuzzled Dom's cheek. "You mean hipsters?"

"Whatever. What kind of person do you have to be to call yourself that?"

Mark laughed. "All I meant is that you two are... nice to look at. Not in a pervy way, but I don't think I've ever met guys who wanna get married, and all that. Everyone always cheats and sleeps around."

"Well, there isn't much to look at in these parts anyway," snorted Domenico, pulling Seth closer. He slipped his hand underneath Seth's shirt.

"Hey, don't..." Seth's breath hitched, and he actually stood up to escape the touch. Mark wasn't sure what that was about.

He licked his lips. "You guys seriously not up for a threesome? I give good head."

Domenico scowled as he followed Seth to his feet. "God! Stop offering yourself up. You're not a bag of Cheetos."

Mark raised his hands. "Okay, okay. Just saying that it's on the table. When do I start training?"

Domenico looked him up and down, slowly pushing his hands into the pockets of his jeans. "Eager. I like that."

Chapter 6 - Domenico

Domenico was walking back and forth at the rear side of the house where he and Dana had enough privacy to do some of their stationary exercise without having local kids asking to join in. This time, it wasn't Dana Domenico was training but a scrawny sixteen-year-old, who was sweating like a pig after just half an hour. "Come on, twenty more," he said, noticing the way Mark fell face-first during yet another sad attempt at a push-up.

"I can't!" Mark cried, with sweat dripping down his nose and his hair in matted streaks, but even as he said that, he pulled himself up yet again.

Domenico kneeled next to him and leaned down to look into the boy's eyes. "You're fucking soft. Really? You can't even manage fifty of them? Don't be a pussy! If I gave up every time something hurt, I wouldn't be doing two hundred each morning. If I tell you that you can do it, it means that you *can*."

"But my muscles burn so bad," Mark whined. Fortunately, for his own sake, he continued doing the push-ups, even if at a snail's pace.

"Dana can easily do a hundred, and she's a *girl*!" growled Domenico as he stood up and placed his bare foot between Mark's shoulder blades. He enjoyed the feeling of muscle contracting under his touch.

To give the boy credit, Mark wasn't as skinny as Dom had thought the first time he'd assessed him. He was lean, but there was definitely some muscle on him. He had the sort of body that could grow if pushed. And then it was hard to know how tall he would be, as he was now several inches shorter than Domenico, but if he was sixteen, he still had the chance of growing much taller.

"Don't you think that's enough, Dom?" Seth yelled from his bench on the porch.

Domenico poked Mark's ribs with his toes. "You heard that? Seth thinks you can't do it! Do you want to prove him wrong?"

Mark rasped as if he was about to cough out his lungs, but he continued with his push-ups with renewed vigor. That was more like it.

"Yes, just like that! I knew you could do it!" cheered Domenico. Inspired, he dropped into the same position across from Mark and started doing push-ups himself. He loved the feeling of his muscles moving with ease, propping him up, only to safely let him go lower.

But what he loved even more was seeing Seth get up from his bench and come closer to the railing to watch him.

"I'm hungry..." Mark moaned, but Dom couldn't care less when he felt Seth's gaze all over his back. It made him want to work harder, keep his hands tighter, his body more ripped, stronger. Maybe strong enough to fuck Seth against the wall one day again.

"Mark, ten more!"

"No... It's too much," Mark spoke, interrupting the sentence with ragged breaths. "Insane."

Domenico gritted his teeth and looked into Mark's eyes, big, brown and mere inches away. "You can do it! Remember one thing—in this life, we're either winners or losers. Your choice, Mark. You wanna be a pussy loser?"

Mark whined but picked himself up yet again. "I'm not a pussy!"

The smile Dom got from Seth was all he needed to spur him on.

"Dom, show him how you do it on one hand."

Domenico grinned and glanced at Seth, immediately pulling one hand back and pumping up and down using just the strength of his one arm. "What will I get in return?" he asked Seth.

Seth smirked. "I'm going off to the shop. I'll get you Nutella."

"Me too! I'm almost done!" Mark whined.

Domenico's heart skipped a beat. "How about Mark getting the Nutella, and you'll give me something else instead," he asked slowly, pushing the words out as he exercised with as much precision as he could muster.

Seth laughed. "Wow. You must really love me to want me more than Nutella."

"Can I get protein powder?" Dana yelled from afar, as she were preparing for her ten-mile jog.

Domenico winked at Seth. "I prefer my protein from a natural source."

Seth bit his lip, and there it was—that blush Dom loved seeing on his face. It instantly brought to mind the expression Seth had on his face when he had an orgasm. All red and moaning for more. Even thinking about it made Dom want to go over there and fuck him over the railing, hear him scream again.

Mark fell to the ground face first, barely catching breaths. "I did it..."

Domenico grinned but didn't stop his own workout. He wanted Seth to keep looking at him, especially now

after yet another horrific dream. This one had Seth shackled to the bottom of a rapidly filling pool. He drowned in front of Dom, who sat in front of the pool, paralyzed from a dosage of drugs Vincente injected into his neck. "Good job. Don't give me that *I can't* shit ever again."

"Yes, sir. I... I'll just lie here until the Nutella comes," Mark choked out, panting like a dying llama.

"I better work on that then." Seth laughed and went into the house, to Dom's disappointment. He was also wearing the fucking baggy jogging bottoms that hid away the shape of his perfectly round ass.

"Seth, we just did shopping yesterday," he called after him, slightly frustrated by the audience he wanted disappearing from sight. What the fuck was up with that?

Mark slowly turned to his back and watched Dom from below, with sweat beaded on his red face. "You are so sexy," he whispered.

Domenico rolled his eyes. That wasn't what he wanted to hear from the kid. "I know, I know. I'm amazing."

"I want to get that way." Mark trailed his fingers up Dom's forearm.

"Stop it." Domenico rolled to the grass and brushed off the hand, as if it were a mosquito.

Mark groaned and put his hands over his face. "Then why did you take me? I don't get it."

Domenico pushed himself up and sat in front of him, evening out his breath in the heat. "Seth asked me to."

Mark looked out from behind his fingers. "He's the one who wants me?"

Domenico snorted in disbelief. Seth wanting a boy like this after having Domenico Acerbi? "Don't be ridiculous. If you want to make yourself useful, you can wash the car."

Mark moaned. "I can't. Everything hurts."

They heard the sound of a motorcycle engine, and Dom was sure it was Seth going off without saying good-

bye. He looked toward the house, but it was only Dana on the porch, drinking some vitamin water.

Dom slowly lay on his back, angry that the air didn't smell of salty water, which was just one more reason why he didn't belong where he was now. At least the sun was behind clouds, so it wasn't as hot as it could've been. "Did he go?"

"Yes, he's gone," Dana said.

But Mark continued with the same stupid topic. "I thought that Seth might want me if you're, like, really religious and don't do sex, or something."

Domenico groaned. "For fuck's sake! Seth just wants to help you. He's a good guy, that's all." His heart thundered so loudly he was afraid Dana would pick it up. "And we fuck enough."

Mark raised his hands and sat up. "Okay, okay! Just asking, 'cause when gay guys stop fucking, things are bad. I know this stuff."

"I've been a gay guy ten years longer than you," growled Domenico, even though he knew there was truth to Mark's words. Each time Seth slid away from his touch felt like a slap to the face. Like he wasn't wanted around anymore.

"I've had this one guy a few times, and we'd fuck for like, five minutes, and then he'd complain about his boyfriend for the rest of the time we were together. And I wasn't even the only guy he cheated on his boyfriend with."

Domenico stilled and looked back at Mark, unsure how that example made him feel. Seth wasn't a cheater. "He went shopping."

And then fucking Dana chipped in, as if it were any of her business. "You don't technically know that."

Domenico frowned at her. "Why wouldn't I believe him?" he asked, even though now that the seed of Seth possibly lying had been planted, the roots were quickly growing all over Domenico's heart.

"Sorry," Dana said, but there was no apology in her voice.

"I probably wouldn't cheat if I had a stud like Domenico at home." Mark gave Dom a dreamy smile.

Domenico scowled at him and pulled himself up. "I'm gonna call him. I want some juice," he added when he noticed a twitch of Dana's lips as he walked past her. The inside of the house seemed dark after spending time outside, but he easily navigated his way all the way to the bedroom and picked up the cell phone he had left on top of the bed. Seth should be in the town center right now, because he'd go to the nearest supermarket, not to the Walmart half an hour away. Dom dialed the number and put the phone against his ear.

He waited while it rang, and all he got was voicemail. He dialed again and then waited for several minutes in the hope that Seth would call him back. It didn't happen.

Domenico bit his lip and looked at the little bedroom. Their few possessions were neatly stacked in the open wardrobe and the drawer where Seth stored all the underwear Dom didn't get to see much anymore. Could it be that he'd met someone, and that was the reason behind him being so disinterested in sex?

Dom didn't want to think about it, but the idea had been planted, and it was screaming at him louder with each breath he took.

"Dana? I'll go into town. I'll be back soon," he said, picking up his gun from one of the drawers.

"Are you getting the juice? Is Seth not answering? Can I come? I wanted some Cheetos, too!" Mark yelled from the backyard, and Domenico thumped his head against the wall.

"As long as you shut up," he growled and stormed outside, heading for the pickup, which seemed a much

brighter red than before, especially against Dana's banana yellow Chevy.

"Yay!" Mark was on his feet seconds later, putting on a T-shirt on the way and stinking of teenage sweat.

"Buy yourself some Old Spice, or something," muttered Domenico, opening the windows as they both settled in their seats.

Mark made a sad face at him. "I don't have money for unnecessary stuff."

Domenico started the car and opened his wallet with his teeth. "I'll give you some pocket money. You can't be dirty while you live with us."

Mark's lips parted in a wide grin, and Dom was sure his words were all Mark had waited for. The kid's manipulation skills weren't very stealthy. "Thanks. I'll wash twice a day."

"Do that." Domenico reached into his wallet and handed Mark a few bills, more than the kid had probably held in a long time. Domenico would make sure to watch what he'd do with the money. For the moment, Mark greedily tucked the bills into his pocket.

"If you and Seth ever broke up, I'd be there for you, you know?" Mark said as if they'd known each other for more than a day.

"You're creepy." Domenico pressed on the gas and rushed toward the town center. Where the fuck would Seth be? Come to think of it, his solitary shopping expeditions were usually quite long. And he'd come back tired. What if Dana and Mark were right? What if?

When they reached the small supermarket in town, Domenico smiled at the motorbike parked in front of it, only to realize it wasn't Seth's. Similar, but not the same one. Seth wasn't here. God only knew where he could be.

When they drove out of the parking lot without stopping, Mark spoke.

"Um... Weren't we supposed to buy shit?"

Domenico turned to look at him and squeezed his hands on the wheel. "He's not there. We'll find him first, and then you can go wherever the fuck you want!"

Mark leaned back in the seat. "Jeez. It's not like he'd vanish. Maybe he went to another store."

"Then look for his bike. You have a pair of healthy eyes, I assume. Earn your fucking keep." Domenico breathed in a big gulp of air and drove toward a small general goods store two blocks away.

Mark looked at him with a stupid grin and new recognition in his eyes. "I get it! You do think he could be cheating. Oh, my God! This is so exciting. It's like this TV show when they find people with lovers. I always wanted to be, like, a detective. Drive around with a spy camera and that kind of shit."

"No, I don't think he's cheating. I'm just worried where he is, you fucking moron! This isn't a game!" Domenico took a sharp turn next to the local museum, which consisted of a single room in someone's spare space. A woman stepped away from the street and called after the car, but Dom ignored it and drove on, leaning forward over the steering wheel. His eyes were scanning both sides of the road, filtering every man and motorbike around.

"There it is!" Mark yelped and pointed ahead, where Seth's sport bike was parked next to a few Harleys.

Domenico frowned as they passed the large compound that housed the local gym, among other things. It *was* Seth's bike. What the fuck was he doing there of all places?

Domenico drove too far, but with the street as empty as it was, he made a U-turn a few yards down the road, at the cost of grazing the pavement with an unpleasant screech of the tires, and rushed straight into the parking lot.

Mark held on to his seat belt and only unbuckled it once Domenico stopped the car. "Maybe he's buying Dana's protein," he suggested.

Domenico froze and looked at him, noticing how shallow his breath was, even though he'd had his ass in the seat for the last five minutes. "Maybe," he muttered and slid out of the car. "Let's check if he's choosing the right one."

Domenico didn't have to see Mark to know he followed him out of the car, but it was something else that made his blood boil.

Seth *was* there.

Domenico could see him through the big front windows of the gym, stretched on a bench and lifting a barbell while a big tattooed guy with a black ponytail spotted him.

Domenico's smile faltered, and he rushed to the door, not wanting Seth to notice him. The powerful pulsing he sensed earlier in his veins was now spreading around his throat, like an ever-tightening noose. He walked past the door and then past the reception desk, straight for the halfway open door that should lead to the weight room. He peeked inside the small space decorated with spots made with dirty hands on the back wall.

Seth's right hand trembled while the left one remained steady, but he still managed to lift the fucking barbell. The spotter looked even more handsome from up close. His hair was gathered into a barely-long-enough-to-tie ponytail, and his stubble gave him the kind of rugged good looks that made him oddly similar to Seth himself. His thick arms were covered with tattoos that didn't look like fancy artwork but ink found in gangs and prisons. Domenico found them appalling, and just watching the ugly, faded drawings near his lover's skin nauseated him.

The spotter's smile, on the other hand, was friendly when he helped Seth put the weight away once Seth was

done. "Good. You keep getting better. Your hand has a better grip now, doesn't it?"

Domenico slowly exhaled a bit of air, but then someone touched his shoulder, and he barely kept himself from punching them back. It was a young woman, dressed in a simple shirt with the logo that he'd seen outside, drawn on the side of the building.

"Can I help?" she asked.

Domenico lowered his eyes. "No. I want to assess it all on my own."

Seth, the bastard, smiled back at the spotter, all red faced and with a sweaty patch at the front of his shirt. "Yes, I can't wait to lift more."

The spotter laughed. "That's such a good attitude."

Domenico growled, staring at that beautiful body stretched out on the bench as Seth clearly flirted with the handsome stranger when all the attention he was giving Domenico was meager scraps. It all made more sense now. Did Seth start despising Domenico because he now knew they weren't blood brothers, and it had been the taboo aspect of their relationship that had turned him on? Or was it just disappointment? Domenico let Seth get hurt. He hadn't been able to stop Vincente from torturing him, even though he had promised. He had failed Seth.

But that didn't explain Seth going behind Domenico's back.

Dom opened the door and walked into the weight room, completely breathless. All he could hear was Seth's soft laugh tickling his inner ear.

"I'm far from your level," Seth said in that lovely Sicilian accent Dom now wanted to choke out of him.

The trainer laughed. "Maybe you need to come more often then."

Domenico grabbed the empty steel rod from a stand and walked straight through the room, which was empty at this time of day. But even if there were men

training all around Seth, Dom would not wait. This could not wait.

"Fuck off him," he growled, walking straight at the spotter, whose gray eyes narrowed when he noticed Domenico.

"I don't know you. Is there a problem?"

"Since when has this been going on?"

Seth looked up at him like a deer in the headlights, and sat up so fast he hit his head on the barbell and fell back on the bench. "Dom? What? What are you doing here?" He rubbed his forehead and rolled off to sit on the edge of the bench. "Are you following me?"

Domenico put the bar on his shoulders, and the cool metal felt so pleasant on his heated nape, he'd be grateful for it if it wasn't for what he just discovered. His heart seemed to grow in his chest, pushing at his lungs and not letting him breathe anymore. It was about to burst like an overgrown soap bubble. "*Are you* buying Nutella?"

The spotter stepped closer. "Hey, what is this about?"

Seth pursed his lips and got up. "Don't worry, I've got this." He put his hand on the spotter's shoulder. *He actually put his hand on the fucker.*

Domenico pulled the bar off his shoulder and put one end at the center of the spotter's chest, pushing him back so hard the guy grabbed himself there and backed away, sinking lower and staring at Domenico, as if he just now recognized that he wasn't dealing with a random crazy.

"Since when has this been going on?" repeated Domenico, staring straight into Seth's big brown lying eyes.

Seth stood between him and the spotter. "This is none of your business. It's private."

Domenico took a shallow breath, keeping Seth's gaze as heat rose in his brain, scrambling it while Dom was still alive. "You lying piece of shit. You're *cheating* on me?"

The spotter blinked and stepped back.

Seth frowned at him and pushed the bar away as if he was asking for Dom to use the piece of steel. "Are you out of your mind? Who gives you the right to stalk me?"

Domenico knocked him aside and swung the bar toward the spotter. The guy had good enough reflexes to dodge, but Dom already knew the man would move and sharply kicked him straight in the unprotected ribs.

The spotter hissed and fell back on the empty bench, rolling away just in time to evade the bar smashing into the floor where the guy's leg had been a second ago. "What the fuck? I'm just his personal trainer!" he yelled loud enough to create an echo in the weight room.

"Dom! No!" Seth yelled at him, and grabbed the steel rod in Dom's hand. He was actually going as far as protecting the motherfucker instead of answering his goddamn questions. Dom could bet Seth was fucking the guy. No wonder he had no energy for his fiancé at home.

Domenico pushed on the rod, hitting Seth just hard enough to put him out of breath. The stinging in his eyes was rapidly becoming stronger, as if someone had blown chili powder on his eyeballs. "You fucking liar! This explains every. Fucking. Thing," hissed Domenico, charging at the trainer, who ducked behind the barbell Seth had used moments ago. Steel met with a power that sent the screeching sound all over the place, attacking Dom's ears and making him even deafer to the world. All he could see was the deception in Seth's pretty eyes when he said *I'm still in pain, Dom*. He imagined those big tattooed hands all over Seth as the guy fucked *Dom's fiancé* in the locker room.

"Stop it," Seth yelled at him. "We're supposed to be lying low!" he added in Italian and grabbed Dom from behind, pulling him back.

Domenico hit him with his elbow, fueled by a fury greater than his body could contain. "I'm gonna rip your

heart out!" he screamed, turning back to Seth. He grabbed the front of Seth's wet shirt and pulled, wanting to look him straight in the eye.

Seth held on to his own ribs with a gasp. "He's not even gay, Dom! You had no right to come after me!" He didn't shy away with his gaze, scowling at Dom. At least Dom felt there was honest feeling still left in the fucker.

Dom could hardly speak loud enough with emotion bubbling up in his chest like a tidal wave. "You keep lying to me, you fucker. I'd do anything for you, and *that's* how you pay me back? You won't let me touch you for three fucking months, and somehow you lift weights?"

That shut Seth up. He made this hurt, tender face, as if he were made of glass, but Dom was not about to treat him like porcelain anymore, since he was clearly fine. Seth opened his lips seconds later, but then yelped and pulled Dom forward so hard they toppled over.

Domenico stopped breathing and pushed away the metal bar, just in time to have his hands free to prop himself over Seth. The clang of falling steel rang in his ears, but the swish behind him became even more prominent in Dom's mind as the moving air touched his skin. He rolled off Seth and jumped forward, grabbing the trainer's waist and throwing him over, along with the metal baseball bat the bastard held in his hand. He swung it toward Dom, his eyes wide with fury, but Domenico grabbed his forearm and bludgeoned the guy's face with his elbow. It wouldn't be so handsome anymore.

There was a blunt sound when the trainer's head met the floor, but Domenico had more to deal with, as another person ran into the room.

"Get off my brother if you want to live!" yelled someone, and Dom could vaguely recognize the voice. "You motherfucker! How dare you show your hairy face here?" screamed the guy, putting Dom on high alert over Seth's safety.

"We were leaving!" Seth answered and pulled on the back of Dom's tank top.

Domenico gritted his teeth and looked back at him through the curtain of his unruly hair. "Are we? You fucking okay to talk now?" he growled, getting up from the trainer whom he had apparently knocked out. That hadn't been the plan, but Dom wasn't sorry.

Seth bared his teeth. "I'm not doing this here!"

"You stole my phone, you little fucker!" Dom looked over Seth's shoulder and recognized the blond prick from yesterday, pulling at Mark's arm. Dom hadn't even known the kid had followed him inside.

The chaos only amplified when Mark started squealing that he didn't know anything about a phone. Seth crouched down next to Domenico, his face going from red to ghastly pale. "Did you kill him?" he asked, but Dom didn't have the time to get agitated as the blond biker heard that. He let go of Mark, pushing the boy away so abruptly he fell to the floor.

"Ryder?" The blond rushed their way. "Ryder! Talk to me, you fucker!"

In the background, Mark scrambled off the floor and ran out of the gym like the chickenshit he was. Domenico hissed after him, but the moment he saw a glint of steel, he pushed Seth back and dove toward the biker, just in time to knock a gun out of his hand with a strategic hit. It clattered against the floor, and Domenico punched the biker under the nose, sending him to the floor.

"You were cheating on him just last night, so shut up, you fucking child molester!" he growled, picking up the fallen gun. He pulled the safety off and pressed the barrel against the biker's forehead. "Don't move, bitch," hissed Domenico, staring into the pale blue eyes.

Seth sat on the floor, gasping for air, but what Dom saw in the corner of his eye truly shocked him. Just behind

the window, Mark drove off in their pickup. He couldn't believe this shit.

The blond biker stilled with his gaze flying between Domenico and the unconscious trainer. "Who the fuck are you? You said you weren't from here. You were supposed to leave." He was heaving. "Ryder?" he asked the unresponsive trainer again, more desperately.

Domenico looked at the bulky body, which was slowly stirring back to life, and then glanced straight into the biker's eyes. "If I wanted to kill him, I would have. Don't be such a drama queen on me, because it's fucking pissing me off."

Ryder groaned and put his hand over the place where Dom had hit him. He rolled to his side and slowly opened his eyes. It took him two seconds to realize something was off, as he suddenly rolled back and tried to rise to his knees, only to fall to the floor. "Fuck... Jed..."

Seth slowly got up, looking around the gym with panic painted all over his face.

Jed looked at Seth, probably sensing he'd be easier to approach. His breath was shallow, his cheeks red, as he spoke without ever moving his head away from the barrel of the gun. "This can all go away. Just tell him to put the gun down. Unless you two have a fucking death wish."

Domenico laughed. He was a panther taking out two dogs. They had no idea how out of their league they were. Only now, being in this fucked-up standoff, he realized just how much he'd missed the adrenaline rush. "You really think you can scare me, boy?"

Jed squinted at him and hissed, despite the barrel against his forehead. "Try me. You gonna kill two people in the middle of town at noon?" He laughed, and there was a hint of crazy to it that Dom needed to watch out for. "Even if you do kill me, you'd be dead men walking wherever you go. The Coffin Nails pay their debts."

Ryder took a deep breath through his bloodied teeth. "Jed, shut the fuck up." Clearly, he was the sane one. With his eyes wide, he raised his empty hands and nodded at Domenico. "I'm sorry for him. He's just... worried. You two go wherever you want. I just want to gather my brother from the floor and have a beer at the end of the day."

Domenico squinted. "Someone still has some brains." Slowly, he looked down at Jed, who still glared at Domenico with his teeth bared like a rabid pit bull.

Seth took a few steps toward the exit, and then a few more. "Come on, Dom," he whispered.

Domenico smirked at Jed and slowly moved to his feet, still pointing the gun straight at the man's forehead. The pleasant buzz in his brain was like a drug he didn't know he missed. "If all of you dogs are like the two of you, I would forget about us, for your own sake. You're not the first to threaten me or my family. I am still here. They are not."

Jed glanced at his brother and then back at Dom. "Fuckin' psycho."

"Dom, let's go..." Seth pleaded, backing out.

Domenico raised the stolen gun to his lips and kissed the barrel. "I'm taking this," he whispered as he made his way to the door, keeping his eyes on the two brothers, frozen in one position like two statues. He could have broken their necks. He chose not to.

He pulled the safety on and followed Seth outside, with a warmth in his chest even as he looked at that lying prick.

"We were supposed to lie low! Are you fucking happy?" Seth yelled in Italian as he ran toward his bike. "Get on. Where's the car?"

"Your fucking stray took it. Yet another decision you totally blew!" Domenico exploded with anger as the truth in Seth's words stabbed into his stomach. They were

fucked. There would be police on their tail soon enough. They needed a new place to stay ASAP. Even before he reached the motorcycle, he had already chosen Dana's number as the addressee of a text message. Blood was thumping in his veins, his head was light from being high on adrenaline for the first time in months, and the motorbike reminded him of another escape long ago.

Seth pushed the spare helmet against Domenico's chest and put on one himself, mounting the bike in rapid moves. "Ungrateful motherfucker."

Domenico exhaled and slid into the slot at the back of Seth's bike. He put his arms around Seth's midsection and pulled hard, now knowing his ribs were fine. He'd been lied to for so long he didn't even know what to say now that he had already expressed his anger toward the two brothers in the gym.

With his other hand, he quickly typed: *Emergency. Find us a secluded spot. We're moving.* He sent it as Seth sped down the main street of the quiet town where they stood out like sore thumbs.

Chapter 7 - Seth

The heat of Dom's body behind Seth was both exciting and unnerving. Seth couldn't believe the outburst at the gym. Dom had actually knocked out Ryder. Sure, Ryder attacked Dom as well, but the whole mess wouldn't have happened in the first place if it weren't for Dom following him. So fucking typical. Seth was sure that the moment they got off the motorcycle, Dom would blame him for all of this. As if Seth didn't have the right to any privacy.

Blood was rushing through Seth's veins at a rapid pace, quicker than the motorcycle wheels could ever spin, and the grip around his body was burning him through the clothes. They were finished in this town. Lying low. *Fuck.* Dom could just never keep his crazy jealousy in check.

And on the topic of lying low, Dom wouldn't even grow a beard. When they moved down here, he'd given it a week but got so angry with the hair on his face he shaved it all off and hadn't tried again ever since.

As Seth arrived at the house, the stolen pickup was nowhere to be seen, and the door opened, spitting out Dana, who walked off the porch and straight at them.

"What's wrong?" she asked before Domenico even dismounted the bike, as if he didn't want his body touching Seth's anymore. It stung more than Seth dared to admit.

"We need to go," he grumbled, running into the house.

Seth got off but wasn't sure what to do with himself. All that he had now could fit into a backpack. He followed Dom inside along with Dana. Maybe he could pack some cans for wherever they were going.

"I've put out a few feelers, and there's a place not far from here that we can go to if things get desperate," Dana said. "But it's not a place to stay at. It's a shed in someone's summer house. They could be coming there at any point, and then we'd be screwed. Where's the car? Is the kid dead?"

Seth grabbed his backpack and started stuffing it with food. "He stole our pickup after Dom decided to pull a gun on two bikers in the middle of town."

Dana frowned, straightening up, as if she wanted to seem taller than Dom. He did exactly the same thing, and for a total of five seconds, they tried to stare one another down like two roosters. It was ridiculous.

"Not a word," hissed Dom in the end and burst into the bedroom, where he opened the wardrobe and yanked everything out, like a teenager throwing a tantrum.

Dana walked off to the living room with her face neutral, as if expressing any emotion was a foreign concept to her.

Seth bent over to grab his leather jacket from the floor. "Watch it with my stuff!" He grabbed his mother's cookbook and stuffed it into the backpack.

Domenico pushed him on the bed, moving around with his face red and a big bulging vein on his forehead. "You have no right to tell me what to do, you fucking liar!" he screamed in Italian.

Seth squinted at him and rubbed his ribs. They still hurt from where Dom had hit him. "I'm not obliged to tell you about everything I do!" he responded in the same language. "What were you thinking bursting in there like that? Now we have to move again! Ryder isn't even gay! He's been very kind to me, and you mess him up."

Domenico grabbed the sides of Seth's head and looked at him with so much venom it almost felt as if Seth's skin was burning. "*Kind* to you? I bet he was! I just wanna peel away all the skin he ever touched on you!"

Seth gasped and tried to pull away from his grip, but Dom only tightened it on Seth's hair. "Let me go," Seth hissed and pushed on Dom's shoulders. "All I did with him was gym."

"Right. You have *me* here, and you go and fool around with some local? I call this bullshit!" growled Domenico and pushed Seth on the bed so hard all the old springs squealed under him.

Seth gave up and watched him from the bed. "I wanted to do it on my own!"

Domenico paced around like a wounded panther, hissing and heaving as he took brief glances at Seth. The sudden movement back toward the bed was so unexpected it had Seth curling up even before Domenico's hand squeezed at the front of his throat and pushed him down.

"Stop lying to me! I deserve the truth! You deserted me and went off with some meathead. What was it that I did, huh?" he screamed, yanking Seth up and pushing him back on the mattress repeatedly, as if he wanted to punch a hole through the bedding. "You don't trust me to keep you safe anymore? Is that it?" he roared, looming above Seth like a furious animal.

"I didn't desert you! I live here!" Seth grabbed on to Dom's wrists, trying to contain him somehow. A part of him believed that Dom would never truly hurt him, but another part recognized that something might happen to him

before Dom calmed down. In moments like these, Seth was reminded that he wasn't on vacation in Louisiana, but on the run from the mafia with his assassin boyfriend.

"You can't keep me safe from *you*!" Seth yelled back at him with a scowl.

Domenico pulled back in one violent move that sent him into the open wardrobe. He grabbed one of the emptied shelves and watched Seth from beneath his thick brows, breathing hard, as if he were about to have a heart attack. "Nothing's left if I can't even trust you." His eyes were intense and piercing even in the shadows.

Seth got up cautiously, rubbing his throat and fighting the stinging in his eyes. How did they get to this point? "You *can* trust me. Why are you so mad?"

"No, I can't. You've *lied* to me," hissed Domenico, but instead of breaking into yet another tirade, he wordlessly grabbed a black sports bag and started randomly stuffing his clothes into it.

Seth swallowed, unsure where to even start picking up the pieces of what had just happened. If he told Dom what his trips to the gym were about, Domenico would regard him as weak. Soon enough, he would resent Seth, and in no time, they'd have no future left at all.

He just stood there with his backpack, but distraction came on its own accord. "Mark pulled up," Seth said, watching the pickup through the window, even though that fact only made him number.

Domenico dropped the bag to the floor and left without a word, gaining speed as he passed the open doorways one by one. Seth followed him like a sheep, but with the tension in Domenico's shoulders, he was now more worried for Mark than for himself.

Domenico jumped off the porch and ran up to the boy, who just exited the cab and backed away against the vehicle with his hands up. His obvious surrender didn't stop Domenico from delivering a punch so hard that it

knocked Mark down to the asphalt. The boy tumbled with a sharp cry and curled into a ball, hiding his head.

"You little shit!" hissed Domenico. "You fucking coward. We could have *died*!"

"Dom! Stop it! He's just a kid!" Seth ran over to him, fearing what could happen next.

"I'm sorry! I panicked!" Mark cried from the ground, but Domenico still kicked him right in the ass, so hard it moved the curled-up body by a few inches.

"He is *not* just a kid! He's a young man," Domenico hissed at Seth, looking back with the wide eyes of a madman. "You could have died because of him!"

Seth grabbed Dom under the arms and pulled him back. "He could have disappeared, but he came back with the car."

"So what? He took it in the first place. It wasn't even his! We could've been shot by some fucking village thugs!" spat Domenico, suddenly hitting the side of the car hard.

Mark yelped and crawled under the pickup. "I didn't know what to do! I felt so guilty after!"

Seth put his hands over his face, and Dom kicked one of the tires. "What did that biker want from you anyway? I'd have protected you, you dumbass!"

Mark peeked out from under the car with his eyes red. "I stole his phone... I pushed it out of his hand when he tried to film me."

Seth groaned. This was the last thing they needed.

Dana spoke from the porch. "We should just get rid of him."

Domenico let out a groan and looked between her and Mark, clearly torn. He was actually considering going with her suggestion!

Seth stepped between Dom and Mark. "Are you out of your mind? We don't need to do that. All we need to do is move. And *you* were supposed to be on that!" he yelled to Dana. "Not fucking drinking your protein shake!"

Dana shrugged and looked at the glass in her hand. "Not drinking it won't speed up anything. I'm waiting for people to call me back."

Domenico sighed and combed back all his hair. It was the most nervous Seth had seen him in a long, long time. "Whatever. Let's just get our stuff in the back of the car, and we're going. We *can't* stay here."

"I know a place we could go to," Mark said in a tiny voice, sticking his head from under the truck, with a bruise already forming on his cheek.

Seth stepped away to have a better look at him, and even Domenico slowly sank to one knee.

"Where?" he asked in a tone so calm, it jarred with his red face and sweaty hair.

Mark swallowed, curling his shoulders in anticipation of another punch. "A few days back, I stayed in this house deep in the swamps. The guy who lived there died, and no one found his body. It was old and dried up, so no one knows about it for sure. But it freaked me out, so I left."

Seth pursed his lips at the thought of staying in the same house with a corpse, but he supposed they could get rid of the body. "He did confess about the phone…" he said to Dom, trying to catch his gaze, but it was useless. Dom hated him now.

Domenico took long, deep breaths. The tension in his shoulders eased, and he reached out to Mark. When the boy took his hand, Domenico pulled his whole body from underneath the pickup. "Will you show us where it is?"

Mark nodded. "Yes, I remember well. I think the biker dude wants to kill me." He slowly got up and hugged himself.

Seth shook his head. "After Dom's stunt, I'm sure he wants to kill us both, too."

"Shut the fuck up," growled Domenico in Italian, before nodding at Mark. "Good. If this works out, think of

yourself as forgiven," he said and headed toward the house, followed by Dana.

Seth sighed and stayed by the truck, unsure where to go. "Do you want me to do anything?" he yelled after Dom, but truth be told, he wasn't in the mood for talking.

"Get our fucking stuff on the back," yelled Domenico from inside the house. Seth whimpered and looked around, stopping when he noticed a face in one of the neighbor's windows. He forced a smile and waved at the woman before casually striding into the house. Sweat slowly beaded on his back. They had made so much noise. What if someone called the police? Domenico would confront anyone he considered a threat, and that included public officials. They needed to get out of here, and fast.

Domenico and Dana rushed outside with some plastic bags, and when Seth walked into the bedroom, it became clear his stuff was all that was left on the floor. Domenico had already taken all of his.

He took a deep breath and gathered the rest of his belongings in haste. So they were now set to entrust their lives to the memory of a sixteen-year-old. Seth hoped he wasn't placing too much hope in the kid. He put his stuff in the cargo bed and sat on its floor, unwilling to face Domenico again.

Dom didn't question his decision about brief separation either, and it almost seemed as if he chose not to look at Seth anymore. He insisted Seth get into Dana's car, and it seemed like the ultimate token of displeasure, but Seth chose to take it like a man and pretended she wasn't there as they drove silently behind the truck. He wasn't alone in this pursuit, which predicted a very long, nervous, and boring afternoon.

There they were, moving again.

Chapter 8 - Seth

The smell of the swamp around them was weirdly pleasant, even though the air was damp and hot. Seth even got a tingle of excitement when he saw a small alligator run into the water when they stopped in front of the wooden house that could only be reached by following a road designed for a comfortable ride in one car. Seth supposed two cars could technically pass one another with their side mirrors folded, but even as Dana drove behind the pickup, it was impossible to avoid touching the overgrown branches of trees growing on both sides. The drive through this green tunnel lasted about twenty minutes after leaving the nearest asphalt road, and clearly no one remembered the dead owner of the place too fondly if his body was still there. In other words, it was just the kind of place they needed.

Just as Mark had warned them, the house wasn't much. It was a wooden shack with a few windows, a door that didn't correctly fill its frame, and a large porch area built on stilts that emerged from the murky water. This part of the house was made of wood that looked newer

than the walls, and with propped roofing over an area with a rocking chair and a small table, it actually looked cozy. There was even a dirty grill they could use.

Seth started unpacking their stuff without a word, replaying the scene from the gym in his head over and over again. Was there something he could have done differently? He wasn't willing to go into the house just yet, not looking forward to seeing the corpse.

"Was he a Christian?" asked Domenico, nudging Mark's shoulder. He already told Dana to look inside, and she hadn't yet run out screaming, which, Seth supposed, was a bad sign about her personality. If there really was a corpse inside, that is.

"I don't know." Mark shrugged, sitting on a bench next to Seth and playing with the weeds that had grown over the clearing by the shack. "I don't think I've seen a cross in there, but there might have been a *Bible* in one of the drawers."

"What does it matter?" Seth rolled his eyes, itching for a drink.

Domenico stared at him with that flat, condescending stare Seth hated so much, even more so in the choking heat of the summer. "If you died, would you rather have a proper Christian burial or be dropped into the swamp?"

"I don't want to think about dying." Seth frowned, unhappier by the second.

Mark was quick to dish out his opinion though. "I would like to be cremated. It freaks me out that someone might bury me alive."

Domenico sighed. "We're supposed to be turned into *ashes*, I suppose." He rustled the curly mane on Mark's head, and Seth felt a sudden pang of jealousy. Why was Mark forgiven when he was not?

"Sometimes, living feels like being dead," Seth offered and got up, too annoyed to even look at them now.

He fished out a bottle of wine from the bag with groceries and started making his way down a path. "Let me know when the body's gone."

"You're not drinking," said Dom quietly. "Put it back."

"You can't tell me what to do." Seth didn't even look back.

A gunshot resonated through the woods, rousing dozens of birds off their cozy places in the treetops. The bottle shattered in Seth's hand, and his leg was suddenly wet.

His lips parted, and at first, he was too shocked to say anything, as his hands trembled. Seth looked over at Dom, who had just shot the bottle in his hand, leaving him alcohol-free. He couldn't choke out a word.

"Fuck you!" Seth finally yelled and spread his arms. "You could have killed me!"

Domenico snorted and waved the gun dismissively, completely oblivious to the wide-eyed look Mark was giving him from a few steps away. The boy was frozen in fear, like a lamb that had just seen its mother slaughtered, and even Dana looked out of the wooden hut to see what was going on.

"Don't be ridiculous. I know what I'm doing," said Dom in the end.

Seth squinted at him and crossed the few steps to the grocery bag. He took it and ran over to the edge of the swamp. He grabbed its sides to open up the hole at the top and threw all the chocolates into the murky water with so much fury he screamed. His mind was still recovering from the shock of having the bottle blasted in his hand as the bag vomited a whole rainbow of colors. The chocolate bars dotted the surface and stuck to the muck floating on the water.

"What are you doing? You want to lure animals to where we're supposed to stay?" asked Dana, and the pure wonder in her voice only infuriated Seth more.

"Why does it matter? I already have a rabid animal in the house!" Seth pointed at Dom and backed away from the swamp.

"He won't eat you," muttered Dana before glancing at Dom, who stood still with the gun in hand. He looked oddly in place with the background of tall trees and lush greenery when he was in a pair of faded jeans and a simple tank top. His face was so handsome, so symmetrical, even despite the scar going across it, that Seth wanted to scream his frustration.

"Just dispose of the freaking body so that we can move in," Domenico said to Dana, never taking his bright eyes off Seth.

"I'm going to cool off." Seth gritted his teeth and clenched his fists. Couldn't his life at least resemble a normal one? He rubbed his eyes and walked down a narrow path leading from the house.

The man who used to live here had to have been dead for a long time because the way was heavily overgrown, but Seth wondered what awaited him at the end of the path nonetheless. At least it wouldn't be Domenico's face, which deserved a hearty punch right now. Branches smacked Seth's face as he walked and wild birds screamed between themselves, but even the calming color of the dark leaves couldn't still the tangle of emotions that settled deep in Seth's chest.

What if this was the last straw for Dom? What if they weren't able to come back from this?

The path led him to an old but steady wooden construction on stilts. Only after passing some bushes, Seth realized it was a small bridge over a part of the swamp, leading to an island sticking out of the water. He brushed some dead leaves from a fragment of the wooden walkway

and sat down on it with a sigh. If Dom dumped him, what would he even do? Would Dom still care for his safety? Would he leave for Colombia alone? Would they travel together and meet other guys? Seth didn't want anyone else. Even now, that fucker was all he could think of. And Dom had become sexier from the constant training he had started doing with Dana back when Seth was still recovering from having his ribs broken.

Domenico wouldn't just leave him, would he? But even if he wouldn't, just the thought of seeing him with someone else, possibly fucking some stranger while Seth tried to pretend to be asleep, was making his heart cry blood. He couldn't possibly take it. There had to be a way for them to be together. For the last month, he'd been doing his best to get back into shape, to go back to being the attractive man Domenico had fallen in love with, but the results weren't nearly as good as he'd hoped, especially since he didn't have the proper equipment to cook the right foods.

A sudden crack turned Seth's attention to the path, but seeing Dom approach brought a mixture of feelings that were making him nauseated.

"You checking if I'm fucking an alligator on the side?" Seth hissed, even though all he really wanted was a hug. His nature was getting the best of him. Dom's first thought at the gym being that Seth cheated on him made him so angry he could hardly breathe. He could have used that bottle of wine.

Domenico groaned and stepped onto the bridge, the old wood creaking loudly. "Why did you lie to me?"

"I didn't know I wasn't allowed to go to the gym. Do I need to ask your permission to pee as well?"

"Maybe if you told me we can't fuck because you have a bladder infection." Domenico frowned and kicked a stray piece of wood lying on the bridge. It plopped into the water close to where Seth's feet dangled above the surface.

"So fucking funny. Ha. Ha." Seth looked at the scar on his right hand and clenched it into a fist. Even now, after hours of rehab exercises, his grip was weaker than it used to be, and he got sudden nerve pains every now and then. *What kind of use was he to Dom anymore?*

Domenico walked past Seth and farther toward the other side of the bridge leading to what looked like a tiny fishing shack. His shoulders were slightly hunched, and it almost felt like each low creak of the wood beneath his feet originated in his joints.

"I just don't understand what I did that you keep pushing me away. What else could there be if not a man on the side?" Dom asked eventually.

The truth was that Seth was terrified of Dom finding out just how much Seth had changed. He didn't feel like his old self with the extra weight on him, and he couldn't even be bothered to shave because that would force him to face the scar on his cheek. He wanted to run with Dom and Dana, or get stronger, but he didn't want Dom to see him fail at it all. He wanted to step up one day and amaze his man.

Domenico put his hand on the railing made out of two branches tied together with a wire. "Why are you not answering? I tried my fucking best to keep you safe, but I'm not a robot. I don't know it all, even if you might think that's the case sometimes."

Seth rubbed his eyes. "You did everything you could. Why would you even say that? I just need some time alone."

"How much time do you need?" Domenico kicked the wood again, leaning over the railing and looking into the water below. "I failed at protecting you twice, and no matter what you say, I can see you don't trust me like you used to."

"I don't know how much time I need! How can you throw a fit like today and now try to be all soft and tender,

huh?" Seth entwined his fingers with a deepening frown. "There's stuff you just can't tell your boyfriend, okay? It's not your fault!"

Domenico hissed and turned toward Seth, approaching so fast, Seth half-expected more violence, but Dom stopped right next to him and just stared. A few moments passed in silence before he walked past Seth and hurried back toward the shack where they had left Mark and Dana. It fell heavy on Seth's heart to be left alone like that, even though it was he who had asked for privacy just moments ago.

He took a long trembling breath, now knowing already that no amount of secluded contemplation could help him. But on the other hand, being around Dom was a constant battle and a litany of *why, why, whys*. Seth threw a few rocks into the water, wishing he had wine for company. He shook his head at the sight of a Mars bar floating his way. He shouldn't have polluted the place like that. Not after always carefully recycling all his trash.

A sound behind him made his senses alert again, but he wouldn't look back this time. He said he wanted to be left alone, and so he'd stand by that decision even if it hurt.

"Rough day?" a voice asked in a heavy German accent. It took Seth a few seconds to realize it belonged to Domenico.

Seth couldn't help a little smirk and threw another rock at the water. "Yeah, my boyfriend's being a dick."

"Tell me about it. Men won't say what they want, but they expect their demands to be met," said Domenico, leaning against the railing in an easygoing, almost sloppy way the real Dom would never do.

Seth dared look up at him, certain Dom had used the same German accent for his Mr. Schwangau persona. "Yeah, I try to go to the gym to get into better shape, and he's angry I even went there in the first place. Can't win."

Domenico shrugged and suddenly pinched Seth's bicep. "You don't seem out of shape to me."

Seth snorted. "You've got to be kidding. I used to be all muscle. He can see that I changed."

Domenico slowly crouched down to be at Seth's eye level. He looked into Seth's eyes so openly, it was hard not to look away. "Maybe he doesn't mind," muttered Dom, and his hand slowly squeezed around Seth's shoulder.

Seth took a deep breath to fight the tingling in his eyes. "I bet he does. He went for my looks first. I wasn't recovering as fast as I wanted after an accident, and he will see right through me."

"We all go for looks first," said Domenico, and his hand opened, slowly moving back and forth over Seth's shoulder, massaging him gently. Seth hadn't recently given Domenico the opportunity to touch him like this, but he missed it so much.

Seth licked his lips. "He looks even better now than he did a year ago. His hair is longer, he's lean, strong, trains all the time. He can even pick *me* up. And I can't even lift a heavy pan sometimes."

Domenico shrugged and leaned closer, then even closer, until their heads touched, and some of Dom's hair tickled Seth's shoulder. He smelled so good too, even without any expensive cologne to mask the natural scent of his skin. "Maybe you should just relax about it. *I* think you're pretty hot."

Seth took a deeper breath and didn't pull away. "You think? But... I wouldn't cheat on my boyfriend." The last words came as a whisper.

Domenico's eyes were so lively and bright when they looked at Seth. The sudden sense of warmth and closeness was rapidly melting all of the defenses Seth had built around himself in the last few months. Domenico had been keeping him under siege, but only an outsider could actually sneak his way in.

"He won't know."

Seth bumped his nose against Dom's, and his heart galloped. "He did go off with Dana. I hate it when he leaves with her for hours..." He dared touch a strand of Dom's loose hair.

Domenico gently nuzzled Seth's nose and pulled him into a loose but sweet embrace. "Doesn't he invite you to join them?"

Seth let his fingers wander to Dom's forearms, shuddering when the dark hairs tickled his skin. "He does, but they both run too fast. I'd be the loser who can't keep up."

Domenico put the other arm around the front of Seth's chest and let the other fall to his ass, comfortably melting into Seth. "I'm sure he wouldn't mind. He must know you've been hurt and need more time."

Seth gently pushed on Dom's chest with a silly grin. "Maybe I shouldn't cheat on him then after all. Since he's such a nice guy..."

Domenico laughed, but then his eyes turned slightly more serious, even though they still carried the same glow. "No? Maybe you're right. Maybe you should show him that you care about him. He must think you got bored with him."

"He's many things, but not boring. He wouldn't like you touching me. He'd go mental if he saw us now." Seth peeled Dom's fingers off his shoulder just to tease him into action.

Domenico exhaled, and his warm breath tickled Seth's skin in the sweetest way possible, rousing all the delicate hairs in anticipation of touch. "Fuck him. I'm sure I could teach him a trick or two," he whispered, pulling his hand up Seth's chest and squeezing his pec through the fabric.

"Are you claiming you're a better fuck than him? You're setting the bar high for yourself." Seth's breath

hitched. Would Dom really not mind his changed looks? Would they actually *fuck*?

Domenico grinned and nipped the tip of Seth's nose, pressing even closer, as if any inch of free space between their bodies bothered him. "I think you should give me a test ride."

Heavy breath parted Seth's lips, and he couldn't blink, too focused on the intensity of Dom's eyes. "Are you saying I'm easy?"

Domenico laughed and started slowly moving his hands down to the pulsing front of Seth's pants, which he was rapidly getting more aware of. "I don't know you. How easy are you? We don't even know each other's names. You wanna keep it that way?"

Seth nodded and put his hand under Dom's collarbone. "I might be easier than I'd like to think, Mr. Schwangau."

Domenico gently squeezed Seth's crotch, sending a flash of sensation all the way up Seth's chest. It felt unreal, just like that moment yesterday when Domenico had sucked Seth's cock dry and cuddled up to him, as if Seth was the best thing that ever happened to him.

"I wanna fuck your ass so bad. I bet it's delicious."

Seth licked along Dom's bottom lip, slightly rocking his hips to the touch. "I haven't done that in a while, so it might be a tight fit," he whispered into Dom's mouth, already imagining those strong arms holding him in place and exploring every inch of his body.

Domenico went straight into the kiss, sucking on Seth's tongue as he trembled in his arms. "Yeah... I have just the right tool to loosen you up for that boyfriend of yours."

"I miss fucking so bad," Seth confessed as he slid his hand down to Dom's solid stomach. The defined muscle was driving him wild every single day, and he moaned in protest when Domenico got to his feet, escaping the touch.

It wasn't long until Dom grabbed Seth's forearm and pulled him up, straight into his arms.

"I can give you all the dick you want. But only as long as we play by *my* rules."

Seth groaned and hid his face in Dom's hair, but he'd say yes to a lot of things right now. He ground his cock against Dom's stomach. "What are your rules?" he whispered into Dom's ear.

Domenico smirked and slowly opened his belt. "Take off your shirt first, and then you'll find out."

Seth swallowed, remembering yesterday's shower through a blur in his mind. He didn't want Dom to see the irregular scars where his nipples had been, or his flabby flesh, but in the end, arousal got the best of him, and he pulled off his T-shirt. The amber eyes twinkled in front of him, and he was relieved to recognize the familiar fire of lust in them. Domenico exhaled and put his hand on Seth's soft, hairy stomach.

"That's more like it. I hope you never ever shave," he whispered, tugging on the hairs.

Seth bit his lip and put his arm over his chest as if to just rest his hand on his shoulder, but he was eager to hide the scars. "Yeah? You like hairy?"

Domenico pulled away his hand and looked into Seth's eyes from up close. "There's no man without the hair. Turn around."

Seth swallowed, but followed the order, getting a kick out of the German accent. His breath hitched when Dom pulled his arms back and tied his wrists with the T-shirt in a few efficient moves. Blood had been trickling down to his dick before, but now the floodgates burst, leaving his brain empty.

Domenico sank his teeth into Seth's shoulder blade and then moved his nose and lips up and down the valley of his spine, leaving wet traces that only made Seth's skin more receptive. "You are pretty easy. A real slut."

"Not always..." Seth tried, but it was hard to think when Dom's tongue teased his skin. He loved being adored by Dom's touch. It sent him flying. That feeling was one of the reasons why he wanted to work so hard on getting back in shape again, but now it seemed like just another excuse not to deal with his own insecurities. Domenico's touch was just as hot and possessive as ever when he pulled Seth off the bridge and propped him against a tree, looking at the scarred chest again, now without Seth's arms interfering.

Seth looked into his eyes, swallowing his nerves. Surely, Dom knew what he wanted, so if he still wanted Seth, his body couldn't be *that* bad.

"I don't let my boyfriend see them," he whispered.

Domenico's eyes immediately shot up to meet his. "Why not?" he asked, and just like that, the strangely smooth tips of Dom's thumbs brushed over the scars, massaging them, as if they were intact nipples. The scars were so sensitive that the touch both tickled and aroused.

"I don't want him to think about them." Seth tried to shy away, but with the tree behind him, there was nowhere to run. Its bark was gently scratching his skin, but the presence of Domenico's smooth, hot fingertips was taking up all of Seth's attention.

"Why?" asked Domenico, slowly pinching the scar tissue and rolling it between his fingers.

Seth looked down with heat burning up his cheeks. "So he doesn't have to remember how they got there."

Domenico sighed. "I like them. They're so fucking smooth, not like all that hair on you. I just wanna bite on them as I fuck you."

Seth sucked in his bottom lip, with his mind rushing toward the fucking already. "The skin is very sensitive there..."

"I know. Would you like it or would it hurt?" whispered Domenico, with a sudden twist to the skin that replaced Seth's nipple.

"I would like... to see how it goes." Seth panted at the mix of pain and pleasure.

Domenico grinned and leaned down, flicking his tongue over the sore flesh. "Oh, you will definitely see how it goes. I'll make sure of that." He stepped back and pulled his own top over his head, revealing his perfectly chiselled chest, tan, dusky, with pale lines of scars in too many places to count, but none of the traces of past combat could ever damage Domenico's beauty.

Only after doing so, Seth realized he gasped. He was so hungry for Domenico's body he wasn't sure a lifetime of fucks could sate that need. His fingers itched to trace the pronounced muscles of Dom's stomach and every little hair on his chest, but with his hands bound behind his back, he was forced to remain a passive recipient of Domenico's attention. Dom put the top over a low hanging branch, and then swiftly pushed down his jeans and underwear. With a bright grin, he hung them along with the shirt and stepped closer, holding only the thick belt he slipped out from his pants. Seth couldn't take his eyes off the pronounced V-shape of muscles, jealousy and lust mixing in him with lust winning when Seth's glance slid down to Dom's cock.

"I'm returning you to your boyfriend soon, and you will be begging him for sex, not the other way around. Is that clear?" Dom asked with a playfulness to his voice, even as he slipped the warm leather around Seth's neck, tightening the makeshift collar very slowly.

All of Seth's senses sharpened, and he nodded fervently, taken by surprise by the placement of the belt. But there was nothing he loved more than Dom taking charge. Seth would hand over his soul to him, just to see what he'd do with it. "He'll have to fight me off with a stick."

"Good. He's probably really missing that sweet, juicy ass, and those pretty lips," rasped Domenico, brushing the loose end of the belt over Seth's lips. His fingers moved to the sides of Seth's body, and just feeling them there was enough to set his senses on fire. Seth got to his toes, pressing his body harder against Dom's hands.

"Now I'm not sure if I should have gone with you after all." Seth gave Dom a cocky grin and nudged him with his knee. The erection in his pants was rock-hard already.

"No?" Domenico stepped closer, swinging his half-hard dick in front of Seth like bait. He was the epitome of masculinity like that—naked in the woods, hairy, scarred, and confident to take what he wanted. "You made your man miserable. That deserves some punishment."

Seth bit his lip. "I didn't mean to." His cock was aching to be out, like Dom's. "I wanted to make him happy."

Domenico shook his head, but the smile didn't disappear from his lips as he gently pulled on the belt around Seth's neck. "You should listen to him next time. He probably feels like you stopped loving him," muttered Domenico looking down between their bodies as he slowly sank down, tugging Seth's pants with him.

"Now that's just dumb." Seth's gaze followed Dom's head, and he groaned as soon as his cock popped out of his underwear. That felt good.

Domenico shrugged. "Maybe. But what was he supposed to think when you wouldn't even fucking cuddle?" growled Domenico, and for a moment, it was clear he was out of character. Two seconds later, Mr. Schwangau was back, stopping Seth from uttering a word with his warm fingers, as he slowly moved his other hand over Seth's dick.

Seth let out a nasal moan, for once not as self-conscious about being touched. He arched his hips forward. He couldn't wait to feel Dom's lips around himself. Even that had been a rare treat lately.

"What was that?" muttered Domenico, leaning in just enough for his hair to tickle Seth's chest. The movements of his hand were so confident, so steady where they touched Seth's cock. Domenico of all people knew exactly the right combination of speed and pressure to get Seth going in no time.

Seth's chest swelled with every hard tug. "I'll do better," he moaned, running his fingers over the bark behind him.

"Do or I'll come back and hand you over to my international friends. You'll be a whore to any man who feels like fucking you," said Dom, before lapping a hot trail up Seth's neck.

Seth's toes curled and he let out a little whimper. "I'm not a whore..." he said, even though he could sense the slight pulsing of his anus at the thought of having Dom's dick push in and fuck him senseless.

"You will be if you don't do as I say. My rules, remember?" Domenico bit into Seth's neck, right where the beard started, and he tugged on the flesh as their naked bodies pressed together. Domenico's cock pushed against Seth's stomach, shocking Seth with the pleasure of it, but the kiss that came right after was even better than the hand on Seth's dick.

Seth leaned into the kiss with a new ferocity. At least he could have this much. He could never get enough of the hint of cigarettes and the scent of Dom's hair when they kissed. The first time had been so aggressive and powerful, it had made Seth's head spin with the comparisons to other men. No one before Domenico had been able to match up to him.

And even now, after so many months together, the closeness they shared was incomparable to anything Seth had experienced before. It was overwhelming him not only with intense lust, but also with the love and safety that Domenico always made him feel. It was as if everything fell

into place when Dom slowly moved to his knees and swallowed Seth's cock with a passionate groan. His hands trailed up and down Seth's thighs, massaging him ever closer to his ass, which was now radiating warmth all over Seth's body.

Seth closed his eyes and let his head fall back as he floated in the waves of arousal. "Fuck yes... Do anything to me..." He moaned when his cockhead pushed into Dom's throat for a second. He'd had such horrific experiences with being bound and hurt, yet there was no claustrophobic feeling when it was Dom who tied him up and Dom who guarded his safety. There was no one to hurt them around here, so he could just relax and enjoy it.

The first brush of fingers against the bottom of his ass made Seth mewl and push deeper into Dom's welcoming mouth, but his lover was already impatient, hard as a rock himself and eager to make up for lost time.

Thick digits pressed between Seth's buttocks, cool from lube Domenico must have had with him when he came here, insistent on gaining entry.

Seth felt a bit shy about the sex when he realized when the last time they fucked had been. For the first month after the ordeal with Vincente, he really was aching so bad even breathing hurt, so they didn't even attempt fucking. He wiggled his ass against the touch, unable to keep still yet elated that Dom would see him as he was and still go mad with lust. It didn't seem to matter at all that Seth's body now lacked definition, or that he had gained a few pounds. Domenico still wanted him, no, needed him the same way he did before. The sudden penetration with one finger sent Seth to his toes, but he was ready and opened his thighs wider, thrusting into Dom's warm, sweet mouth at the same time. And from the start, it was clear Mr. Schwangau wouldn't have mercy on him. Those fingers were determined to get him ready as fast as possible, drilling, thrusting, moving around out of sync, and Seth

would take it. He wanted all the rough touch Dom would offer.

He bit down on his lip, revelling in the harsh thrusts stretching him. "Oh, fuck! Yeah, like that," he mewled, hardly recognizing his own voice. Dom had a way with his fingers that was pure magic when he wanted to squeeze as much pleasure out of Seth as humanly possible. The loosely tied belt around Seth's neck felt tighter with every deep breath he took. A thousand scenarios of how Dom would actually fuck him ran rampant in Seth's brain, none of them winning over the reality.

Seth squealed when his pulsing cock slipped out of the warm, smooth lips, but when he looked down and met Domenico's scorching hot gaze, his whole body went up in flames. His fingers moved out of Seth's stretched ass, and when Domenico got to his feet, he spun Seth around so that he faced the tree. There was no lengthy preparation after that. One moment, Seth's shoulder was propped against the tree trunk, the next—there was a thick, hard dick pushing deep into his body, unrelenting even as Seth's body spasmed around it.

He moaned and arched his ass toward Dom's hips for a better angle. Sweat beaded on his skin from the intensity and the damp heat in the air. "Yeah..." was all he could utter at the mixture of strain and arousal. Most of all, his thoughts were on Dom. On just how eager Dom was to fuck him. All conversation was bullshit in comparison to this fuck. The way their sweaty bodies connected expressed more than words ever could.

A sudden yank on the hair at the top of Seth's head took him out of his thoughts, and he was kissing Domenico again. His body molded to the warm muscle behind him, even as the cock was only halfway inside Seth. They both moved back and forth, desperate for more, and Domenico forced Seth back against the tree, following it with a series of slow yet powerful thrusts, which sent Domenico's

cockhead deeper and deeper. When Dom's balls slapped against Seth's ass, it almost felt like fireworks exploding above their heads.

Seth bit down hard on Dom's tongue just to mess with him and writhed on his cock, rubbing his ass against Dom's hips. He couldn't think of anything that felt better than being taken by Domenico. Every tiny sensation grew to combine into one powerful experience. The way Dom's hair tickled Seth's shoulder, the coppery taste of blood from Dom's tongue, and Seth's hands being tied, leaving him helpless to take whatever Dom had to give. And the intense throbbing of Dom's thick cock inside of him. Even the way his own dick brushed against bark didn't bother him.

Domenico turned Seth's face so that it would lie on the bark for Domenico's easy access whenever he wanted to kiss and bite as he drilled his way into the depths of Seth's body. Each thrust was punctuated by a slight tug on the makeshift collar around Seth's neck, and the way that made him lose his breath for a fraction of a second every time was so unexpectedly exciting, all of Seth's senses became agitated. He already knew he'd want more of that in the future.

Skin slapped and breaths combined as Domenico drank air from Seth's lips, looking at him from below half-closed eyelids. It was wild beyond belief, and as pleasure built up in Seth's body, Domenico's movements grew in intensity.

"You're mine, remember. I'm gonna come inside you, and you're gonna take it."

"Yes, yes," Seth whimpered between one thrust and another. "I will take anything from you. Fuck me hard. Leave a mark."

"Yeah, you think your boyfriend would want that?" hissed Domenico, driving into him at a crazy pace. The friction was driving Seth insane, and with his cock

swinging between his thighs, slapping against the flesh over and over, he was slowly climbing toward his ultimate high.

"He'd see it and fuck me even harder for it." Seth grinned against the tree, spacing out into a reality where it was just the two of them, and Domenico fucked his ass so relentlessly it felt as if they were becoming one body.

"You want that, don't you? Provoke him into screwing you with everyone else to see," rasped Domenico, working behind Seth like a machine. He grabbed Seth's pec and squeezed it hard.

Seth let out a moan, on the brink of coming as Dom's cock brushed over his prostate over and over again. He hadn't come this way in months. "Yeah, no mercy for me," he uttered.

Domenico turned Seth's face to the side and bit into his bearded chin. Sharp pain tipped Seth over the edge, and he shuddered in Dom's arms, completely falling apart. Domenico was soon following him and slammed his hips against Seth's harder, quicker, turning Seth's body into a puddle of warmth. When they both stilled, the rapid pulsing of the thick rod inside Seth told him Domenico was coming, and when they kissed just after, there was a coppery taste to Dom's mouth.

"Yes…" Seth whispered, thinking of the thick cock still deep inside of him. He grabbed Dom's lip between his teeth and pulled gently. This was the fuck he needed and craved all along.

Domenico sighed, relaxing against him, all warm and smiling, as if Seth hadn't seen him in ages. "When you get rid of that beard, there will be a mark for everyone to see."

Seth tickled Dom's stomach with the tips of his fingers. "I like it when everyone knows I'm yours."

Domenico grinned. "Maybe you should get a tag with my name then?" He slowly pulled out of Seth, and the

sudden sense of emptiness sent Seth right into Dom's arms. He could hardly keep himself straight.

"I already have a tag on my finger." Seth gave him a dreamy look, and for a moment, even the silly marriage idea didn't seem all that bad.

Domenico chuckled and kissed Seth's shoulder while he slid his hand down Seth's back, delving straight into the vacated hole. "Yes."

Seth didn't have words left in him, just gasps and trembles when Dom took his time slowly drilling his fingers into the dripping hole. He bit his lips and put his forehead against the tree so Dom wouldn't see his face. Seth often lost all inhibitions during sex, too horny to care once they fucked, yet all sorts of insecurities crept back in after orgasm.

"*Danke schön*," Seth whispered with a silly grin.

"You must meet my friend, Mr. Gribov. He fucks like a madman," said Domenico, massaging Seth's anus with absolute tenderness as they both slowly cooled off.

"Oh? Yes. Yes, tell me more about him." Seth looked over his shoulder, overwhelmed and excited with fucking Mr. Schwangau. What else could Dom possibly have in store? "I mean... if I manage to sneak away from my boyfriend." He gave Dom's nose a kiss.

"Oh, that guy. He's so possessive, isn't he?" Domenico rolled his eyes but slowly pulled his fingers out of Seth and freed his hands from the shirt.

Turning around was a slow, lazy process, but Seth finally wrapped his arms around Dom's neck and planted another kiss on his lips. "Greedy fucker. Doesn't wanna share me. But what he doesn't know won't hurt him."

"I can introduce you to interesting people. You'll be too sore to fuck him afterward," whispered Domenico, gently nipping on Seth's lips. He smelled of fresh sweat, and Seth hoped they didn't have to move anytime soon. His

veins were still hot from the sex, and he really didn't care for reality.

Despite Dom being a tiny bit shorter than him, Seth still got to his toes as they kissed and leaned his weight on him, knowing that it wasn't too much for Dom to take. The whole new array of possibilities was making his head spin. "That's what he gets for proposing to a slut," Seth said into Dom's lips.

"Just make sure to be available once you two marry. Can't wait to breed a married man," whispered Domenico, gently tugging Seth closer and kissing him over and over.

Chapter 9 - Mark

Mark sat in the rocking chair on the porch, and the thing squeaked every time he tipped back. He was watching Dana dig some holes in the ground around the shack. The grass and weeds were so tall her blonde head kept popping out, then hiding from view as she worked.

"What are you doing?" Mark asked out of boredom, since it didn't seem as if Dom and Seth were coming back any time soon.

Dana straightened her back. "Explosives," she said, looking at him with the same contempt she had displayed when she bullied him into sleeping on the floor last night.

Mark groaned, giving a wistful sigh when he saw another bar of chocolate float by in the water beyond the railing. He considered using the dead man's fishing equipment to try to get some of the chocolates out of the swamp, but he was still in the planning phase for that.

The shack was small and dirty, and there were creepy gator skulls hanging from the ceiling but Mark wasn't complaining, since he didn't have to dispose of a

dead body. He didn't want to ask what Dana did with it, but at least it wasn't floating about amidst all the candy.

"Oh, come on! Just tell me what you're doing. I'm bored. I could help you if you told me."

"I don't need your help. It's not like you'll be sticking around," said Dana, covering the hole with dirt before moving a bit farther in the overgrown grass.

"I might be!" Mark protested. "With this whole mess going down today, I could be staying longer than a few days."

Dana snorted. "Don't kid yourself. I know Domenico, and if there's one thing he hates, it's cowards. He'll want you hanged with a hook through your ribs after that stunt you pulled today."

Mark stilled, but the chair he was in kept rocking, propelled by his weight. "No... he said he forgave me."

Dana shrugged. "He's just waiting, so that Seth doesn't suspect anything. He'll make you disappear, and nobody will ever find your body," she said casually, her pale hair hardly visible from behind all the weeds growing in front of the house.

"I was gonna call the cops and come back for them..." An uneasy feeling settled in Mark's stomach. Such a lie. He *was* a coward. He had completely lost it when he saw Jed.

"Doesn't matter. The moment you put Seth in danger, you're done." Dana slowly rose to her feet, looking weirdly Instagram-worthy with her fair hair in a mess and her perky nipples poking at the front of her shirt. "If I were you, I'd just go now."

Mark swallowed, trying to keep his gaze on her face. "Would you go with me? It can't be that nice living with two gay guys who are practically married."

Dana smiled and slowly walked toward him, playing with the tips of the plants on the way. She was incredibly attractive, an adult woman who most likely

knew what she wanted. Unlike him. He bit his lip as she approached on those long tanned legs.

"Go with you?" she asked softly.

"Y-yeah." He straightened up in the rocking chair, but it was useless, because the chair instantly tipped forward. He got up to spare himself the embarrassment and leaned against the railing. "I'd steal a car for us, and we could go on a wild road trip all over the country."

Dana climbed up to the porch and leaned against the wall right next to him. This woman had disposed of a dead body not that long ago. She was adventurous, and they could surely have a lot of fun together. For now though, Mark was stuck looking at the very revealing cutoff shorts she was wearing.

"What about your future husband, Fred?" she asked.

Mark laughed. "Him? I'd ditch him in a heartbeat for a girl like you." He stood on his toes, just ever so slightly, to look taller, yet they still weren't equal in height. At least with guys, being short wasn't an inherent disadvantage.

Dana scratched her head and playfully moved her hand over the top of his head. "You're funny."

Mark's smile widened. He'd never been with a woman, so even the thought of being alone with a naked girl made him nervous. As attractive as it seemed in his fantasies, he didn't even know how he'd like it, but Dana was pretty and blonde. Even if she did have the abs of a personal trainer.

"I'd take you all around the country. We could go to California and surf. And when we run out of places to go to in the US, we could go to Europe."

Dana chuckled and poked the middle of Mark's chest, for once dropping the icy attitude she had when anyone else was near. Mark even got why she didn't want to sleep in bed with him last night. Unlike Domenico, she saw Mark was interested in her, and it was probably

blatantly obvious. Maybe she didn't go about it the most pleasant way, but it was understandable.

"I don't even have a passport."

Mark trailed his fingers over the top of her hand and shrugged. "That's fine. You could get it sorted once we stop somewhere."

Dana smirked. "But wouldn't that be weird for you? I mean, I'm much older," she said, and her eyes suddenly went softer, so close to Mark's face. She smelled so good, of flowers and fruit and shampoo.

Mark waved his hand dismissively. "Nah. How old can you be? Twenty?" She was probably closer to twenty-five, but a bit of flattery never hurt anyone.

Dana chuckled and playfully slapped Mark's shoulder. "You're too sweet. And I like feeling comfortable. I can't do everything I want with Domenico and Seth around. Could you take it?"

"Take what? You? Are you kidding? Totally!" Mark grinned. So he didn't have a cent to his soul, but he did have Jed's phone. That could give them a head start. At least two hundred bucks.

"You sure? Because you might have noticed, I'm not that much into this whole bra thing. I'm actually a nudist," confessed Dana, poking at her lip with one perfectly manicured finger.

Mark's eyes went a bit wider, and he licked his lips. "I'm cool with that. I'm a bit of a nudist myself."

Dana blinked and then shrugged. "Really? You're just saying that to make me trust you."

"No, really. I don't have many inhibitions. I like to be free. Like, if I was born fifty years ago, I'd be a hippie."

Dana grinned at him, and all of a sudden, the pink top was up, and Mark faced a pair of small, perky breasts with gloriously pink nipples. Already hard. Waiting for his touch.

Mark exhaled loudly with his gaze glued to her body. His own top was off before he even knew what he was doing.

Dana chuckled and stepped away. "Wow, that's a start!"

Mark grinned and unbuttoned his pants after a quick glance to the path where the other guys had disappeared. "We can do whatever. It's not like anyone's here."

"Can you, really?" asked Dana, and her perky breasts stirred when she moved, hypnotizing Mark. Oh, wow, maybe she was actually interested now that she knew he wasn't some creep?

"I mean... a moment of freedom. Why not indulge in our nudist nature?" Mark grinned and pushed off his shoes before letting his pants fall down. He wanted to see if she had pubes or not so bad it hurt. Not that he'd mind it either way. He was just interested how it would feel. He'd sucked many dicks, but pussy was still unknown territory, exotic as the white beaches of the Caribbean.

He stopped talking when he noticed Dana's gaze glued to the front of his boxer shorts.

"I know." Mark laughed nervously and pushed his clothes to the side with his foot. "You're so hot I can't think straight. A guy can't really hide liking someone."

Dana exhaled and nodded at the underwear, biting her lip as she leaned back into the wall, her breasts moving as she took deep breaths.

"You take yours off?" Mark put his thumbs under the waistband of his boxers.

Dane shuddered. "Be a gentleman. You first."

Mark's gaze went from Dana's face and down her chest as he took off his boxers. Even if he was to just see her naked, it would make his day.

Dana raised her hand to her lips and chewed on the tip of her finger. "This is a bit awkward, with you being only sixteen..."

Mark breathed hard and threw his boxers to the pile of clothes. "Come on, just pretend we're in Europe." He reached out to her breast, feeling its warmth without even touching.

Dana looked away and covered herself. "Wait... we must be quick. There should be condoms in one of the bags on the back of the pickup."

That one word sent echoes of trembles all throughout Mark's brain and then his body.

Condoms.

Mark gave her a furiously quick nod and ran down the two stairs from the shack and off to the pickup truck, as though the world was on fire and the only water to save humanity was in the truck.

His mind was scrambling. He'd get to fuck a girl. No, a grown woman. Clearly, she saw something in him. Maybe she wanted to teach him all about sex, the way she liked it. He had once read an erotic book with a similar theme, and it'd been one of his most prevailing one-handed reads. Looking through the bags, he was getting increasingly anxious. Clothes and other items were flying all over the place, but none of them bore even the slightest resemblance to condoms. Surely, Domenico and Seth used them? And Dana? Shouldn't she know best where she kept hers?

He wanted to smack himself when he realized he had them in *his* bag. The condoms Dom had bought for him. He jumped off the pickup truck, holding on to his raging hard-on.

The smell of gasoline or something similar confused him for a second, but when he spotted Dana closer to the shore, with her top on and air trembling with

heat next to her, his erection faltered as quickly as it had appeared.

"Hey! What are you doing?" Mark rushed toward her, through the weeds and pieces of dry wood that dug into his feet. When he arrived at the shore of the swamp, his blood froze in his veins at the sight of his only outfit burning down with a blue flame.

For a second, he considered running to put out the fire, but it was too late to save any of the clothes. He stood there, covering his crotch, completely out of his depth. He had been played like a freaking banjo. "Why would you do that? That's fucking evil!"

Dana was back to her usual icy self, with eyes so sharp they could make him bleed just by staring. "You're not wanted here," she said quietly. "You should go."

Mark turned around with his eyes stinging from the smoke and shame burning his cheeks. He quickly made his way to the shack, as he could already hear voices from the path at the back. His heart ached as much as his pride.

He couldn't believe he just fell for it. Now that he thought about it logically, it did seem wonky that her attitude had changed so quickly, but his mind had forgotten all logic at the prospect of sex. What was he to do now? He had two more pairs of underwear and two pairs of socks, but no pants or shirts. He couldn't face Domenico and Seth like this.

He got to his bag as fast as lightning and pulled on a pair of black briefs. His pride hurt so bad he could hear it weep. Dom asked Dana about the holes in the ground, and Seth was actually laughing, so they must have made up somehow. Mark had to go out and face the music.

When he walked out, Domenico was standing right next to Seth, all smiley as if he just won the Super Bowl, with his arm around Seth, who chattered about an alligator trap he wanted to set up in the area. It was a surreal image,

especially with Dana having gone back to digging holes, as if nothing had happened.

Domenico must have noticed Mark, as he looked toward the house. "I wouldn't bathe in this water."

"I was thinking more about sunbathing, to be honest." Mark gave them a fake smile, hugging himself, unsure what to do now. He was afraid to even look at Dana.

Domenico shrugged. "If you're staying with us, you might as well get rid of all those weeds. Can you do that for me?"

"Um... You remember how you told me I stink? I wanted to wash the clothes in the water, but they only got more horrible, and... I kinda had to let them go." Mark was not about to admit that he had been played like a kid in preschool.

Domenico frowned. "Let them go? As in, you thought they'd stay on the surface?"

"No... I think a gator might have grabbed them in the water or something..." Shame pierced Mark's skin when Seth laughed, even though the chuckling probably wasn't mean-spirited. Mark could see Dana's smirk in his imagination.

"Well, then wear something else," said Domenico, pulling Seth toward the house, which only made Mark feel more like a loser, because there was no way he could keep his pride in this situation.

He swallowed and dared to speak when the two men reached the porch. Being a shorty hurt now even more as he stood next to their towering figures. "It was all I had..."

Domenico and Seth looked him up and down, and Dom smirked, shaking his head. "What's the matter with you, kid? You lose the only clothes you have?"

Mark looked at his feet, fighting the massive tears forming under his eyelids. He was such a failure. How could

he even think someone like Dana would give him the time of day?

"Hey, Mark. Chill out." Seth put a hand on his shoulder. "I'll get you something. Can't promise it will fit."

Domenico chuckled and slapped Seth's ass. "Mark could wear your T-shirts as dresses. He really needs more muscle on him."

"Hey, Mark! I could lend you *my* stuff!" Dana yelled in her fake good-natured voice, but Mark knew all too well this was yet more mockery.

He rubbed his eyes as soon as the first two tears dropped by his feet, leaving clear dark dots on the dry wood. His whole body shuddered when he saw Domenico's boots across from his toes.

"What is that? Don't be a baby," hissed Dom, poking Mark's shoulder.

"I'm just… This is horrible," Mark uttered and kept rubbing his eyes.

Seth opened the door to the shack. "Come on in. I'll give you a T-shirt."

Domenico rolled his eyes and pushed Mark toward Seth. "I'll get our stuff inside," he said and walked off toward the pickup.

"No! I—there was a badger in the stuff!" Mark looked at the back of the pickup where he had scattered everything as he mindlessly searched for condoms. "I scared it off."

Domenico's roar tore through the air, and all Mark could do was cuddle into Seth's big strong chest.

"Oh, no, you should have let Dana handle it. Those things are dangerous," said Seth, but he didn't seem all that bothered and took Mark deeper into the house. It was old and smelled of decay with two plates of rotten food still on the table as if the owner had left them on the day he had died in his chair. They opened all windows for a free flow of air, but what the additional light also did was reveal the

dirty state of the hut. Spiders and other bugs they could deal with, but there had been a lot of damage to some of the items inside. Earlier Domenico had decided they needed to test all the chairs before using them, and many of the metal items showed signs of rust.

Seth told Mark to do weeding later, and as soon as Mark got a T-shirt, he was set to work on the inside of the shack. Dom brought in their belongings from the back of the pickup truck, and as much as Mark hated cleaning, it was actually nice to get their temporary residence in better shape.

Seth brought in the gas stove, and smiled all the time, even when not talking to anyone. He cleaned the table to make some space for cooking, which was the last thing Mark expected to see here. He was sure they'd be having granola bars for dinner, since Seth hadn't thrown those out. As Mark cleaned, he kept stealing glances at Seth and was amazed by the proficiency with which his savior was cutting vegetables and preparing food despite the spartan conditions.

And as hours passed, the shack really did start feeling homey, thanks to the combined effort of four people. Domenico used one of the beams underneath the sloped roof to hang some blankets close to the back wall, in order to create some privacy around the only bed, where he and Seth would be sleeping, no doubt about that. They'd taken their own bedding from the house in town, so that was sorted, as the former owner of the hut didn't die in the bed and it seemed usable. The walls and sparse furniture had all been dusted with old clothes found in the only wardrobe. Domenico was whistling some melody Mark didn't know, and to his surprise, Seth soon joined in, filling the single room with pleasant noise. By the time it was slowly getting dark, the house seemed livable, especially now that it smelled of fresh tomatoes and spices.

Seth even found some candles in the cupboard and set them up on the table. They only had paper plates and plastic cutlery, but it was better than nothing. Mark hated the pretend truce with Dana, but decided to avoid her as much as he could. Seth and Domenico, on the other hand, were ridiculously tender to each other, taking into account the fight Mark had witnessed before. Sometimes they would speak softly to each other in Italian, and he wished he could understand all the sweet words rolling off their tongues.

"Everyone ready? It will come bit by bit, because I only have one pan, but I have everything prepared." Seth smiled and gave Dom a kiss in passing.

Domenico stopped him, only to solicit one more smooch before settling by the table, smiling as though this wasn't a dead man's house they had decided to occupy. Things like that didn't seem to bother any of Mark's new friends.

Domenico pulled him out of his thoughts with a little poke. "You're in for something really good."

Mark raised his eyebrows. "I mean... it's canned food."

Seth shook his head. "Sure, that's part of it, but it's how you prepare it that counts. The vegetables I got from a farmer's market a few days ago. And when you have good olive oil, that's half the success."

Dana raised her hand. "Can I have mine without oil?"

Seth glared at her. "No."

Domenico smirked. "Dana, you're pretty no matter how much oil you consume," he said and opened a bottle of Sprite.

Dana sighed. "It's unnecessary calories."

"If Seth says oil's necessary, you'll eat the oil," decided Domenico, and Mark didn't really understand why

she listened to him in the first place, but that ended the discussion.

The cozy atmosphere around the table, the candlelight, and finally, the food, all created good momentum to start asking questions. But before Mark could do so, Seth served what he called *bruschetta*. Hot crispy bread made in the pan with olive oil, topped with tomatoes, aubergine, and some spices Mark couldn't name. Their names didn't matter. The food was so delicious that eating it actually cheered him up.

Even in a massive shirt with an alligator print, after being almost raped, humiliated by the first woman who showed him her tits, and having lost a big part of his belongings, he could smile again as he looked at Domenico and Seth by the table together, so completely happy but still open to talk to him as well. It was quite overwhelming, though the best part of the evening came when Dana excused herself after the starter, which apparently went over her daily oil allowance, and Mark could properly relax again.

"How did you two meet?" Mark asked, but his eyes followed the large bowl of pasta with tomatoes and anchovies being served. After weeks of eating fast food, chocolate bars, and occasional leftovers fished out from trash, the simple dishes served by Seth felt undeniably fresh. His arteries were unclogging by the second.

Domenico looked up from above the bowl, which he dug into first, moving two large portions of spaghetti onto his paper plate. His gaze transferred to Seth. "Ah, we're from the same town. We went to school together, played together as kids, and all that."

Seth gave Dom a tender smile. "Love at first sight."

Mark rolled his eyes at the sugary sweetness of what he was hearing. "Not really if you knew each other as kids."

Domenico dismissed Mark with a gesture. "Details. We always had this... connection. When I realized I was gay, I would watch him in his window, sitting under a tree by his house."

Mark wanted to say something, but when he started tucking into the food, he was too busy chewing.

Seth smiled at Dom and ran his fingers through his hair. "Oh, did you now? I used to find any excuse to visit Domenico in his father's antique store."

Domenico grinned and ate some of the food before kissing two fingers with an appreciative murmur. "That is amazing. Thank you," he said, petting Seth's nape.

As Mark watched them, for the first time he wasn't fantasizing about a threesome, but feeling a bit like a third wheel instead.

"Wait till dessert," Seth said with a wide smile, and his love for Dom seemed to glow on his skin.

Mark stuffed his mouth with more pasta, only now realizing that no one had ever actually cooked for him. His parents had given him TV dinners, and then, on the road, any warm meal was one bought at a diner or some other cheap place. "Why'd you leave Italy then?" he asked with his mouth full.

Domenico's eyes dimmed and he leaned back in the chair, pulling Seth against him. "Homophobic violence. Our town wasn't too open-minded about our relationship."

Seth nodded. "Being together back there was impossible. I would rather lose everything than not be with the love of my life."

Domenico sighed and kissed Seth's temple, staring into the dark shadows of the ceiling, high above the beams. He slowly pulled his fingers over the pronounced scar on his face. "We were repeatedly attacked, and in the end, I wanted us as far away from it all as possible."

Mark raised his eyebrows. "But all the way to another continent? Must have been pretty bad."

Seth gave Dom a kiss and got up as they were finishing the pasta. "Dom protected me, got shot in the process. I had to carry him through the woods in the middle of the night. I was so scared that he would die."

Domenico's face went grim, and he slowly raised his gaze at Mark. "I lost so much blood back then."

The sweet smell of crêpes filled the room the moment Seth poured some of the mixture into the pan. Mark's mouth watered, and his heart thumped like when he first kissed a guy. He wanted to stay here forever. Even with the spiders. Even with Dana.

"Maybe we can go back to Italy one day, but it's all too fresh now," Seth said.

Domenico ate his spaghetti slowly, chewing every chunk of food. He seemed a bit absent, maybe remembering the violence he left behind. "Yes. I would like to go back home at some point."

"I don't think it's realistic, but maybe in ten, fifteen years." Seth was putting the finished crêpes on a separate plate.

Mark was tempted to steal one, but he imagined Domenico shooting a bullet through his hand before he could even reach them. "Come on, it can't be that dangerous."

Domenico gave a dark chuckle. "Tell me that when you see the man *you* love cut up and bleeding," he muttered, staring at the table. The temperature seemed to have dropped by ten degrees.

Seth flipped the crêpes in silence, but Mark wouldn't give in to this grim talk and shrugged. "I don't think I'll ever fall in love. I'm too logical for that."

Domenico snorted. "Like fuck. Logical for crêpes."

Seth shook his head and put a stack of crêpes in the middle of the table, along with a bowl of cut-up bananas and caramel sauce. He wiggled his eyebrows and placed a

jar of Nutella next to those. He must have been hiding it until dessert, because Domenico's eyes grew wider.

"We'll see how you'll talk in a few years."

Mark pouted but was quick to put food on his plate. They wouldn't be there in a few years. They would be only a memory he could maybe hold on to when someone told him good people didn't exist when clearly they did—even if they came in the form of two foreign weirdos. No one who made crêpes like these could be evil.

Domenico shoveled down the rest of the pasta and reached out for a clean plate with the enthusiasm of a hungry puppy. "I said the same thing when I was your age," he said as if he were seventy. "I thought I'd just fuck all my life, but when we started dating, everything just came together."

Mark closed his eyes for a moment, delighting in the dessert melting in his mouth. "Oh yeah?" he asked as soon as he swallowed. "How many guys did you fuck?"

Domenico shrugged. "I was traveling a lot, so I guess... many. I'm attractive, so it wasn't a big deal."

The face Seth made suggested it was a bigger deal than Dom thought.

"So what? You'd just go on Grindr wherever you traveled to? While your hometown sweetheart was withering away?" Mark snorted and didn't even care when Seth slapped the back of his head.

Domenico cleared his throat. "Our relationship was a bit on and off. We had a fight after high school and only got back together later."

"So who was the most interesting guy you ever fucked?" Mark pushed, eager for juicy details.

"He's right beside me," said Domenico, tugging on Seth's wrist. He swirled his thumb over the hair at the back of his hand.

Seth smiled back at him and raised Dom's hand to his lips for a kiss.

Mark rolled his eyes. Of course Dom would say that. "Okay, okay, but I mean like looks-wise or something."

Domenico squinted at him. "Seth."

Mark groaned. "Yeah, right. You're just not allowed to say anything else now, are you?"

Domenico shrugged and pulled Seth down into his seat. "Why is that so strange to you? He is perfect to me. I'd never swap him for anyone else."

Mark gave up and settled for eating more crêpes. "But don't you miss the thrill of meeting other guys?"

Seth answered before Dom could. "No. No one else could ever understand me the way Dom does. When you share so much past with someone, the relationship itself becomes a part of you."

Domenico smirked with half his mouth and nodded, absent-mindedly twisting a small coin in his fingers. "Seth is the heads to my tails." He looked up and into his lover's eyes. "So tough but so sweet at the same time. I can't ever get enough of that."

"Oh, my God. Any more sugar, and I'm gonna barf." Mark made a gagging sound.

Dom laughed loudly. "Don't eat if it's too sweet. More for me."

Seth sighed, playing with the banana on his plate.

Mark frowned. "So what do you do in the US? Live off savings or something?"

Domenico looked at Seth. "More or less, yeah. I'm trying to be frugal."

"We're kinda drifting. Working out the details of what to do next," Seth said without looking up from his plate.

Domenico sighed. "Yeah, we have some stuff to figure out, I guess."

"So where are you going to next?" Mark wouldn't mind hanging around a bit longer. They were nice and gave

him free food. And he deserved the smack he got, since he did steal their car. Fred could wait.

"South. We have no plans that can't be moved. Just drifting for now." Domenico kissed Seth's cheek and ate some Nutella straight out of the pot. Mark kind of regretted he hadn't thought of doing that.

"Yeah, it's all up in the air right now," Seth muttered and pulled away slightly.

Dom blinked and held his hand. "What is it?"

"Never mind. Maybe we can talk about it later."

Mark sat up straight, ready to hear something juicy.

Domenico gestured at him even as he kept his eyes on Seth. "We could put him out the door."

Mark crossed his arms on his chest and frowned. "Hey! I'm sitting right next to you."

Domenico glanced at him with a slight frown. "Then you should have gotten the hint that it's time to go for a walk."

Mark groaned and got up. "Yeah, whatever! I can go." A crappy ending to a lovely meal. He was never on the inside of anything. All anyone ever allowed him to see was surface-deep.

"Don't eavesdrop. I'll know if you do," said Domenico, unfazed by the outburst.

Mark grabbed a packet of Cheetos from the cupboard and went out, slamming the door behind himself. So much for being included.

Chapter 10 - Domenico

Domenico looked back at the closed door, but then shifted his gaze to Seth, to the table that was still littered with remains of food, which they couldn't really store anywhere, as the shack had no electricity. Or running water. It was like the Middle Ages out here, and while Domenico enjoyed some time with nature, he'd much rather be in a nice penthouse somewhere. Or in a villa close to a large city. But this shack would be their home for at least a few days, until things in the outside world settled down a bit, and Domenico was intent on enjoying his time with Seth now that they had come to a consensus about what was going on.

Domenico couldn't believe Seth had been pushing him away all this time because he somehow didn't consider himself attractive enough. It was such a ridiculous concept that Dom would have never come up with it if Seth hadn't told him. Looking at that gloriously big, tan body, at the thick arms, and the hair he knew was sprouting beneath Seth's clothes, Domenico would gladly feast on him all the time, with or without the few extra pounds he piled on

since the confrontation with Vincente. He was just as hot as when Domenico had first laid eyes on him in New York City.

"What is it?"

Seth rubbed his forehead. "Nah. It's not like it's anything new. Just the talk of all your flings had me thinking again."

Domenico stepped back, unsure what to make of this confession. "You know it's only you and me now, right? I promised you that."

Seth sucked in his bottom lip and chewed on it. "I know… but what about the consequences? You told me that you slept with several *hundred* guys. I mean, if you got anything from them, then I have it too. I didn't want to think about it, but it might be time to stop living in the dark."

Domenico stepped away, taken aback. They had talked about it before, and he'd assumed Seth had followed his example and chosen to go with the flow, not think too much about things they couldn't really control, but clearly that wasn't the case.

"What would this change?"

Seth swallowed and got up as well. "If you… *we* have HIV or something else like that, there are treatments we could start now."

Domenico took a deep breath that burned his lungs even as he looked at the wall, which was bathed in the pleasant light of the candles. "We're not staying in one place anyway. It would be complicated."

"It doesn't have to be tomorrow. But you can do a checkup at any clinic we come across. I would really rather know." Seth looked out the window with a sigh.

Domenico swallowed hard, but now that he had let off some steam, it didn't feel like that unreasonable of a request. And yet, when he saw the worried look on Seth's face, it suddenly struck him that he could have put Seth in

danger. No, he *did*. From the very beginning. What if Seth's worries came true and they were ill? What if *he* got Seth ill? That thought had him holding his breath.

"Will you do the checkup?" Seth asked, rubbing dust off the window with a frown.

Domenico gritted his teeth and squeezed his hand on the edge of the tabletop. "I'm sorry."

"I know. But what's done is done."

"What if we aren't okay? You'll hate me. You won't say so at the beginning, but you will start resenting me," whispered Domenico as the black hole spread through his chest.

Seth wouldn't look his way. "If I was to hate you for what you did to me, I'd be hating you already."

Domenico couldn't make himself answer. His thoughts went to times past as he looked through the window, into the darkness outside. He'd never worried about the future. He'd always smoked like a chimney, gorged on food, and drank too much caffeine. And he fucked a lot. He fucked strangers without protection. All that because his life had been meant to be a short and intense one. But now? Without any imminent danger to his life, if he and Seth hid away somewhere, there was a chance he'd live to old age. Seth would be with him, and if Dom got ill, Seth would have to take care of him. Days would be subtracted from his life for every crime Dom had committed against his body, and the precious time he was to have with Seth would be lost.

"You're right. I'm a fucking coward for not thinking about it," hissed Domenico.

Those words made Seth instantly turn around, and he crossed the space between them, welcoming Dom into a hug. "I love you, no matter what, okay?"

Domenico shook his head, his whole body burning on the surface. "Don't say that. You can't know how you'll feel if you're right."

Seth kissed the side of his face. "There's no way to take it back now. I try not to dwell on things I can't change anymore."

Domenico exhaled, increasingly frantic on the inside. He hated not being able to act. This thing was already out of his grasp, and it was all his fault. He hadn't cared back when they had met after years of estrangement, when he was still holding a grudge over something that hadn't been Seth's choice. Dom hadn't even known that his real father *had* always been around and instead tried to prove himself to someone who resented him. Back then, he had wanted to hurt Seth, humiliate him, put him in his place, and he didn't care about any possible damage. Now he had to deal with the consequences of his actions. Did Seth think back to those first months often? To the harsh words and brutal fucking so different than the rough, steamy sex they both enjoyed now?

The sweet kiss Seth gave him pulled him out of the quicksand of grim thoughts. "What's Dana doing?" Seth stepped back toward the window.

"Setting up traps around the house. We don't want any wild animals knocking at our door," said Domenico and petted Seth's back.

"*Fuck*. Traps. I left some bait on a hook over the water. I thought it was a good opportunity now that we're staying here. I'll go tell Mark to stay away from the shore. I'll be back in a sec." He pulled away but then came back to give Dom one last kiss. "Don't worry so much."

Domenico sighed and held on to Seth's fingers, not even wanting to comment on the alligator hunt. His brain was scrambling with worry as it was. "I love you."

Seth smiled at him and disappeared behind the door. Fucking him today had felt like a visit in heaven. It made Dom remember why it had been worth it to leave everything behind to be with him. Seth's body was so pliant in his hands, yet so tight around his cock, but it was the

way Seth opened up to Dom, parted his lips for kisses, and mewled in pleasure that told Dom the whole story of his affection.

Voices outside suggested Seth must have found Mark, but when he heard screams, all his senses went into high alert. The gun was in his hand before he even reached the door. The safety was off as he jumped off the porch, desperately trying to blink away the darkness that clung to his eyes after leaving the candlelit house. The ground was soft and uneven where he landed, but that would not stop him, and he rushed blindly toward the screams. Toward the murky water of the swamp.

Mark cried out something Dom could not understand, and just as Dom was reaching the shore, he started picking out the contours around him. Seth's bulky body writhed around in the grass, struggling with something... large. Dom's first instinct was that it was an assailant. Someone who followed them here and decided to take them out one by one, but seconds later, an even more awful truth emerged from the thick darkness along with a bone-chilling hiss.

Seth rolled toward the house, with a scream on his lips, but an alligator the size of Mark wouldn't give him the chance to get away. It grabbed Seth's leg, pulling him toward the swamp in sharp, merciless tugs, and wouldn't let go even when Seth kicked its eye. The animal shook its head, tossing Seth about like a heavy rag doll and pulled him toward the murky water that would do the work for the alligator.

Domenico's first instinct was to shoot the beast's brains out, or at least distract it with a bullet to the back, but with shadows moving like snakes in the darkness, he could not risk injuring Seth further. He dove for the beast's rear, spraying water all over when he accidentally stepped into the swamp. Its temperature sent a flash of electricity all the way to Dom's spine, only fueling the force with

which he pulled the thick tail while holding the gun with his armpit. Wet, it felt slippery in his hands, even despite the hard, rough skin that was nothing like the crocodile skin shoes Domenico had once owned. He yanked the beast back to the shore as hard as he could, and a raw, hoarse cry tore out of his throat from the effort. To his horror, the alligator kept his jaws tight on Seth's calf, and within a second, rolled its freakishly strong body in the mud. Seth cried out but had enough clarity of mind to follow the alligator's movements even as the tail slipped out of Dom's grasp.

Out of breath, Domenico charged at the reptile, jumping on top of it as soon as it showed him its back. Pushing his shoes under the rear legs, Domenico grabbed the alligator's nape and pushed, feeling it stir between his thighs. He could almost sense the claws scratching against the soles of his combat boots, but at this point, Dom's sole focus was Seth, whose eyes were so wide they seemed to glow in the dark. Noises morphed into a mush in Domenico's ears as he punched the beast's head with the handle of his gun repeatedly. If he shot the thing dead, its jaws could squeeze, crushing Seth's leg, so he pulled his arm back, and shot the alligator's tail. The reptile writhed under him, turning Dom's world on its head, and throwing him into the water. His gun slipped out of his hand as he fell, but there was no time to look for it when the alligator turned its jaws his way.

At least Seth was free. With mud in one eye and the darkness not helping, he could still see Seth's shadowy figure crawling out of the water.

"Dom! Come out!" Seth yelled from the shore.

Domenico stumbled forward trying to reach his gun, but the jaws of the alligator were all too close. He jumped to the side and straddled its back to be out of the reach of the deadly teeth.

"Domenico!" Dana screamed from the shore, her voice a higher pitch than usual.

As soon as he gave her a glance, she expertly threw a gun his way, and he caught it in the air, just in time to put the barrel against the top of the alligator's skull and pull the trigger.

The moment the familiar sound tore through the air, Domenico's face warmed with peace as the animal slouched under him, stilling in silence. With the five-foot beast finally eliminated and its heavy, hard body limp beneath Domenico, Seth's moans became all the more pronounced, drilling holes in Dom's brain and pulling him close on hooks that dug deep into his flesh.

Dom rolled off and found his gun in the mud, rushing away from the swamp and more reptiles approaching at the scent of blood.

"Light! I need light!" he screamed, scrambling in the mud that soaked through his jeans and bit his skin. He reached Seth and grabbed him below the arms, dragging the heavy, struggling body away from the water. His spine screamed with effort, but he refused to let go and pulled Seth farther and farther onto the shore. Ignoring his struggles to get up, Domenico only let him go by the porch, pulsing with primal fear as he dropped to his knees and cradled Seth to his chest. It was even hard to breathe, but he made himself speak anyway.

"You... alive?"

"I'll get a flashlight from the car!" Mark yelled and ran off.

"What's happening?" Dana yelled, but Dom was much more focused on finding out what Seth's injuries were.

Seth's first words made Dom livid. "Is Mark okay?"

Domenico gasped and looked around. "I—he ran for the flashlight. What are you talking about?" Domenico couldn't stop choking on air as he patted Seth down,

searching for wounds, but with their bodies completely wet, it was a difficult task. When he reached ripped fabric on Seth's calf, he understood he found what he was looking for. "Dana, give me the fucking first aid kit!"

Seth screamed when Dom pushed on a tender spot. "Don't touch!" He clung onto Dom's tank top for dear life.

Dana disappeared in the darkness, but soon, the engine of the pickup came to life, and the cool white glow of the headlights illuminated the scene. It was a smart move that Dom would have appreciated much more if it wasn't Mark who had lured the gator in the first place.

Mark jumped out of the car with an extra flashlight, which uncovered the horror that was Seth's leg. Blood was pouring out of the torn flesh, and for a moment, even Domenico couldn't tell what exactly he was looking at.

"I-I'm taking him to a hospital," was all he was able to choke out as he looked into Seth's lovely face, now twisted in pain. "I need to go..."

"Wait, I'll secure the wound," Dana said as she slid into the mud on her knees, working fast on Seth's leg with bandages. At least she wasn't distracted by Seth's moans of pain and his squirming the way Dom was.

He scrambled closer to Seth and embraced him hard as his own heart went into overdrive. He kissed the wet hair on top of Seth's head, happy to hear him breathing. "It'll be fine. I've got you."

Dana was very quick, that much he could see, but subjectively, it still seemed to take far too long. All he wanted was to get Seth in the car and drive so fast no animal would be spared if it crossed their way.

Mark helped Dom transfer a shaking Seth to the pickup. Each step of the way, Domenico's ears filled with the frantic rattle of Seth's teeth.

"What else can I do?" Mark whined.

"Nothing. Just don't do anything stupid," said Dom, unable to focus on anything else other than getting Seth

into the passenger seat. His muscles protested, but he managed to position him eventually, and as soon as Seth's seat belt was buckled, Domenico ran around the car and got inside, immediately rushing to the only road there was. He switched on the high beams to light the way and bolted into the narrow channel of the road at as high a speed as he could muster. Leaves and branches were black and golden as they slapped the windshield, and Dom leaned forward, desperate to see as much of the road as he could.

"Seth, talk to me."

Seth took a shaky breath. "I didn't know alligators liked Cheetos."

"What? What are you talking about?" hissed Domenico, afraid that Seth was getting delirious. It was still a long way to the nearest hospital.

"Mark was hanging out around where I set bait. He threw them Cheetos. And they came." Seth's words came after pauses, as though it was hard for him to gather his voice.

"*They*?" Domenico felt as if the blood drained out of his body, fear suppressing anger at the irresponsible kid. "There were more?"

"Just small ones." Seth took a deep breath and squirmed in his seat to have a look at his leg. "But I saved him."

Dom wanted to say that he should have let the little fucker die, but he knew Seth would hate him for it, and there wasn't anything he could do now anyway. Frustrated, Domenico hit the side of the steering wheel and bit his lip. "Yes, you did. But now your leg's hurt, *Hero*."

Seth gave him a weak smile in the darkness. "Now I'm a hero, too. But my leg doesn't hurt."

Domenico swallowed hard, stiffening immediately. Could it be Dana had made the dressing too tight? "But can you feel it? Is it numb?"

"N-no. I don't feel it very well... I'm dizzy." Seth's breaths were shallow, and Dom was sweating enough for them both. After all they'd been through, this would have been the stupidest way to die.

Dom stopped the car and switched on the light, leaning down to look at the dressing. He slipped his hand under the bandage, to the tune of Seth's moans, but the dressing was fine. It had to be shock. *It had to be.* Seth had enough nerve damage in his hand already. Domenico couldn't believe something like this could happen to them again. It wasn't as if people were bitten by those things all the time, was it?

"You hold on," he whispered, starting the car again. "It's gonna be fine. I'm gonna get you anything you want once the doctors are done with you."

"Can I get a hammock?" Seth muttered, getting paler by the second in the faint light from the front of the car.

Domenico nodded, and spoke, his voice thick with emotion. "Sure. I'm gonna hang it for you myself."

Seth smiled with his eyes closed. "You're the best..."

Domenico sighed and forced a smile, grabbing Seth's hand over the gearbox. "No, *you* are the best thing that happened to me," he said, as his thoughts trailed to all the deaths he cared about, to the countless fallen brothers, and funerals, the kisses good-bye. Seth wouldn't be one of those lost. Domenico refused to let that happen.

Chapter 11 -Domenico

Seth was pale, thin as an old, starving man. His body had given up way before Dom's did, even though it was Dom who had let the illness loose in Seth's body. And as Seth's cool hand slowly relaxed and slid from Domenico's fingers, the heart rate monitor flatlined, with the most horrifying of sounds.

Domenico stared at his peaceful face and gently petted the bony jaw line. He had been ready for this for a long time, and yet watching his beloved deteriorate and suffer for such a long time had been the most horrific experience. Now at least, he was not in pain anymore.

Blinking back the tears, Domenico walked up to the door and locked it, before returning to the bed and slowly moving Seth to the edge of the mattress and climbing in under the blankets. Seth's body was still warm, and he cuddled up against it, kissing the dry skin of the stubbly cheek.

"We're going to be together soon," he promised and slid his hand underneath the fabric of his pants, pulling out his small knife. Domenico had never told Seth, but as soon as

he realized his partner was dying, he made a promise to himself that he would follow. There would be no life for him without Seth. He did not want to continue his earthly existence alone and lost when his beloved was waiting for him in purgatory.

Dom winced when the sharp steel pierced through skin and tore the muscle and vessels down from his wrist. The numb pain radiated all over his arm, but he wasn't finished and soon the other forearm was open as well.

The blade clattered against the floor, and Domenico gently nudged Seth's face toward him. The brown eyes were still open, and though unfocused and lifeless, they were still as warm and beautiful as the day Domenico understood just how much Seth meant to him. Dom kissed the parched skin of his lips and waited, covering Seth with his scent minute by minute.

Domenico shivered, pressing tighter against Seth as he looked into his face, growing increasingly colder. But that was good. They would be together soon. His eyelids felt like they were made of lead when the freezing cold turned into warm numbness in his fingers and toes. He was slowly fading, but as he curled around the lifeless shell that remained of his man, he couldn't be calmer. Just before darkness swallowed him whole, Seth blinked, and his mouth twisted into a thin line. Domenico stopped breathing.

"You killed me," said Seth harshly, just before Domenico fell down into the tar-black clutches of death.

He woke up to moans and whimpers, trembling skin sliding against him like a swarm of vipers, but when a cold hand squeezed around his dick, Domenico jerked to his feet with a scream. It was completely dark, and yet he could see for miles and miles on end. Dozens of bodies with skin white as paper were crawling his way. Their faceless heads were wet with saliva spilling from identical, gaping mouths. They dragged their fat cocks on the black ground and touched the

huge, pink holes between their buttocks. His name was on all their mouths.

Domenico kicked back a hand reaching for him and dashed toward a rock nearby, screaming Seth's name with growing despair. His open wrists were dry, his veins devoid of blood. He was dead, but Seth was nowhere in sight, only thousands of faceless creatures in heat.

Dom cried out so loud even his stomach ached with the effort, but no one answered him as his scream resonated over the monotone chanting of his name.

He was trapped here forever.

Domenico jerked out of the dream, almost falling off the chair as his heart rattled with panic. Seeing Seth fast asleep made him relax into the backrest, desperately trying to calm down. His first instinct was to cradle Seth's hand in his and find peace in its warmth, but he didn't want to disturb his lover's sleep. In the end, it took him several minutes to chase away the nightmare that clawed at the most fundamental fears in his life. But there were so many plaguing him recently that he was starting to consider them a fact of life.

He stared at the peaceful face of his lover pressed against a pristine white pillow. It was now slowly growing brighter outside, and after a long procedure, Seth had dozed off due to an IV with some kind of sedative. Fortunately, the damage done by the alligator was reversible, and for what happened, Seth had been lucky. The surgery went fine, and all the stitches would eventually be gone, leaving even more scars. It choked Domenico up to think that maybe there was truth to the dream, and if he had something lying dormant in his blood, his bad seed could do what the alligator couldn't, and neither could the

Villanis. If Seth's worries were true, Dom would be the one to kill the man he loved.

He had lied about being Seth's brother to be allowed to stay, but that only happened after security tried to throw him out for being aggressive. He wasn't 'aggressive' he was just scared for Seth. How was he to even know if the doctors here knew what they were doing? It was too far to any of his contacts, and he didn't want to risk revealing himself anyway, so he needed to trust the staff of the hospital, but trusting strangers wasn't in his nature.

Constantly being on the move was not optimal to say the least. They needed to finally make the move to Mexico and put roots down, so that in an emergency they would have more people around, more of a structured environment. Everything was up in the air right now, and they needed a home, not a damn pickup truck.

Seth was now on a diet of antibiotics, and Domenico was determined to check every single pill that went into Seth's mouth. He'd heard a lot about situations when the wrong drugs were administered or wrong quantities, and now that he was here, in an uncomfortable chair at Seth's bedside, it was his mission to ensure his lover would get well as soon as possible. He was lucky to have hidden cash in the seats of their pickup, so at least he didn't have to worry about payment for any services the doctors could come up with. A young pretty nurse was clearly interested in Seth's health, and Domenico couldn't blame her—she had no idea her chances with the best-looking patient at the ward were zero. But if that strictly non-professional interest would get Seth better care, Domenico was ready to butter her up. Even though she looked more like an underwear model than a nurse and Dom wasn't all that certain about her credentials.

She came over again, this time with a tray of food, and put it on the little table next to Domenico. As she

leaned over, he noticed a black pattern on her skin where the shirt she wore under the scrubs rolled up a bit. "Don't tell anyone I got this for you," she whispered and winked at him, to Dom's utter confusion. Did she want a threesome? And since when were people with tattoos allowed to work in hospitals? Was this not a health hazard?

He smiled back at her though and shrugged. He'd make sure she used latex gloves when handling Seth's leg. "It's good to have friends in high places."

She left Domenico with a tray of cut roast chicken in some kind of sauce, macaroni and cheese, a biscuit, cooked corn, and other delicacies Domenico despised. Only now that the fear was over, he was also hungry. On second thought, Dom dug in, watching Seth rest with drug-induced slumber. At least when Seth woke up, Dom could surprise him with good news—he'd done the test, just to pass the time waiting for Seth to come back from surgery. And even though he still dreaded that the results could come out positive, at least he was trying to meet Seth's expectations. A step in the right direction. Maybe he would not lose Seth. Maybe there was still a chance everything would be fine.

"What's that smell?" Seth groaned before he even opened his eyes. "Fuck, it hurts…"

Domenico put the tray on the table and shifted closer, grabbing Seth's hand. "I'm here. It's just food."

Seth opened his eyes and squeezed Dom's hand, yawning. "I'm so happy it wasn't the hand this time. I've done so many rehab exercises…"

Domenico kissed Seth's palm and cuddled his face up against it, breathing in the scent of skin, along with a faint aroma of disinfectant. "Yeah, it should be fine. You'll just have to stay here for a few days."

"Did you wrestle an alligator, or did I dream that up?" Seth frowned, but at least his gaze seemed more focused.

Domenico laughed and kissed the middle of Seth's palm again. Now that he thought about it, it had been a crazy thing to do, and he might have ended up dead. "I'm your personal crocodile hunter."

"I was angry about the pig, but I'm happy you killed the gator. Did you make sure to keep the body?"

Domenico sighed but then broke into a laugh that just wouldn't stop. He couldn't believe Seth was still upset about the damn piglet. "I was busy taking you to the hospital."

"Maybe call Mark about it. Fuck, we need to get him a phone. Dana?" Seth was getting more flustered over the gator's body than over the fact it was Mark's fault that he would be limping for a while.

Domenico groaned. *"We need to get him a phone?* Really? What next? Maybe we should decorate a nursery for him at our new home?" And he didn't really want to speak to Dana at the moment.

Seth shut up and fell back to the pillow. "You're sure he's fine?"

"Pretty sure." Domenico cleared his throat. "You said he got the alligator to attack? If it wasn't for that kid's stupidity, you and I would be lying in a bed right now." Domenico frowned at the one Seth lay in. "A dirtier one, but at least there would be space for me. And your leg wouldn't have any holes."

"He didn't know what he was doing…"

And speaking of the devil, there was a knock at the door, and Mark walked in with his hands in the pockets of a new pair of jeans. "Hey…"

Domenico's smile dropped, suddenly replaced by a blaze of fury. He got up and walked up to Mark, grabbing his hair. "Cheetos? Are you for fucking real?" he hissed, shaking the kid.

Mark grabbed Dom's wrist, trying to wiggle out of the grip. "Ouch! Ouch! Dom, please. I wasn't thinking," he whined.

Seth sat up in the bed, propping himself up with both hands. "Dom, come on, let go of him. He'll know better now."

Domenico pushed Mark at the bed, pacing in front of the door. "Eat the damn mac and cheese. That shit smells," he groaned, watching Mark and Seth as they both stared at him.

"I just wanted to say that I was so sorry..." Mark bit his lip, glancing at Seth. "I've caused so much trouble, and you still saved my life."

"That's fine, kid," Seth said even though his new set of scars wouldn't be fine at all.

Domenico sneaked the carrot cake out of the tray and pushed it whole into his mouth. Of course, now it would be *poor Mark* who'd be the center of attention. How typical.

"Did you take Seth's bike?" he asked once he was done with the cake.

Mark swallowed and turned his gaze to Dom with guilt painted all over his face. "I climbed into the back of the pickup yesterday. I needed to know Seth was fine," he whined.

Domenico exhaled and rubbed his forehead. But this time, there was no anger in him. He was exhausted, and all he wanted was to doze off next to his man. "You know where we are? Let's fucking hope no biker needs to have his appendix removed," he said, looking at the door. Of course, the nearest hospital would be in the town where they made enemies. That was just their luck.

Mark pulled a phone out of his pocket, catching shallow breaths. "I've got that Jed guy's phone, and I looked through it. He's got a gay dating app on there, and I've got the video he tried to make of me in that restroom. When

the phone fell, it caught his face as well. I'd blackmail the shit out of him, and he wouldn't dare touch us!"

Domenico saw red. He rushed to his feet and slapped Mark across the face. Breath caught in his throat as he snatched the damn phone from the boy's hand. "There's no *us*! What the fuck? This is just another reason for him to go after us. And by *us,* I mean myself and Seth. I am not about to take a bullet for you, and my fiancé's suffered enough because of your idiocy!"

"Dom, come on... He's still a child," Seth tried.

Mark held on to his cheek with his other hand, which probably ached even more than Domenico's palm. "I just meant—"

Domenico tossed the phone on the chair and angrily messed up his hair. "Stop getting on my nerves! Wait at the main entrance, and I'll have Dana pick you up. Go with her and stay the fuck in the swamps! You and I are gonna talk once Seth gets better."

Mark opened those stupid pouty kid lips, but said nothing in the end and stormed out of the room, as if he was about to cry again. Babysitting him was the last thing on Domenico's agenda.

Domenico rolled his eyes and looked at the tray of food. "And he didn't eat the fucking smelly noodles," he muttered, still buzzing on the inside.

"I don't think he came here for them," Seth grumbled, pulling up the comforter to look at his leg.

Domenico shook his head and slowly walked up to Seth, choosing Dana's number. "You know he can't stay here anyway. Let him lay low at the swamp with Dana, and then he'll go where no biker will get him."

"I know, I know. It's just nice to have people around. Make *connections*." Seth made an attempt at the macaroni and cheese but pushed it away after the first forkful. "Even Ryder. I liked talking to him. Sure, I couldn't

tell him even a quarter of the stuff you know, but I didn't feel so disconnected anymore."

Domenico looked at Seth's sweet, handsome face and gently brushed his fingers through his hair. "I get it, he was a straight guy."

Seth smiled and went for the roast chicken in the end. "I knew he wouldn't stick around in my life, but I enjoyed his company."

Domenico couldn't stop feeling a tiny bit jealous anyway. Couldn't *he* provide everything Seth needed? "Only as a friend?"

"Yes, Dom. Only as a friend. Not everyone wants to fuck me, you know?"

Domenico rolled his eyes and sent the message he typed in the meanwhile. At least Dana would get Mark out of his sight. "Yeah right. You're like the fucking gay Holy Grail. Can't think of anybody who wouldn't want to fill you at least once."

Seth's jaw dropped as he looked up at Dom. "And why's that?"

Domenico leaned against the wall, uncomfortable with the topic. "Because you're so fucking radiant. Sweet, hard, fucking pretty but not like a doll."

Seth nodded. "I like that. I can live with that."

Domenico walked up to the bed and sat in the chair, slipping the biker's phone into his pocket as he touched Seth, watching him eat. If only he could stop constantly worrying and give Seth the kind of life he needed.

Domenico hadn't moved from the hospital the next day. He only left Seth's room to use the cafeteria and buy some snacks. Other than that, he spent about fifteen hours dozing off in the chair, watching TV, and playing cards with

Seth. Seth was in pain, but the pills helped him enough to actually be eager for distractions, which Domenico was happy to provide. It was rather nice to have this time to spend with only each other. Seth told him all about a food blog he wanted to run one day, where he'd pay homage to his mother's cooking, and how he was already looking for cameras online to take great photos of his creations. It was the sweetest, non-mafia related conversation and reminded Domenico just why he was so grateful to have a man like Seth when they were surrounded by sharks.

A call from Dana came not long after dark, and Dom hoped it wasn't any more gator news. He picked it up while browsing through his giant hand of cards in yet another round against Seth. "What is it?" he asked, holding the phone between his head and shoulder as he chose the right cards.

"Mark's gone. I thought he went out to pee or something, but he hasn't been back for a few hours now. I'm worried he might want to rat us out to the bikers."

Domenico gritted his teeth. "Fuck!" He tossed the cards on the blanket, and the rotten cogs in the depths of his brain started moving. "Don't you have both the car and motorbike? What the hell's going on there? You let him pee for hours?" Suddenly, a cold feeling spread through his muscles. "Did you kill him?"

Dana groaned as Seth sat up in the bed, trying to listen in on the conversation. "I didn't! He's an annoying shit, but I wouldn't *kill* him. I was surprised you didn't after he put Seth in danger."

"Don't you try to turn that on me," hissed Domenico, getting to his feet. "It's bad enough that you can't keep an eye on one kid."

"Well, I don't have maternal instincts," she huffed. "What do you want me to do?"

Domenico laughed, even though his gums were itching with rage. "I don't remember asking you to give him

a tit to suck. All you were supposed to do is make sure nothing weird happens. And now he's gone, and you're telling me this hours later."

"He was sulking all day! I just thought he wanted to sit around alone. He's a teenager. Why do you care? He's out of our hair now."

"Don't fuck up anything else," said Dom and ended the conversation, biting into the silicone case of his phone as soon as he was done. "Fucking fuck."

Seth looked up at him, searching for an answer in Dom without even asking the question.

Domenico dropped his hands. "The kid's gone. She let him get away, and he's been missing for hours now."

"What do we do?"

Domenico slid into the chair, feeling somehow queasy about the whole thing. He didn't believe for a second Mark would rat them out, but nevertheless, the kid would get in trouble again, that Dom was sure of. And even after all the bad blood, and maybe even because of it, the disappearance felt like a waste after Seth risked his life to save Mark.

Domenico exhaled, feeling much better when he made his decision. "You'll have to entertain yourself while I'm gone."

Chapter 12 - Mark

Mark wasn't sure what was worse, complete darkness of the woods with the added soundtrack of insects and animals he didn't dare imagine, or turning on the flashlight and actually seeing what was there. He didn't know how long he'd been walking for, but the drive to town took half an hour, so if he hadn't taken a turn in the wrong place, he had a chance of getting there tomorrow. At least he'd bought pants with the money Dom had given him for groceries earlier. He tried hard not to get nervous, but he could hardly see where he was going and stumbled several times on his way as he followed the shallow dip in the ground made by tires. He tried to keep one arm up, in case yet another young branch wanted to smack his face good-bye.

He was not about to stay where he wasn't wanted, and Dana made damn well sure he understood just how much he wasn't wanted. Mark spent too much time doing nothing anyway. He needed to get to Fred's house and start a new life, not attach himself to a bunch of criminals. He hadn't stayed home for the abuse his parents dished out,

and he wouldn't take it from strangers. He didn't even know if Dom and Seth were legally in the US. The last thing he needed was to be taken by the police as well, or accused of assisting illegal aliens. Clearly, Domenico had something to hide. Sure, when they told him the dramatic story of their love, he was feeling for them. He was enamored with the way they touched each other, and putting Seth in danger made him feel like the biggest idiot, but the truth was that he wasn't really wanted in that strange group.

Dana clearly despised him, Domenico had hit him more than once, and even Seth seemed to treat Mark like a charity case. He'd been wrong to include himself in their *family*, and Domenico had showed him exactly what he thought about that.

After a long time of walking through the dark woods, with plants constantly slapping against him like stray snakes, Mark was shocked to hear a low roar ahead. Was he getting close to the asphalt road already?

Before he saw the headlights, there was a white glow penetrating the forest and making all the narrow trees look like black thorns. When a truck emerged from behind the hill and moved toward Mark, it felt as if he suddenly woke up in some kind of artsy animated movie where armies of cars and tanks trampled over every living thing, leaving behind a burned wasteland. Mark swallowed hard and stepped to the side of the road, giving up on the idea of catching a lift, as the car was driving in the opposite direction.

But then it stopped, just a few steps ahead of Mark, blinding him with the headlights.

He covered his eyes and squinted at the dark silhouette of a tall man emerging from the driver's seat. Mark took a few steps back when he realized the stranger was carrying a gun and then another few when the man stepped into the light and revealed himself as Domenico.

This was not good at all. Had Dana been right? Was Dom just waiting to be out of Seth's sight to dispose of Mark?

Domenico shook his head, looking even more powerful with the bright background, like a villain from a serial killer movie. "I'm surprised nothing ate you on the way," he said coolly.

Mark crossed his arms on his chest, even though all his joints were frozen with fear. "What do you care?" He eyed the gun and took a step to the side. He'd be less of a target between the trees.

Domenico exhaled and waved the gun toward the car. "Get in."

Mark crossed the road and started walking toward the asphalt road to town. He'd had enough of being told what to do and then getting nothing but shit in return. At least when he sucked dick, guys loved it.

Domenico turned toward him and the metal clang that followed had Mark's heart freezing. The safety was off. "I changed my mind about you," whispered Domenico.

"How come? You don't like anything I do." Mark watched Dom, slowly taking steps back, into the darkness of the forest.

Domenico shook his head, and his hair had a halo in the bright light of the headlights. "Now that you put Seth out of commission for a while, I think I might have a use for you."

"What kind of use?" Mark didn't like the sound of this at all. The hot air was choking him just like Domenico's gaze.

Domenico stepped closer but stopped when Mark moved back to maintain his distance. "What kind of use could I have for you? You made it clear you're just a cumrag."

The cruel words hit Mark harder than a bullet ever could, and he was not about to wait and find out what exactly Dom wanted him around for. He was a sexy guy, but

this was not what Mark wanted. Not like this. He froze for just half a second before he turned around and ran faster than ever before, straight into the forest. He kept tripping, branches hitting his face, and he didn't even know whether he was heading into the jaws of another gator, but he didn't care at this point. Cold fear had him dashing in a zigzag pattern as he hoped to lose Domenico far behind.

He had no idea how long he ran, but when he finally slowed down, there were no sounds of hurried footsteps to be heard. Mark allowed himself a second to catch his breath. He'd seen Dom wrestle an alligator and shoot a bottle in his lover's hand. He would not hesitate to—

A large hand grabbed Mark by the back of the neck, and he was shoved face-first into a tree. All and any words were stuck in his throat when the cold barrel touched him behind the ear.

"On your knees," whispered Domenico, but it didn't even sound like his voice. It was cold, devoid of any emotion whatsoever. *Nothing* like when Seth was around.

Mark squealed in panic, but followed the order, unwilling to become gator feed just yet. "Please, don't... I won't tell anyone about you two. I'll just disappear."

"So you thought you'd get away?" hissed Domenico, poking Mark's head with the gun over and over, as if he expected it to finally give a hollow sound. "Rat on us? That's how you wanted to buy your safety?"

"No, I was scared. I'm so sorry I put you two in danger." Mark whined as cold sweat dripped down his back and his heart rattled in his chest.

Domenico groaned, and Mark was shocked when a small packet of Milky Ways dropped by his knee.

"Then what? You wanted to find this Fred guy? Be his bitch?"

Mark looked at the chocolate bars unsure what to think. "I'm not going to be *your* bitch for sweets!"

"What about money then?"

"You'd need to pay me *a lot*." Mark's breath hitched uncontrollably. It felt as if the whole forest were reaching out with its branches to grab him and squeeze the air out of his lungs. He had no skills. Sex was all he had to offer.

He flinched when Domenico switched on a flashlight, but moments later, breath pumped out of his lungs when a thick wad of hundred-dollar bills landed on top of the Milky Way bag. The silence was unbearable, and Mark was surprised that with all the shock and fear, what hurt him most was that Domenico's devotion to Seth was fake.

He slowly picked up the money to see if it was real. He'd never seen so much cash in his life. It had to be thousands of dollars. Who was Dom to have this kind of money in cash? Did Seth even know about this? And was all the love between them just for show when more sex was on the table?

Beggars couldn't be choosers. "And... what would I have to do for this?" he whispered, turning around to look straight into the barrel of the gun, forcing himself not to look away from the blinding light of the flashlight shining at him from above.

Domenico's face was partially hidden in the shadows, and the sharp scent of rotting leaves made the situation even more surreal. His voice sounded as though it came from some kind of underground tunnel. "A fantasy of mine. It's hard to find someone willing to go with it."

Mark could only imagine Domenico's fantasy being cruel and twisted if he wouldn't subject his *fiancé* to it. He swallowed. "And what's that?" he whispered.

Domenico slowly sank into a crouch in front of Mark. The smile on his face was enough to send a tingle of fear down Mark's back. "Lick the barrel, and I'll tell you more."

"Put the safety on," Mark whimpered, wishing he could just disappear, vanish from the face of the earth, and

never meet another man. Or woman for that matter if they were all like Dana.

Domenico shook his head. "No. I need to know if you're worth it first. Come on, give it good head."

Mark looked into Dom's cold eyes, but they were like a reptile's. So frightening he quickly gazed down to the gun and kissed the cold steel without thinking much. His insides did a twist, and he didn't even want the Milky Ways anymore.

"That was pretty lousy," muttered Domenico. "I thought you wanted that money."

Mark could barely breathe when he opened his lips for the gun. He did want the money. He wanted the freedom that would come with it. He could rent a room somewhere and live on delivery pizza for a year. Or two. Or five, depending on how thrifty he'd be. He could fuck people he liked, maybe even date someone, and he wouldn't be forced to drift anymore.

Domenico put one hand on top of Mark's head and slowly pushed the thick barrel between Mark's lips. It was so cold, and the weird smoky scent of gunpowder made Mark's stomach clench as the cock replacement moved back and forth. He dropped the flashlight to the ground.

"Yes, that's more like it. It's the risk of it that turns me on most," whispered Domenico.

Mark waited for Domenico to let him back out, fighting the tears that were threatening to spill from his eyes. What risk was it to Dom? The risk was all Mark's. His toes curled and he wished for it to be over. What was even the most horrible discomfort if he could have a better future? He would endure, even despite his body shaking and his teeth rattling against the gun.

"Think of it, I could pull the trigger now, and your brain would be splattered all over the place. And just for a split second, you'd know you are about to die," rasped Dom, looking at Mark intently as he pushed the gun in so

deep the metal clanked over his front teeth and dug into his soft palate, like a strange parasite ready to rush into his brain.

Mark panicked and pulled back, but then he thought that the sudden movement could have Domenico pull the trigger, so after the first impulse, he froze still, whimpering and not even trying not to cry anymore. Tears fell from his eyes and slid down his cheeks as Domenico withdrew the gun slightly and pushed the tip of the barrel against the inside of Mark's cheek, moving it back and forth.

"Good. I will fuck your ass like that, and you will cry for me," Domenico whispered.

Mark took a deep gulp of air as soon as Dom pulled out the gun. "You'd have to pay me more!" he whined with snot running down his chin. This had to be the most evil man he'd met to date. The mere thought of having that loaded steel up his ass had Mark needing to hug himself. He felt sick.

Domenico grabbed his throat and pulled Mark's face into a spot with more light. "Don't test me. I will pull the trigger on the last day of our agreement!"

Mark broke down sobbing. His mind melted into a chaos of misery. "Please, let me go. I'll suck your dick if you want, I'll suck the gun, just let me go."

"What's the worst thing you did so far, just to get money or whatever else you wanted?" asked Domenico, holding him in place, but he lowered the gun.

Mark couldn't stop sobbing, too overwhelmed, too trapped. "I let a guy pee on me," he uttered. It had been disgusting back then, yet now, in comparison to the gun fuck, sounded like a funny fetish.

Something clicked right next to Mark's head, and he cowered, for a moment certain Domenico would put him down now and leave his body to be ripped apart by animals, but instead, it was a loud shout straight into his

ear that sent him on his hands and knees, vomiting as his stomach revolted.

"Are you fucking insane, kid? You're sixteen! You'd let me—anyone—do those things to you for a lousy few thousand?"

Mark threw up even more before being able to look up. "I don't know! I don't have anything!" His body was shaking, and he wheezed while crying and spitting out the bitter taste of bile. He'd never experienced such a visceral meltdown. And did this mean Dom didn't want to kill him after all?

Domenico grabbed Mark's shoulder and shook him. "Clearly, you don't have any respect for yourself either. You're walking on such, such thin ice kid..." Domenico trailed off, and for once, his face lost its sharpness. "You will die if you don't change. Someone will hurt you, cut you up with a chainsaw, and dump you somewhere. No one will ever hear of you again."

Mark's teeth clattered. He couldn't believe someone would fool him like this, make him humiliate himself so badly just to prove a point. "I thought... that if only... I had money..." He could barely catch a breath to speak.

"And what? How long could you live like that? You won't be young and pretty forever."

Mark looked at his trembling hands where they curled into the muddy ground. "I'd go back to school if I had money. I wouldn't have to worry all the time. I could be free." He sniffed loudly.

"And you would never forget the things you did. Your body might never be the same either. Don't be stupid, Mark. You can't just regain self-respect after you throw it off the cliff." Domenico pulled him close until Mark fell into the warm embrace that smelled faintly of sweat and the hospital.

Within seconds, Mark hugged him back so hard he could feel his nails digging into Dom's back. And for once, it

wasn't a sleazy attempt at feeling him up. Mark just needed a friend. At least one person in his life who wasn't by his side because he wanted to pimp him, fuck him, or steal something.

Domenico exhaled and patted his back. "You're so fucking stupid. I can't believe it," he said, but this time, there wasn't any malice in that statement. "Come on, you need to eat something."

Mark let out a long breath and could barely stand on his shivering legs. So Domenico still wanted him around? He rubbed his eyes. "Is Seth feeling better?"

Domenico helped him up and started walking back toward the light coming from the road, leaving Mark to pick up the chocolate bars and the wad of cash. "He's fine, but they want to keep him in hospital for a few days, just in case."

Mark spat out the taste of vomit and couldn't wait to wash it out with some water. "Will he be able to cook when he comes out?" He loved how much care Seth put into the food he'd made for them before.

Domenico chuckled as if he hadn't just made Mark nauseated with fear, and he climbed the small slope ahead of them. "Getting hooked already? He always cooks."

Mark gave Dom a glance from the side. He wasn't even sure how to talk about what had happened just minutes ago. His heart was only slowly going back to its normal rhythm. Domenico was surely not some average antique dealer. Mark washed out his mouth with a bottle of water he found rolling about on the mat underneath the passenger seat and sat down, strangely numb. Would he really let a guy fuck his ass with a gun for money? Was this who he was? Who he *wanted* to be?

Domenico was there to distract him. "There are chocolate chip cookies in the glove compartment. Feed me," he said, maneuvering the car back and forth on the narrow road. He was trying to turn back toward town.

Mark frowned at the four different packets he found and chose chocolate chip in the end, passing it to Dom slowly, as if he were feeding a shark.

Domenico ripped the packaging with his teeth and grunted happily when he finally managed to make the U-turn by going back and forth on the narrow road. With one cookie in his mouth, he hummed some melody. Assaulting Mark in order to prove a point didn't seem like a big deal to him.

"I'm always hungry..." Mark muttered in order to say *something*. He grabbed a cookie as well and started munching on it. He felt elated and miserable all at the same time.

Domenico glanced back at him, and something in his gaze changed, just before he smiled. "Seth doesn't get it. Whenever we eat out, he's always taking those tiny desserts, and he can make a bowl of delicious pasta and not eat it in one go."

Mark dared to smile back. "It's funny that he's the pudgy one."

Domenico sighed. "Don't tell him that. He used to be very lean, but then he had the accident, and he hasn't gotten back to the way he was yet. But even then, he was always the one who'd rather eat a tuna sandwich than one with Nutella."

Mark raised his eyebrows. "What? That makes no sense. Nutella and peanut butter are like the Holy Grail of all spreads."

Domenico let out a groan that reminded Mark of a bear. "I loved this spread with marshmallow and caramel, but with real bread, not some cotton-like toast. They had it in Italy years ago. I was so pissed off when they stopped making it. Fuckers."

Mark nodded at this true understanding. "I love French pastries, like they have in cafés and stuff. If you come at closing time, they will sometimes give them out for

free." Though Mark doubted someone with a wad of money to throw around cared for free pastry. A wad of cash that Dom didn't ask to get back for that matter. "Does Seth bake too?"

"He's the god of baking!" Domenico winced like a needy puppy as he drove into the asphalt road. "I mean... his lemon cupcakes are unreal."

Mark smiled. "Maybe it's for the better that he doesn't have any place to bake in that shack."

"Why? You'd fucking love them."

"'Cause I might just fall in love if he fed me that stuff every day." Mark snorted.

Domenico shrugged. "Yeah, well, that wouldn't work out for you. But what is a broken heart when you can eat homemade lasagna? *Peperonata* with chargrilled chicken?"

Mark could already imagine all that food even if he had no idea what a *peperonata* was. "So he cooks, and what do you do?"

Domenico chewed on his lip, and he slowed down when they approached the bright site of a diner on the side of the road. Mark had eaten there once, and they had amazing breakfasts.

"I can tell you, I suppose. No one would believe you anyway," said Dom, driving into the parking lot and stopping the car in front of the building. "What do you think I do?"

Mark raised his eyebrows. "You are either a vigilante superhero, or you make lamps out of human skin."

Domenico barked out a laugh and slowly combed his fingers through his hair. "No. I used to be in special forces," he said and jumped out of the car.

Mark stalled for a moment. That made some sense. The way Domenico used a gun, the way he pacified two bikers on their own turf... Mark followed Dom out of the

car with questions buzzing in his skull. "For Italy?" he uttered.

Domenico nodded and locked the truck. They walked into the diner, which looked so standard Mark automatically made his way to the booths at the back, where he usually sat, while Domenico stopped at the counter, glancing at the pies on offer.

Mark was busier eying the clientele around. He'd usually look for a paying hookup in a place like this, and once he caught himself surveying the room, an overpowering feeling of shame settled in his chest when he realized that it was the first thing he looked around for. So instead, he glanced at the group of teenagers not far away. Old guys were easy to hook, but would a normal guy his age ever actually like him? A glass wall stood tall between him and the group of high school kids. He would never fit in with them. They seemed so normal drinking their floats and eating waffles. He on the other hand was with a guy who not long ago had made him suck a gun. Talk about different circumstances.

When Mark was walking past the group, a dot of bright blond sucked in all his attention. As if sensing something, the guy looked up, and his blue eyes briefly met Mark's before he got distracted by a friend.

Mark was sure the blond hair was dyed, but he didn't care either way. He liked the guy's piercings and his undercut. Not that it mattered. He sat down in the empty booth at the back and settled for ogling. At least he was wearing a cheap-but-new top instead of a Seth-sized T-shirt.

Domenico walked up to the booth and sat with his back to the window, taking the menu in hand. "Not hungry?" he asked, pushing one of the other menus at Mark, who got a bit distracted by the pretty blond biting on his lip piercing.

"Yeah, yeah, food." Mark looked into the menu. Now that the prospect of eating was so close, his stomach seemed to try to suck itself in out of hunger. "Would you teach me some special forces moves?"

"Sure. It was pretty pathetic that you couldn't fight off that biker. He was horny and distracted."

Mark frowned at him. "What? He was so much bigger than me. You're so unfair."

Domenico shrugged, going through the menu with ease despite still talking sense. "It's not about the size. Once you know the right spots to hit, as long as you're not blocked, the guy's going down, no matter how big he is."

Mark pondered that for a moment. He'd love to know those spots. "Maybe if I learned, I could become a bodyguard in the future or something."

Domenico chuckled. "You'd have to get bigger for that job. Size is good for intimidating people, and your face's just too nice," he said. Mark wanted to protest, but the tired waitress chose that moment to fill their presence with too much perfume and questions. She was very helpful and nice though, so they soon ordered a whole mountain of food.

"So, to sum it up, you think I'm pretty but stupid. I don't have an education, and I don't have skills. What do you suggest I do, Mr. Special Forces?" Mark slurped his shake as soon as the waitress brought it.

Domenico sighed and picked up his sparkling water. He also asked to get his pie as a starter, and in retrospect, Mark was sorry he hadn't done the same as he watched Domenico dig in.

"Some jobs are unglamourous, but they're honest, and if you work hard, you can climb up the ladder. That's what I did," said Dom.

Mark sighed, unhappy about the prospect. "What if you never climb up and you're just stuck at the bottom of the pile forever?"

Domenico sucked on the fork, looking at Mark across the table. "Look. I know I said you're stupid, but you're not. You're sixteen. You're trying to get by, but you chose the wrong way to go about it. You're damaging... your future. You have no idea how hard it could be to climb out of an arrangement with someone who holds power over you," said Domenico slowly as he ate the pie. "The world's not kind to young boys like you."

Mark held his milkshake closer. It felt strange to have Domenico talk to him so seriously. Like he really cared. He swallowed, all of a sudden overwhelmed by the need to voice his worries. "That's why I'm not sure about Fred. I mean, he seems really nice, but I can't help thinking that there could be something else for me out there."

Domenico's eyes narrowed. "Good. I think you're right to be worried. You're underage, and he's asking you to come over from across the country to meet him. It stinks."

"But he didn't say anything about sex or nothing like that. He said he'd help me find a job, and we'd see what happens. No pressure."

Domenico smirked. "But you don't believe him. He might be honest, or he might be one of those creeps who will start out giving you a back rub after a hard day. Trust me, there are shitloads of creeps out there."

Mark sighed and went quiet when the waitress brought their food. Dom was right. Mark wasn't sure about Fred, yet at the moment, the guy seemed his best bet. "I'm pretty sure he wants to fuck me. Most older guys do. I know how to navigate it. He seems like a really nice guy, so at least he's not scary. He sent me a photo from a barbecue last Sunday. Wanna see? He drank juice instead of beer."

Domenico smiled. "I think even if you want to meet him, maybe you should cleanse your palate with someone young and pretty? I think you have a fan at that table over there."

Mark looked over to where Dom indicated and instantly got that rush of excitement followed by heat all over his neck when he caught the blond's gaze for a split second. He squirmed in his seat so hard he curled his toes.

"No... I—um..."

Domenico laughed and ate his pie. "No? I bet you your ass he does. He would suck your cock so hard."

Mark bit his lip and kicked Dom's foot under the table. "Don't say that. I bet he's nothing like that."

"Come on, Mark, look at him. He's hooking you. You've had plenty of sex in your life already, so how can you not see that?"

Mark leaned closer and started munching on the fries. "But not with guys like *him*."

Dom ate some of his hot dog, licking mustard off his lips. "What do you mean?" he asked with his mouth full.

"Like... that young. And normal looking. He's probably gonna get grounded tomorrow for being out on a school night. Me? No one cares if I live or die."

Domenico's mouth stretched around an especially big piece of food, but his eyes remained on Mark, burning holes in his skin until he swallowed and could speak again. "Surely, you've had sex with other boys before..."

Suddenly, Mark felt like even more of a loser. "Yeah, yeah..." he muttered and looked away quickly to spare himself the judgment in Dom's eyes.

"No—" Domenico shook Mark's shoulder. Of course, a guy that used to be in special forces would spot a blatant lie like that. "Seriously? Never had sex with a guy your age?"

Mark ran his fingers through his hair. "That kind of guys aren't out to buy sex, they didn't hang out where I did, or didn't like *me*. I've got a bruise on my face. I look like I'd cause him trouble."

Domenico smiled and shook his head, patting Mark's back. "Oh, no. Listen. To him, you look like a bad

boy. You are exciting and different. You are cool. Not controlled by parents, hanging out with your older brother at the diner."

Mark straightened up slightly, encouraged by Dom's words. He always thought it would have been nice to have siblings. An older brother who would look out for him. Or even a younger one whom Mark would support and never let anyone touch. He gave the blond another glance, a longer one this time, and he caught the guy staring as well. This time he dared to smile at him, and the way the guy's pale face went red just before he quickly turned around had butterflies erupt in Mark's stomach.

Domenico smirked. "I think you should finish your food soon and make use of those condoms I bought you."

Mark got to his burger in a flash. He'd need the calories in case he did manage to score. "I think he's really hot," he whispered between one bite and another.

Domenico drank some water and smiled lazily. "Just remember to ask him if he wants it. You know, enthusiastic consent."

With the idea of fucking the blond firmly planted in Mark's head, he nodded at Dom. "He's gonna consent *so* hard."

Domenico discreetly looked at the table from behind his hair. "Yeah, I'm pretty sure he will," he said and reached into his pocket, pulling out a small packet. Lube. "Just in case."

Mark was getting horny just thinking about it, so he ate faster. "Can we do it in your pickup?"

Domenico laughed. "In front of the diner? Think."

Mark took his time chewing. He wouldn't risk actually fucking in the diner toilet. But maybe a blow job? Where could they possibly go though? "Maybe he has a car." His dick made a little twitch when the blond winked at him.

Domenico shrugged and pushed the car keys toward Mark. It was the sound of victory. "If you do use my car, go into the road leading to our shack. Police won't look there. And pick me up within one hour. I need to see Seth at the hospital."

Mark put the keys in his pocket. Fuck! He'd also get to pretend he had a car. This was his night. "Thank you *so* much," he said and licked his fingers before getting up. It was time to bring his flirting A-game.

Domenico nodded and leaned back like some kind of Godfather. "Make me proud."

There was nothing in the world Mark wanted more.

Chapter 13 - Domenico

Domenico sat down at the windowsill and looked out into the parking lot. They were in the biggest hospital in the area, so there was plenty of traffic outside. He was happy Seth would finally be going home with him and that the alligator bite hadn't left him with infection or worse. According to the doctors, Seth would limp for a bit, but everything should go back to normal with time. Domenico brought Seth some much-needed shaving supplies to celebrate his release. Now that they had settled the problem that was eating at their relationship for the last few months, Seth was happy with the idea of getting rid of the beard. Domenico doubted anyone in the rural areas of the South could ever recognize them anyway, and he was looking forward to seeing his man's face again.

Seth was already dressed when Domenico came to the private hospital room that ate their savings at an alarming speed. But even the scent of disinfectant wouldn't put Dom off Seth. Months of frustration were not settled with one fuck, yet the circumstances never seemed to be

right. He missed having personal space, a room, a bed, even a kitchen counter that was just theirs.

"Ready?" Domenico slowly opened the leather bag he kept his shaving supplies in. He pulled out the leather strop and his straight razor, smiling up at Seth, who looked much healthier than he did just a few days ago. Color was back in his cheeks, and his eyes shone as he approached Dom.

"Let's do this." Seth took a deep breath. "I'm just worried how the scar looks. Don't cut into it, because it seems to be this raised lump."

Domenico stretched the belt and slowly slid the steel razor back and forth. "Yeah? Does it hurt?" he asked slowly, putting aside the razor after a few strokes. He got up and reached for Seth's face. He was now beginning to think that Seth not wanting to give head because of the scar 'still healing' was yet more bullshit he'd been fed, even if he tried not to be angry about it.

"A bit... I guess it's slightly tender." Seth looked at his feet and hooked his thumbs in the back pockets of his jeans.

Domenico got up and walked up to him, quickly pushing Seth's face up by the furry chin. The brown, warm eyes pulled Domenico into their endless wells, and for a moment he was just staring, overcome by a shiver he couldn't control. "Look, I didn't tell you, but I did the test."

Seth blinked a few times, but then nervously found Dom's hand. "Oh. *Those* tests. And what do they say?"

Domenico chuckled and pushed his fingers into Seth's beard, then farther, to curl around his warm ear. "That you can safely use my razor."

Seth exhaled so hard his breath tickled Dom's wrist, and he pulled Dom into a hug so strong it could crack ribs. "You lucky fucker. I was so scared. Only you get to fuck half of Grindr and not catch an STD." He petted Dom's hair and kissed his ear, with his heart pounding against Dom's.

Domenico frowned. He had caught some STDs on the way. But he'd never gotten one that wasn't treatable. He supposed that did make him lucky. "What's Grindr?"

Seth stalled, but then snorted. "It's a hookup app. Something you will never need." The way Seth licked the side of Dom's ear sent shivers down Dom's body.

Domenico chuckled and pulled Seth closer, letting his eyes shut. "I suppose not. I'm more of a hands-on type of guy."

"As in, you see a guy you like, you put your hands on him?" Seth asked, and Domenico could hear the smile in his voice. As much as he'd avoided testing, it was a relief to know that he and Seth were clean.

Domenico grinned and grabbed all the shaving supplies, pulling Seth to the bathroom. "Pretty much. I grab them. They want me. And then I fuck them."

"And that's what you've been doing when I was stranded here the last few days?" Seth's hands kept roaming all over Dom's back as they entered the small bathroom.

Domenico smiled and made the lock sound especially loud as he turned the key. He pushed his nose into Seth's sweet-smelling beard and closed his eyes. "Securing the house. Did some repairs. Mark helped me a lot."

"*You* did repairs?" Seth snorted, but finally wasn't resisting when Dom gave him a kiss. Just as the doctor predicted, the limp wasn't very pronounced either, which Dom was relieved to see.

"Why, am I not manly enough?" asked Domenico, pushing Seth against the sink.

Seth laughed and put his arms around Dom's neck. "Nah, you were just never good at that DIY stuff. Unless we're talking about constructing a weapon out of a toothbrush and a CD."

Domenico laughed and pulled out the newest addition to his grooming kit—one he intended to dispose of in the nearest trash can. A beard trimmer. "Throw in a shoelace, and I'm good to go."

Seth eyed the trimmer like he wasn't yet sure if he wanted to take the plunge. "What can I help with? My hand gets better every day. I need to use it so it gets better. I could fix something on the roof, see if there's any electricity cables that got disconnected…"

"No." Domenico shook his head and put his hand on Seth's throat, focusing on the Adam's apple moving beneath the middle of his palm. He switched on the trimmer, and a buzzing sound filled the small room, echoed by blue tiles. "You're hurt, and you're not climbing anywhere."

Seth sighed but gave up and let the trimming commence. Dom enjoyed Seth's stubble, but the whole beard thing was getting out of hand. He'd bear with it if need be, but Seth didn't seem to have that much of an issue with letting it go. The facial hair was a disguise in Seth's mind, but Dom knew it wouldn't matter much. Just like wearing glasses wouldn't help much if they actually met Frederico or someone who knew them well.

"I just want to help…" Seth muttered.

Domenico leaned in and touched his nose to Seth's, drawing in his lover's delicious scent. "I know, but I'm not letting you botch your treatment now." He put the trimmer against the unruly black hair, and soon, subsequent layers of the beard were falling to their feet, uncovering more and more of the beloved skin, which now seemed paler than it used to be.

Seth closed his eyes and gently petted Dom's stomach with his knuckles, spurring lazy pleasure spreading all over the covered skin. Dom had never noticed just how thick Seth's eyelashes were, despite being short

and straight, and he was surprised to find out yet another new thing about the man he loved.

"Feels good? I bet you were melting in that thing with the heat outside," said Dom, noticing how his own voice dropped.

Seth looked back at him and chuckled. "A bit like wearing a sweater on the face."

"Your skin will be so soft once I get to it," said Dom, chopping off even more hair, which tumbled down Seth's chest and to the floor.

"Why do you even use the old blades anyway? Wouldn't it be faster with the regular ones?" Seth ran his thumb along the ridges of Dom's muscle.

Domenico closed his eyes as the slightly coarse skin rubbed him in such a sensitive place. He switched off the trimmer and put it in the sink. Memories flooded his mind like a tidal wave and spilled into every nook and cranny of his brain. "Tassa taught me. He thought men shouldn't take the easy route. For a straight razor, you need a steady hand. He was the one to give me my very first shave."

He'd never shared this with anyone, and the way Seth's eyes filled with understanding had Dom's heart skip a beat. It didn't matter that there were still things they didn't know about each other. No one could ever be to him what Seth was. They could banter for hours, and yet later share the most intense silence.

"No one's hands are as steady as yours," Seth whispered and pulled Dom's palm up for a kiss. "He did a good job."

Domenico curled his fingers around Seth's and held them, savoring the warmth streaming between their bodies. He exhaled as the pressure in his chest rose to a level that he couldn't bear anymore, and he looked up. "And then I busted his skull."

Seth swallowed, but didn't even blink. "If you knew what you know now, would you have acted differently?"

Domenico squeezed Seth's hand tighter. If he hadn't done what he did, he wouldn't be holding Seth now. He'd be alone and grieving. "I'd try to reason with him earlier. But if that couldn't change things, I'd still do the same."

"And who taught you that? He did. You can't blame yourself for what happened." Seth leaned closer, for a kiss that left a few tiny hairs on Dom's lips. "He made you into a man who doesn't stop, who goes for what he wants at any cost. It was his choice to stand in your way."

Domenico smiled, but there was a bitterness rising in his throat, and he slipped his arms around Seth, pulling him close. "I just wish he'd died proud of me."

Seth hugged him back and kissed the side of his head. "I know. If it helps, I don't think my father was ever proud of me. I actually think that electing me to follow in his footsteps was some cruel joke to spite me."

Domenico snorted, immediately remembering the moment he had been shot for the first time, by the hand of someone he had thought was his father. "He was a fucking maniac."

Seth ran his fingers through Dom's hair. "What do you think would have made your father proud?"

Domenico sighed and backed away slightly, not wanting his emotions to get the best of him. He brushed stray hair off Seth's face and slid his fingers over the scar that was now visible. It was still pink, still raised, but it did seem to have healed well. "If I were the don," he whispered, looking up into Seth's eyes. "He wanted me to take over."

Seth frowned. "But if I died, Vincente would have taken over. He killed our father for that."

Domenico smirked. "Vincente would have been easy to get rid of. I would have done it."

Seth backed away, but he didn't get far, bumping into the sink. "Oh. Is that what you would have wanted?" he whispered.

Domenico kept his gaze, unsure what was happening now, and he wasn't entirely sure how to respond either. "I wanted to stop being a pushover."

Seth put his hand on Dom's hip. "You? You were never a pushover. You were father's best man."

"He still could've killed me for the slightest error. He never included me in the game of inheritance, even though he thought I *was* his. I could've gotten my accounts straight with Frederico."

Seth looked at their feet, but kept his hand on Dom. "Don't you ever think there could have been another man for you? You could have had Tassa on your side, your revenge on Frederico… I can't help thinking I'm a burden. I keep fucking up your life. You warned me about the alligator, I still set up the bait, and then you had to pick up the pieces. You always sort out my mess."

Domenico smiled and rubbed his face with his free hand. "You always do something to keep me entertained. There's no way to get bored with you around." He leaned in and pressed his mouth to Seth's, relaxing into the embrace. "There could never be anyone else for me. There's no one else as sweet as you."

Seth chuckled but hugged Dom. "So you're saying I should keep causing mayhem, to keep you on your toes?"

Domenico grabbed the shaving brush, and nuzzled Seth's nose as he started working the dollop of shaving cream in a plastic bowl. "That's exactly what I'm saying."

Seth smiled wildly and pulled away to let Dom work. "Okay, I can do that."

Domenico chuckled and petted his neck before starting to work the cream all over Seth's face. The foamy lather had never failed to make the young Domenico feel like a grownup, and his liking for the traditional wet shave had never faded. He'd never let anyone else near his neck with a naked blade after Tassa. The blade had been a present from Domenico's real father and was one of

Domenico's most important keepsakes. It was an expensive item, with a tortoiseshell handle and an elegant engraving of the words *Life or Death. Now in Your Hands.* on the blade that Tassa had purchased for him in a specialty store in Palermo shortly after Domenico got made. "You're gonna like this."

"Just watch out over the scar." Seth took a deep breath and straightened up.

"I'm not gonna hurt you," promised Domenico, finally cleaning the brush with water. The bright white lamp above made the setting a bit too clinical for his liking, but it would have to do. He opened the razor and smiled as the blade reflected light into his face.

Seth watched it, and though Dom noticed Seth's Adam's apple bob a bit faster, he stayed still. When Dom put the blade against Seth's skin, he imagined what it would be like to shave the hairs all over his body, but as exciting as the process could have been, Dom wouldn't have liked the effects. He loved Seth's body hair. Perhaps even a bit too much sometimes.

The first strokes underneath Seth's nose made him freeze, but Domenico shushed him with a few calming words and slid the thin blade in short downward strokes, gradually removing all the excess hair. The cheeks were fairly easy to do, even with the scar, and Domenico couldn't help but smile when Seth's lovely tan skin emerged in its full glory.

The neck and throat were last, and Domenico pushed Seth's chin up to give himself better access. Even with no intention of hurting Seth, the sense of power that came with holding a blade against a man's neck gave Dom an adrenaline rush of the best kind. It made him think that he'd need to find *something* to do once they left the United States. He wasn't a man who could sit idle all day, even if he'd have the money to do so once he gained access to his Colombian account.

Domenico pushed his hand into the hair on Seth's nape and moved the razor over the arch of his Adam's apple. "How does that feel?" he whispered.

Seth exhaled deeply and spread his lips into a smile. "Like you could push the blade in, but you won't."

Domenico's stomach melted with heat, but he held his hand steady, slightly shifting the blade in a way that would make cutting Seth's throat all too easy. "I won't. I'd never do that."

"I love the steady way you hold me," Seth whispered. "Like you'd catch me whichever way I fall."

Domenico exhaled as he made the last stroke. When he put the razor on the side of the sink, it clattered slightly, and he held onto Seth's arm. "I would," he agreed, mindlessly grabbing the towel with his free hand.

"I want you to feel something..." Seth purred and leveled his gaze with Dom's. His shaved face made Dom's heart skip a beat.

Air left Domenico's lungs, and he smiled, petting Seth's pec through the shirt. "What?"

Seth grabbed Dom's clean hand and led it to his mouth. He parted his lips and invited two of Dom's fingers to touch the scar inside his cheek. He never even blinked as his dark eyes glazed over, and he petted Dom's fingers with his tongue.

It was like lightning shooting straight from the digits, all the way down Dom's spine. His breath caught in his throat, but he slowly thrust the fingers back and forth over Seth's silky tongue, and then very gently brushed them over the scar. The flesh was tougher there, and he could sense where the cheek had been pierced.

Seth gave Dom a moment before forcing his fingers to back out. "It's all healed, Dom. Doesn't hurt anymore."

Domenico glanced at him, suddenly flustered even with the wetness cooling on his fingers. His cock stiffened in response to that veiled invitation, and he wasn't even

sure where to begin with this, but then his mouth opened on its own. "Why don't you kneel then?"

Seth watched him and his nostrils flared as he slowly went down to his knees. Seth made the prettiest picture down there, all cleaned up and ready to take a cock, with streaks of the shaving cream still visible on his face. And it wasn't just *a* cock he was waiting for. It was all about *Dom's* cock. Seth raised his eyebrows and leaned forward to give the front of Dom's pants a kiss.

Domenico gasped and put both his hands on top of Seth's head, gently thrusting forward and brushing the bulge at the front of his jeans against Seth's mouth and nose. "Look at me."

Seth's trusting brown eyes were up in an instant. He slid his hands up Dom's legs, all the way to the front of his thighs.

Domenico smirked and massaged the top of Seth's head as he gently humped his face, arousal bubbling up at a rapid pace. "Do you still remember how to do this?"

Seth sucked his lips in, and only now Dom realized how he missed seeing Seth's face redden in full glory. "You will have to show me," he whispered and put his lips over Dom's erection through the denim.

Raw lust exploded in Domenico's brain, and for a few seconds, he wasn't even sure where to start, but the blatant invitation was enough to pull his cock to complete hardness. He didn't care about the smudges of cream Seth was leaving on Dom's clothes at all. "Take it out," he rasped, squeezing his fingers on Seth's hair, which was longer than usual, and easy to grip.

Seth unzipped his jeans slowly, as if to tease him and force Dom into action. "Like this?" He pulled Dom's jeans down along with his briefs, just enough for his cock to be released. Seth took a deep breath and licked the slit on the tip as his hands traveled to Dom's angular hips.

Domenico groaned and reached down, grabbing his cock and jerking it a few times, less than an inch away from Seth's face. He couldn't help but moan at the sight of that handsome face so close to his cock. "Touch my balls."

But instead of his fingers, Seth used his lips to dive to Dom's balls, teasing the sac, sucking the balls into the heat of his mouth, making them so wet they cooled in the brisk air.

Domenico curled his toes in his shoes when Seth lavished him with so much attention. His hand kept working his cock at a languid pace, but it was only preparation for the main act. Seth had never been an enthusiast of cocksucking, but it seemed that even he was missing the hot meat of Dom's prick on his tongue. "You've dreamed of this, haven't you? Now I'm sorry I haven't come all over that beard before I shaved it off you."

Seth groaned and nuzzled the underside of Dom's cock. "You're so fucking perfect every time you do those hundreds of push-ups." The adoration in his eyes when he looked up was what Dom lived for. The essence of his existence. "I watch you and I imagine you pumping your cock into me. Every day." Seth's voice went quiet as if he was afraid to say that out loud, but he finished off the sentence with a wet kiss to Dom's balls.

Domenico's mouth stretched into a smile as his body tingled with the pleasure of such praise. He did know his worth, but at the same time, hearing it from the man he loved never failed to get to him in the best possible way. "You want to serve me, don't you?"

Seth nodded as his breath grew shallower. "I remember that one time when you fucked my mouth so hard I couldn't breathe. I almost came from just that." The way his nostrils kept flaring told Dom just how hard Seth was. He didn't even need to look at the front of his pants.

It was almost as if a thousand hands caressed Dom's cock for him. He'd long suspected that Seth liked

force when they had oral sex, but for him to admit it...
Domenico would have never counted on that. "Is that what
you need? For me to take what I want, come in your mouth,
and make you swallow it all?"

If the redness of Seth's face was anything to go by,
it was exactly what Seth wanted. "I like when you're in
charge," he confessed and opened those plump lips, making
Dom's heart beat faster. No one else but Seth would ever
do.

Domenico exhaled, and it felt as if there was lava
gathered in his chest. He jerked Seth's head back by the
hair and pressed his uncovered cockhead against Seth's
lips. "Kiss it like you'd want to kiss my lips."

Seth's hot breath tickled Domenico, but that
sensation was soon replaced by the wetness of Seth's
mouth around his cockhead. He closed his eyes and
murmured as he sucked on the tip of Dom's dick. His hands
went all the way up to Dom's stomach, followed by a groan
of pleasure that crawled up Domenico's chest and tugged
on his nipples. Dom was ready to make sure he had
pronounced abs even if just to hear that moan again.

"You like that?" he whispered, slowly moving his
hips back and forth. He put his hand on top of Seth's and
guided it all over his skin, enjoying the warm touch. Seth's
hands were so huge, bigger than his own, with hair at the
back and on the forearms. Domenico would love to
worship them all night.

Seth looked up with his eyes glazed over and let out
a nasal whimper as he took more of Dom's cock into his
mouth. His breath tickled the base of Dom's dick, and Dom
was ready to test Seth's limits, see how far he could push.
Dom had missed the eager touch over the muscles on his
stomach so badly, but he hadn't even realized that until he
felt it. He'd been so fixated on not getting to come in Seth's
hot tight body he forgot how much he'd missed Seth's lust
in itself.

"You won't be pushing me away again, understood?" rasped Domenico, pulling Seth closer by the hair. He loved the way Seth's tongue massaged his cock, teased the corona, the slight suckling around it. It was so perfect it hurt.

Seth exhaled deeply and nodded with his mouth full of cock. Domenico needed to make up for the weeks of missed opportunities. Of lazy days spent reading books or training Dana when he could have been fucking Seth's brains out. Now that he was finally cracking Seth's shell again, he couldn't care less about all the bickering and fights they'd had.

Domenico grinned and pushed in deeper, making sure to pull Seth closer with every thrust. "Now suck it. Show me how much you love my cock," he demanded, leaning over Seth with pure pleasure streaming through his veins.

He caught the sight of his own face in the mirror and couldn't help a smirk. Young, handsome despite the scar, with the man of his life sucking his cock with the eagerness of a teenager. No wonder Seth fell in love. Domenico was a stud in the prime of his life and wouldn't be denied what he deserved. He tore his eyes away, all too aware of his own vanity, and looked down at Seth, who was swallowing more of his cock and sucking around it, with loud moans filling the bathroom. The way Dom's cock dove into his cheek was perfect, pushing out the scar, only to retreat and rush straight into Seth's throat.

This time, Domenico grabbed Seth harder, remembering what Seth had told him that he loved about the oral sex. He held him in place and pushed, watching the brown, loving eyes glaze over.

"Take it. You know you can."

Seth whined, gagged, but didn't even try to back away, watching Domenico with a whole new intensity. His hands slid to Dom's back and then to his ass, squeezing the

cheeks as Dom forced his cock into Seth's throat. Seth had never mastered deepthroating. He kept gagging, and a few tears slid down his temples from the exertion, but he stayed put where Dom held him, even as his freshly shaved chin dribbled with spit.

Domenico could hardly breathe as the fervor of fucking took over his mind and body. He held Seth in place and slammed his hips against his mouth, repeatedly. He couldn't help noticing that the more ruthless he was, the more Seth shuddered and shifted around, and so he moved his cock out, smiling when Seth followed it with his open mouth, still connected by a thread of saliva. "Will you be coming?" uttered Dom.

Seth panted with his lips widely parted and watched Dom as if he were God himself come to Earth to answer his prayers. "Y-yes," he uttered and unzipped his pants in a frenzy, pushing them down to reveal his engorged dick. It had Seth's briefs sticky with pre-cum.

Domenico smirked and gently nudged it with the top of his shoe. "I want you to come when I fuck you, and I want to feel it," he muttered, gently swirling his thumb over the head of his cock. Now that he was so far gone, each touch felt like stepping onto a minefield.

Seth quickly nodded and covered his own cock with his hand, squeezing it slightly. Domenico loved seeing him so obedient. It wouldn't have been the same if there were no contrast to how Seth was in everyday life. If he always followed orders, it wouldn't be so special to have him so agreeable now. Knowing it was Dom's touch and actions that got Seth this way was a big part of Dom's pleasure.

"There, open up," whispered Dom and grabbed Seth by the hair without waiting for an answer. His cock was back in that welcoming throat right away, pushing farther into the pulsing, twitching hole. The power of it gave Domenico a rush, as he slammed in so deep that his balls met Seth's chin with ease. He was slowly becoming

mindless, focused on the sound of Seth jerking off as he worshipped Domenico's dick.

Seth made groans, which Dom knew by heart, and he came when Dom held his head still by the hair. His mouth didn't exactly tighten the way his anus did when Seth came, but Dom could feel Seth's body spasming around him during the orgasm. Seth dug his fingers into Dom's hip, and Dom wasn't sure if Seth could breathe in more than shallow, stolen gasps through his nose. No professional deepthroating slut had ever felt better than the sloppy head Seth gave.

Domenico bit back a moan and cradled him even closer as his vision suddenly became brighter and more colorful. He came deep in Seth's throat, and with the orgasm so powerful, he had to lean against the wall for support. His temples were pulsing like crazy, and only after a few seconds, he slowly pulled Seth back, remembering that his lover needed to breathe.

Seth gasped for air, panting and bright red. He curled his arms around Dom's midsection and put his smooth face against Dom's stomach. His shoulders rose and fell with the deep breaths he was taking, and moments later, he gave Dom's hairy skin a kiss.

Very slowly, Domenico sank to his knees and pulled Seth in for a deep, wet kiss. His mind was racing as he sensed the familiar salty aftertaste, and it only made him hold his lover with more force as their blood cooled.

"Was that good?" he asked in the end, pushing two of his fingers into Seth's mouth.

Seth sucked on them and nodded, gazing into Dom's eyes shamelessly, soon smiling around the digits as Domenico nuzzled his face.

"Come, I'll finish with that shave, and we can go home. You'll love what I did there."

Chapter 14 - Seth

Seth smiled at the road, even though it was getting dark fast and alligators could be lurking in any shadow. At least he was out of the hospital. On the other hand, he didn't know what to make of Dom talking so much about Mark, the brat he hadn't even wanted to take in the first place. The brat who stole their getaway car. The brat who, in Dom's words, got Seth bitten. Seth needed to keep a close eye on the boy. Not that he was afraid Dom would stray, but it was better to be safe than sorry.

"He's really dedicated. I was impressed that he actually tried to keep up with me and Dana. This kind of determination can help him get far," said Domenico with enthusiasm, slurping a shake they bought on the way home.

Seth raised his eyebrows. "In the whoring business?" He wasn't happy to hear that even a sixteen-year-old kid trained with Dom and Dana, when he was walking with a limp.

Domenico stretched in the seat and dumped the empty cardboard box next to the shotgun. "This kid is

seriously messed up. He's only fucked a guy his age three days ago for the first time. Can you imagine? This is insane."

Seth took a second glance at Dom. "What? That makes no sense. I bet he's lying. He's not bad looking. Why would he not?"

Domenico shrugged. "He's not lying about this. There was this kid at the diner. Blond, with rings in his face and those denim leggings," he said with a scowl that reminded Seth what Domenico thought of the fashion choices of today's youth. "The kid was kinda pretty for what he was, he was into Mark, but Mark got all shy all of a sudden, so I intervened." Domenico's face stretched into a smile so smug it could have been sported by someone who just found the cure for cancer. "I got him laid."

Seth shook his head. Good, so at least the kid wouldn't be too horny around Dom. "Mark got shy? That boy's got a mouth on him the size of a block of *Parmigiano-Reggiano*. And there's been no money involved, nothing? Did they date or go at it like rabbits?"

Domenico leaned forward and finally switched on the high beams when it became too dark even for him. "He fucked him in the car. And they met up twice since then. One of those times they had shakes, or something, so I'd count that as a date."

Seth nodded. That also meant Mark wasn't spending *all* his time with Dom. "That's kinda cute, actually. I'm guessing you gave him money for those shakes?"

Domenico pursed his lips and nodded. "Kid needs some pocket money. You know, since you decided to *take him in*."

Seth snorted. "Our responsibility, right? Let's hope this week or two gives him the kick in the ass he needs for a better start."

"Yeah. He needs that," Dom said, somewhat flatly.

"And how's Dana?"

"She's as boring as usual. I swear that woman has only one focus. To be better at my job than me."

"At least she seems loyal. And doesn't try to kill me, so there's that." Seth frowned at the rearview mirror when he spotted a light. "What are all of you eating?"

Domenico laughed. "Mark's bringing us takeout food when he comes back from his sex dates, and Dana's mostly having rabbit food." He stopped talking for a second. "Did you see that movement behind us?"

"It's not like we'd have the postman visit the swamp at this time. Maybe it's a fisherman?"

Domenico snorted, but his voice dropped, and it gave Seth goose bumps. "At night? No, this is something else. Pick up the shotgun."

Seth sighed but reached back. "Do we have to do this?" Scaring the life out of some lost guy was the last thing he needed tonight.

"Just hold it," said Dom, and stepped on the gas, suddenly going much faster on the quiet, narrow road through a gully surrounded by woods.

Seth buckled up his seat belt and gripped the gun. The adrenaline suddenly spreading in his body went all the way to the stitches in his leg and made the wounds throb. "Did Mark have his dates out of town?"

"Yeah, I told him to, and he didn't want to meet this Jed guy either." A curse ended the sentence as a shadow moved behind them on the road. Now even Seth couldn't deny that the person behind them accelerated to match their speed.

Seth was about to go on a rant about the town being small, about everyone knowing everyone around here, but gunshots killed those thoughts in an instant. A bullet tore through the back window of the cab, and Seth screamed out reflexively. Another shot must have hit a tire in the back because part of the truck sank down, and before

Seth knew what happened, Domenico stopped the car so rapidly he was grateful for the safety belt. The lights died.

"Stay low," hissed Domenico as he yanked the shotgun out of Seth's hands. They were at a spot where the road changed direction, and the bright light behind them only came to full view in the rear window after Domenico fled the cab without another word. Seth heard every detail of his own rapid breathing as he realized just how alone he was in the quiet cab, with the mascot from the milkshake carton laughing at him from the floor. His skin tingled as blood fled to his legs, making them throb painfully.

He unbuckled the seat belt and watched the single headlight approach the pickup, too shocked to think of anything on his own. His eyes lingered on the hole in the windshield as his heart sped up, galloping in fear as the single headlight approached behind the rear window. Seth gasped, suddenly fumbling with the glove compartment. He brushed over a map, two packs of cookies, and some used wrappers, but when it gripped cold steel, a little confidence streamed back into his veins.

God knew how many bullets this guy had on him, and how good he was. Was he even alone? A motorcycle could easily take two men when needed. What if one of them surprised Domenico? After all, it was their turf. Seth took a deep breath that didn't help the pounding in his chest and slid to Dom's seat, which was turned away from the road and shouldn't be visible from the back. He slowly opened the door, making use of the fact that the motorcycle engine was still running and swiftly jumped off, curling into a ball behind the tire. It took him a while to be able to breathe again, but he made sure the beam of light coming from behind the truck didn't touch his body.

Blood was rapidly pulsing in Seth's temples, and even as he forced his shallow breaths to be as slow and quiet as possible, his hands shook when he pulled off the safety, staring toward the shack that at this point should be

at walking distance. The dirt road was disappearing in the darkness ahead, but the light coming from around and under the vehicle caught small plants growing on the steep, muddy walls of the gully, creating an eerie picture. Seth touched the steel to his hot forehead, trying to think and listen as the engine suddenly died. Shouldn't Dom have attacked by now? Seth could barely inhale any air when he realized the shotgun could have been empty. What if Domenico had no bullets out there?

Seth flinched, squeezing his hand even harder on the grip when someone shouted with a very pronounced local accent. "Get the fuck out of the car. No tricks! I wanna see your hands!"

Fucker didn't know they weren't even in the car anymore. Did he seriously think they'd just wait for him, like two pigs at the slaughterhouse? The guy didn't seem to be in a hurry either. Seth rolled into the dirt and crawled under the pickup, breathing in the faint scent of dead leaves. He moved slowly, making sure he was silent, but even though he had to look silly moving forward like an ancient tortoise, at least the car provided some shelter as long as he stayed in the shadow. His throat was aching with worry, as he held on to the gun, ready to help Domenico in any way he could. Big leather boots thudded as the unknown man dismounted the bike and came closer. Close enough for Seth to touch if he wanted to reach out.

Seth's heart worked at twice its normal speed, and at this moment, he wasn't sure whether he wanted Domenico to appear and risk his life or stay in the shadows. The boot nearest to Seth worked itself deeper into the muddy ground.

"Get the fuck out of the car, and I'm not gonna kill you!" yelled the guy, clearly unwilling to get close enough to see there was no one hiding in the cab anymore.

Seth held his breath, set on making no noise, but then, in the silence of the swamp, Dom's phone rang, far off

to the right, on the edge of the slope. Seth now regretted setting it to Avicii's *Addicted to You* despite Dom's protests. The sound traveled, as Domenico threw the phone to the other side of the gully, but it was too late, and the biker fired that way. The gunshot was followed by a loud splash that told Seth the cell was lost.

"Told you to stay in the car, motherfucker!"

Seth's mind went into panic overload when he thought Dom could actually be in danger, and he reached forward, shooting the biker right in the foot.

A roar of pure panic filled the walls of the gully as the man fell over, shooting two more times during his tumble into the mud and swinging his injured leg in the air. "Fuck! Don't shoot! This can still end well for you!"

Seth rolled out from under the pickup scared of what he'd just done, yet set on protecting Dom at any cost. He crouched behind the back wheel, praying to God for the man not to shoot his way.

"Fucking fuck," mumbled the biker, and Seth could clearly hear him scrambling to his feet. "I'm goin', all right? You must be the wrong people."

Seth tried to swallow, but his throat was too tight for that. Their hideout was screwed the moment this fucker left. Where was Domenico? Cold sweat covered Seth's back. What if Dom was down, grazed, or shot but keeping quiet? It was just Seth now having to make sure they were safe. At least for long enough to get Dom to Dana or to a hospital, depending on the wound.

Once he managed to get a breath of damp air into his lungs, he got up and pointed the gun at the biker who was already approaching his bike. Their eyes met.

"You're not going anywhere," Seth hissed at him, spurred on by pure adrenaline.

The man's eyes widened, and he too pointed his gun at Seth, but with the way his eyes kept straying to the dark edges of the gully, it was clear his attention was

divided. He knew he was outnumbered, but there was nothing he could do to mend the situation now that he understood how out of his depth he was.

"Told you, I'm going. You're not the man I'm looking for," hissed the biker, his thick arms shaking. He was still very young, younger than Seth, with a second chin visible underneath the thin blond beard but a firm-looking body that still had some baby fat on it.

Seth took a step closer, trapped in a problem of his own making. He couldn't let the guy go, but he didn't have cuffs on him either. "Put down your gun and you can go." He could only hope he sounded confident enough to pull this off.

"Listen to him or I'm gonna take you down," came a hollow voice from above. Domenico. He was alive! Seth had no idea how Dom managed to sound like that, but it gave him the shivers.

The biker clenched his jaw so hard that the muscles of his cheeks twitched, but he slowly raised his hands and bent over at an agonizing pace, finally leaving the gun on the ground. But before Seth could breathe in peace again, the guy dashed for his bike in a viper-like move.

Seth darted toward him from the other side and crashed against the other man. The motorcycle tipped over, taking them both down to the ground with a screech of metal. A fist smashed into the side of Seth's head, and the biker scrambled to freedom, kicking and jerking out of Seth's hold. The light of the motorcycle was shaking as the two of them constantly pushed on the vehicle, struggling in the mud.

Seth used his sheer size to force the guy down and locked his elbow over the biker's neck like Dom had taught him, but the problem was, he didn't know where to go from there. "Stop. Fucking. Moving," he hissed.

A sudden thump close to his head had him scared shitless. A pair of legs passed in the light, and then

something large and dark fell straight on the biker's head. The body went limp in Seth's arms, leaving him with a weird sense of dissatisfaction. Like when Domenico had shot the damn piglet for him.

Dom grabbed Seth's arm and jerked him up to his knees. "What the fuck did I tell you? Did I tell you to leave the car?" hissed Domenico with a scowl so deep he looked wrinkled like an old man.

Seth panted, still in a state of shock. "I—you weren't making any movements. And he was shooting… I just thought—"

Domenico kicked the unmoving body at his feet with a growl. "I couldn't do anything because I could've accidentally shot you in the dark. What the fuck?! Can't you listen for once?"

Seth got up slowly, annoyed by the tremble in his knees. "Was I to just sit there like a target? He knew I was in the car!"

"If you'd stayed in the fucking car, I'd have gotten rid of him! It's the fucking rooster all over again!" hissed Domenico and pushed Seth back.

Seth spread his arms and only then realized he'd dropped his gun somewhere. But he was not about to tell Dom about it and make a fool out of himself. "It's nothing like the rooster! Maybe if you told me what the plan was, I could be in on it!" He looked around discreetly. "And if Lucrezia had survived, you'd have been fucking happy to eat her eggs every day!"

Domenico rolled his eyes. "Which one of us has actual combat experience? Well, it's not you. It's not like I had plenty of time to draw a fucking map so that you know the strategy!"

Seth groaned. "I didn't know you were my superior officer. Sorry, *sir*. But I had a good plan! I was under the pickup. He'd have never known. I shot him when your stupid phone rang, and he could have killed you!"

Domenico sneered at him and walked up to the pickup, collecting something from the back. "Really? It was you who could have ended up killed! What possessed you to think this was a good plan? I relied on you being in the fucking car, and then I was afraid to act, you moron!"

"I can't just always rely on you! I have to do my own thing." Seth made sure Dom faced away when he made a dash to pick up his gun from the mud.

"Oh, really?" snarled Dom, and the item he got from the pickup turned out to be heavy-duty duct tape, which he was now using to tie down the unconscious biker. "How about you take up crocheting, huh? You wouldn't get us killed that way."

Seth's nostrils flared, and he started cleaning the gun with his T-shirt. "So, I finally know what you think of me. That's what I'm good for? Making fucking doilies? Your bad, because I can't even do that."

"No, *your* specialty is catering," hissed Domenico, dragging the biker toward their car.

Seth made sure the safety was on the gun and held it in his hand out of a lack of better place for it. His pride was now much more badly injured than his calf. "Catering and giving head. Great talents." Dom really did think Seth was good for nothing but making pasta.

"And bringing me close to a fucking heart attack. Every week, you do something that puts your life at risk. What the fuck am I to do with you, huh?" asked Domenico, slowly taping the biker to the punctured tire. He shook his head and looked back at Seth in the bright light of the motorcycle. Too handsome for his own good. "Let me do my job."

"Do you want a blow job now? Or should I get you a cookie from the car?" Seth crossed his arms on his chest, heaving with the anger boiling up in him.

Domenico exhaled and slowly, very slowly got to his feet. He pushed back the hair that got into his face. "Stop fucking with me. This isn't funny."

"I clearly can't do anything else right!" Seth passed Dom to get his backpack from the car. In the background, he saw Domenico collecting the biker's fallen gun, but he followed Seth soon enough, his movements silent like a ghost's.

"You're not very good at keeping yourself safe. That's why you have me."

Yes, Dom was just as necessary in Seth's life as oxygen, but what could he offer in return? Anything he did backfired. "It looks like I'm not very good at anything," he grumbled, and was even angrier at the fact that he now waited for Dom to decide what they should do next.

Domenico stopped next to him and leaned against the car. He knocked on the closed window. "The thing's fucked," he said, not commenting on the source of Seth's anguish, which made sense. What was he to say? He was stuck with Seth for better or for worse. Five languages, excellent marksman, great in bed, well-traveled, and stuck with the most boring man on the planet, who made an average-to-good pizza and struggled with keeping himself alive. Oh, and Dom also excelled at fucking ballroom dancing, whereas Seth couldn't even properly deepthroat.

Seth groaned and kicked the tire. Something needed to change.

Domenico sighed and scratched his head. "Is *your* phone working at least?"

Seth patted his jeans. The phone was gone. He started searching in his bag, but he was pretty sure he'd had it in his jeans before, so it was a search for show. He was getting redder by the second.

Domenico groaned and bumped his forehead against the car. "For fuck's sake... what else? Will there be an earthquake with the epicenter at our shack?"

"I don't know. Let's just go. Do we take him, or what, *sir*?"

Domenico scowled. "Oh, fuck you. That's the last fucking thing I need right now. If I wanted a sex slave, I wouldn't go for a hothead like you."

Seth squinted at him. "Who'd you go for? A priest maybe? All nice and kind and obedient?"

Domenico grabbed Seth by the neck and pushed him against the car. He stepped so close that his warm breath tickled Seth's lips as if it were his tongue. "You're questioning my choices?"

Seth groaned but didn't fight the touch, as Dom wasn't choking him. "I'm saying I don't know how any of this will look like in two years. I don't know where I'll be tomorrow." He spread his arms despite Dom's grasp.

Domenico smirked and let him go, putting the shotgun over his shoulder. "You think I know any of that shit? I want to keep us alive. And have a good life, that's all I can ask for."

"You claim to always have a plan. And we don't even know when we're going to Mexico. We've been putting it off for weeks. You haven't even told me what town we're going to!"

Domenico shrugged. "I don't know either. We'll figure it out. Stop worrying." He leaned closer to Seth, and his warm hand cupped the side of Seth's face, running his fingers over the new smoothness of his skin. "If you can't find a purpose in life, just think about me like I think about you."

"How do you think about me?" Seth couldn't fight the warmth crawling into his chest at the touch.

Domenico shrugged in the darkness and pulled Seth down the road, toward their hut. Even without anything to light their way now, Seth felt confident Dom wouldn't let him fall and hurt his already injured leg further.

"I gave up on my plans to be with you. Whatever I do know, you are a vital part of those plans."

Seth swallowed and his hand found Dom's, cradling its warmth as anger evaporated. "What if I bore you, because I'm proficient at so little? I can't even go study anything right now..."

"You will never bore me. I told you already," said Dom, and his grip became stronger around Seth's arm when Seth's sore leg made him stumble a bit. "You are my purpose. Can't I be yours?"

Breath caught in Seth's throat at the thought. The concept was so simple yet slightly scary. It was something everyone always sneered at, defining yourself through a relationship, losing yourself in it. But with the life they led, wasn't Seth lost in it already? It wasn't as if he was about to do media studies, or start a food blog. Domenico was all he had, and it would have to do. Even thinking that had him embarrassed. It wouldn't *do*. It was everything and more. A core to his being. Wherever they would go, whatever they would lose on the way, they would be there for each other. One constant in a life that kept changing from hour to hour.

"Can being the best I can be for you be a purpose?" Seth whispered, embarrassed by how needy it sounded.

Domenico laughed and led Seth on, down the dark, dark road that smelled of wet leaves and dirt. "You are already the best for me, Seth."

"I'll try and be a better boyfriend." Seth sighed. "Listen to you and all that shit. I kinda see how it could have ended badly tonight."

Domenico rested his head on Seth's shoulder for a moment. "Well... there is always room for improvement, I suppose."

"I'll try. But it's hard to hold back when I'm thinking you could be somewhere out there, shot, or dead..." He squeezed Dom's hand harder.

Domenico snorted and squeezed Seth's hand as they walked in the darkness. With him, even the menacing shadows seemed like nothing. "Me? I'm Domenico Acerbi. I'm invincible."

Seth pushed his elbow into Dom's ribs. "You're so full of yourself." Truth was though, that Seth kind of wanted to think of Dom as indestructible and their relationship as one to last forever. He could be the one to fuel the fire to keep it going, but Dom would be the wall between them and the world.

They kissed, just before entering the clearing by the shack, to the background music of Mark and Dana bickering like a bunch of kids. With the moon high up in the sky, it was rather bright out here, and Dana spotted them immediately from the rocking chair on the porch.

She raised her hand in greeting and slowly moved through the now-clear patch of land, which during Seth's absence had been weeded.

A few oil lamps illuminated the house, one right next to Dana. Seth wasn't sure whether he should start explaining what had happened on the road, so he left that to Dom.

Dana's face was hidden in the shadow as she approached. "Did the car break down?" she asked, stopping with her hands on her hips.

Domenico exhaled and pulled Seth closer, playing with the hairs on Seth's arm. "We need to go. Again. They sent a fucking scout after us, and he busted the back tires. There's only one spare at the back."

Mark burst through the front door with his curly hair in an unruly nest. "Why didn't you tell me they're back?"

"Are we going back for the guy?" Seth asked.

Domenico sighed. "*He's* not going anywhere. I think we should gather all the important provisions and go tonight. We still have the bike and Dana's car."

Dana nodded, and Seth noticed her smirk when Mark spread his arms.

"What can I do?" Mark complained. "And move now? Seth hasn't even seen how I cleaned inside."

Seth snorted. "Dom made you clean?"

Mark crossed his arms across his chest. "I mean—I wanted to. You need a clean place if you're wounded."

Domenico laughed and led Seth to the shack. "Told you he has potential to become an actual human."

Seth smiled at the sight inside covered in warm, yellow light. The place was as spotless as a swamp shack could be, equipped with two new chairs and two futons on the floor. Seth looked out to the terrace over the water and raised his eyebrows at the construction made out of rope, water containers, and a watering can.

Mark followed him there, all bright-eyed. "It's a bit like a shower. I made it," he was quick to say, and explained how the thing worked. Now Seth was regretting not being able to stay here for even one night.

"Dom's been using it?"

Domenico laughed. "I have. It's pretty good, actually. He's one smart boy for someone who didn't even finish high school yet," he said and ruffled Mark's hair, as if the boy were a dog.

Dana leaned against the doorframe. "We should have at least two hours to spare. They will be waiting for the scout to return."

Domenico nodded. "Pack the most important things: weapons, some snacks, your documents..."

Dana went off, along with Dom, but when Seth wanted to follow, Mark grabbed his arm.

"Seth? Can you stay a moment?"

Seth stopped and had a better look at Mark. "Sure, what is it?"

The kid glanced back nervously, as if checking if no one was eavesdropping on them and looked up with his

huge, dark eyes. "I never got to thank you for saving me from the alligator. You could have died, but you came for me. Dom told us to get rid of the gator's body, but I saved this for you." The boy reached into his pocket and pulled something out. He was smiling, but it felt different from when they had met and he kept trying to flirt with Seth and Dom.

Mark presented Seth with a large alligator tooth fastened on a piece of leather string. "No one's ever risked themselves like that for me. Thank you."

Seth put on the pendant and leaned down to hug him with a wide smile. "You're welcome, Mark. Just never throw Cheetos at baby alligators again."

Domenico popped in his head. "Are you two done making out? There's work to do," he said calmly, and Seth was ashamed that he'd felt jealous of Mark earlier that night. Of course, Domenico wouldn't consider Mark a threat, especially with the number of times he called Mark out on being a stupid kid.

"Only take what you can carry," said Dom, but then his eyes lingered on Mark. "You're going too. If they find you here, it's gonna get ugly."

Mark's smile widened even more, as if this weren't a life or death situation, but his face fell the moment something that seemed like background buzz turned into a roar. They all froze in place, and even Domenico's face seemed to lose some color when it became clear what they heard was an ever-louder symphony of engines.

Seth looked over the railing and into the alligator-infested water. There was nowhere to run.

Chapter 15 - Domenico

Domenico's blood trembled to the tune of the engines, and he pushed Seth down, covering his head as he did so. There weren't many items that could provide them with protection, so he knocked over the table, uncaring about the sound of breaking glass as he pushed Seth behind the makeshift barrier.

"Switch off the lights!" he yelled, pulling the safety off his Beretta. Just the weight of it in his hand made him feel much more confident. Why were the bikers here already? Did the scout inform them exactly which way he was going before the showdown in the gully? His and Seth's walk couldn't have taken more than twenty minutes, so the bikers must have been on the way here already, without waiting for intel. Clearly, the fuckers didn't work with as much caution as the organizations Dom was used to, and while he considered that crazy, surprising the enemy had its merits.

He squeezed Seth's shoulder and pushed their foreheads together, breathing in Seth's panting. "Promise me to listen this time," he uttered, staring into his lover's

wide, dark eyes as the revving engines became much louder. The bikers were almost here, but Domenico wouldn't run.

"Only if you don't get yourself killed," Seth whispered and stole a kiss. "You better sort this shit out. If you die, I *will* go and get myself killed."

Domenico blinked and wanted to protest, but it hit him that he wouldn't act any differently, and it warmed his heart to see just how much he and Seth were on the same page sometimes.

He pressed a quick kiss to Seth's mouth and started crawling along the wall, wary of getting a splinter in his hand from the raw wooden planks. The gas lamps inside the house were off, but he cursed, noticing a bright glow on the porch. All of a sudden, the shadows moved as bright white light slipped into the room, making all cracks in the wood painfully obvious.

The sound of engines was now at its peak, and it wasn't moving anymore. It was a choir of revving, meaty and low enough to give him a visceral shiver. He knew the science behind using sound to intimidate your enemy, and he hated that it still made his body react with disproportional agitation. No wonder those people used it to their advantage. Dana was ahead of him, by the window close to the exit, and Domenico sought out Mark, just to make sure the boy wouldn't do anything stupid.

"Do you need backup? What can I do?" Dana whispered, with her gun in hand. "I can stay here. Whistle if you need me."

Domenico exhaled, and his breath burned when the roars came to a halt, leaving only a silence that clawed into his heart. Would they try to break in through the back? "Keep the remote control ready to use," was all he said before a loud, tubal voice broke through their whispering.

"We've got you surrounded, and you're outnumbered. Come out *now*, and keep your hands where we can see them!"

A warning shot broke something on the porch, and the heat in the shack was becoming too much to bear. Dom took one more glance at Seth, to make sure he was where he was told to stay, and got up, leaving his Beretta next to Dana's feet.

"I'm coming out unarmed. Don't shoot!" he yelled and crawled to the door. Very slowly, he pulled himself up and pressed on the handle while standing against the wall, just in case. As much experience as he had, most of his missions involved stealth and combat in close quarters. Little as the bikers had to gain from just shooting him on sight, they were still a group of dumb fucks who came here like a horde of mules ready to trample whatever they encountered, without a proper plan. Could he trust them not to do anything stupid? No.

But they didn't shoot at the door, and so he pushed it open and slid outside, making sure it shut behind him. The bright headlights blinded him so badly that it was impossible to tell how many men were there. He raised his hands and stepped forward, squinting to get at least some visual cues.

"Where's the rest of you fuckers?" yelled the same thick voice as before, not Ryder's or Jed's. The man got off the bike and into a puddle that splashed around his boots. He was big and quite overweight for someone who apparently led a party of fighting men. Silver-haired under an eggshell-shaped helmet, the man sported a thick horseshoe moustache worthy of an eighties porn star.

Domenico narrowed his eyes farther, quickly counting human-shaped shadows around. There were ten of them. Ten men against four, only half of whom were proficient at fighting. It did not look good at first glance. "They're civilians. It's me who you have a grudge against."

The biker took a few steps closer and pulled out his gun. "You don't disrespect the Coffin Nails in their town and get to leave with a slap to the wrist, you dumb fuck!"

Domenico took a deep breath but made sure for it to be drawn out, so that none of the men knew that having a huge chunk of steel and gunpowder pointed at his forehead did in fact affect him.

"I meant no disrespect," he said calmly, looking into the man's pale eyes, hidden behind a pair of simple glasses. "As you can hear, I'm not from here." He was assessing the situation as well as he could. Rarely had he been forced to play a submissive role in a confrontation, but he was unarmed, and he didn't want to end up having his teeth knocked out with a gun. Or shot. His sense of decorum demanded a cleaner end to this confrontation, and from what he knew of biker gangs, they could be negotiated with, provided one had the right arguments.

"Are you fucked in the head? Who are you to be taking down two of my men? Not to mention you knocked out my Prospect. Ryder, come over."

Domenico watched Ryder dismount his bike and appear from the shadows behind the lights of the motorcycles. He pulled out a gun as well and walked up to Domenico with a grim expression. "You think you can pull out a gun on my brother? Accuse me of fucking your fag boyfriend?" Ryder hissed, and his words were followed by a few laughs.

Domenico looked at him, and this time he got slightly worried. For this guy, it was more personal. There was no room for negotiation. "I know this looks very bad for me, but I have been here for a long time, and I'm prepared for uninvited guests," he said, looking straight into the eyes of the leader.

The man with the 'President' patch on his leather vest laughed. "Is that so? You have snipers around? Somehow, I doubt that."

"Where's the kid?" grumbled a voice still behind the blinding lights. Jed.

Domenico was sweating like a pig in the heat that his body produced, but he kept as calm as possible. He thought about Seth, hidden behind a table that couldn't possibly withstand much enemy fire. "No snipers. Bombs."

The bikers started laughing.

"That's a good one. A nobody from nowhere has bombs?" the president asked with a smirk under the thick moustache.

"Any more bluffs?" Ryder took the safety off his gun.

Domenico straightened but stared at the president, just as seriously as before. He started counting. "Ten. Nine. Eight—" and he hoped that Dana would get the cue.

When the shack door slammed open, Dom's heart dropped, and he was sure he'd see Seth, but it was Mark who burst out like a little idiot.

"Jed? You better call off your fucking dogs!" he yelled, as if he were in a class C action movie, and approached them quickly. "Yeah, I stole your fucking phone! And I still have it! I will tell—"

Domenico spun around, hardly breathing when he noticed Jed raising his gun, eyes open like those of a deer in the headlights. He grabbed Mark's face and pulled him against his chest. "Shut the fuck up," he whispered, staring back at the bikers now that he knew both their lives hung by a thread. "Now!"

An explosion to their side ripped through the ground, covering them in a rain of mud as the earth shook beneath their feet. Chaos erupted in the group of bikers as they dropped to the ground for cover. The first explosive had been placed far away, as a show of Dom not bluffing. More were closer to the house. Once they were detonated, arms and legs would fly.

Mark whimpered and pushed into Dom's body, and Domenico held him, standing his ground even as he mentally examined his whole body. Did someone shoot after all? Sometimes, adrenaline would make it impossible to feel pain at first.

"I am not bluffing," he said as soon as he knew he could keep his voice completely steady, and this time, no one laughed. He hardly suppressed a snort of his own and pushed Mark away. "Go back to the house. It's just grownups talking."

The president got up from the ground, as well as Ryder, and Mark looked like he wanted to say something but shut his mouth and ran back to the shack.

The president looked into Dom's eyes, much more serious now. "I see your arguments. But all that went down can't stand with no retribution. You must see this."

Domenico stretched and made a small gesture toward Jed. "There were mistakes made on both sides. All I want is to take my family out of your hair."

Ryder stood between Dom and Jed like a muscle mountain. "What does that have to do with him?"

Domenico frowned. "I think he should be the one to come into my shack and talk on your behalf."

That caught the president's attention. "Why am I to trust you won't take him a hostage?"

"Jed's not going anywhere," Ryder hissed, but his brother passed him without looking into Dom's eyes.

"I'll go."

Domenico frowned. "You are all my hostages. You stand on unknown ground that is loaded with explosives that my associate can detonate at any moment. If you ask me, *Jed* here will be the safest one of you," he said, slowly relaxing now that he had assumed control. It was just like the good old days.

Ryder gritted his teeth but slowly put the safety back on and looked away.

Jed stepped forward with his handsome face twisted, as if he'd just bitten into a hundred lemons. "I'll be fine," he muttered to Ryder before following Domenico into the shack.

Domenico walked up the stairs with a pleasant burn in his stomach and made sure to be especially gallant when he opened the door for Jed. "It's not much, but it's home," he said with a wide smile.

Jed didn't return the courtesy as the door closed behind them. "You better come up with something good," he hissed at Dom. "The Prez doesn't take bullshit offers."

Domenico smirked and gave him a slap on the ass. "Maybe you should bend over for the boy you assaulted, as part of the agreement."

Jed flinched and went pale. Dom enjoyed imagining that the guy was a virgin. All cooped up in the closet and wriggling around in its confines. "I—It was..." All the attitude he'd been giving before vanished, and he looked a bit younger with vulnerability in his big blue eyes. He couldn't be older than Dom.

"I wouldn't fuck him now. He's an asshole," Mark hissed from a shadowy corner, as Seth crawled out from behind the table.

"Isn't a hole just a hole anyway?" asked Dana from her place by the window, where she sat with a small tablet they used to program the explosives. "You all like fucking so much that it shouldn't matter."

Domenico raised his brows at her, enjoying the sight of Jed's ego shrinking by the second. The guy was terrified, and for good reason: if they wanted to humiliate him for his sexuality, they could, and there would be no one to save him, as he would most certainly not look for help.

"Mark, look out the window, and watch if they're moving," said Dom, lighting the gas lamp.

Mark nodded and quickly moved to the window. With the face he was making, Dom could just see him imagining that he was James Bond.

"He told me he was eighteen," Jed hissed, now getting red in the face again.

Domenico rolled his eyes. "Oh, fuck you and that *eighteen year old* bullshit. A sixteen-year-old knows whether he wants to fuck or not. The problem is that he said *no*, you moron," hissed Domenico, pushing Jed hard at the wall. He reached into his pocket and pulled out the biker's phone.

Jed eyed it as if it were toxic and didn't push back, which for a hothead like him had to mean he was terrified. Dom had to admit to getting a slight buzz from it. "He's the one who offered. He walked up to me about it. I'd have never come up with this bullshit."

Domenico opened the dating app Jed used and looked at the first message in a row. "I wouldn't expect that after reading your conversations. You actually block people who send you dick pics," he said, as he read through pretty much everything on that phone that could come in handy. "But then when push comes to shove, you never actually meet any of these guys. Even Cory, who you've told you're 'the loneliest guy on the planet.'"

Jed's eyes went wide, and he rushed at Dom with quite the proficiency, but Domenico still managed to spin around and shove his elbow against Jed's spine. He pushed him at the table and pulled his arm back so hard the joints crackled.

"Stay," he said in a commanding voice and switched off the app, only to go find the piece of media that Jed was probably so worried about. The short clip Jed had recorded during the night they all met.

Dom put the phone in front of Jed's eyes, holding him down against the table, and the video showed a kneeling Mark and Jed's voice pushing him to do the blow

job on camera. When Jed dropped the phone, the camera kept rolling, actually catching his face on video as he pulled up his pants before the end of the clip.

Jed was heaving under Dom, as if he was about to have a heart attack.

Domenico sighed and put the cell back into his pocket, crooking his head at Jed. Just seeing him so worried, so afraid, made Domenico want to get a piece of Seth behind the curtain. "Blackmail isn't my favorite way to deal with things, but I won't shy away from it."

Jed slowly pulled up, massaging his thick, tattooed arm. "I just want this to go away," he whispered. "But the prez won't let it go. Ryder won't."

"Well, then it's in your interest to convince your friends to negotiate, because if they won't, I will kill them."

Jed nodded, his eyes becoming blank walls guarding the turmoil that was no doubt tumbling through his mind.

Domenico snapped his fingers to get Jed's attention. "Focus. This will be the agreement between us and you. Whatever we demand, you will support, or I will make sure this video will be very, very public, along with your full name."

"But we don't mean any harm," Seth butted in all of a sudden. "We also want to settle this as quietly as possible."

Domenico frowned at him. "Maybe offer him cocoa while you're at it?"

Jed licked his lips. "I'll do everything I can."

Domenico smiled. The Loneliest Man in the World wasn't lying, and so it was time to push. "And you will take the lovely Dana as a hostage."

Dana gasped. "You're fucking kidding me."

Domenico looked back at her and shrugged. "I'm sure Jed here will ensure your safety. And you will soon be back anyway."

Mark grinned and made a fist pump, but Dana hit the back of his head for it.

Jed gave her a surprised look but didn't comment. Dom was pretty sure Jed would eat a live eel if it would prevent anyone from ever finding out the truth about his sexuality. It was a loss for the world, really, with Jed's face so handsome. He could make some guy happy with those pretty lips.

"Can we agree on that?" asked Domenico, looking between Jed and Dana. She eventually gave a weak nod, pressing her lips together.

Domenico rolled his eyes. "Make sure no one tries to fuck her. She's not a fan of sex," he said to Jed.

"I could say I have a thing for her," Jed suggested with a weak laugh.

"Good. Do that," said Dom and crooked his head. "Who should we invite for more open negotiation? Who can you influence?"

"Ryder," Jed said with no hesitation, and then, "and the prez. The VP's my dad, so don't get him in on this, he's most pissed off."

Domenico smiled. "If I didn't know better, I'd think you and Ryder are fucking," he said and slowly walked up to the door. He switched on two more lamps and opened the door to look out.

"He's my brother, you shit," Jed hissed behind Dom's back, but Dom just waved his hand dismissively, glancing at Seth with a small smile.

The bikers immediately stood up straighter, but none made a move to raise any weapons. "I would like to talk to your president. I think both sides agree that there are a few things to discuss."

As expected, Ryder pushed forward. "I'm going too! This is some fucking bullshit!"

Domenico opened the door. "Good that you volunteered. I was about to ask you to come as well."

The president first carefully lowered his two guns to the ground and stood up, staring straight into Dom's eyes. He'd strangle Dom if he could, but at the moment, the situation was safe.

The man who had to be the VP spoke up from behind the lights. "You fuck with any of my sons, you faggot bastard, and I will make sure you all end up six feet under!"

Domenico sighed and made room for both men he had invited in. "I've got no interest in your sons. Their virtue is safe."

Seth snorted, and Dom was happy at least someone was getting amusement from this messy situation. There weren't many jokes to be made once Dom closed the door.

"Gentlemen, I hope you don't carry any weapons," said Domenico, gesturing toward the table.

Ryder scowled at him, and his eyes immediately went for Jed. They shared a nod, but it wasn't the time for brotherly love. Domenico cleared his throat. "Sit," he said, taking a seat at the top of the table.

They all sat down. Dom and the bikers. There weren't enough chairs for anyone else. He could only hope Seth wouldn't ask the men if they wanted tea. That wouldn't do great things to Domenico's image.

"There needs to be retribution and payment for the wreckage in the gym," the president said.

Domenico leaned back and looked at him, all business-like. "I have not introduced myself yet. Domenico Abate," he said and reached out his hand to him.

Prez eyed him, but did shake Dom's hand. "Ripper."

Domenico squeezed the thick fingers in greeting. "I've heard quite a bit about your club. The Sicilians are raving about it," he said, consciously trying to throw the man off guard for the second time in a row. Domenico wasn't very familiar with this, but the Villanis were supplying the Coffin Nails MC in the northeast, and he wondered how much he could win on this.

Ripper's eyes opened a bit wider. "What could you know about that?"

Dom didn't miss the way Ryder glanced at Seth, but he ignored it for the time being. "I am not just some tourist. I am willing to give you some kind of payback, but there is only so far that I will go with this." He let this settle in, and just before Ripper opened his mouth, utterly confused, Domenico continued. "I can tell you some interesting things about the people you do business with."

"That depends on how good the leverage would be..." Ripper said, stroking his moustache, but Dom could see the cogs were turning in the old head.

Domenico nodded, looking over at Seth, who sat down on the bed and watched them intently. "Absolutely. What do you want to know?" he asked, suddenly very happy with himself. If he hurt the business for the Villanis, that would not only make Frederico's life more difficult, but also divert their attention further away from Domenico and Seth. Domenico wouldn't mind if Frederico suffered a heart attack from overexerting himself.

"I want to know who Mr. Tropico is. He's the biggest drug provider from the south. We know he's connected to the Villanis, but we're not sure how," Ripper said slowly, weighing every word.

Ryder glared at Dom. "Don't give him intel, J. This snake is a nobody who knows nothing. I bet he heard the name 'Villani' while fucking some mafia pimp. Or was it Seth who fucked them?"

Jed shook his head but Dom was first to speak. "Shut your fucking mouth, breeder! Don't you *dare* talk shit about my fiancé!"

Seth got up from the bed with a scowl. "Really, Ryder? That's what you think now, 'cause you know I'm gay? We were friends!"

Ryder got up so fast Dom almost grabbed a gun, but fists didn't fly. "We were friends before your *fiancé* put a gun against my brother's head!"

Domenico narrowed his eyes at Jed, who got up as well and pulled on Ryder's arm. "Shit got a bit heated, give it a break. Can happen to anyone."

Even Ripper frowned at those words coming from Jed's mouth.

Ryder visibly tensed in Jed's grip. "You can't be serious. Those guys attacked us on our turf."

"I honestly didn't know who you were," said Domenico, trying to do some damage control. "If I did, I'd have never done what I did."

Ripper sneered, and Dom wondered if his lack of knowledge hadn't been considered an insult. "So you have insider knowledge about the Villanis, but you claim to be some jealous tourist? I don't buy it."

As Dom opened his mouth, Seth butted in and stepped up to the table. "*Tourist*? You have no idea who you're dealing with!" He pointed at Dom. "He doesn't even need the explosives to get rid of all of you if he wanted to. Fucking hell! I saw him kill five armed men with a cleaver, so just say what you fucking want as retribution, and let's get on with it!"

Dom's eyes met Mark's, which were wide as saucers, but he leaned back and looked up at Seth, hardly containing the anger rising beneath his skin. They really didn't need anything that blatant.

"That was supposed to be a secret, *darling*," said Dom somewhat coolly. "I'm retired."

Ryder gave a barking laugh. "Stop fucking around. You're a Villani goon at best."

Ripper didn't seem so sure though. "Boys, sit back down on your asses," he said and only continued when Jed and Ryder resumed their places at the table, throwing

stormy looks at each other. "Can you get me the details on Mr. Tropico?"

Domenico sighed and shook his head. For a very long time, he'd believed Vincente had been Mr. Tropico, but facts clearly indicated Dino Villani. It was he who had sent the Chinese after Seth, and it was he who had given Vincente the credit card with the fake name. The man was long gone.

"Dead," said Domenico.

Ripper frowned. "When?"

"Four months ago."

"He's been in contact with our brothers in Texas last month."

Domenico blinked, but his heart skipped a beat and he saw Seth's shadow move on the floor. "Can't be. Someone must be impersonating him. He's been eliminated in the power struggle within the Villani family."

Ryder spread his arms. "Clearly, we have no reason to believe you one way or another!"

Jed frowned at him. "Can you calm the fuck down?"

Ripper ignored them. "If you can't be of use with intel, maybe you can be of use as an outsider if you really do claim to have balls. One of ours has been missing for a while now, right, Ryder?"

The young biker's face fell, and he slouched in the chair. "Yeah. A few months now."

Domenico swallowed. Getting involved in some lengthy local problem wasn't on his to do list. "What can *I* do? I'm not clairvoyant. I don't know how to find missing people."

"We have a meeting set up with a trafficker, but we need a complete outsider to talk to the guy, because our faces end up in newspapers sometimes. He seems legit, and so he would check the background on any of the locals, see that they're connected to us. It's the sister of Ryder's girlfriend who's missing. We will give you all the info about

her, and if you manage to get a real lead from the trafficker, you can all go. Just pay damages for the gym and leave the state." Ripper nodded at Domenico and straightened in the chair. "Until that's done, we're gonna keep a hostage so that you don't try to fuck us over. Him." Ripper pointed at Seth, and Dom's blood began to boil. He'd rather break the fucker's neck than give him Seth.

"No, no. I want her." Jed pointed at Dana with a cocky grin, and Ripper rolled his eyes, glancing at the other biker. To Domenico's immense relief, he nodded. Maybe Jed wasn't as stupid as Dom had thought.

"Can be her."

Domenico growled and crossed his arms on his chest, pretending to ponder it. Eventually, he looked into Dana's face, which was a bit less expressionless than usual. At least she was trying to look frightened.

"Dom?" she asked, and he looked up at the bikers across the table.

"Can you guarantee she won't be hurt in any way?"

Ripper frowned. "I can't be responsible for her pussy twenty-four-seven. That's why I wanted the guy."

Jed nodded with a silly grin that jarred with him being The Loneliest Guy on Earth. "I'll keep her to myself."

"Do that," said Dom. "She's my cousin, so if anything happens to her, I'm gonna pull you behind your own motorcycle."

Ryder scowled. "Shut the fuck up. Nothing's happening to her. She's a hostage, not a club slut."

Jed raised his hands. "I mean, I can't be held responsible if she falls for me."

Domenico squinted. "She does like blonds. But I'm gonna ask her."

"Whatever," hissed Ryder, for once seeming more cooperative. "If you find out what happened to Jo, I'm gonna deliver that bitch of yours in a fucking limo."

Ripper got up from the table and extended his hand to Domenico. "So we have a deal?" He snapped the fingers of his other hand at Dana, and she slowly got up with a slight pout that managed to hide her usual lack of facial expression.

"I'll just gather my things."

Domenico nodded and grabbed Ripper's rough, calloused hand, shaking it firmly. "Any more details?"

"I don't want to text about this, so show up at our club tomorrow, and I'll tell you everything you need to know, in case the contact gets cold feet over night. The club's down the street from the gym."

Domenico nodded. "I will be there." He was already wondering how to turn this situation to his advantage, but with lack of sufficient intel, it was a difficult task. He'd have to rely on Jed and Dana.

Ryder also squeezed Dom's hand, unpleasantly digging his finger between the soft flesh between Dom's index finger and thumb. Domenico didn't react and just nodded. Jed was first to leave, despite Dom imagining him to have the heaviest of hearts.

Dana gave Dom a glare as she sat on the back of Jed's bike, but he just gave her a brotherly kiss on the forehead and made sure to make his *It'll be all right* loud enough for everyone to hear. He eventually stepped back and regarded the bikers as they prepared to leave, eyeing him suspiciously. Ripper would have a lot to explain once they went back to their clubhouse.

Once they left in a thundering of engines, the patches on their backs were the last thing he saw of them as the roar slowly died down. The swamp silence filled with buzzing of insects and noises made by small animals was all he was left with as neither Mark nor Seth spoke.

Domenico pushed his hands into his pockets and watched the road, wondering how it would all play out tomorrow. Were they honest about wanting his help, or

was it just a trap to get rid of him? Both possibilities needed to be taken into account.

"Men only night, huh?" he asked eventually, wanting to disperse the tension that settled on his shoulders with all its weight.

Mark looked out of the shack with his eyes still wide. "Do I know too much now?" he whispered.

Domenico slowly turned back to the shack and rubbed his forehead. Fucking fuck. Seth couldn't keep his mouth shut, could he? "Are you asking me if I'm going to kill you?"

Mark pouted and looked away. "M-maybe…"

"I'm sorry, Dom," Seth muttered. "It got heated."

Domenico rubbed both his eyes as fatigue overcame his limbs and sent sand beneath his eyelids. He'd been furious back when the bikers were still here, but now all he wanted was to touch Seth and feel that he wasn't hurt. He called him over with a gesture.

Seth was quick to come over despite his limp and hugged Dom tight. The mud on his clothes had dried and now just left a mess of sand on Dom. Domenico embraced him anyway and rested his head on Seth's shoulder.

"Mark, I have no idea what you're talking about. Told you I'm special forces. When I kill people, it's for the right reasons"

"And I thought you were an antiques dealer," Seth whispered into Dom's ear, rubbing his smooth cheek against him.

Domenico groaned. "That wouldn't fly after all he's seen." He breathed in Seth's scent and lost himself in the heat of the embrace, in the calming effect of the slight movement back and forth. Very soon, he was serene as a baby.

Mark licked his lips. "Aren't you scared for Dana?"

Domenico laughed and looked into the wide-open eyes of Mark. "I believe Jed is her hostage more than she is

his. Knowing that we have his phone, he'd rather put his own ass on the line than let anyone near her."

Mark nodded and sat on his futon with a bag of chips, looking strangely thoughtful. Seth pulled Dom behind the blanket hanging from the ceiling, into the cocoon of their small bed.

It was all the consolation Domenico needed.

Chapter 16 - Domenico

Domenico woke up to the sound of frying and the pleasant aroma of eggs. He shifted on the uncomfortably soft mattress and rolled on his back, looking up at the beams that held up the curtain dividing his and Seth's sleeping area from the rest of the room. Seth was gone, and it only made the longing in Domenico's chest stronger. Last night, Seth wouldn't let Dom fuck him with Mark in the room, and since both of them felt queasy about kicking him out after the whole biker thing, they settled on blow jobs.

And blow jobs were nice. No, they were amazing, but what Domenico really wanted was to cover Seth's body with his and get that physical connection that he'd craved for such a long time. And for once, Dom's sleep was peaceful.

"Hey," he whispered, slowly pushing the sheet off his legs.

"I didn't want to wake you," Seth said from behind the blanket. "I took a shower in Mark's invention. It's pretty good actually, because in this weather, the water is lukewarm anyway."

"Yeah, it was pretty smart. Maybe he could become an engineer," muttered Domenico, slowly getting to his feet. He brushed off a bit of crusted semen from his chest and pushed back the curtain, squinting when the bright morning light hit him head-on.

"No, it's just a hobby," Mark said with his mouth full, but then went silent and just stared.

Domenico yawned and walked up to Seth, who was busy turning something in the pan. Domenico slid his arms around his back and molded their bodies together, happily enjoying the lazy morning.

Seth gasped, almost tipping over toward the gas stove. "Dom, Mark's at the table," he hissed.

"I'm fine. It's all good. I like the view." Mark chuckled.

Domenico grinned and rubbed Seth's shoulder with his chin. "That's all right, it's not like he's never seen a naked man before." Dom wished he could have woken up to a naked Seth, but he had to settle on feeling Seth's bulky body through his jeans and T-shirt.

"But this is *you* we're talking about," Seth groaned, but didn't truly push Dom away.

Mark considered himself part of the conversation. "I've seen a very hot naked man just a few days ago, and I hope to see him again soon." There was no conclusion or point to what he said. Pure bragging.

Domenico laughed loudly and looked over Seth's shoulder at the loveliest frittata with tomatoes and mushrooms. He kissed the shoulder that smelled of simple soap and closed his eyes. "Must be exciting. A hot new boy. Who doesn't like that?"

Seth snorted, focused on the cooking. "Dom, clearly. Stuck with the same old guy for almost a year."

"I was his first, you know?" Mark continued. "I made sure it was really good for him, 'cause my first time was pretty useless. And now he totally loves it."

Domenico held Seth tighter and kissed his nape. "I hit the jackpot with my old man."

"Dom, please stop being naked," Seth said, but Dom could swear he wiggled his ass against him.

"How can I stop? It's not an action," chuckled Domenico, gently scratching the front of Seth's stomach.

Mark wouldn't stop trying to hoard attention. "And he makes these cute faces when he comes. He's so pale, so his skin gets really red."

Domenico looked at him with a slight frown. "Should you really kiss and tell?"

"I mean, we're all guys here. And it's not like you'll ever meet him." Mark shrugged with a wide grin. "Have any of you ever de-virginized anyone?"

Domenico tickled Seth's stomach, and his ego immediately expanded. His mind flooded with the image of Seth's face, contorted in a mixture of pain and pleasure over the twisted bedding of their Berlin apartment. The need to have Seth again came back, and Domenico couldn't help but discreetly cup Seth's ass where Mark couldn't see it.

"Yes."

"It gives this amazing feeling, right? Like, he looks at you like you're the god of sex if you do it right." Mark wiggled his eyebrows.

Domenico smiled and quickly reached his hand to steady Seth's when he struggled with the pan. Was he as distracted with memories as Domenico was? Dom wanted to ask him and tickle Seth's ear with his tongue, but he didn't want Mark to be there. "It is pretty amazing."

"Do you ever top, Seth?" Mark's question was so blunt Dom could hardly believe it for a second.

Seth glanced at Mark with a frown and turned off the gas. "What? And you don't have to help me with the pan, I'm fine." He seemed angry for no reason.

Domenico still held on to him, but when the warm pan came too close to his naked skin, he decided to let go. Behind Seth's back, he showed Mark the cutthroat gesture. Christ, how could anyone be so stupid?

Seth put the pan on the side and turned around. "Go put on some clothes," he hissed at Dom before looking to Mark. "And for the record—"

"Seth, our sex life is private," said Dom, with his jaw locked almost completely. "You don't have to tell him anything."

"I was just asking…" Mark groaned.

"Fine." Seth tensed up, looking like a bomb about to go off. "If you want to eat breakfast, go put on pants!"

Domenico rolled his eyes. "Why? I'm not gonna flip my dick over the plate."

"Because the kid doesn't need to be staring at your junk! Or is this not as private as our sex life?"

Domenico frowned. "It was you who went all *private* yesterday. What if I don't care that much?"

Seth squinted at him. "Oh, don't you now?"

Domenico rolled his eyes. "It's hot. I'm comfortable. It's *my* junk, not yours."

Seth nodded and put his plate with frittata on the table and pulled out a chair for Dom. "Here you go, honey." He turned to Mark. "Since things are not private around here, yes, Mark. I do top."

Domenico froze, and it seemed as if his heart slowed down, almost stopping to pump blood to his brain. He couldn't look at Mark, and his eyes focused solely on Seth and the ugly scowl on his face, so condescending and full of disgust. That was not something Dom deserved after saving his life so many times.

"And I am the only one to *ever* fuck your tight, hot ass."

Seth sneered at him. "Mark, take your food and get out of the house."

For once, the boy didn't have a stupid comment and did as he was told, dashing for the door as soon as he gathered his plate.

Domenico could hardly breathe, stiff in the joints as he watched Seth move. He couldn't believe he'd tell Mark something this personal.

Seth crossed his arms on his chest. "We can't have one normal morning, can we? Even on a day like this you can't do one simple thing I ask you to?"

Domenico exhaled and stepped closer, clawing his fingers over the backrest of the chair. "You think you can just tell me what to do? After all I have done for you?"

"I wasn't *telling* you. I asked. It wasn't a hard request."

Domenico hissed and pushed Seth's chest, stepping right into his personal space. "Fuck. You. I repeat: *you*."

Redness rose up Seth's neck. "Yeah, 'cause I'm the one who gets fucked by King Domenico the First."

Heat spread all the way to Domenico's head, and he rapidly spun Seth around and propped him on the table. With one hand on Seth's nape, the other on his hip, Domenico bit into his flesh through the fresh cotton shirt. "You can talk like that to your boyfriend. Not to me," hissed Domenico, following the first thought that came to his mind. The German accent seamlessly replaced his own as he moved his hand to squeeze Seth's ass.

It was a gamble, and Dom half expected having to block an elbow flying his way, but Seth stilled under him, swallowing loudly. Seth's nape was hot as hellfire, and he slightly parted his legs. Un-fucking-believable.

"Good boy," said Domenico breathlessly, suddenly overwhelmed by having that amazing body all to himself. "I'm back for you. And I'm gonna fuck your ass hard. I'm gonna come in you and leave that cum for your boyfriend to discover later," he muttered, jerking up the back of Seth's shirt and lapping at the fresh skin.

"Oh, fuck," Seth whimpered and put his forehead against the table. Dom was amazed at just how many times he had tried to reason with Seth, only to get nowhere, or worse, in the case of the last months, only to get the cold shoulder in bed. Yet the moment he lost the will to be the nice guy, Seth actually stopped arguing with him. Not only that, he was ready to surrender his body to a hard fuck just moments after they had started arguing.

Seth put his palms flat on the table. "I can't have him know..." he whispered, already panting. Dom could only imagine all the filth going through Seth's head right now, but he wasn't sure he cared as long as this new discovery continued to work in his favor. He didn't mind having a horny Seth on his hands one bit.

He pulled the shirt all the way off Seth's body and grabbed the flesh at his sides, holding him in place as he nipped all over his back, tasting and yanking at the skin as his cock quickly came to life. "No? What if he finds out? He wouldn't want you anymore, and you'd be all mine."

"He wouldn't. You have to come outside. I only bareback with him..." Seth's voice was low and heavy with lust. It was as if he was setting up the rules just to see Dom break them. So typical.

"All right," said Dom, even though he didn't intend on keeping that fake promise even as he searched to Seth's front and pinched the scar tissue on his pec. He moved his hips against Seth's ass, moaning when his growing cock fit into the valley between Seth's round buttocks so well. "Not wearing underwear? Were you expecting me?" Dom asked.

Seth arched his back, making his spine more pronounced, and he whimpered at the touch to the scars. It looked like Dom would finally get to touch them without listening to a litany of complaints. "No, I just—Fuck, your dick is so hard."

"It is. And you know how long it's gonna take me to get it into your ass?" asked Domenico, yanking Seth's pants

down, uncovering the beautiful tan globes. He wanted to continue, but the temptation was too strong, and he ended up on his knees, eating the warmth between the cheeks.

Seth moaned and curled his hands into fists as he stood on his toes, arching those strong calves and thighs. "Fast, it's gonna be fast."

Domenico hummed in delight, spreading his cheeks wide open, and gently swirled his tongue all around the entrance, teasing the little folds of skin, so warm and inviting. Seth was completely open to him now, and he'd probably say yes to anything Dom came up with. "Yes... I need to breed you before your boyfriend comes back."

"You're such an asshole. Told you not to," Seth hissed and only spread his thighs more. Dom loved how pliant Seth could be in sex, yet strong enough to take everything Dom had in store for him. He'd be dripping by the time Dom was done.

"I'm not gonna do what you tell me to. Next time I see you, I'm gonna grab you and fuck you right there, wherever we are," whispered Domenico against the tiny hairs that tickled his face. He nudged Seth's anus with the tip of his tongue, over and over. He had no idea how long it took him to get to the point when he was alternating at fucking Seth with his tongue and fingers, but at this stage, neither of them cared.

Seth moaned and writhed on the table, losing his inhibitions to his own lust, just the way Dom loved to see him.

"You can't," Seth murmured into the table, and Dom could swear there was a hint of a smile to his words.

Domenico spat at Seth's hole and got to his feet, pushing him flat on the table, but he would not just take him from the back this time. He needed to see that lovely face go red and contort with pleasure as Domenico hit Seth's prostate over and over again. Seth squealed in surprise when Dom grabbed him under the knees and

pulled them up, consequently turning Seth's chest up as well. He was just as proficient at this move as Seth was at turning pancakes.

Fortunately, the table was old but sturdy, so it held Seth well as Dom looked at his wide pupils and red face. Dom was Seth's drug, and Seth was waiting for his high. His plump lips were parted, letting out breath after shallow breath. Dom loved making Seth so irrational.

Domenico reached to the kitchen counter to grab oil and spilled a generous amount on his hand. Shoving his fingers up Seth's tight ass, he watched light flicker in those big brown eyes. "I'm not gonna have any mercy on you, you fucking cheater." Adrenaline spiked in his veins, even though they were just acting. The kick of arousal came both from the fantasy of stealing another man's property and the carnal look on Seth's face. Domenico didn't mind being Seth's weakness.

Seth moaned and half-closed his eyes, sucking in his bottom lip. "I only did it once." He ran his hand up Dom's forearm and kicked his own jeans to the ground.

Domenico grinned at him and pulled out his fingers. Three strokes of his hand up and down the length of his painfully erect cock, and he was pushing into the softest, sweetest ass he'd ever fucked. A gasp left his lips as his eyes locked with Seth's during the long push inside. Once completely embedded in the vise-like tightness of Seth's body, Domenico pulled on the skin of Seth's pec, twisting it gently. "Twice."

The weight of Seth's legs on his arms was pure pleasure. Dom had always liked big guys, as it gave him an immense sense of power to be topping someone like Seth, making him squirm and go wild for Dom's dick.

Seth gripped Dom's arms, his face a thing of beauty with his brows gathered, lips parting with a moan every time Dom stirred his hips. Watching the effect he had on Seth never failed to turn Domenico on.

"But it won't happen again," Seth moaned, locking his eyes with Dom's. Fucking tease. Always setting a challenge.

"No?" rasped Dom, slamming into Seth's hole at full force. He loved the melody their bodies created together as they moved in unison, covered in sweat. He could do this forever. Once he died, this moment could be his heaven. "I'm not gonna ask. I'm gonna take your tight virgin ass whenever I want, you understand me?" he uttered, grabbing Seth by the jaw. He didn't even think much of the word 'virgin' slipping off his tongue, but it made his dick twitch to think that he was the first to ever make Seth give up his ass and squirm for cock. Maybe they could role-play *that* one day.

The whimper his words elicited told Dom all he needed to know about Seth's hidden desires, just like the way Seth's ass squeezed around him did. "Yes, don't ask." Seth panted and reached down to his own cock, not shying away from Dom's grip. "He never fucks me like this," he moaned, just spurring Dom on. Of course, they fucked like this. Hard, rough, sweaty. From the very first time, Dom didn't spare Seth, and Seth lapped it up like a hungry pup who was finally getting what he needed.

Domenico smiled, watching Seth's big hand moving over the thick, slightly curved cock. The tip was already wet from the milking Dom was providing with every thrust, but watching it disappear and emerge from underneath the hood of foreskin had Domenico salivating. He grabbed Seth's hips hard and started a deep, punishing rhythm, galloping toward orgasm. "You're mine now, Seth. Completely mine."

"Oh, God! Yes, like that!" Seth moaned, jerking off like a horny teenager. He reached out to slide his other hand over Dom's abs. "You can cream me if you want. I don't care. I love your dick so much." He squeezed his eyes

shut, completely spacing out. And all because Domenico knew exactly how to fuck the horny bastard.

"Come first," hissed Domenico, kneading the flesh of Seth's thighs as he bit Seth's thick, hairy calf.

Seth wasn't even talking back anymore and milked his own cock ferociously until he came between their bodies, with his muscles tensing before a shiver. Spurts of cum covered his stomach, and a droplet even reached Seth's chin. His ass throbbed around Dom's cock, hot and hungry for cum that Dom was more than eager to provide. He came seconds after, squeezed hard by Seth's tight ass, which milked every single drop out of Domenico's balls.

Seeing double, Domenico dropped on top of Seth, nuzzling his face against his sweaty chest and covering it with lazy kisses that tasted of sweat and cum.

Seth seemed to only be catching every other breath, and his heart drummed at the speed of light against Dom's skin. He opened his lips, but nothing came out. Dom didn't mind, still gently grinding his cock into Seth's hole.

"So," he started, cuddling up to Seth when his cock started shrinking. "When are you gonna have sex with *me*?"

Seth snorted, and seeing a smile on his flushed face was the best thing after fucking. "I'm sorry, I don't mean it like that. You took me by surprise." He lowered his legs to allow Dom closer.

Domenico pulled Seth up and made him sit on the edge of the table, with Dom standing between his spread thighs. Locked in a loose embrace, they kissed, and now that Seth had lost his nasty edge, Dom was more willing to talk.

"I just... miss us making love too," he whispered, stroking Seth's back.

"I know, there's a lot of time to make up for." Seth wrapped his arms around Dom's chest and kissed his nipple. "But fuck, that was good. My ass is still feeling it," he whispered the last words and gave Dom's neck a kiss.

"I sure hope so, considering I'll be going to work now and leaving you on your own," said Dom, caressing Seth's ass.

Seth stood up and wrapped his arms around Dom's neck. "Look at me, seeing my future husband off to work." Not a hint of the earlier argument was there, and the tender kiss to Dom's jaw did in fact make him feel like a king.

He grinned and nodded at the frittata. "Maybe you should pack that. I don't think I'll have the time for dessert now."

Seth gave him a long kiss that spoke of his devotion before pulling away to do as Dom asked. He had that silly well-fucked grin on his face as he wrapped the frittata in paper. Dom took his time watching spunk trail down Seth's thigh. He loved it. If he could only make sure it stayed inside him forever, without using some silly toys, he would.

Instead, Domenico rushed to take a quick shower and dressed in casual clothes, in case they wanted him to meet up with the trafficker on the same day. But no matter how tiring dealing with the bikers could get, at least Dom got his share of happiness for the day. He was completely elated.

When he got back from his quick cleanup, Seth was there, in just the jeans he wore over bare skin, smoking a cigarette with a lazy smile as Domenico's lunch waited for him on the table. "You want one?" Seth pointed at the smokes.

Domenico kissed Seth's shoulder and nodded, caressing the warm body once more, just to gather more energy for the day. Seth put the cigarette between Dom's lips and lit it for him. Dom knew Seth too well to assume every morning would be like this, so he took his time reveling in Seth's newfound good attitude. Maybe Dom needed to fuck him before asking about the marriage again.

K . A . M e r i k a n | **235**

"Be safe." Seth stroked his back between the shoulder blades, and at that moment, Domenico truly felt invincible.

He poked Seth's forehead with his and walked out of the house with the packed frittata in hand. Even the bright sunlight shining straight into his eyes couldn't get to him now.

He saw Mark sitting behind the railing of the porch, and he could swear the boy had just moved there judging by the redness of his cheeks. He was doing that pretend 'I-am-just-sitting-here' expression of disinterest.

Domenico squinted at him and slowly raised his hands, shaking his index finger in warning. The boy was unbelievable. Then again, at least he got to see what a stud Dom was. "Watch and learn."

Mark laughed nervously and slowly got up, not daring to meet Dom's gaze.

Domenico lowered his voice, but he didn't have the right mindset to be angry. "That's what you did, didn't you?"

Mark followed Dom as they walked to the bike. "Not all the way, I mean... curiosity got the best of me, but it seemed intense, I didn't wanna totally pry."

Domenico raised an eyebrow at him and shook his head. "We're not your personal porn show."

Mark hid his face in his hands. "I'm so sorry. I didn't wanna lie, 'cause you read people and all that."

Domenico nodded, happy to keep Mark in the dark about his lack of telepathic capabilities. "Don't lie."

Mark put his hands down and reached into his pockets with a deep breath. "About that..." He cleared his throat. "I kind of... You forgot this," he muttered and pulled out the wad of ten thousand dollars Dom had thrown at him in the forest.

Domenico looked at the cash, surprised. He wanted to take it away before they left Mark, and even though it

was a test of what the boy would do, he hadn't really hoped Mark would return the cash without prompting. He even thought Mark could have buried it somewhere to pretend he lost it and retrieve it later. "Is it the whole thing?" asked Domenico, mounting the bike.

Mark rolled his eyes. "Yes. You gave me other money for shopping and stuff."

Domenico grinned and slapped Mark's shoulder as he put on the helmet. "Good. Give it to Seth. He'll know what to do with it."

Mark stood still, watching him intently. "I wouldn't take it now. Your offer. I'd rather be poor than do what you asked."

Domenico swallowed, and a smile resurfaced on his face immediately. And the warmth in his chest? It was pride.

Chapter 17 - Domenico

The clubhouse was an ugly compound, hidden away behind a row of trees. Its gray, grainy-looking walls reminded Domenico of the concrete walls of cheap housing in the eastern part of Berlin. The clouds had grown unusually thick in the last hour, big puffs of dirty white, with a layer of gray at the bottom. Add the sickly humid air, and all Domenico could think about was the storm that would surely leave him drenched on the way back home.

To reach the compound, he drove down a narrow road lined with large cement blocks. The gate was open, but he slowed down when someone appeared from behind the fence, as if ready to block Dom's way. The young man had a large bruise spreading all over the left side of his head from beneath a white bandage dressing, and Domenico soon realized it was the scout from the night before. With the senseless bravado he'd shown yesterday, he had been lucky to get out of it with as little harm as he did. Even the eye, which looked freakishly dark because of a burst blood vessel, should eventually go back to normal.

His foot was probably the worst. The guy was lucky to still even have one.

Domenico stopped the bike and stretched, looking at the prospect as if it were the first time they met. "Domenico Abate. Your president's waiting for me."

The guy gave Dom a stormy look and limped to the side to make way. "Follow me," he muttered, eying Dom's motorcycle.

Domenico did as he was told, and soon he parked Seth's sleek sport bike right next to a row of big, powerful Harleys. It looked good, though he needed to have Mark wash it. With his breakfast in hand, Domenico pushed on the heavy steel door that was probably almost impossible to get through without a bomb. Domenico knew the type— with thick locks that went deep into the wall for extra protection and a frame that was a part of the construction of the building. This meant that the compound was built for protection, not merely modified for it.

A few bikers looked up at him from a game of cards when the prospect led him in. "Your girl's not much fun!" shouted a large man, who resembled a Viking with his long red hair and beard.

Domenico straightened his back, quickly assessing the space. The common area consisted of a kitchenette of sorts, with two huge fridges and a whole stack of chips bags next to one of the cupboards. A deep fryer sizzled with something, adding the scent of oil to the smell of cigarette smoke, booze, and leather. But there was also a large area with mismatched sofas and chairs organized around a few beat-up coffee tables. Three closed doors led into more private parts of the clubhouse, but Domenico didn't let anyone notice his quick assessment and smiled.

"No, she's not. I'm happy you noticed."

One of the doors opened, and Jed walked in, followed by a grim-faced Dana. "Ripper will be here soon. Want a beer?" he asked, as if Dom hadn't almost made him

cry yesterday. For someone who called himself the Loneliest Guy in the World, he did have a lot of friends. Dom didn't really understand why he wouldn't simply fuck guys on the side if that was what he wanted. That's what Dom had done, and it had worked out well for him.

He shook his head and raised the packed lunch. "A fork perhaps?" he asked, walking up to Dana. He squeezed her arm, and making use of the sudden commotion, he asked in a low voice. "Okay?"

She gave him a quick nod. "It's fine, just a pit of stupid. Do I have to be here?"

Domenico nodded. "We couldn't be doing this without you."

Viking gave an appreciative sound, batting his pale eyelashes at them. "That is one touching reunion."

A girl showing more cleavage than Dom wanted to see approached him with a plate and fork. "Here you go, sweetie," she said in a voice so high-pitched and childish, Domenico got the mental image of her playing with Barbie dolls and rubber ponies. It was not a good thought.

Dom thanked her and sat in a free chair by the table. The smell of cheap tobacco and beer would cling to his hair for weeks, but he chose to ignore it and calmly unpacked the frittata.

"And now you're eating at our table? Who do you think you are?" asked a raspy voice from across the table.

Domenico looked up into pale eyes hidden away behind wire-rimmed glasses. The man was big, muscled but with a potbelly stretching the front of his black T-shirt. The white beard that reached halfway down his chest had single streaks of pale brown in it, a sharp contrast to the man's completely bald head, which shone in the light coming through the window behind him. He had a few random-looking letters and symbols tattooed around his eyes and on his neck, and from their faded state and crookedness, Dom guessed they'd been made in prison.

"I've been invited to come here. Didn't have time to eat on the way," said Domenico, digging in.

The other bikers were oddly silent, which made Domenico believe this guy was someone important in the hierarchy, and sure enough, there was a vice-president patch at the front of the old man's leather vest. So that was Jed and Ryder's father. No wonder he wasn't Domenico's friend.

"Just wait until I show you how welcome you are—"

"Ripper *has* invited him." Jed sat down next to his father, blocking his way out if he wanted to make a sudden move for Dom.

Dana on the other hand sat next to Dom and looked at his plate. "What is it? They have nothing good here."

Viking's lips parted. "*Nothing good*? Are you fuckin' crazy, bitch? I should make you some barbecue ribs, and then I would see you talkin'."

Domenico scowled and let Dana have a bite. That was the least he could do.

Dana frowned at Viking. "Be my guest and eat them all yourself, Axe. Not to mention that all the cooking I saw here so far was deep-frying. Greaseball"—she pointed at the young prospect who was tending to whatever sizzled in the fryer—"seems to be obsessed with it, but I want to have clean arteries at sixty."

The other guys hissed out mocking laughs, and if Dom heard right, even the word *hipster* fell from someone's mouth, but he just ignored it. He looked up at the VP. "Your sons are alive, and I am ready to settle any scores with them. They are big boys."

Ripper came in through the same door as Jed did before. "I hear we have guests." He rubbed his hands together. "You wanna get the van, Wolver?"

The VP, or *Wolver* as he was apparently named— why did those people call themselves the stupidest of

things anyway?—slowly got to his feet. "Is Ryder still in the office? Shouldn't he be here? It's a family issue."

"I'm here," grumbled Ryder as he slowly walked through the door, his stare hitting Dom in the face with a generous portion of contempt.

Wolver nodded and walked off, kicking the table Dom ate at on the way. It felt like kindergarten all over again. Only the food was much, much better. Seth was a wizard of the pan to create something this smooth, this fresh and delicious, with a shaking hand, in a hut without electricity or running water.

"Give 'im a break," Jed muttered at Ryder. "The guy could help."

"Can I come?" Dana asked Dom, but Ripper was first to answer.

"You ask *me* about this shit, bitch. Understood?"

Domenico wasn't about to defend Dana's honor. He did, however, need to talk to her before he left. "I think you'll be safer here," he said, not ready to disclose her abilities.

She seemed a bit deflated by the answer, but had another bite of Dom's frittata.

"I've got a wire for you, come on," Jed said and got up.

Ripper nodded. "Everyone coming, be ready outside in ten."

Domenico stuffed his face with the remaining food and chomped on it as he followed Jed, pulling Dana along.

"Don't get too busy back there," someone called behind them, but Domenico just ignored the lecherous comment and entered the corridor behind the door. It was short and smelled of stale air, but as they walked into a tidy-looking office with a bright carpet and some framed certificates hanging on the walls, he was slightly confused about where he was. He wasn't about to ask though.

Domenico raised his eyes at Jed. "I think you've forgotten the wire from the other room," he said, wanting to speak to Dana on his own.

Jed groaned and rolled his eyes. "Really?"

"Yes. Go and find it," said Dom. He pulled Dana's athletic body closer, and scowled when her tit flattened against his chest.

Dana blinked a few times, stiff even when Jed left, grumbling beneath her breath. "What is it?"

Domenico leaned to whisper against her ear. "If something happens, use him as a hostage. They won't touch you then."

She exhaled and raised her eyebrows. "I thought *I* was the hostage. But to be honest, I was planning just that. He seems pretty tough, but his sexuality paralyzes him completely."

Domenico hissed through his teeth. "What did you learn about them? Did they mention Mr. Tropico again?" he asked hurriedly, eager for any scrap of information. As much as he hated the former Don, it sickened him to know someone impersonated him using all the old contacts. There was something deeply disturbing about the whole thing.

Dana gave him a self-satisfied smirk. "I wasn't wasting time. I don't know about Mr. Tropico, but Ripper must have lied about the drugs. They don't mule them here. They deal with heavy arms. One-off short operations and transport. I batted my eyelashes at Axe long enough yesterday for him to take me to... wait for it... a tank they have stored in one of the units in the woods."

Domenico stepped back. "A *tank*? Who the fuck would buy a tank around here?"

Dana groaned. "I don't know. He tells me it's legal, although I've seen ammo for it, and I'm pretty sure that's not allowed. They also have a helipad here, and it looks like it has been recently repainted."

Dom shook his head. "They're probably getting off on just the idea of having it." He went silent when they heard Jed coming back, but whispered, "Find out about Tropico."

The way Dana nodded was like seeing a soldier take an order, and he liked her attitude. "I'll do everything I can."

Jed looked at them with a grave expression as he closed the door. "Take your time. What's the plan now? Fitting me with a bomb that goes off the moment I say something that you don't like?"

Domenico raised his brows. "That won't be necessary."

Jed shook his head. "And by the way, how am I supposed to protect her pussy if she throws herself at the first guy she meets here? Axe told me she half-fucked him. What the actual fuck?"

Domenico squinted at Dana, and she mouthed *tank*. Domenico nodded with a small smile. "You should work on satisfying her curiosity then."

Jed shook his head. "This is bullshit. Take your top off. I've got a different shirt for you as well, to hide the wires better."

Domenico groaned but pulled up his shirt. Tempted by a sudden burst of humor, he twisted his body gently, tensing the muscles of his stomach and torso, just to fuck with Jed. "I hope it fits."

Jed frowned. "You have to be shitting me. One fucking misstep and here I am. Should 'ave known the boy was a trap..." His mumbling sounded more like he was talking to himself rather than anyone else in the room. He attached the wires proficiently, as if he was afraid to touch Dom for more than a second.

Domenico snorted. "That's what you get when you fuck *boys*, not men. Where's my shirt?"

"He offered," Jed said his mantra and shoved an oversized shirt at Dom.

Dana laughed loudly. "He's too cute, Dom. Can I keep him?"

Domenico rolled his eyes and buttoned up the new shirt. It was made of some kind of artificial fabric mix, and he already hated it and its ugly olive-green color. "He offered me, too. But I'm a responsible adult."

"Okay, you dick. Lesson learned. Never again," Jed hissed and wouldn't even look into Domenico's eyes.

The staring contest only lasted a few seconds before Jed dashed outside, bringing in the Barbie girl. Domenico was squeamish when he realized her purpose was to cover his face with makeup. But as emasculating as it was to have a layer of thick foundation covering his skin, he supposed it made sense to make the scar on his face less visible and this way make him look more generic. The end result made him sneer at the weirdly flat features of a man staring at him back from the mirror, but Barbie had done her job and transformed him into a very tanned mannequin.

"Let's go," said Jed, as if annoyed by Dom looking at his reflection.

"At your service," said Dom and followed Jed out of the room. The other bikers were already outside, but not on bikes. They were all packed into the back of a yellow van with dark windows and a picture of a smiling man with tools in his hand. The huge letters next to him read *Call John the Handyman* and were followed by a telephone number.

Domenico slowed down slightly, asking himself how he'd ended up in this dump. Was this how his life was going to be from now on? Hiding away in vans? But he walked into the back anyway, ignoring the strong smell of sweat and leather.

"So, what is it that you actually want me to do?" he asked Ripper.

"Be safe, Dom!" Dana said before Ryder pulled the door shut.

The van was off to a shaky start, and Ripper sat down on a bench inside. "You need to ask the guy about buying a girl like Jo, or an experience with her. She is around twenty, with green eyes and blonde hair, very small, flat chested. She has a large gap between her front teeth, so that could help make the search more specific." Ripper passed Dom a photo of the girl. "If you get the chance, ask him to let you have your pick. Maybe they have a cellar or a facility where they keep people, and you could find her there. Though I doubt he'd take you there on the day." Ripper let out a sigh. "This is a long shot anyway. Do a foreign accent, dangle more offers in front of him if he provides good service."

"What kind of accent? Russian?" Domenico straightened up, looking at the girl. She looked like a child with makeup, but he assumed she could be an adult and just had a baby face.

"As long as it works," muttered Ryder from the back of the van, his brows drawn tightly together.

Domenico sighed and looked around at all the men. The girl might as well have been snatched away by a lone wolf. There would be no trace of her then. "This is your turf, so how can you not know what happened? Aren't you staying in touch with those people?"

Ripper grunted. "Don't test my patience. We're not pimps, and we don't get dirty with human trafficking. Those fuckers stay away from us for a reason, and this is literally the first time we have a lead on a group like this existing in the area. We checked, and other than Jo, there were no missing girls in the county in the last few months. I would not have kids from our area pulled into the hands of some deviant fucks."

Domenico spread his hands. "I'm not saying that. I'm just wondering if they would really take someone close to you? Risking war? Maybe the guy who took her isn't affiliated? And the man I am meeting? How much do you know about his organization?"

Ryder cleared his throat. "They're *not* on our turf. We wouldn't allow that. The guy you'll be meeting traveled here just for the meeting. He thinks you're a pimp."

Domenico pressed his lips together. "All right." They wouldn't admit they were clueless, but he was already sensing that the girl was a lost cause, and they were grabbing at air in the dark to find any *leads*. Unfortunately for them, from Domenico's experience, the girl was by now probably dead or smuggled out far away. Sad story, but such was life, and Dom had his own problems to worry about, so he'd do the meeting, hope for no follow-up, and he, Seth, and Dana could leave. It was about time. Seth needed to be somewhere where he wouldn't constantly get in trouble.

"Do any of you have a gold chain, or ring, or something?" asked Domenico, gathering his hair into a ponytail that lay low on his nape. If he were to convince the man he was meeting that he was a serious Russian client, he needed to look the part of an Eastern European gangster. He opened the gold chain on his neck and removed the cross.

Ryder shook his head but passed Dom a signet. Jed spread his arms. "Don't look at me. I don't wear this kind of stuff."

Domenico snorted. "I'm guessing no one here's orthodox?" His joke fell flat, but he chose not to worry too much and just waited, remembering bits and pieces of a persona he'd used a few times. Gribov. Dom couldn't help a smirk as he thought this was the man he told Seth would come for him.

The bikers didn't bother him, and none of them had even tried to search him for a gun, so he supposed they really wanted his help. It took a good half an hour to get close to the meet-up place, so Dom figured it was somewhere out of town.

When the car eventually stopped, he was eager to get out of the van that smelled of far too many men in warm leather, but when he jumped out, he couldn't help but laugh. It was the same diner he and Mark ate at after the lesson he had given the kid in the woods. Without asking any more questions, he casually marched across the parking lot, hoping they weren't being watched. It was a big risk to just unload him at the venue. Now that he was Sergey Andreyevich Gribov, his gait became slightly slumped, his knees softer, even as each subsequent step was longer than the previous one. He kept his hands in his pockets and smiled as he entered the diner with his sunglasses on. The meeting was supposed to start in one hour, so he decided to take his time and have a look around the place.

He had some coffee and pie, he talked to two elderly ladies, who told him they came here every Tuesday, he spoke to the waitress, and he examined the large window in the toilet stall. Ultimately though, he sat down at the back, in the same place where he'd eaten with Mark, and pretended to read a newspaper, looking at the empty parking lot and sipping even more coffee. He was quite relaxed.

A man in his thirties approached him slowly from the moment he entered the diner. He wore a T-shirt too tight for his muscular chest, and his bald head glistened with sweat.

Domenico leaned back, sliding his arm over the backrest of the seat. His heartbeat picked up. This had to be the guy. He gave a slight smile and looked at his watch. It was five past. "And there I was, thinking you chickened

out," said Domenico and removed his sunglasses to wipe off a smudge.

The man was halfway to sitting down when he stalled in the awkward position, staring at Dom as if he'd seen a ghost. "I know you..." he whispered.

Chapter 18 - Mark

A few hours earlier...

Mark sat on the porch, unsure how he felt about going to talk to Seth now. He wasn't lying. He'd stopped watching them fuck at some point, as even he felt that he had overstepped a boundary, but the images were in his head, and he couldn't get them out. Even with the sex being so rough, he could sense both of them being so *there*. Not getting sex over with, not like when Mark fucked for money, not like on porn clips. Also not the way he fucked Raj, since Raj was a newbie to it all, and their sex was fervent but not that harsh.

Domenico and Seth had a connection much deeper than he'd initially thought. Their story was like something out of a movie. So much so that he wasn't even sure if he hadn't been lied to. Yesterday's showdown with the bikers revealed a new, darker side of his new friends that Mark was still dubious about. And the explosives? No one had told him about *those*. Wait, Dana had, but it was such an outrageous claim that he hadn't believed her.

Mark got up with a deep sigh and knocked before entering the shack. He needed to give Seth back the money.

"Come in," chirped Seth, and Mark pushed the door, peeking inside.

The table was so pristine one could eat from it... again, and the whole room smelled of soap. Seth's muscular forearms flexed when he squeezed out excess water from one of Dom's T-shirts.

Mark cleared his throat, unsure how to approach Seth about the topic. The image of Seth so pliant, with his skin a dark pink hue, kept running through his mind as if it was stuck in a loop. "Um... so you've made up, I guess."

Seth licked his top lip and smiled. "Yes, just a small misunderstanding. We both have tempers, I suppose. There always needs to be some compromise. Come, help me hang the laundry."

Mark frowned when he thought back to the way Domenico just suddenly shot down Seth's anger with sex talk. He supposed that meant Seth's ass was the compromise in this equation. "Sure," he said and grabbed a stack of wet clothes, following Seth outside. To be fair, he rarely saw Seth as laid-back. As if there was absolutely nothing he could be worried about. "You two seem close... after the homophobic bullies from your hometown, and all that."

Seth shot him a glance and carried out the rest of the laundry in a plastic bag. "Of course. Things like that bring you close. You have to know you can depend on the other person." He approached the clothesline Mark had earlier hung between the house and a tree.

Mark scratched his head. He couldn't quite work out how their bizarre relationship worked. "I mean, Dom's retired now? Does he plan to find another job?"

Seth frowned and put some clothespins in his pocket. "Um... yes, I suppose. At some point. He'll have to assess his options."

Mark cleared his throat, and the thick wad of cash in his pocket burned him through his jeans as he tried hanging the clothes one by one along the line. "Is there something he knows how to do, you know, except for shooting people?" muttered Mark. Judging by the confidence with which Dom pulled the trigger at a bottle in the hand of his beloved man, his proficiency was outstanding.

Seth hid behind a T-shirt he was hanging. "You shouldn't say that. He's got... people skills."

Mark sighed. "I don't know. I mean... he's telling me and Dana what to do, and then you do all the work at home, and he's just reading in the chair. Doesn't that bother you?" he asked, looking for any cracks in that perfect picture. There *had* to be a catch.

Seth's face became less cheerful, and Mark was almost sorry that he was the reason behind the change, but he had to know.

"He does *stuff*."

Mark swallowed hard. This was what he had suspected all along. Domenico wasn't a normal person. Many of the things he did for Mark weren't *normal*, even if they were good for him. "Illegal stuff?"

Seth groaned and hung up a few more pairs of underpants before answering. "That's not what I said. He's retired. You know, sometimes your partner needs support in finding himself and all that. Dom has been there for me, and I am there for him. It's his money we live off now. He does all the research on the places we're going to and makes sure we're safe. Sure, I could work on that, but he's better at it. You have to know your limits."

There it was, the key word that normal people didn't have to use. "Why do you need to research safety? You guys keep your money in cash, and you live in those rundown places. Is someone after you?" asked Mark, stalling for a moment when he looked at a pair of Dana's

panties, with a cute human-like melon at the back. They were the last thing he'd expect her to wear.

"Don't ask questions you don't want answered. Why can't you just take it one day at a time?"

Mark exhaled. He needed to know this before they would part ways. Something unexpected had happened since he met Domenico and Seth. He'd been made to work for his keep, but he also knew he'd be fed, that he'd have a place to sleep without anyone molesting him, that he was safe, and Domenico wouldn't let anyone hurt him. On the contrary, he was given money for his own needs, a car, and a lot of encouragement. Even if some of the things he experienced were unconventional, he still couldn't help but think that he'd miss this stability in life. Not of place, as this changed, but of Dom and Seth around. Maybe after parting ways with them, he could just knock at the gates of that cult he heard about from Raj. If he told them he wanted to rethink his life, maybe they would take him in? He could help them with farm work and even pray to the wooden statues they apparently worshipped. Then again, it could be one of those cults where they sacrifice people to demons, and as an outsider, he was obviously more at risk. After a moment's thought, he decided he'd rather not tempt his luck.

"I don't know, maybe because Domenico told me to give you this," Mark said and whipped out the cash.

Seth slowly took the money, watching it intently as the smile melted off his face completely. "Did he give you anything else? Did he say anything?"

Mark stepped back and shook his head. "No. He just told me to give it back to you as he was leaving."

Seth's Adam's apple bobbed, and he put the money in his pocket. "Okay," he muttered and went back to hanging laundry.

Mark bit his lip, surprised by the way Seth suddenly deflated, instead of being happy he got money. He cleared

his throat. "You could get married and have a luxurious honeymoon for that," he offered.

"There will be no one to get married to if he doesn't come back." Seth's breathing became shallower.

Mark opened his mouth, and his brain went empty. "W-what? Why are you saying that?"

Seth gave up on the laundry and sat down on the ground, his eyes strangely empty. "He doesn't usually give me a lot of money, because he takes care of things. He's gone to do something dangerous and gave me this just in case. Fuck!"

Mark stopped breathing. "W-what? But he didn't say anything. He even took his food with him."

"Well, he's not gonna go to McDonald's for what's potentially his last fucking meal, right?" Seth hissed, ripping a weed out of the grass. He was heaving and so utterly lost even Mark could see it.

Mark looked at their feet as his heart sped up. Would this mean he'd have to take care of Seth now? Why else would Domenico have given the money to *him*? "Maybe just call him?"

"He lost his phone yesterday. Don't ask. He's out there, doing some bullshit task, and I'm stuck here doing laundry like some 1950s housewife! Fuck! Fucking fuck!" Seth got up but didn't look like he knew where to go.

Mark hugged himself and looked around the swamp. "I—so what do we do now?" he asked, suddenly as unsure as when falling asleep in the street.

Seth took deep breaths, and the gator tooth pendant Mark had given him moved on his chest with each inhale. "We have to find him. Be there as backup, just in case. He'd kill me if he found out, but I'd rather have him angry than dead. He hasn't left long ago. And he's going to the club, that we do know."

Mark looked at his feet, trying to get his heartbeat in order. He was surprised to see Seth so decisive for once.

Had he too been in special forces? "But... isn't the pickup blocking the way?"

Seth nodded. "We will make it somehow. We can try to bring it back here despite the fucked wheel."

The plan was getting more extreme by the second, but if Seth was going to these lengths, Mark was beginning to think that Domenico really was in danger. Especially as Seth was limping on the way to the shack.

"Okay," he said quietly. He wanted to help after all the support he'd received, even if his stomach quivered at the thought of danger. "Will I get a gun?"

Seth turned to look at Mark all of a sudden, as if he'd seen him for the first time. "I mean... sorry, Mark. I got carried away. You don't have to go."

It was like being a spanked child, and Mark gritted his teeth in anger. "No, I *have* to go! You two really made a difference, I—" He swallowed hard, embarrassed by the outburst. What Seth and Domenico had done was probably nothing for them, and it was just him who put so much meaning into their friendship. He didn't want to imply this should continue. "Domenico helped me talk to a guy I like for the first time, and you cook for me... I wanna give back."

"Can you use a gun?" Seth asked, and his serious side was surfacing by the second.

Mark opened his mouth and wanted to say yes with all his heart, but in the end, he shook his head, deflated. He couldn't even shoot at someone who threatened Domenico's life.

Seth pulled out a gun from his bag and removed the bullets. "Take this one, so you can at least threaten people if necessary."

Mark bit his lip and nodded, squeezing his hand over the hard steel. "O-okay."

"Dom taught me to shoot, you know. He was a real bastard during training, but a good teacher nevertheless." Seth looked around the shack and in the end stuffed a

medium-sized, tattered notebook into his messenger bag, and headed for the way out. Seeing him so determined was a new side of him Mark didn't expect.

Seth did limp, and his face was twisted with discomfort when Mark ran up to him, but he moved with a purpose. It was clear nothing short of dying would stop him from getting to the Coffin Nails clubhouse.

Mark sat at the steering wheel of Dana's car, and they drove off, reaching the truck soon after. It was blocking the way, and so they moved it a bit, despite the flat tire. Seth even found his phone under the pickup, but the battery was dead. Seth swore when he realized Dom had taken the shotgun home last night, and he ended up getting a small gun from a hidden compartment under the seat. Mark was beginning to wonder how many more weapons they had, and whether Domenico and Seth, as foreigners, had the right to carry them. Not that he would ever testify against them.

"Dom would know what to do," Seth hissed and rubbed his forehead as they climbed into the car and immediately drove off, grazing the pickup with their side mirror. At least it only slightly changed position.

"You're not Dom. Don't beat yourself up about it," Mark tried, pressing on the gas to speed up on the empty road.

Seth just nodded, but by his expression, Mark was guessing Seth was drowning in grim thoughts. Mark had never truly loved anyone, so he wasn't sure how it felt to care for someone so deeply, but he could try to imagine what the risk of losing that person could do to someone.

About half an hour later, Mark parked down the road from the clubhouse and kept the windows open, as the old car had no air conditioner. Seth wore a cowboy hat, and Mark got a big pair of round sunglasses from the glove compartment. On the way here, they needed to stop at a gas station to refuel, and Seth got Mark a caramel

frappucino, but even with the sweetness melting on Mark's tongue, his adrenaline levels were rising. He felt like he'd landed a part in a spy movie.

In front of the clubhouse stood an ugly colorful van that from afar looked like child bait that should never be parked in front of a playground. Mark slurped the delicious and expensive drink and squinted at the men in black clothes, who boarded the back of the car one by one. They were too far away to recognize anyone though. "They're going somewhere."

Seth squinted. "Did you see him? I didn't see him. The motorcycle is still there. Fuck. I don't know if he's in there or not. What if they're going in two batches, or something?"

Mark flattened his back against the seat to make it easier for Seth to look through the fence. Sweat was soaking through his shirt at the back. "Maybe we could just... you know, go there and ask about Dom?"

Seth groaned. "Yeah, right. And if they're actually torturing him right now, they'd just hand him over. Oh, look. Dana. Yes, she's waved at the van. Let's go." He started the car so abruptly Mark spilled some of the iced coffee on his chin.

"W-what? How do you know he's in there? Maybe she fucked one of the bikers, and she's on their side now?" muttered Mark, though his heart did hope that Seth was right. That even despite Dana's treacherous and mean nature, she would not betray Domenico. She was obviously enamored with him. Mark was sure her I-don't-fuck attitude was just an act to make Dom want her. Pretty foolish, as Dom only had eyes for Seth.

"She doesn't fuck. And surely, doesn't fuck bikers," Seth said as they drove at a steady distance from the van. "Then again, I remember her saying she fucked this one guy at a gas station, but that was for favors."

Mark shrugged. "I suppose she doesn't have a high sex drive. Or she's in love with someone," he said, watching the van as they followed it discreetly. This was quite exciting. Would they witness a takeover of some dirty underground brothel?

Seth shook his head. "Highly doubt that. I sometimes look into her eyes, and sure, they're nice and pretty, but it's like looking into the eyes of a fish. A dead one."

"Yes!" Mark smiled and patted Seth's thigh. "She's so unpleasant. It's only Domenico she tiptoes around." He fell silent for a second, suddenly realizing he had no idea why she was even with them. "Who is she to you anyway? Neither of you seems to like her."

Seth groaned. "You know Dom was in special forces. She really wants to train under him. So she's his little pet project, I guess. Which is kind of strange, because he's a terrible misogynist otherwise. The mere concept of pussy offends him."

Mark pouted, unsure whether he wanted to share the embarrassing story about Dana tricking him with not even her pussy but tits. He chose not to. "Why? What is her job? Does she even have one, or does he pay for her food?"

"She's extra security, I guess." Seth pouted.

Mark nodded. "From who?"

"Mark, please. Is this really the time for this? Bears and alligators, okay?"

Mark crossed his arms on his chest and fell silent, making sure Seth got the point. He would not be denied information. "Are you in witness protection?"

"If I was, I wouldn't be allowed to tell you, would I?" Seth gave him a meaningful look.

"You gave me a gun!" mewled Mark, but he did see the reasoning behind Seth's words. It kind of made sense: Domenico and Seth were alone, hiding away in small towns where they were least likely to be recognized.

"Desperate times, Mark! Christ!" Seth gripped the steering wheel so hard his knuckles went white.

Mark scowled, but he bit his lip when the van's brake lights went on, and Seth drove into a parking lot in front of the very same diner where he and Domenico had once eaten dinner. And where Mark had first met Raj. It was a lucky place, so he relaxed slightly. Nothing could go wrong here.

Seth stopped in the empty road for a while, behind trees, and only drove into the diner's parking lot a few minutes later, making sure to find a place away from the van, in the far-off corner at the back of the diner.

Mark blinked, and breath caught in his throat. "I can see him," he said, noticing Domenico's profile in the window. He chose the same booth they used last time. Maybe it was for good luck?

Seth lowered the cowboy hat onto his forehead, but looked where Mark pointed. "Okay." He slumped into the seat. "Let's just make sure everything goes smoothly."

"See? He's alive," said Mark, squeezing Seth's shoulder, though relief was also his. Now he could relax and drink the remaining frappe in peace.

Seth took a deep gulp of air. "I hope I just overreacted, and we can go home after this whole thing and pretend in front of Dom that it never happened. I can't lose him. He's my whole life now." And the way Seth looked at Dom told Mark just how in love Seth was.

He swallowed hard, jealous of a feeling he didn't understand. "But... isn't it really making you feel miserable that you're so addicted to him?"

Seth's lips stretched into a tender smile, and he slurped on a smoothie he had bought for himself. "No. It's the best feeling on the planet. He can set my skin on fire by just brushing against me."

Mark felt heat rise up to his cheek at that confession, which sounded more intimate than any

detailed story his hookups told him about fucking. He looked down at the melting crystals inside the plastic cup, and for once felt completely empty. As if he was not a person but a shell that the sea tossed around.

"I wish I had that."

Seth finally tore his eyes away from Dom and rustled Mark's hair. "I thought you said you'll never fall in love?"

Mark hugged himself, more grateful for the touch than he should be. "I don't know. I mean, I met Raj, and when I think about kissing him, it's like my body gets all hot. He has this creamy skin, he's so slim and tall. Taller than me, actually." Mark cleared his throat, remembering the last time he had met up with Raj, in the woods again, and they fucked on a blanket. "It's so great, but... I don't think it's the same," he whispered, slowly turning his eyes back to Seth. He got all the attention he craved, as if Seth really cared and truly listened. He wasn't just a dude who listened to Mark because he wanted to fuck him later.

"Why not? You just met. Maybe it could deepen if you gave it a chance. Me and Dom... we had lust, but it wasn't like we exactly fell into each other's arms. We fought quite a lot at the start."

"You still fight."

Seth groaned. "But every time we fight, we both know that we want to make up. It's different than arguing with someone and breaking up over it."

"I guess." Mark shrugged, still thinking about Raj's smile. The guy was so normal, with the biggest problems he listed being the fear of coming out to his adoptive parents and bad scores in math. Raj lived in a world so different from Mark's everyday reality of fear. "But me and him... we're not like you. If I told him how I got here, he wouldn't want to date me anymore," Mark whispered, only now noticing that his voice was dropping with every word.

Seth took a deep breath. "You're only sixteen. It would be great if you met the love of your life now, but you still have time to figure it out. If you worry so much about what he would think about your lifestyle, maybe you need to work on changing it to what you want it to be. You'll feel more confident, and you'll be able to find someone right for you. And if the sex is fun, you can still fuck in the meanwhile, right?" He smiled at the end and slurped his smoothie. These were the kind of things Mark's dad should have told him, though he doubted there was a grand future ahead of him. All his bets were on Fred's kindness and willingness to help Mark through school, so that he could get real job in the future, when Domenico and Seth would be long gone from his life.

"Domenico brought me here once. That's when I met Raj," Mark said with a small smile. "I wouldn't have talked to him if Dom hadn't told me to."

"You shouldn't listen to everything Dom says though." Seth laughed and gazed toward the diner for a moment. "But I can see he was pretty spot on with Raj."

Mark sighed, and for a few seconds, he too watched Dom, who was too focused on something he ate to notice a guy in a cowboy hat and one in women's shades. "My parents never took me out anywhere. I mean, a few times when I was really young, and then they just... got too focused on themselves, I guess." It was a mild euphemism for violent alcoholism.

"Even your mom?" Seth looked at him with care painted all over his face. "Wait. You said they died...?"

"I lied." Grief rose in Mark's throat, and he looked away as his eyes welled up. He'd had a shitty family, and if they had ever loved him, they'd forgotten about it over time. "They're drunks. I couldn't stay with them anymore."

"Oh, Mark..." Seth quickly unbuckled his seat belt to lean closer and hug him. "I'm so sorry to hear that. You could have told us."

"You would have told me to go back," whimpered Mark, stiffening in the embrace. It felt too honest to be true. "And I can't. I won't. I'd rather be on my own than anywhere near them. My dad is the worst. He beat me if I wouldn't bring him booze, so I had to find ways to make the extra few bucks, and then it just got shittier, and shittier, and I *hate* him so much..." The last word made his throat clench, and he grabbed onto Seth, as Seth gently stroked his back. And listened. Just fucking *listened* to him.

"That's how I got into... you know." *Fucking for money.* "How I got here. I want to turn my life around, and Fred has a job for me. He promised—" Mark took a deep, raspy breath and used the hem of his shirt to wipe the wetness off his eyelashes. He didn't want to be such a baby in front of Seth, but he just wasn't used to anyone being so *kind*.

Seth didn't pull away and let Mark cry for as long as he needed to. "That's good. That's a good attitude, Mark. Or you could always start a company, building watering can showers." He laughed, and it deflated some of the tension in the best of ways. "Seems like a pretty good idea to me if you market it right. It is eco-friendly and uses little water."

Mark chuckled and rubbed his face, just to have an excuse for how red it was. He raised his eyes to look at Domenico, who was still sitting at the table. "Maybe you're right. Domenico said I have a talent for that. And he's *never* wrong, as we know."

Seth snorted and fake-clinked his smoothie against Mark's cup. "Never."

They both looked up when a big, bald guy approached Domenico's table. Slurping sweet drinks, it almost felt like being in the cinema. Domenico slipped off his shades and started polishing them on his sleeve like some kind of movie star. The other guy pulled away the chair and stopped with his ass halfway to the seat, as if he were imitating a duck. Mark snorted.

Domenico leaned forward and put his glasses back on his nose as the other man finally sat in the chair. Sharp glances were exchanged over the table, and Mark liked to imagine they were talking like two characters from an action movie. With Dom being the hero, who you'd see use controlled violence. He would grab his opponent by the head and slam it against the table. And then he'd take out the gun, put the barrel against the bald bastard's head, and roar, "*Where are they?*"

He was swallowing another sip of the frappe when Domenico made the swiftest movement Mark had ever seen. It was like watching an alligator grab its prey, only to pull it into the swamp for a certain death. Domenico shot forward and hit the guy in the neck, only to stand up and casually leave the table. Mark blinked, surprised that the baldy hadn't followed and just sat there against the backrest, staring ahead like an idiot. But then a cold hand grabbed at Mark's heart when he noticed a red stream falling down the man's neck, from beneath something slim and dark.

"Fuck," Seth hissed. "Fuck! He was supposed to talk to him. What's happening?"

But Mark didn't have an answer. Seth just expressed his own worries. He frowned, and it only sank in now, after he replayed Dom's action in his head forty times. The baldy was dead. Dom had killed him before their eyes. Stuck something in the guy's neck and killed him. Mark managed to unglue his gaze from the victim and followed Dom's elegant-looking silhouette all the way to the colorful van, which opened with a slamming of the backdoor, and two massive arms forcibly pulled Dom in by the shirt.

"No, no, no, no..." Seth whimpered and threw his cup out the window, starting the engine.

Mark fell back against the seat, feeling unreal. His life really had become a movie.

Chapter 19 - Domenico

Domenico's flesh stung where he'd been manhandled, and his Beretta was temporarily with Ryder, but at least he managed to prevent the bikers from cuffing him. That would have been too risky, but fighting six armed brutes in a van? Even he could not come out of that alive. Back at the clubhouse, at least Dom had the space to think, even with the bikers all tense and ready to take him down. He exhaled, trying to keep his breath level and his senses alert to any violence as Ripper paced in front of him like a bloodthirsty lion. "Who are you, huh? You offed the guy just when he was about to say your name. How do you explain that?"

Domenico shrugged. "My name's not your concern. I don't want it on tape."

Ryder got up with a snarl and swung the Beretta in the air. Domenico didn't like it when his weapon wasn't shown proper respect. "Can I just kill this cocky motherfucker?"

Jed jumped to his feet as well. "Let him explain!"

"You in love with him or something?" Ryder came forehead to forehead with Jed, who slouched, as if his brother was about to smack him. It was painful to watch.

"It's not all over yet. They will send people to investigate, and that could be the chance to trace where those bastards have come from," said Dom, even though he was already thinking about ways to leave Louisiana as soon as possible. The girl was long gone, and he would not waste his time chasing after a ghost.

Ryder shook his head. "She's one of ours. We can't just let him fuck it all up again!"

"Yeah," Axe grumbled from his place at the counter. He picked up a piece of newly fried chicken and patted Prospect, who poured oil into a second pot and wordlessly continued his artery-clogging spree. Upon their return, the guy had declared there would be deep-fried chocolate bars for dessert. Domenico was so eager to try them that for a moment he stopped listening to the conversation until Axe raised his voice. "We don't even know if he doesn't work for them. The trafficker knew him."

That much was true, and it chilled Domenico to the bone. "I have no idea who this fucker was. This has never been my area of expertise."

Ripper leaned down to look into his eyes. "What *was* your area of expertise?"

Domenico closed his mouth and smirked as his hands itched to smash the old man's face in for the impertinence. "Don't you have an idea already?"

Ryder looked at him, his eyes going darker. "You're no ordinary goon, that's for sure."

"Maybe he's like Grim?"

Ripper showed his teeth without looking at Dom. "A killer, huh?"

Domenico said nothing. If anything could improve the situation now, it was staying calm.

Axe snorted and wiggled his pale eyebrows. "Maybe being a fag also comes with the profession." No one laughed. "Tough crowd, eh?"

Domenico stretched his back and looked at him. "I would laugh if I knew why it was funny."

Axe groaned and rolled his eyes. "It's funny because Grim fucks boys as well."

"And if you called him a *fag,* he'd put a bullet through your skull," Jed hissed and clenched his fists.

Domenico chuckled. "I'm sorry I don't have any bullets at hand. If I did, it would make for a great punch line."

The bikers stilled, seemingly too confused to know whether they should laugh or try to beat him up.

Ryder growled. "Fuck off. My woman's sister is missing. Stop fucking around!"

"How do you plan to make up for today's stunt? I'm afraid we're running out of options." There was no humor in Ripper's voice.

Domenico met his gaze, tired of constantly being pushed out of control. He'd been reluctant to get in touch with his old contacts, but maybe approaching those who only knew his fake personas was an option. At this point, he was ready to do a lot for a newly cleaned slate. "I'm retired, but if I wanted, I could use you as my shield right now, so stop. Pissing. Me. Off," he yelled, keeping an eye on the men around him. He would not take Ripper. He would take Jed, unsuspecting and standing close enough. He had enough of wasting time.

Jed held his hands up. He was trying to keep up his part of the deal. Good. "Come on, guys. If he's some badass killer who was known to the bald guy, I'm sure he can make some calls to his friends high up, get some contacts?" He looked at Dom.

Domenico groaned and gave a slight nod. "I am a man of honor, and I pay my debts, but I will not be scolded

like a ten-year-old who pissed his pants. That guy needed to go, so I got rid of him. End of story."

Ripper's nostrils flared, but he stood in place, watching Domenico, with his body tense and ready to fight. He probably wasn't threatened very often but was smart enough not to let his anger lead him. Clearly, that was why *he* was the leader of this gang. The other bikers stayed silent, taking the hint from their president, and Domenico nodded.

He could see the Coffin Nails were relatively well organized, but their efforts to find the girl were undermined by the fact they didn't have much to do with the shadiest corners of the crime world. He supposed that made them the good guys in this equation, though the lack of knowledge of what was happening under the surface of the normal world was hardly excusable for an organization as large as this. Domenico wasn't proud of it, but he occasionally did contracts for groups connected to large human trafficking rings. As sorry as he felt for the victims, the world was an ocean, and predators occasionally caught fish that strayed too far away from the protection of their school. A shark like Domenico generally considered it beneath him to target the defenseless, but it was his policy to stay away, unless he had a reason to intervene. He supposed that getting Seth away from here without yet another organization on their tail was reason enough.

"I will make calls. If this man knew me, then there must be a connection between some of my former associates and those people. If there's anyone who can help you find that girl, it's me." Dom was sure she was as dead as the canned fish Seth put in pasta.

"Do that, and you can leave Louisiana in peace," Ripper said, as if he were the president of the US granting Dom amnesty. "I don't even care about the money for the gym damages. Just work on this. Do we have an understanding?" He held out his hand.

Ah, the man clearly respected his betters. That much played in his favor.

Domenico squeezed the thick hand and shook it firmly. "I will find her for you."

"That's more like it!" Jed said with a wide smile and drifted off to the kitchenette. "Let's drink to this."

Ryder gave Domenico a dark look, but everyone else seemed more at ease now that agreements were made. "I'm watching you," he growled and pulled out Dom's gun. Domenico accepted it, and Ryder slowly drifted toward the fridges, with his shoulders slumped. The scent of fried meat was overwhelming as Prospect served his associates the food, and Domenico scowled at the thought of the oily scent clinging to his hair.

A scream outside made everyone face the door, and Dom was glad he had his Beretta back, because fuck only knew what was happening out there. Maybe Baldy had friends watching, who followed them?

No one got to act before the door flew open, and Seth burst in, red in the face, holding his gun up and pointing it all around like a flustered newbie. "Nobody move!" he yelled, but a few of the men had already pulled out their weapons, clearly not very intimidated by the display. To Domenico's horror, Mark was right behind Seth, holding a gun against the head of the Barbie-like girl who Dom had spoken to earlier. His face in contrast was pale as a sheet, and his big eyes were so wide they looked like they were about to pop out of his head.

Domenico raised his hands, including the one that clenched around the grip of his trusted Beretta. "Nobody shoot, for fuck's sake!" he uttered with cold fear turning his limbs into ice. As calmly as possible, he looked at Seth and Mark and shook his head.

"I've got this," Seth muttered, but then spoke up to the confused bikers. "He's coming with us, or Mark will shoot the girl!" He was heaving, and the barrel of his gun

trailed back and forth, without aiming at any specific target. It would have been humorous if that wasn't a loaded gun in Seth's hand.

Anger exploded in Domenico's chest and streamed through his mouth. "Put down those weapons, now! Are you two brain-dead?" He stepped closer and yanked the girl out of Mark's hands, sending her at Axe. His brain was pulsing with images of red splatters. Of Seth's body jerking against the wall with each bullet that tore through his body. He wanted to slap the stupid bravado out of that lovely head.

Seth's Adam's apple bobbed, and he looked at Mark, not that confident anymore as he lowered his gun. "We came for you..."

Ryder snarled at them. "How fucking romantic."

Domenico shook his head. He pulled the gun out of Seth's hand and put on the safety. His gaze trailed to Mark, who stared at him like a mouse caught feeding on cat food. He returned his gun as soon as Domenico reached for it. The thing was light, and Dom rolled his eyes. "Unloaded? Really?"

Seth looked around at the bikers' smug faces. "I didn't want him to kill someone by accident," he whispered, but everyone could hear, and the laughs got louder.

Domenico hung his head, frustrated beyond belief. He grabbed Seth's wrist and pulled him toward the corridor. His eyes met Jed's who was too busy peeking at Mark to even notice until Dom approached him. "Someplace private?"

"Let them into the office, Jed," Ripper said in an amused tone.

Seth wasn't even resisting, just followed like a kid who knew he'd done wrong. His skin was so warm, his pulse so lively beneath Dom's thumb that even this was enough to somewhat stifle the fear.

Domenico burst into the office and pushed Seth forward, slamming the door behind him. Even his throat was desperately pulsing in tune with Dom's heart. "Are you insane?" asked Domenico, surprised by the tremble in his own voice. He could hardly catch a full breath as he looked at his lover's remorseful face. "You could have *died*. They could have drilled a fucking hundred holes in you!"

Seth grabbed his hand, holding on to his own forehead with the other. "I can explain, Dom. I'm so sorry... We had a plan..."

"You had a plan?" Domenico squeezed Seth's hand so hard he was afraid he'd juice it. "You saw me off in the morning. What the fuck possessed you to go after me?" he rasped, holding onto the front of his shirt. It hurt him to even think about what could have happened.

Seth opened his mouth and frowned. "Are you wearing makeup?"

Domenico twisted his lips in displeasure, and his anger was already fizzling out. "Yes," he said eventually but immediately changed the topic, "Why did you do this?"

"Mark brought me that money from you, and I panicked." Seth rubbed his eyes, never letting go of Dom's hand. "You always lie about the danger you're in. I thought maybe this was money you wanted me to have in case you died. I couldn't take it, I had to act..."

Domenico bit back a gasp, shuddering slightly as cold overcame him despite the summer heat. There was some truth to Seth's words, but Domenico only omitted certain facts to spare Seth the worry. "Why don't you ever trust my judgment? It happens over and over. One more stunt like that, and I could lose you. Do you understand me? I could lose you, and if I lose you, I might as well be dead!"

"Because you don't include your own safety in your judgment. You don't trust that I can handle the truth, so how can I believe you? One day you'll lie that you're just

going out for a walk, and you'll never come back, and I will never know what happened to you!"

Domenico frowned. "I always include my safety in my judgment. I like my life," he said, pulling Seth closer and squeezing his shoulders. His head was clouded after the scare, and it wasn't going away. "You're brash. Stop doing this. Stop endangering yourself. This is not something you can handle." Domenico's breath shook as he swallowed his pride. "I can't see you hurt again. It's coming back to me at night."

Seth sat down on the desk. "What? The alligator?"

Domenico dropped his hands off him and shook his head, emotionally exhausted. He felt as if he had just pushed a huge rock to the top of a hill. "No. Vincente."

Seth looked at the floor and started playing with his fingers. "I'm so sorry, Dom," he whispered, even though it was him who had gotten tortured back then. Truth was they both had been, in different ways.

Domenico pinched the bridge of his nose and squeezed his eyes shut, suddenly overwhelmed with the urge to just collapse and sob. And he couldn't do that. He was Domenico Acerbi. He wouldn't cry. "Those dreams are so fucking vivid. You bleed, and I... I'm there. I can't do anything."

Seth was quick to get up and hug him. Maybe Dom couldn't cry, but the heat of Seth's big body, alive and warm, was a huge relief. "We did our best back there."

"I fucking failed. I shouldn't have called Mother. I was fucking stupid," hissed Domenico and shook his head, pushing his face against Seth's shoulder. Even sensing the warmth of his skin and the scent of him wasn't enough to fully compensate for the fear of the last few minutes. "It wasn't worth it. I wish I could take it back, so you wouldn't have to go through it all."

"You're not a machine, Dom. You couldn't have predicted what was gonna happen," came the soothing

words as Seth stroked his back. "I was, and I always am, ready to risk everything for you. If it wasn't for you, I'd be dead in the first place. If not by your hand, then by Tassa's. You sacrificed everything for me, and all I want is for you to know that I would also do everything I can to save you if necessary. I don't know what's necessary if you don't tell me the truth."

Domenico exhaled and squeezed his arms so hard around Seth he couldn't push anymore. "I'd tell you if I needed help. I just... please, trust me. I know what I'm doing." He took a raspy breath and pulled his lips over Seth's shoulder. "There's nothing worse that could happen to me than losing you. You need to keep yourself protected for me," he whispered, letting his hands climb all the way to Seth's face.

Seth exhaled and slowly nodded, looking into Dom's eyes. "I know you're proficient at all this. I can trust you, but I need you to promise not to lie and ask for help if you really need it, not just go down with the ship." Seth slid his hands up over Dom's. "I'm not useless."

Domenico swallowed hard, holding on to Seth's face now. His brown eyes were so open and sincere that Domenico couldn't help an ache forming in his heart. Maybe there was some truth to Seth's words. Time after time, keeping things from Seth had proved disastrous. If Seth were close and knew all Dom's secrets, it would be at least easier to keep an eye on him.

"I know," he whispered, slowly leaning in for a kiss, and Seth's lips opened without protest, inviting Dom into the safety and pleasure that Seth's body provided. For a while, they just kissed, without need for words. The serious talk they had taken some of the edge off Dom's nerves, and the confession about his nightmares made his heart lighter, but it was the long, slow kisses that eased the fear Dom had for Seth's life. Seth was here. Safe.

He nuzzled Seth's cheek and rested his head on Seth's shoulder, enjoying the sense of safety it gave him, even if it was just emotional safety. Before he and Seth had gotten together, his life had been much easier, but now that he looked back at it—also painfully empty. No weekend fling with the most handsome of men could compare to what he shared with Seth. No amount of partners could compare to Seth giving in to Dom's lust. What they had was too precious to even compare with anything that had happened before.

"Don't worry," whispered Dom in the end. "This will end soon. Once we're across the border, it'll all be fine."

Seth took a deep breath and slowly pulled the hairband off Dom's ponytail. "We followed you to the diner. Why did you kill that man?" he asked in a voice as soft as when he wanted Dom to tell him what topping he wanted for his *crêpes*.

Dom stiffened and shook his head. "Fuck. Mark saw it?" That was *the* last thing he needed.

Seth sighed. "Yes, Dom. I'm sorry. Please tell me the truth about what happened."

Domenico bit into the flesh of Seth's shoulder with a low groan. What was he to do now? He didn't want to hurt the kid. "He knew me. I don't fucking know how, but he knew my face."

"Fuck. I get it. You didn't have much time to talk then? Why are the bikers okay with this? I thought I would need to pull you out of their claws."

Domenico rubbed his face and pulled back, somewhat calmer. "They aren't okay with it. They're fucking furious, but I'm gonna try and nudge some of my contacts who know people dealing with human trafficking. That's the only thing that comes to my mind."

"As one of your alter egos?" Seth guessed. "Frederico doesn't know them all, does he?"

Domenico smirked and looked at Seth. "You might be the only lucky man to meet them all."

Seth let out a silly laugh. "I can't wait. But I promised to fuck a certain Domenico Acerbi first, so they have to get in line."

Dom punched his chest gently and laughed. "Don't make him wait too long."

Seth leaned down for another kiss. "He's waited long enough already."

Chapter 20 - Seth

Seth sat on a bed in a guest room in the Coffin Nails clubhouse and listened to Dom making phone calls and changing his accent, or even the language he spoke, quite a few times. It was so strange to see his body language and facial expression change with each conversation, as if he were truly becoming different people, not merely acting. Seth felt like an idiot after the failure he had made of himself that afternoon. Then again, it was still better than actually having to pull Domenico out of the bikers' clutches. The talk they had afterward also gave him some peace. He would at least try to trust Dom. He imagined how he would feel if he had to watch Domenico suffer, and even thinking of it gave him a shudder. They'd been through so much together already.

Domenico sounded like he was getting somewhere with the phone calls, despite Seth not catching all of it because of the changing languages. He wrote a note for Dom on a piece of paper, to not bother him, and put it on the shabby desk next to the bed.

It read: *Take your time. I'm going to grab a beer.* He waited for Dom to acknowledge it and pressed his lips against Dom's cheek in silence. His lover squeezed his hand and smiled as he told the man on the phone that he didn't like brunettes and only fucked blondes. Seth couldn't help but smile back. He walked out of the room and took a deep breath once out in the corridor, facing a portrait of a naked girl straddling a motorbike.

He didn't like the stuffy atmosphere of the clubhouse, although he supposed it was only stuffy for him, Dom, and Mark, who hadn't left his assigned room since he was led to it. They were prisoners here, as there were far too many police officers investigating the murder of the trafficker for Domenico to walk around town. There were no cameras in the cheap diner, and the public announcements stressed his Eastern European accent, without mentioning the scar, Dom's most identifying feature. But on the other hand, his looks were quite striking, especially in a small town where everyone would easily identify him as an outsider. They were treading on thin ice just by staying in proximity of the diner.

Seth knocked on the door of Mark's tiny room. "It's me. Wanna come out and breathe a little?"

Moments later, Mark opened the door and looked around, as if he suspected this was all a trick to lure him out. Seth was pretty sure Mark was still embarrassed by the failed hostage stunt, but being under one roof with a guy who had assaulted him wasn't helping much either.

He took a deep breath. "Might do, I guess. I was just texting Fred that it will be another few days till I can see him."

Seth nodded, pretending that he didn't mind the Fred guy. He couldn't help a bad feeling in his gut about the man, but it wasn't his place to tell Mark what to do. "You're not in a rush."

Mark shrugged, stepping out of the room that looked more like a prison cell than anything else, complete with bars behind the windows. He made sure to lock the door, too. "I don't know. What if he gets tired of me constantly pushing it off? It's like I'm dissing him."

Seth sighed. That was somewhat true. A part of him actually wanted Fred to call it all off with Mark, but then again, it wasn't as if Mark had anywhere else to go. Even if Seth gave Mark some cash when they parted, it wouldn't be the same as providing a safe home.

"I know… But as long as you keep in touch, a few more days won't hurt him."

They walked all the way to the end of the unnecessarily dark corridor with only two small windows letting in the light—one at each end, both reinforced with steel bars, just like the ones in their rooms. Seth supposed the Coffin Nails had their reasons to plan their headquarters like that.

They continued down the staircase that led toward the lounge area downstairs. As much as Seth was uncomfortable with the idea of taking hostages, he was glad he didn't have to spend much time with Dana. Even after so much time in her company, she never failed to make him uneasy. For once, he was slightly irritated at Dom for keeping his promises, even to people he didn't seem to really like having around.

He and Mark were instantly met by glares once they entered the lounge, and Seth didn't like it one bit, but he couldn't show Mark just how uncomfortable it made him. He put his hands in his pockets and sat on a bar stool by the counter, staring at a stack of cold fried meat. He didn't like that his first thought was that if Dom were here, he'd feel more comfortable. Seth had never wanted to be this dependent on someone, yet he couldn't help liking the feeling of safety Dom provided. Domenico always knew what to say, and more often than not, his confidence was

enough to put others in their place. Domenico didn't take anyone's shit, and just thinking about it made Seth's cheeks warmer. He was sure Mr. Schwangau didn't take any bullshit either.

"So how does that work?" asked someone, and when Seth looked up, he realized it was the redheaded guy they called Axe. He was pressing his lips together, as if trying to stifle a laugh. "Are you forming a fucking centipede?" Everyone else burst out with loud laughter, as if it were the funniest joke they had heard in a while.

Seth glared at him. So that was the warm Southern welcome. "He's *sixteen*, you dumb dick. He just hangs around with us." His eyes trailed around the common room, searching for Ryder, and there he was, leaning against the wall with his grim gaze focused on Seth, as if he were regarding a huge rat that he couldn't get rid of because it was his sister's pet. All remainders of a smile dropped from Seth's lips. He couldn't believe the guy would just turn on him like that. The gym thing was a misunderstanding, and Ryder had to see that.

"Yeah, right," said Axe, who apparently was the nominated voice of the masses. "Two guys traveling with a good-looking sixteen-year-old chick and nothing happens? You gays are no better."

Mark bit his lip. "I'm not even gay," he said weakly, much to the amusement of everyone gathered.

Seth sighed. Denial wouldn't help Mark much right now. "It doesn't matter, Mark. You don't have to explain yourself." He got off the stool, even though he knew Axe most probably had a lot more experience in fights than he did. "Are you saying you're a pedo?"

The boos and hisses around them added to the laughter

Axe smirked. "If she's got tits and the whole shebang, she's no little girl."

Ryder rolled his eyes at the wall, and it seemed that even Axe's friends were split on the subject, even though no one tried to support *the gay*.

Seth sighed theatrically, even though he wasn't comfortable with this situation at all. "Okay, so I fuck guys. Can we get this over with, so I can get a beer?"

Axe shrugged, but he looked Seth up and down as if he hadn't expected this. He waved his own bottle toward the kitchenette. "The fridges aren't locked."

Mark slid off the bar stool and rushed to the fridge. Out of the whole thing, only one shelf didn't contain stacked bottles. Mark took two beers.

"Whoa, shouldn't we protect the innocence of sixteen-year-olds?" asked Ryder.

Seth finally got a way to pick a fight with him. Maybe it could at least clear the air. "I don't know. Should we? You didn't seem to care seconds ago?"

Ryder straightened and pushed his chest forward. "If it were up to me, I'd let him get wasted and see how that ends for him," he growled, and one of the guys slapped his thigh.

"Don't give him the wrong idea." It sounded more like an explanation that no one here wanted to reenact gangbang porn than a promise of leaving the boy alone.

Mark pressed his lips together and put back one of the bottles before walking back to the counter.

Seth spread his arms, never taking his eyes off Ryder. "I don't get what you're saying. That he's gonna get a lesson in hangovers, or that one of your brothers would actually be up for a little boy-on-boy action when drunk?" Seth's feet burned on the explosive territory, but he couldn't just leave the issue alone.

The room exploded with rage, and Axe jumped right into Seth's face, pushing at his chest. "What did you say, fag? No one wants your dirty gay asses, but if you fucking insist, I can show you my baseball bat!"

Ryder did nothing. He smirked and looked away, clearly not interested in maintaining the easygoing friendship he and Seth had shared. It was a slap in the face worse than Axe's offensive words.

Jed came between them, pushing at both Seth's and Axe's chest. "Give him a break. It's not like he's a Nail. Who cares how many dicks he sucks? It doesn't matter."

"Doesn't it?" hissed Ryder, pushing through the crowd. Jed stepped back immediately, and his body language betrayed just how much it mattered to *him* what his brother thought about it. Seth felt a pull at the back of his shirt, and he realized it was Mark prompting him to leave, but only then, Domenico's booming voice cut through the noise like a cleaver.

"How the actual fuck am I supposed to work when all you do here is bicker like a bunch of old ladies at the marketplace?"

Ryder faced Dom but held on to Jed's shirt in a gesture that suggested they weren't done with their conversation. "Someone's fucking *precious*. Can't be that loud up there. Don't worry, no one here is gonna hit on your boyfriend. As I think we've already established over a week back."

Domenico looked at him, completely serious. "I'm glad you remember," he deadpanned and walked up to the counter, casually rustling Mark's hair. "Since it's you who wants my help, you should make sure my contacts don't think I'm buying cattle while talking to them."

Jed pulled out of Ryder's grip and pushed him away. "I'm so done with all this gay talk. Anyone wants to play some pool?"

Axe watched Domenico with his arms crossed. "You know they're searching for you. Can't you at least cut your hair or something?"

Seth's eyes went wide at the suggestion. He loved Domenico's hair so much. Smelling it, pushing his fingers into its silky texture... "He's not cutting his fucking hair!"

"Why? You like pulling on it as you fuck him?" growled Ryder.

Seth scowled. "You're such an asshole, you know that?"

"Fuck off," said Dom calmly and approached Ryder with his hands casually down his pockets. It was almost as if he intended to push away Ryder with the power of his deadly gaze alone.

Ryder took a deep breath as if to say something, but Jed pulled him away again. "Give it a rest! He's looking for Jo. Sure, it's fucked up that they're just flaunting themselves like that, but... they're foreign, they don't know any better."

Domenico smirked and pulled Seth closer by the waist. "Excuse me, gentlemen. I think it's high time to go fuck," he said calmly in an insanely proper British accent and walked Seth toward the exit.

Seth snorted and grabbed his beer on the way. "Jed, keep an eye on Mark, will you? We don't want anything *improper* happening to him."

"I'll be fine," Mark muttered, and Jed didn't look one bit happy with how the situation had developed, but Domenico didn't seem to care. He pushed the door open and took Seth back into the quiet staircase. It was an immense relief.

"Rough day, isn't it?" asked Dom, slowly pulling Seth's hand up to his lips.

Seth groaned, and looked at his bottle, hoping he'd find a way to open it in their room. "I kinda wish they didn't know. But since they do, I can't be timid about it, or they'd eat us alive. Ryder's been a dick to me. It's not fair."

Domenico kissed Seth's shoulder and molded his body to Seth's side as they climbed the last few stairs. "Not that good of a friend now, was he?"

"Not really, no." Seth sighed and wrapped his arm over Dom's shoulder. "I guess you will have to spot me after all," he said as if it were a tedious task.

Domenico smirked and nuzzled Seth's nose as they walked up to their room, but his face got slightly more serious when he unlocked the door. "This could've escalated."

Seth pursed his lips as he walked into their little trap of a room that really only contained a bed and a desk. "They were picking on Mark. I had to do something. That Axe guy is like three times his size."

Domenico locked the door behind them and softly put his arms around Seth's waist. "I know. But Jed's gonna protect him with his own ass now, if needed."

Seth nodded. "I thought I could find a way to hang out with them, but it was as if I had Ebola." He stroked Dom's hair. It was smooth as silk—Domenico's pride and Seth's joy. He'd never let Dom cut it off.

"Fuck them. We're gonna be out of here soon," whispered Domenico, stroking Seth's hips in slow, circular motions.

Seth bit the inside of his lip and put away the beer. "I suppose this can wait."

Domenico stretched his neck so far something crackled, but he smiled and sat on the mattress, while holding Seth's hand. "I'll wait with telling them what I found out if they can't behave."

Seth followed him on the bed and pulled off his T-shirt. He still wasn't happy about how his body had changed, but he was now determined to get back into shape, and feeling firsthand just how much Dom had wanted to fuck him gave him the confidence boost to stop worrying about it too much for now.

"So I will be the first to find out?" He smiled and straddled Dom's hips.

Domenico rested his head on Seth's shoulder and just let his hands stay around Seth's chest, like the strongest of armors. Domenico would never let anyone hurt him.

"There's an abandoned military base about thirty miles from here. I will tour it. Apparently, they're a transfer point, so they don't really keep people long-term. One of my former colleagues used to do jobs for them, and it seems like a trustworthy piece of information. They're saying they can show me the stock," he muttered, looking at the grated window. Domenico's gaze was clouded, as if he too was worried about the implications of such a find. Maybe they should inform the police? But then again—how would they do that? As an anonymous tip? And if the local police were somehow involved, the business and its victims would be gone before anything could be done about it.

Seth sighed and hugged Dom's head to his chest. "And you will try and see if she's there?"

Domenico shrugged and gave Seth a weak smile. "She won't be there. But maybe I'll find proof so that they can stop searching. As much as I fucking hate Ryder, I am sorry for him. No one deserves to lose their family," he whispered, more and more lax in Seth's arms.

"I know." Seth kissed Dom's hair and gently rocked on his hips. "At least you can give them closure. You said you regret calling your mother, but at least she heard from you. That's the important part. There's nothing worse than the uncertainty." He let his hands slide down Dom's back and explore each hard ridge of muscle.

Domenico hummed and fell over, taking Seth with him. The mattress was too soft, the bedding not fresh, but at least it seemed clean, and the privacy of the tiny room made all the disadvantages unimportant.

"I'd still rather have her grieving than you hurt," whispered Domenico, touching his forehead to Seth's. "I need you in my life."

Seth was quick to wrap his legs around Dom's hips. Only now, he realized they kept being interrupted or having problems with privacy lately. It was either Dana always there or Mark lurking somewhere around. Even if the walls in this room weren't all that soundproof, they were solid, and the door had heavy locks. It would be just the two of them.

"You are the best thing, and the worst thing, that has ever happened to me." Seth arched up for a kiss and closed his eyes, as he explored every vein on Dom's forearms.

Domenico muttered his approval and rolled on top of Seth, sliding between his legs and slowly moving his hand up and down Seth's chest. His touch ignited more heat with each moment, a slow burn that would surely explode within Seth's chest soon enough.

"The worst?" asked Domenico quietly and pressed his ear to Seth's ribcage, as if he needed to listen to the heartbeat beneath.

"Because I used to be independent, and now I'm addicted to you," Seth whispered, loving Dom's heavy body on top. He was like a machine made out of pure lean muscle. Seth's fingers traveled all the way to Dom's ass, and he squeezed it, already anticipating doing that when Dom fucked him. Seth thoroughly enjoyed the attention of Mr. Schwangau, but it was Dom's love he most craved. "I get all twitchy when you're not there." He laughed.

Domenico's mouth curved into a wide smile, and he raised himself up, trailing his hair up Seth's neck and cheek in the process. There was a glint of wickedness in Dom's bright amber eyes, and Seth couldn't wait to have it unleashed on him. "I'm sorry I haven't always told you the truth," Dom whispered and slid his nose to Seth's ear.

Seth smiled back and put his hands lower, to Dom's thighs. "Oh, I know you will still lie to me at one point or another. Just keep it to a minimum."

Domenico laughed, and the sounds he was making trailed all the way to Seth's cock. Domenico reached down and pulled his fingers up and down Seth's thigh before hooking it over his hip. "All right. But I want to trust you tomorrow, when I go and investigate the base."

Seth sighed, instantly deflated, but he tried to pretend he didn't mind. "Yes, I promise I'll sit here on my ass and look after Mark."

"No. You will not do that. I hope." Domenico raised himself on his elbow, just high enough to look Seth in the eye as their noses touched. "If something goes wrong, I need you with me, so that we can disappear." Domenico swallowed, and he placed the gentlest kiss on Seth's mouth, just a dry brush of sensitive skin, but it made Seth's arousal skyrocket. "Will you go with me?" breathed Dom.

Seth nodded quickly, and his heart skipped a beat. Visiting an abandoned army base where a prostitution ring had a transfer point was the last thing on his bucket list, but accompanying Domenico at a risky venture like this was what he wanted with all his heart. He'd follow Dom's orders, do as he was told, but at least he would be able to act if push came to shove.

"In case someone else recognizes you?"

Domenico nodded and kissed Seth again, making a small but very well-aimed movement with his hips. Seth gasped as warmth spread all over his stomach and thighs. He couldn't help but rock against Dom.

"I'd go to the depths of hell with you."

Domenico grinned as if they'd just agreed to elope to Hawaii, and he grabbed Seth's wrists, putting them over Seth's head. "You'd be safe in hell with the devil himself."

Chapter 21 - Domenico

The walls around the former military base were high and barely visible in the darkness as they approached them in the car. Only from up close was Dom able to tell that they'd been crafted out of cement blocks, probably with metal scaffolding at the back, and he was sure the wires at the top of the fence weren't merely for show. There were lamps on both sides of the tall solid metal gate, and he slowed down the car as they approached. There was no one visible between the dark trees all around them, but the moment Domenico stopped a few yards from the gate, it slowly started opening with a rusty creak. It was a lucky coincidence that one of his personas was in the business of dealing with illegal brothels and human cargo, so the contacts who knew Dom as Mr. Adler could vouch for him. Clearly, the references had been enough.

He and Seth had shopped for the best suits they could find at such short notice in the middle of nowhere, Louisiana, and despite the mission being so stressful, Dom took peeks at Seth's hairy forearms revealed by the rolled-up sleeves of his black shirt. He was sure that the last time

he'd seen Seth wear anything this official was at Seth's own wedding. It looked hot on him. No matter how much Dom enjoyed seeing him in jeans and funny T-shirts, there was something about seeing Seth in formal clothes that had his adrenaline revving. It made Seth look older, more dangerous, like a true mafia man. Domenico could only imagine how it would feel to be naked against Seth when he was dressed to kill.

Despite having a persona for the meeting, Dom felt strangely comfortable back in a suit. He wore a tie and wouldn't take off the jacket, even in the heat. He felt like himself again, as if the sharp lines of the suit gave him back his true form. He was not the Russian mobster who killed a man who presumably was a member of the same organization as the people at the base. He was a confident businessman, dressed to kill. At the back of Dom's mind was a hint of fear that despite the makeup he wore the day before, his facial scar could have been mentioned in some reports. Then again, who would expect a man to do something as insane as going into the hornets' nest right after slaying one of theirs?

He didn't hesitate and drove in with the most expensive car they could get their hands on—Ripper's wife's car for that matter—after a quick change of license plates. The area surrounded by the fence was vast, and due to its remote location, rarely visited by locals. From time to time, teenagers loomed around its perimeter, only to be arrested for attempted burglary, at least that was the intel the Coffin Nails managed to gather throughout the day.

People were saying that the place was the headquarters of a cult, or a training ground for security specialists. Some even believed it was yet another UFO research site, but what no one reported was that there were people kept here. Obviously all the staff consisted of outsiders with no ties to the local community, and even

when they got out of those walls, they never spoke about the place.

A man in a gray jumpsuit approached the car and waved for it to drive on, deeper into the fenced area. Streetlights produced an eerie glow over a row of elegant cars and a few SUVs, but they extended farther, shedding light over an asphalt road that disappeared between the trees, leading deeper into the private woods.

Domenico let out a low breath as he parked alongside the other cars. "Ready?" he asked, adjusting his tie. It always calmed him down to know he looked good. Because there was no way for him to take a gun inside, or even the knife he frequently wore strapped to his calf, Domenico had some fishing line in his pocket, in case he needed an inconspicuous weapon, but other than that, they were unarmed, not to let anyone read the serial numbers on their guns or otherwise examine them.

Seth gave a quick nod, with a completely focused expression. Dom usually preferred Seth to be playful, sexy, maybe even slightly tipsy, but in this situation, it calmed him down to see that Seth could take things seriously.

Domenico left the car and nodded at a handsome man in a shirt and slacks. He was in his early forties, with his hair already graying at his temples, but Domenico would do him anyway if the situation were any different.

"Mr. Adler? Mr. Abate?" asked the man with a nod of acknowledgement.

Domenico smiled and squeezed the man's hand first. "We almost lost our way, but at least we're here," he said with a barely-there Russian accent. Mr. Adler was half Austrian and spent most of his life in the United Kingdom. Domenico enjoyed making up all the personas he had up his sleeve. A lot of the ideas for personality traits and quirks came to him during sniper assignments, when he had to watch his targets for hours on end.

Seth played the part of a rude Italian, and instead of shaking the man's hand, he looked at his expensive watch first. "How long do you think the tour will take?" he asked, and Dom was positively surprised by the concise persona having an added gruffness to his voice. Since he knew Seth so well, it reminded him of Seth's voice when he was angry and sulking.

Their guide smiled and shook Seth's hand too. "It will take however long you'd like it to take, although I believe it won't be more than two hours, unless you have other wishes or want to have a drink in pleasant company. My name's Jackson. Follow me to the car, please," he said, leading the way to a black Range Rover.

Domenico looked at Seth to express his appreciation for his act, but didn't otherwise acknowledge his presence. They were associates, not friends.

Before they went inside, a man in a simple gray jumpsuit patted them down, but once inside the vehicle, they were offered drinks like any other business partner in the real world. Seth had some wine. They were on a business trip, but since this was part of their lifestyle, it would have been seen as suspicious if they both rejected the notion of "fun." Domenico entertained Jackson with small talk about the area as they drove deeper into the giant fenced base. They all knew what Mr. Adler and Mr. Abate were here for, and jumping to the topic would make them seem too eager, not used to the business. Domenico and Seth had had a lengthy conversation about the workings of such rings, and Domenico was sad that Seth got visibly upset with Dom for knowing so much about them.

The drive wasn't long, but they passed a few security gates, where Dom discreetly counted guards and watched for big guns.

Seth finished his wine, but instantly rejected a line of coke when Jackson offered. "Are you fucking kidding? I puke like a cat after this shit."

Domenico let out a laugh. "Damn right. He can't handle anything stronger than wine. Must be something in his blood."

Jackson smiled at them in the rearview mirror as he drove through a tunnel of trees.

Seth shrugged. "Besides, I don't know about you, Mr. Jackson, but I don't want to wake up next to some kind of butterface tomorrow."

Jackson chuckled. "That is quite right," he said as they drove into a clearing where they could see several block-like buildings on the background of the dark trees. Lights shone in some of the windows, and there was even a group of umbrellas open in an area with small tables.

"You have a bar here?" asked Domenico, surprised.

Jackson nodded. "Our associates need to let off some steam somewhere, and we'd rather keep them on the premises. Besides, it's always nicer for the guests who end up staying longer."

"Do you have good rooms? How much for the night?" Seth asked and leaned forward toward Jackson. His bulky body worked in his favor. No one needed to know Seth was a big teddy bear most of the time.

Jackson slowly parked in a row of identical cars and unbuckled his seat belt. "It's complimentary, if you'd like to stay. Are you not happy with your current accommodation?"

Domenico sighed. "We can't stay, as much as we'd like to. There's urgent business we have to attend in Jersey, and we need to catch the flight early in the morning."

Seth groaned, as if Dom was the boring one out of the two of them. "Can't win. Maybe next time."

"If we're happy with your services, that is," added Dom, and Jackson was quick to assure him that he probably

would find what he was looking for. They exited the car and walked down a tidy walkway framed by small LED lights, all the way to the biggest building, which had a modern front with large windows in the second floor.

The cheerful music coming from the bar made Domenico sick to his stomach, but he did an obligatory double take at a young woman serving cocktails completely naked.

Seth's dark gaze lingered as well, but Dom was pretty sure it was because he was assessing if the girl was here by choice and quickly coming to the conclusion that she wasn't when a red-faced man pulled her close and slid his fingers between her thighs. Seth's nostrils flared, but that was it. If someone was paying close attention to them, it could have been interpreted as interest or arousal.

They entered through smooth glass doors, which Dom could imagine were cleaned by sex slaves during their "time off," and entered a lobby with tasteful landscape pictures.

"It's quite late. Most guests come during the day," Jackson explained, as if not wanting Domenico and Seth to think there wasn't much demand for the product he was selling.

"That's understandable," said Domenico. "It was a last-minute decision to come here."

"We're looking for a girl with a few particular features, to gift to someone who made us very happy in business." Seth put his hands in his pockets. "So he feels appreciated."

Jackson nodded as he led them to the elevator. Why they had an elevator in a building with only two stories, Domenico had no idea, but he walked inside anyway. "You're not looking for anything yourself?"

Domenico looked at Seth and shrugged. "Depends on what you have. I could be tempted to come back if I see the right *arguments*."

Seth waved his hand dismissively. "I've got special taste when it comes to this kind of thing. I doubt you'd have what I want. But who knows." Every time Seth spoke, Domenico was more relieved. He could actually keep a *façade* when he wanted to, which meant it had to be a choice that he didn't usually act this way at home. Even when they argued, and he claimed he wanted to be left alone, he never manipulated Dom into truly believing that. Domenico was relieved to see that, and as strange as it was, it only made him appreciate Seth more. He didn't want to live with someone who wore a mask in front of him when all Dom wanted was the possibility to be sincere with that one person.

On the second floor, Jackson led them to an office with a wall lined with concrete blocks and a translucent bar that glowed dark purple. Jackson sat down behind a massive desk made of dark wood and indicated two chairs of luxurious leather for Domenico and Seth to sit in. The light was discreet and pleasant on the eye, and Domenico knew that their opponents were not only business-minded, but they also probably had clients with deep pockets.

Seth leaned his elbows on the desk and sat closer. "The girl we want to get should have a diastema. You know, a gap between her front teeth. Our business partner goes for these skinny chicks with thigh gaps. Like those anorexic models, but short. Blondes mostly. Young, but not girls anymore."

Jackson gestured to a collection of bottles on the coffee table in front of them, and Domenico got himself some juice, as it was in the only unopened container. One could never be cautious enough about drugs.

"What's the age range you want, approximately?" asked Jackson, typing something on the keyboard.

Domenico shrugged and purposefully gave a wider window. "Between fifteen and twenty-five, depending on her looks." He quieted down Seth's staged protest with a

gesture and went on, "Some girls just keep looking like they're barely legal, and it's not like he's gonna keep her around for a long time."

Jackson walked up to a shelf with identical leather-bound catalogs. He pulled one out, and when he did, Domenico noticed the one behind it had 'Losses' written on the front. Jackson sat back behind the desk and pushed the catalog their way. "See if anything catches your eye here. I'd recommend the pages marked blue."

Domenico discreetly scanned the room for cameras, but as far as he could see, there were none. No wonder, it was a business aimed at people who wouldn't want their privacy compromised in any way. That was the reason why their files were on paper, and they probably only kept digitized records written in code. It wasn't the first time Domenico had encountered this kind of practice, but it only confirmed his suspicions that this was a high-profile operation, possibly with more locations across the country.

He opened the folder, leaning toward Seth so that he too could look inside, and they were faced with rows of pictures, nine on every page, of blank faces and haunted eyes.

Seth pouted and leaned back in the chair. They had discussed that in a situation of this kind, it would be preferable if Seth got Dom a chance to be alone in an office with the computer, or whatever they actually encountered, but Dom's gut still clenched at the thought of separating in a place like this.

"Can we leave the bore here to look through all this and go see the real thing? I have an eye for this stuff, but you don't get the *vibe* of the girl in a photo."

Jackson looked between them, and Domenico made a show of rolling his eyes. "Be my guest. I'd rather take care of this myself."

Jackson switched off the computer and slowly got to his feet. "I don't want to leave Mr. Adler alone for too long, but I suppose I could show you the girls we keep on call tonight. They are the prime stock, but we haven't yet catalogued them properly."

That meant they were new additions to the stable, but that only worked to Domenico's advantage. He hoped the Losses catalogue would actually reveal something about Jo's fate, or he and Seth wouldn't be able to leave here in peace. As sorry as he was about what was going on in this place, his prime goal was to get Seth to safety. The bikers could deal with this shit once he showed them proof.

Seth patted Domenico's shoulder. "Yep, sounds like a job for me. It's tough, but someone's gotta do it."

"Have fun and don't get anyone pregnant or her owner will sue your ass," chuckled Domenico, even though he didn't find this joke even a bit funny. Jackson apparently did, and he hid his mouth behind his hand as he walked Seth out of the room. Each of their footsteps resonated down Domenico's back, and the moment the door closed, Domenico dropped the folder and went for the open cabinet, reaching for the catalogue he had spotted earlier.

He browsed through it quickly, with his heart drumming, but page after page, Jo was nowhere to be seen. From the name of the catalog, and the black Xs on each of the photos, he could safely assume these girls were dead, but he sneered even more when he passed the halfway mark and discovered the remaining pages were filled with photos of boys and young men. He cursed and wondered how he could access a full list. He was no computer specialist, so even knowing the codes written on every single photo, he wouldn't be able to hack into the database, which he was pretty sure was offline anyway, just in case. Domenico knew people who could do this for him, but there was no way he could reach out to them now, as they knew his true identity. It was a lost cause.

Each photo was a person, either dead, or shipped off, or hidden away against their will. What surprised him was the number of people who were at best average looking, but he supposed everyone had their taste, and they weren't to be reasoned with.

He made it through half of the catalogues containing women when there was a distinct noise outside, and his blood froze. He pushed the folder in its place and jumped back on the chair so rapidly he hit himself on the arm. But the pain was worth it when Jackson walked in without noticing anything. Dom congratulated Seth in his mind for making some noise as they approached, but most of all, he congratulated Seth for still being alive. As afraid as he was for Seth, it was high time to put some trust in him when needed. Dom might not ever let him become a free-range boyfriend, but he could let him graze freely once in a while, just to satisfy his instincts.

"Did you find one he'd like?" Seth asked with a grim expression. "All of the ones downstairs are too curvy."

Domenico sighed. "To be completely honest, none of these caught my eye. Do you have more? I didn't want to invite myself to look through anything else without your permission," Dom said, waving the folder in the air.

Jackson shook his head. "These are in the right age range and available now. This isn't Walmart," he grumbled.

Domenico exhaled. "Well, my associate told me you have *everything*."

"We could make sure you get the girl that suits your needs, but that takes time. If it can wait, just leave a description, and we will contact you on the same number when we find her," said Jackson.

Seth nodded but looked at Dom, waiting for his decision.

Domenico chewed on his lip, but eventually shook his head. "We need her sooner than a week from now, but I'd love to come back and maybe find a little something for

myself in the future. Should I contact you beforehand when I want to stay over?"

Jackson got up, though he didn't seem very pleased with how it went. "Yes, a day's notice will be enough."

Seth got up as well. "Hate leaving empty-handed."

"We will stay in touch," said Dom, squeezing Jackson' hand. "I might need a regular helping of girls for my own business, so I would be interested in talking about that another time."

That seemed to lift the clouds from Jackson's forehead, and he nodded. "We could definitely talk about this in the future."

They walked out and headed for the elevator, but a man in a suit stopped them and whispered something to Jackson.

"We will have to take the stairs. Excuse the inconvenience," Jackson said with a polite smile.

Domenico didn't comment on the ease with which pretty much everyone should be able to take one flight of stairs and followed, asking Jackson about his watch, just to leave more pleasant memories behind. They walked all the way to the end of the corridor and down a set of very average-looking stairs, only to emerge on the first floor.

Domenico tried hard not to be disappointed with the outcome of this experiment. True, he wouldn't call it finished before they exited the gates, as they could still be gunned down at this point, but there was no way for him to see more photos. He didn't even have any idea how far back the Losses folder went. Maybe it was created every three months, with the old one being moved into the archives or destroyed.

He wondered what his next course of action should be. The Coffin Nails wanted him to get proof of what had happened to their girl, and he had none. Getting away with Seth was out of the question, as none of them knew the area well enough, and if the whole club banded against

them nationwide, their life could become very difficult. And then there was Mark. As much as Domenico had tried to keep the kid away, he had still crawled under Dom's skin, and it didn't feel right to abandon him at Jed's mercy.

A female scream tore Dom right out of his calculating thoughts, and Seth turned his head as well. It came from a corridor leading downstairs, but then two men emerged, carrying a wooden box with holes into the elevator. They went back for another one and stacked it on top. The scream came again, and the box rattled slightly.

Jackson sighed. "Excuse the disruption, the other elevator keeps breaking down, and transports need to be made with this one instead."

Seth got a bit tense, and Dom worried that the horrors were making him crack. "They're girls right? You haven't showed me those."

Jackson frowned. "They're... damaged."

Domenico's stomach turned into ice. "What do you mean?"

Jackson shrugged. "You could say they're... returns, in a way."

Domenico quickly shot Seth a glance and grinned. "That's interesting. How do you utilize them? Can we see?"

Jackson pursed his lips. "Maybe. If you insist. They're really not much to look at. Though... One of them does have a gap in her teeth, but I doubt your client would want her. There's no way to clean up the mess." He turned around and headed for the open elevator.

Dom and Seth followed, and despite the neutral expression, Dom was happy Seth was naturally so tan, because he was turning slightly pale.

The workers, two bull-like men whom no one would want to meet after dark, gave Jackson an expectant look. He walked up to them and looked at the boxes, one of which was twitching as the girl thrashed inside. It was making even Domenico deeply uncomfortable to look at,

and yet the three men in front of him didn't seem moved in the slightest. "Which one has the girl with rabbit teeth?" asked Jackson.

One of the workers, a bald giant in a red shirt indicated a still box on the side. "She's in her calm phase today," he said, chewing on gum.

Jackson knelt next to it and pulled out a tiny flashlight. There was a movable flap on the upper part of the box, right over the tip of a red arrow drawn over a sign that read *This way up*. He opened it with a small latch and looked inside.

"That's her," he said, moving away and presenting the flashlight to Domenico and Seth.

Dom took it first, in case he needed to discourage Seth from looking. He crouched and shone the light inside, but the girl didn't even look his way.

She didn't need to. It was her. The girl they were looking for.

Dom was so shocked he just stared. Not because of the bruises on her collarbones and neck, her sorry state, her hair unevenly cut off to shoulder length, or the fact that one of her arms ended below her elbow on an ugly-looking stump. He was shocked that she was alive at all. In his experience, a girl lost wasn't easy to find after a month, not to mention after a few more than that. There had to be a reason why they didn't move her from here. Too risky with the Coffin Nails around, looking for her? Could taking her have been a mistake in the first place?

"Can you open it so I can see her teeth better?" Dom asked, and the goon in red groaned but reached for the hinges when Jackson nodded.

Domenico got up, hoping his face didn't color too much from the excitement and joy that they could possibly at least come out of this doing something good. He shot Seth a glance full of warning and then smiled. He prayed to

God for Seth not to lose composure now. "This one might be right up your alley, actually."

"Oh, yeah?" Seth came closer, and Dom raised the girl's chin up slightly as soon as the lid was off the box. She didn't react to the light or to the touch, staring blankly at the wall across the corridor.

Seth licked his lips and leaned down with his eyes wide.

"Her?" Jackson frowned. "Not very modelesque, if you ask me. She's short. Don't even get me started on the rest of her."

"No, no!" Seth said excitedly, and Dom was increasingly worried that the moment was getting the best of Seth. "This one won't be for him. She's for me. I'm into... stumps." He swallowed, watching the girl as if he was hypnotized.

Seth's choice of words was slightly odd, so Domenico let out a barking laugh and slapped him on the shoulder. "Nailed it. She looks like the bitches on those drawings you have in your office. Equally thin too."

Seth groaned and kicked him slightly, putting on a show. "Ah, shut up. She's perfect. I can never find one who has it *all*. Look at those ribs," he whispered, pushing Jo back, only to move his fingertips over her purplish side, feeling up every protruding bone.

Dom looked up at Jackson and didn't dare exhale deeply, but he could see it. Jackson was buying it and already calculating how much more he could charge for Seth's excitement.

"Can you... package her somehow? Make her seem like she's sleeping, in case she starts losing it on the way?" asked Domenico, knowing this would be a buyer's primary concern.

Seth kept staring at the girl without even blinking, but it worked with the act.

"Sure, absolutely. We will sedate her for you, but you have to take her yourself," Jackson said. "How will you be paying? She is very special, after all."

Domenico burst out laughing. "Why, you take credit cards?"

"We charge for *luxurious vacation package*," said Jackson calmly.

Seth shook his head and pulled out a wallet pre-packed with Coffin Nail money. "I'll just pay cash."

A giant weight fell from Domenico's shoulders as the gate closed behind them, and they drove off into the darkness. Now they could finally breathe freely, and Domenico pressed on the gas pedal, eager to be as far away from this fucked-up place as possible. Jo was asleep in the trunk, and he'd be much happier with himself once she was out of there. Or better yet, in the hands of the bikers. He still couldn't believe that they got her. She was alive. Damaged, yes, but she would eventually get better, or at least he decided to believe that as he sped down the straight road ahead, hoping no big animals chose to run into his way.

Seth wasn't very talkative and just sat there with a grim expression. A good ten minutes later, as they drove on an empty road between two sides of a forest, he spoke out all of a sudden.

"Stop the car, Dom."

Domenico squeezed his hands on the wheel. "What? Why?" he asked, even though he was already hitting the brakes.

"I just need some air. Can we stop, please?" He closed his eyes and put his hands over his face.

Domenico nodded and opened his own door as soon as they weren't moving anymore. He burst outside and quickly walked over to Seth's side. He opened it and offered him his hand, closing his eyes as the cool night air filled his nostrils with its fresh scent. It was a different world out here.

Seth pulled himself up and took a deep breath but then let go of Dom and walked a few steps away from the car. "Jesus Christ." His breaths were so intense they sounded a bit like wheezing.

Domenico rubbed his face and looked from between the fanned-out fingers at Seth's silhouette looming in the white light of the car. It didn't seem like he wanted touch now, but Domenico chose to speak at least. "You're a fucking hero. I couldn't have pulled this off alone," he said, and it was true. The fact that he had a crazy partner helped to rationalize the taking of a damaged girl when they came looking for one that was fresh. As much as Domenico was usually worried about Seth not thinking long enough about what he was about to do, it did seem that when put under pressure, he could step up his game.

"I can't believe we've got her," Seth uttered but then straightened up for a long, deep breath. "But all those other people in there... I was shitting myself." He looked at Dom, and it wasn't Mr. Abate in those eyes but Seth, with all his emotion and vulnerability.

Domenico rushed over to pull him into his arms. He quickly kissed Seth's cheek as they embraced. Oddly enough, with all the tension and a fear for Seth that he hadn't wanted to acknowledge while they were at the base, Dom needed the touch just as much as Seth. "I know. I know. The club will retaliate. They will deal with this."

Those words seemed to help Seth, because his body relaxed slightly into Dom's hug. He still took yet another deep gulp of air by Dom's ear. "I hope so. I hope all those

fuckers just fucking *die*." Seth squeezed the back of Dom's jacket.

Domenico nodded, swallowing a curse word. He held on to Seth, watching tiny particles of dust, or maybe something else altogether, slowly fall in the glow of the headlights. A whole minute passed until he was ready to let go.

"We need to tell them. Come on."

Seth swallowed and grabbed Dom's hand. A strange thought came to Domenico's mind when he trailed his thumb along the scar on Seth's palm. Thanks to it, he'd be able to recognize Seth in the dark just by holding hands. He pulled him to the car.

Chapter 22 - Seth

Seth was still elated with the success of their mission as they approached the club. Seeing the insides of that gateway to hell had his heart rattling and his stomach turning, but right now, his chest swelled with pride. He had pulled off his act and they'd gotten Jo out of there. She was alive, even if hurt. Her family would take care of her, and the biker club would deal with the trafficking, show those monsters that they should have never started their enterprise. A part of Seth knew things like that were going on. Everyone did, but seeing it in person, closer than he'd ever wished to, had him confronting a reality he never wanted to be a part of.

Even Domenico had been impressed with Seth's acting skills. Seth was on top of the world, with adrenaline still releasing into his bloodstream, almost an hour after they'd left the base. Dom looked so cool and collected in his new suit and didn't even loosen his tie. Seth loved Dom in all his many forms, but Dom had been wearing jeans for so long that seeing him in formal wear brought back all sorts of memories. How Dom had sneered at a Hawaiian shirt

even after memory loss, and how they had gone shopping at an Emporio Armani store and Dom had looked good enough to eat. Sadly, even the memory of Dom's look at the funeral of Seth's mother was impossible to forget. All black, sleek, and dangerous.

As they drove into the uneven path leading to the main asphalt road to the compound, in the faint light of the lamps outside, they could see a swarm of men, and the gates opened for them before they even got close to the fence. Domenico exhaled and finally stopped the car, walking out right away. He moved like a machine: elegant and efficient wherever he went, and Seth didn't want to fall behind. When he walked out, Domenico was already speaking to the crowd of bikers.

"They have a fucking catalogue of girls and boys, and they had us pick and choose."

Seth looked around and headed straight for the trunk. "It was just luck that we found Jo. They didn't want to show her to us. Said she was 'damaged goods.'"

Ryder pushed away two other men and touched the car in a jerky move. There was a big, bulging vein pulsing on his forehead as he approached Domenico. "You *found* Jo?"

Seth swallowed and wouldn't look into his eyes. "Yes, but be gentle. We don't know what her injuries could be. She's... sedated now. I bought her off them on the spot," he said and opened the trunk where the young woman lay under his jacket, which made her look even smaller than she was.

Ryder peeked right in and froze, squeezing his hands over the rim of the trunk. "Fucking fuck..."

Ripper, Axe, and the others joined right in, pushing Seth away with their sheer volume. His mind muted out most of the buzzing voices, but he still flinched when someone noticed Jo's stump.

"What the fuck? Who does this shit?" roared Wolver, walking off and casting a mean glance at Seth, as if he expected an actual answer.

Ryder wasn't paying attention to that though. "Brother, call Jess. She can assess if Jo needs to go to the hospital or not. We want to keep this under wraps if possible, so the fuckers don't know we're coming for them." His voice was raspy, and he looked like he wanted to reach in and pull Jo out but wasn't sure how to go about it.

Seth backed away by a few steps and crossed his arms on his chest. He felt so elated he could fly. He didn't even notice Domenico coming over until he touched Seth's shoulder. "It wouldn't have happened if it weren't for Seth."

Ryder stopped, staring at the ground under his feet, and then slowly raised his eyes, pinning Seth in place. His big chest was rising and falling, and by this point, he probably knew that they'd been here all this time and hadn't rescued her, while two strangers did it on their first try.

He nodded and rubbed his face, turning back to the car.

Seth looked at Dom with a new intensity filling his chest. No matter the failures Seth had caused or the messes he got himself into, Dom still praised him. He took a deep breath. "How about we give them a moment to deal with all this?" he asked and hooked a finger under Dom's belt.

Domenico let out a whiff of breath and glanced down at Seth's hand before slowly, very slowly, moving his gaze up Seth's chest. He sank his teeth into his bottom lip as their eyes met. "We should," he rasped in a way that had thousands of phantom ants crawling all over Seth's back.

Looking at the commotion around, and with another car arriving with a shriek of tires, Seth truly did feel like the hero. He pulled on Dom's belt, and every step he made toward the clubhouse was quicker, more intent, more filled with need to show Dom just what kind of guy

he was. That he still had it all together despite insecurities or the limp left after the bite. The wounds were still healing, but since no bones were broken, somehow he would eventually make a full recovery.

No one noticed that they left, with Dom following Seth for once, led on the leash of his belt loop, all the way through the lounge and toward one of the exits on the other side. Even through the fabric of his slacks, Dom's body streamed heat into Seth's fingers.

"You think you can just pull me around like that?" asked Domenico, and Seth's insides screamed in anguish when he pushed down the handle leading to the inner corridor and found the door locked. All of a sudden, having to go and ask for keys and then come back seemed like far too much hassle. He groaned but he wouldn't lose momentum to a fucking door. He looked at Dom over his shoulder and yanked him toward a restroom behind the kitchenette.

Power and purpose were flooding Seth's veins. "I'm the hero, right? I can do whatever the fuck I want." He licked his lips, already imagining Domenico with his hair loose and sticking to his face.

Dom's eyelashes fluttered as he stepped closer, tickling Seth with his sweet, warm breath. "You are the hero, so I guess all the spoils are yours."

That was all Seth needed to hear, and the words streamed arousal down his body. Fuck yes. Domenico would be his in a matter of seconds. His perfectly shaped, strong body would be Seth's, and he'd take everything Seth chose to give. Seth's body was awaking from a lethargic state that had lasted much too long, and he was feeling more alive with every step. He grabbed a massive container of cooking oil with his other hand as he kicked the restroom door open.

Domenico stepped inside first, leaning against the wall next to the toilet. His cheeks were flushed, as if

smeared by dark cherry juice, and his eyes drilled bright-colored holes in Seth's face. His breath was coming in sharp gasps, and in the confinement of the tiny stall that was too narrow to even fit a small trashcan next to the toilet bowl, there was nowhere he could run from Seth's insatiable lust.

Seth put the oil container down on the closed lid and locked the door behind them, trapping them in complete darkness, which seemed oddly fitting with Dom's black suit and his tar-colored hair. Seth found Domenico's mouth, uncaring about looking for the light switch or that he hit his head on the low ceiling when he rose to his toes. He instantly slid his hands under Domenico's suit jacket and pulled him close as their lips opened up to each other.

Dom hummed into Seth's mouth and slid his arms around his neck. He didn't even attempt to keep all of his own weight and just hung on Seth, moving against him like a stud in heat.

Being so aggressive in the kiss and showing Dom just how much Seth wanted to fuck him felt like getting back something he'd lost. In the past months, he'd always felt he wasn't good enough to attempt topping a hottie like Dom. That he'd make a fool of himself—that he wasn't fit enough to fuck the way he wanted to. All of that nonsense was gone from his mind now, erased, and to be hopefully quickly forgotten. He slid his hands to Dom's ass and couldn't wait to unbuckle Dom's belt, pull down his pants, and feel all that was underneath. Seth was the luckiest man alive to have someone like Dom, and no amount of hurdles on the way to getting here could change that.

Domenico arched into Seth, grabbing at him, as if there was nothing in the world he wanted more than Seth. He sucked on Seth's lips with a dedication that required no words. He needed Seth so badly he wanted to pull his soul out of him. "Fuck..."

"I know, I missed this too." Seth chuckled into Dom's lips. He wouldn't leave Domenico wanting for too

long. All those nights when he'd been lying next to him and considered just turning around, climbing on top, and fucking his ass seemed like an eternity. And every time Seth had ended up thinking he wasn't good enough. Or worse. At the beginning, when his ribs still hurt, he had such problems breathing that even getting aroused hurt. "There's not much time," Seth murmured. "But I'm still gonna fuck you senseless."

Dom bit down on Seth's lips, and the sudden pain miraculously transformed into a meaty wave of arousal that made Seth's cock even stiffer.

"Go on then," rasped Domenico, pushing the side of his nose against Seth's. "You're so fucking big you could just hold me down."

Seth knew Domenico probably had ways of dealing with a bigger guy if he needed to, but it didn't matter now. All he wanted was to feel Dom's muscular back against his own chest, slide his cock inside his fit body, and know he owned Dom's mind and soul. He gave Dom's nose a gentle nuzzle, but then spun him around in his arms, and pushed him flat against the wall.

Dom didn't resist and voiced his approval with a buzzing grunt. His ass nudged Seth's crotch and rubbed it up and down, making Seth want to just jump out of his slacks and take what was clearly his.

Seth found the band in Dom's hair and pulled it off, freeing his long hair so he could sniff it. Just the scent had his cock hardening even more. His whole body filled with power and confidence when he pushed against Dom, flattening him against the wall, and he sniffed Dom's hair while unbuckling his belt. The fuck would have to be quick, but Seth was sure he'd remember every minute.

Domenico cursed beneath his breath, and his hands met Seth's as they too pushed down his pants and briefs. He was almost wheezing, and the sound created a rhythmical music in the confines of the tiny restroom. Seth

gasped when Dom's hair smacked him across the face, bringing in the earthy, masculine scent that made Seth crazy.

"Do it."

Seth didn't need to be asked twice. Feeling Dom's naked ass against his crotch was heaven. He quickly leaned down to find the oil canister, and as he opened it, he turned his face and bit into Dom's asscheek.

Domenico groaned and rolled his ass against Seth's already stubbly face. Just the sound of their skin touching this way had Seth's cock twitching. So close to Dom's groin, his own distinct scent was even stronger, and it spurred Seth into action.

"Yeah? You think you can take it fast?" Seth whispered in the darkness and quickly got his own dick out. He loved being fucked by Dom, and he found bottoming such a pleasure he often daydreamed about it. More than he'd like to admit actually, but at times like this, something completely primal took over, and all he wanted was to claim his beloved partner in the most visceral way. He oiled up his own dick and got up, ready to push it in. He spread Dom's ass with his cock and groaned against his fragrant neck. With all the men Dom had fucked, Seth was one of the few who would get to top this magnificent beast of a man, and he loved the thought that he'd now be the only one to ever be allowed this.

Domenico stifled a moan and stiffened against Seth, but even as the muscles of his ass clenched against the invasion, driving Seth crazy, Domenico pushed back, forcing more of Seth's cock inside him. He writhed and trembled even as Seth's stomach docked to Dom's buttocks. Every shaky breath came with a harder squeeze around Seth's dick, but Dom voiced no protest, bracing himself against the wall. It'd been months since Seth got to do this, and they both wanted it like mad.

Seth put his hands on the wall, on the sides of Dom's torso, trapping him with his own body, and making slow circular movements with his hips. His thinking process was deteriorating by the second, as pure lust overcame his body. His cock throbbed in Dom's tight hot body, and he smirked as he began slowly pulling back.

Domenico arched his shoulders, and he climbed to his toes, still as tight as the first time Seth took him in a New York City church. He moved forward, as if trying to escape Seth's clutches, but Seth wouldn't have it and rammed his cock back in, pushing Dom flat against the wall. As his hands slid lower, his fingers found the light switch. *Bingo.*

With the room suddenly illuminated by ugly yellow light, Seth pulled his chest away to look down at his own cock buried deep in the most perfect of asses. He grabbed Dom by the hips and began a harsh rhythm of thrusts, each time milked by the tight sphincter.

Domenico's hair was everywhere, spilling down his shoulders and covering his face as he hunched by the wall, jerking off to the rhythm of thrusts. Still in the elegant jacket and shirt but with the slacks pooled around his ankles, Domenico was all but bending over to be screwed hard. Each time Seth slammed in, Dom's ass opened for him, and his buttocks shook in the most enticing way.

Seth only strengthened his grip on Dom's hips, arousal skyrocketing in his body at the sound of Dom rapidly moving his fist over his own dick. Seth let one of his hands travel to the front of Dom's body, and he grabbed the sleek black tie around his neck. He pulled it back over Dom's shoulder, and forced Dom to look back, only to kiss his trembling lips, and catch his shallow breaths. Seth intensified the pace of his thrusts, pushing his cock in and out at a rapid pace. He'd come any moment now, but with his brain scrambled, it was hard to decide where exactly he wanted to leave his spunk.

Domenico kept his eyes closed, but his face was the most magnificent sight. With his brows drawn together and mouth hanging open, he whimpered each time he breathed, pushing his hot skin against Seth. They were both so close now, and Domenico's face kept twitching each time Seth slammed home, but it was the touch of Dom's hair that made Seth go completely mad with the need to come.

Seth pulled out of Domenico's hole and turned him around, pushing him back against the wall. He grabbed his cock in his slippery hand and pulled Dom's shirt up with the other. He wanted to come on that amazing ripped stomach and see his spunk drizzle down the short dark hairs. But it was also Dom's dick that competed for attention. Thick and dark in Dom's hand, with the head pushing out from between tan fingers, as Dom jerked off.

Domenico's eyes were much darker than they usually were, and they shone with determination and love as he looked at Seth, playing with the head of his dick. He reached for Seth and pulled him into a rough, demanding kiss, as they stood even closer. Seth moaned when his dick touched Dom's. He let their cockheads rub together and moaned into the kiss.

He jerked off, making sure that their dicks touched, but it was the thought of Dom's ass, of his hole now well fucked, hot, and raw that pushed him over the edge. This would never get old. He made sure to keep Dom's shirt up as he came on his muscular stomach, biting on Dom's lip with a groan.

Domenico's eyes got a devilish glint that only became brighter seconds before those beautiful amber eyes closed, and Dom came, carelessly spraying cum all over Seth's clothes. He stumbled back against the wall and held on to Seth with one hand, catching his breath.

Seth smiled, not caring about stains just yet. All he was focused on was Dom's chest, and he reached out to smear his cum up all the way to Dom's pecs. He was still

panting as he watched the beautiful man before him, who was always more than willing to fuck at a second's notice.

A smile danced on Domenico's lips, and he opened his eyes again, looking down at the white streaks on his skin. "That was over quick," he said with a joyful undertone to his voice and put his hand over Seth's, moving it all over his chest.

"Sorry for being an overeager teenager about this, but we don't exactly have much time." Seth sighed and leaned down for a kiss as he rubbed his thumb against Dom's nipple.

"I know," said Dom, slowly pushing his shirt back over the drying seed. He kissed Seth's mouth, soft and loving like a well-fucked man should be. "But I fucking missed this."

Seth's smile widened, and he couldn't help the butterflies in his stomach. Being in love with Domenico never got old. "Me too. I kept watching you do those push-ups every day... And wanted to be on you, under you, all over."

Dom grinned and pulled Seth down with him as he picked up his pants, twisting Seth's neck into an uncomfortable angle. But that didn't make Seth break the kiss. "There will be plenty of that once we leave here."

Seth smiled into the kiss, and got some toilet paper for a quick cleanup before pulling his pants back up. "Oh, yeah? After all, I have many of your associates to meet."

Domenico purred and nipped on Seth's lips again before breaking away to sort himself out. Their bodies were still buzzing with excitement as they left the restroom and sneaked into the deserted lounge. Domenico's shoulders seemed so relaxed Seth knew he needed to provide this kind of service more often.

He tried to wash off the spunk with water, but just ended up with half of his shirt wet. Not that it mattered in the summer heat. He watched Dom's back as he led the way

and imagined his ass still feeling the afterglow of the rough fuck. And it was high time for them to be coming back, as Greaseball was already looking for them.

"What is it?" asked Domenico as they approached him outside. "Where is everyone?"

Grease scowled at Dom, still with a huge bruise that looked like a tentacled beast sliding from beneath the bandage. "In church."

Domenico frowned and looked back at Seth. "Why the fuck would they be there? What are they thinking? That her arm's gonna grow back if they pray hard enough?"

The guy frowned at him, as if Domenico was the stupidest person on the planet, whereas *he* knew it all. "It means they're in a meeting…"

Seth took a deep breath, still a bit lightheaded. "Where's the girl?"

"Her sister's taking care of her." Grease pointed at a distant part of the lounge, where a woman leaned over Jo and spoke something quietly.

She had dark hair that covered her face, and she was facing away from them, but even now, he could recognize the tattoo on her arm—a unicorn on a motorbike. Domenico scowled but turned around and went straight at Grease.

"We kept our end of the bargain. Where's Dana?"

"Here." Dana's voice crept out of the shadows behind the pool table so suddenly Seth cringed.

Jo's sister looked back finally, and her wet eyes widened when she recognized them. At least it was now clear how the Nails had found them in the hospital. It was Jess, the damn nurse who always seemed to make pretty eyes at Dom.

Domenico casually walked up to her, and only Seth was able to pick up the slight hesitation in his gait. "How is she?" he asked, not addressing the elephant in the room.

Jess rubbed her eyes and looked at her unresponsive sister, who was now dressed in a black band T-shirt that she could easily use as a dress. "I—she's in shock."

"But she must be well in general? Since you're not taking her to the hospital..." Seth asked and put his hands in his pockets.

"Y-yes. She has no broken bones, no cuts. Just... scars and bruises." The last words came out trembly, and Jess sank to her knees by the couch, squeezing her sister's limp hand.

"I'd run a battery of blood tests on her, if I were you," said Domenico, as if he weren't speaking to a medical professional.

Jess's eyes narrowed, but she didn't comment on that and hugged her sister. "I'll take care of her, but the guys need to move first."

Domenico shrugged, and a low groan escaped his lips. "I'm happy we got her. I was convinced we wouldn't."

Seth stroked Dom's back, enjoying the warmth of flesh underneath the fabric. "I'm happy it all worked out this way. We will probably be moving as early as tomorrow."

Jess hunched her shoulders. "Thank you," she said in a small voice. "She's the only family I have left around here. I'm... I'm sorry about Ryder. He can be pretty stubborn."

"No shit," said Dom.

"I can't believe she was so close, and we didn't know." Jess sniffed and gently ran her fingers over Jo's hair.

There was a roar of bikes outside, and moments later, a few more men in leather vests poured into the lounge.

Domenico shook his head. "Those people don't recruit locally, and they don't advertise within the state. Just take care of your sister, and leave the rest to your

men," said Domenico, and even Seth cringed at his way of thinking. Thank God Dom wasn't straight. He'd make some girl either crazy or miserable.

Jed blinked as he entered, his eyes settling on Domenico and Seth before moving to the women. The bikers stilled, poking each other as they stared at the miraculously found girl.

"Oh, fuck... Jo," muttered Jed, pushing past Dom and kneeling in front of her. The girl didn't even blink—her eyes as empty as a porcelain doll's.

Seth didn't want to imagine the horrors she must have been through. The door to another corridor opened, and more bikers came in, including Ryder, his father, Axe, and their club president.

"We're getting more Nails here from other states," Axe said with a frown. "This shit will not fly on our territory."

The newly arrived men roared their agreement, and Jo gave the tiniest flinch, but it seemed only her sister noticed and quickly pulled her to her feet. As strange as it was, Jo moved once expressively prompted, and they walked out, closing the door behind them.

Ryder followed them to the door with his gaze and shook his head, massaging his temples as the president spoke about the people he'd called over for support. It seemed like quite an impressive number, but with the way the traffickers were organized, it was hard to say whether the small army of Coffin Nails would be enough.

Jed walked up to his brother and put an arm around his shoulders, speaking softly.

"We need to be smart about this," said Ripper, looking at his men with a glare that promised blood. "As far as everyone outside this room's concerned, Jo's still missing. Don't talk about this to anyone. Not to your women, not to Jo's friends, not to random strangers who seem to be just passing by."

Domenico spoke up, "I'll sketch the plan of the base for you, at least what I saw of it."

All eyes turned toward him, even Ryder's, whose flushed face seemed forlorn as his gaze strayed to Seth, who just frowned at him in return, remembering all the hurtful words thrown his way. Seth was proud of Dom wanting to still help them some more, as he could be a spiteful bastard when he wanted to.

Ryder pulled away from his brother, and as Ripper finished his speech, he made his way to the fridge and pulled out three beers. Seth stood closer to Domenico when Ryder approached them with a grim expression.

Dom squinted. "What?"

Ryder showed his teeth, and it was clear that admitting his mistakes didn't come to him easily. "Thought you two wanted a cool beer after doing the job, but you don't have to if all you drink is some fancy-schmancy European wine!"

Seth finally looked into Ryder's eyes and dared a smile as he took the beer. "I could use one."

Jed walked up to them with a glass of brown drink in hand already. "I'm guessing you'll be leaving tomorrow?" He sounded so eager about it, Seth could imagine that Jed would even give them a ride to Mexico if it meant the video was to never surface. It was kind of sad, really.

Domenico nodded. "Yeah. We'll be out of your hair very soon," he promised, and Jed's shoulders all but sagged in relief.

Ryder took a few big gulps, as if interacting with Domenico and Seth cost him a lot of courage. "Hope it works out for you," he said eventually.

Jed looked up at his brother. "I told you they were all right," he grumbled.

Seth was pretty sure it wasn't what Jed was thinking, but a try at regaining Ryder's trust.

Ryder gave them both a sideways glance. "I suppose. For guys who fuck other guys."

To his credit, at least he didn't use the F-word. Seth couldn't help a silly grin. Never in a million years would he admit it to Dom, but in fact, he did find Ryder handsome. With his tats, short ponytail, and the stubble, his looks and good attitude had always provided entertainment during tedious gym sessions. Especially when he'd take his shirt off. It was nice to get some kind of conclusion to the weird way their acquaintance had developed.

"It's not like you can choose it," he said, looking at Dom. Being attracted to Domenico Acerbi had definitely not been a choice.

Ryder smirked and gulped down more beer as Jed's eyes grew even bigger. "Spare me that propaganda. You two do whatever you want, but I don't wanna see it, and neither does anyone else."

Jed nodded quickly and downed his drink.

Seth sighed, feeling sorry for him already. One day, this problem would blow up in Jed's face, and it wouldn't be a pretty sight when it happened, and his own brother cast him out. He raised his hands. "Okay, okay. Just saying. It's hard to think about rules and morals when you're horny."

Domenico chuckled, but Ryder didn't seem the least amused. "Jesus fuck! Don't put that in my brain. Not gonna happen."

Seth's smile widened, and he couldn't help but reach for the low-hanging fruit now that he was sure he wouldn't get punched in the face for it. "Of course, it won't. I have a boyfriend."

Ryder shoved him, but it wasn't menacing, so even Dom didn't feel the need to straight-shame him.

"Congratulations," said Ryder dryly and wet his lips with the beer again. It seemed he would be much more

content about being anywhere else, and so was poor Jed who avoided eye contact.

"I deserve it," said Dom, and Ryder walked off after waving his hand in resignation. Jed was quick to follow in his brother's footsteps.

Seth clinked his bottle with Dom's. "Let's find Mark?"

Domenico smiled and led the way to the staircase, which was already open again. He snickered when Grease asked about the oil in the restroom. They held hands as soon as they were out of sight and climbed all the way to the second floor. Domenico said nothing as they approached the door next to theirs and knocked. No one answered, so Seth knocked louder.

"That's how you do it," he whispered to Dom when the door opened.

Mark looked up at them with big eyes, and Domenico forced his way into the tiny room. "Are you okay? No one bothered you?" he asked, sitting on the bed.

"No, I'm fine." Mark waved his hand and backed up against the wall. "I even forced Jed to get me these." He pointed at a big pair of earphones on his neck.

Seth closed the door behind him and leaned against it.

Domenico caught his gaze before looking at Mark again. "Have you talked to Fred?"

Mark shrugged. "Yeah, told him it's gonna be a few days. Better tell me about your mission. How did it go?"

Domenico nodded at the earphones. "You need to stop using these. They'll damage your hearing. And you'd already know we found the girl if you listened to what was going on downstairs."

Mark's eyes went wide. "You found her? Oh, my God! That's amazing! I bet they're all licking your boots *now*."

Seth smiled and raised the bottle he had in his hand. "Ryder got me a beer."

"Yeah, he'd probably suck your cock too if you asked him long enough," said Dom and pulled Seth into his lap so hard the bed creaked under their combined weight.

Seth laughed and wrapped his arms around Dom's neck. "I wouldn't go that far. I just feel a bit sorry for Jed."

Mark rolled his eyes. "Seriously?"

Seth groaned and hugged Dom. "I mean, the guy seems lost." He gave Dom a kiss and grinned. "He just needs to find the right cock to suck."

Domenico shook his head. "Not gonna give him mine or yours, so he's got to fend for himself." He kissed the side of Seth's neck and cuddled his face up against it. Having regained that close physical bond they had shared before Vincente caught up with them was making Seth feel like he was walking on cotton candy.

"So we can move back to the swamp house?" Mark asked. "Since, you know, the police is looking for Dom..." He made a gesture of neck cutting.

Domenico stiffened, and all of a sudden, Seth's chest overflowed with fear that he'd want to get rid of Mark, and it would be Seth's fault. He had taken Mark into town.

"The fucker was about to say a name. I didn't know if he knew me or one of the other guys," Dom muttered, casting a heavy glance at Seth. He had to mean the fake personas. "I couldn't risk exposure."

Mark twirled his thumbs. "What name? You killed him for knowing a name?"

Domenico squinted and patted him on the ribs. "Names can kill. Some decisions just need to be made, and that man was no innocent either."

A silly smile surfaced on Mark's lips. "So you're not Domenico? Are you, like, Percival or something?"

Domenico exhaled and rubbed his eyeballs as if the question sucked the life out of him. "It is Domenico. You really think my fiancé would be calling me by a fake name?"

"I'm sorry," Mark mumbled. "I mean, I suppose he must have deserved it if you killed him..."

A small smile curved Domenico's lips, and he ruffled Mark's hair. "He did. He was a bad, bad man."

Seth licked his lips, embarrassed to hear that and eager to change the topic. "We won't be going back to the swamp house. I think it will be time for us to move on from here. Take you where we promised in the first place."

Domenico exhaled and gave a nod that made Seth sag with relief. "Yes, I think we will be safer out of the state."

Mark's smile faded, and he watched them with wide eyes. "Oh, okay. I suppose that makes sense."

Domenico looked at his nails, and it was one of the most un-Domenico-like things Seth had ever seen. "We can talk to him, if you'd like. You know, to make sure he's all right."

Seth stroked Dom's nape. He was pretty sure Dom had developed an attachment to the kid that he wouldn't admit to. Domenico treated outsiders like potential threats, so it was strange that Mark would have found a way to weasel into Dom's calculating heart.

Mark shrugged. "Nah. I mean... It's *Fred*. The worst he's gonna do is bore me to tears with some documentary series on sea life..."

"It's fine either way. I want to go early so that I can have a look at him," said Domenico.

Mark nodded, and Seth passed him his beer. "You should party tonight. Chill out before the big trip."

Mark squeezed it in his hand and nodded. "I think I'll just relax."

"It could be a long day tomorrow, so do that. And make sure to let Fred know you're coming," said Dom,

pulling out a cigarette. The flame danced in front of his face, but in the end, the cigarette burned red, and he took a drag of smoke.

Mark licked his lips, playing around with the bottle in his hands. "Would it be all right if I borrow the car first? I wanted to say good-bye to Raj."

Domenico fumbled with his pocket and threw Mark the keys. "Give back that beer."

Mark flashed him a stupid grin but passed the beer back to Seth. "Probably gonna try and sneak in some last-minute BJ or something."

Seth shook his head and got up from Dom's lap.

Domenico followed him to his feet and ruffled Mark's hair again. "Have fun."

Mark nodded without looking up, too focused on the keys. Seth wasn't truly happy about how things had developed with the boy, but they had saved him from Jed, stuck out their necks. There wasn't exactly much they could do anymore. They'd probably give him some money. Maybe a used car... but it wasn't as if they could keep in touch.

Domenico's hand squeezed around Seth's, and they walked out the door.

"See you later."

Chapter 23 - Mark

Mark took a deep breath and threw a little pebble at Raj's window, hoping to catch his attention, since he wasn't picking up calls. Knowing him, he was probably gaming and lost track of the reality around him. Mark didn't have that luxury. He was stuck, desperate, and so anxious he had a stomachache. Despite the night's chill, he was so hot he half suspected himself to be feverish. He'd hoped for at least a few more days with Seth and Domenico. At the back of his mind had been a glimmer of hope that maybe they'd feel sorry for him. Take him in. Maybe help him find a job? But he couldn't force himself on them when they clearly had problems of their own. There was a cash prize from the police for anyone who helped find the *diner killer*, but Mark wouldn't betray Domenico no matter what money was on offer. It wouldn't be fair after all that Dom and Seth had done for him.

Raj's home was a massive building in a row of similar two-story houses with nicely cut lawns and clean driveways. The only thing that differentiated it from the other buildings in the same street was a stone figure of

Ganesh in the garden, as Raj's family was Hindu. When he
drove Raj here once, he imagined what it would be like to
live here. He'd sat in the car and watched the light go on in
Raj's room, illuminating all the posters of games and TV
shows. Raj had already had a plate with some food in hand
as he waved to Mark and sent him a kiss in the air. It had
been Mark's cue to leave, even though all he'd wanted was
to stay in Raj's bed forever. He was so pretty with his blue
eyes, blond hair, and pale skin that Mark wanted to cover
with kisses. His mother and younger sister were so nice,
too. They had been making sweets together, and Mark got a
whole plate of them.

Yet another pebble bumped against the window,
and Mark hugged himself, standing beneath the tree by the
wall. In his mind, he saw himself climbing all the way to
Raj's room and sweeping him off his feet.

His breath caught when the window opened, and
Raj looked down, dressed in a pale shirt. "Who is that?" he
asked.

"Raj, it's me," Mark loud-whispered, looking up
with a smile. He loved how Raj's nipples would go hard
under his touch, and he could see them through the top Raj
was wearing.

Raj's soft, silent laugh tore through the air. "Wait.
I'm coming down," he said and disappeared from sight,
closing the window.

Mark grinned, even though his heart was in his
throat, and he rushed up to the door. Fred never excited
him half as much as Raj did, with his pink lips, long fingers,
big blue smiley eyes, and hot body.

He had only walked up to the door when it opened,
and he was immediately pulled inside, into a kiss of sweet,
warm lips. Raj pushed against Mark and his long fingers
slid to Mark's nape. "You're crazy. My parents are here."

Mark smiled into the kiss, slightly pushing Raj
against the kitchen wall. Maybe if he fucked Raj the way

Dom did Seth, Raj would also get 'addicted', and he'd let Mark stay with him. "I'll be very quiet. Can we go up?"

Raj bit his lip and nuzzled Mark's forehead as he silently locked the door. "Just... let's be quiet, okay?" he asked, pulling Mark up the staircase. Even the carpet beneath Mark's feet felt so soft and luxurious. It was unreal.

Mark put a finger against his lips with a smile and followed, devouring every family photo with his eyes. Raj had been, technically, an unwanted child, given away at birth. But what did that matter, when a family like this adopted him, and he was now their son? There were pictures from a trip to Mexico, from a birthday in Disneyland, and a photo of Raj with his dad in a car he got from his parents for his sixteenth birthday. It had Mark so jealous and upset that he stopped looking and focused on the pretty guy in front of him and on his ass in just a pair of white briefs.

Raj pulled him into his large room, complete with cool furniture that Mark would just love to own himself. Raj had everything Mark had never gotten from his parents, and as much as Mark didn't want to think it was unfair, he still felt that way.

Raj locked the door and turned to Mark with a wide grin, which showed that he had already forgotten the hot new game that was frozen on the television screen.

"If someone comes, I'll leave through the window, so don't worry." Mark put his hands on the sides of Raj's warm body, both enamored and horny just thinking of Raj's orgasm face, yet so anxious about what he wanted to talk about.

Raj grinned and pulled Mark close, resting his head atop Mark's. "No one will come in here as long as we're silent. They never come in without knocking."

Yet another thing Mark's dad had never respected. Not that Mark had a room in the first place. Back home, he used to sleep in the living room. He wrapped his arms

around Raj and kissed his shoulder. He needed to focus, stop thinking about Raj's perky ass. He couldn't decide if it was better to ask Raj now, when the tension was high, or after sex, with endorphins still coursing through their bodies. "Oh, fuck. You're so perfect."

Raj grinned and pulled Mark to the dresser. He opened a drawer and reached deep inside, eventually pulling out a pack of condoms. "You too..."

Mark bit his lip and couldn't help but slide his fingers to Raj's ass. He'd never rimmed anyone, but if there was someone he wanted to do that to, it was Raj. "Raj? You have a garage for three cars, right? But your family only has two."

Raj blinked, and the smile froze on his lips for a moment. "Er... yeah?"

Mark gave him a kiss, but the tension in his chest was already becoming too much. "If I, like... stayed there for a few days... Is that something you could talk your parents into? I know a guest room could be a bit much, and they don't really know me, but maybe if I could stay there first... I wouldn't be a burden."

Raj's arms fell from Mark's shoulders, and he stepped back with a slight frown. "Are you serious?" He blinked. "Oh, God, did your parents find out you're gay?"

Mark swallowed. Raj didn't need to know the whole story just yet. If he only got to know Mark better, he'd have the time to adjust to the details. He reached out to grab Raj's hand. "They kicked me out." He took a deep breath, but the desperate fluttering of his heart was making him want to throw up. "I mean, it's fine, whatever. I can take care of myself. I just need a place to stay for a while..." Mark stared into Raj's beautiful blue eyes, hoping he could hypnotize him into love.

Raj sucked in a breath and looked away. "You're underage. They can't just kick you out. This must be illegal..."

"I'm not going to the police about it. I don't want to end up in some homeless shelter or whatever. Your parents are good people. I'm sure they'd understand. You could just tell them I'm a friend. They'd never find out. And I could be so close to you..." Mark squeezed Raj's hand, but his heart broke when it slid out, and Raj took another step back. He was pale now, and the gaze he was giving Mark wasn't something he wanted from Raj at all. It was full of pity.

"I can't do that. I can't ask them to let you stay over. I'm not even sure it's legally allowed. And you don't even go to school."

Mark grabbed his own fingers and twirled them with growing nausea. He just needed a helping hand that wasn't from an adult who wanted to fuck him. Was that so much to ask? Didn't Raj want him around?

"Yeah, but I'd get a job. I wouldn't be in your hair all the time. And we could have sex, like, every day." He was disgusted with himself the moment he said it. Did he really have no other assets to offer? Sure, he wanted to fuck Raj every day, but not on these terms.

It was as if that last sentence stripped Mark of all sexiness in Raj's eyes, as he moved back and quickly picked up a pair of jogging bottoms that he hastily pulled on. "I mean... I really like you, but I don't know you, really. I don't know, maybe I could... help you find a motel?" he asked, looking up at Mark with an awkward smile.

Mark's world slowly crumbled around him, yet again in his life. Staying with Raj was the only thing he could think of other than ending up at Fred's. Mark wasn't stupid. Even if Fred was a nice guy, Mark couldn't evade him forever, and he'd have to fuck him eventually. He hugged himself, humiliated. It was worse than being peed on for money.

"No... I just thought that... I don't know. With the big house... You could spare some room for a week, or

something." Mark gulped a breath of air, but still felt as if he were drowning.

Raj wet his lips. "It's not my house. It's my parents', and I already told them I just met you, and that you're not from around here. There's just no way they would agree to this." He drew in a sharp breath. "Maybe... I have some savings, if you need money for a motel," said Raj, walking over to the dresser yet again.

Mark's face got hot, as if someone had burned it with hot coals. The shame of it all hurt just as bad. "No. I don't want your money," he uttered, forcing back tears. "I just wanted... something else." *Some fucking affection.* He quickly headed for the window. He wasn't staying here a minute longer. He'd been an idiot to come here in the first place. To this pretty boy in a pretty house, with a pretty family, and a lovely trimmed lawn. He should have known better than to put his grubby hands all over this piece of candy.

Raj went after him and looked out the window just as Mark slid down the slightly sloped roof, feeling fear choke the life out of him. He might as well break his legs falling to the ground. "Mark, please! Don't be angry!" Raj whispered in the darkness.

Jed had no idea what it felt like to be the loneliest man on the planet. At least he had family, good people who would catch him if he fell. All Mark had was a leap of faith. "I'm not angry." *I'm just so sad.*

"You sure you want to do this?" asked Raj when Mark got to his feet, shakily reaching toward the dark arms of the tree. He could only hope they were thick enough to hold his weight.

He looked over his shoulder at Raj's pretty face, partially obscured by shadows. "I hope you find someone nice soon."

Raj didn't answer and just hung his head, so shapely with the background of light, but it wasn't a picture

worth dying for, so Mark looked ahead and jumped. He lost his breath when one of his feet slipped, but the other landed steadily, and he regained balance by holding on to a different branch. They moved slightly but held him up just fine, and he could breathe again.

As he climbed down, he tried to be positive. At least he had one good accomplishment to his life now. Taking Raj's virginity. But as much as he tried, the forced thought didn't cheer him up. By the time he was heading for the car, which was parked down the street, he could barely breathe, and tears streaked down his face. His life was so worthless. If he disappeared tonight, no one would notice.

As he finally climbed into the cab, for almost half an hour, he was unable to move, staring ahead and thinking of just how much he overestimated his worth. He could see it now that to Raj he was just a hookup. Someone so pretty, so smart, so middle class, could have anyone. He didn't need to settle for a street kid like Mark. And he sure as hell wouldn't want Mark roaming in his picture-perfect home, no matter how well Mark fucked him.

It was easy for Dom to say that Mark shouldn't sell himself short when he had wads of cash lying around. Mark could fantasize all he wanted, but Fred was his best option now. He was trembling all over as he pulled out his phone and texted his old prince charming.

I made it early. Probably will be around tomorrow :)

The reply came within five minutes and was enthusiastic yet boring as always. *Fantastic! I can finally squeeze your hand in person. It's my day off so we will get to know each other better.*

Maybe Mark would be able to put sex off for a long time? Maybe Fred would be one of those guys who just wanted blow jobs? Even thinking about it made Mark gag, so he started the car, ready to get back to the Coffin Nails clubhouse and get drunk for free. At least he wouldn't be exactly taking money for sex anymore once he started

living with Fred. It would be more like... barter. His life sucked so hard.

When he arrived, the party was in full swing, complete with loud rock music and a couple fucking on the hood of a car in the shadows of the main building. Mark contemplated staying in the car, but in the end, the thought of a bed he didn't have to share with anyone and four walls that enclosed a space he could use as he wished, was too big of a temptation.

He grabbed a bottle of rum from the shelf, and no one even noticed him on his way through the lounge. He was just as invisible to these people as he was to the world. He took the first swig of alcohol as soon as he was in the corridor and headed up the stairs with his shoulders heavy. The liquor burned Mark's throat, but he didn't care. Maybe if he was completely hungover tomorrow, Dom and Seth would decide to stay one more day and take care of him.

"Hi," said a smooth feminine voice that he knew all too well.

When he looked up, Dana was standing in an open doorway opposite to his own room. It seemed she wasn't a hostage anymore.

"What's up?" she asked.

Mark looked up at her but wasn't able to force a smile. "I'm fine." He shrugged and opened his door.

"I heard they're taking you to your friend's place tomorrow."

Mark drank some more rum and leaned against the doorframe. "Why do you care?"

Dana shrugged. "Look, I know I haven't been the nicest person, but I need Domenico to train me, and you were taking away some of the attention I needed. It's not personal."

Mark took a deep breath. "Okay, I'm leaving tomorrow anyway, so whatever."

"That's what I wanted to ask about," said Dana, closing her door and walking over. "It is the other way. We'd have to do a loop to get you to your friend."

Mark looked up at her, slightly worried by her approach. He'd seen her wrestle Domenico, and it was pretty scary what she could do. In comparison to her, the training Dom gave Mark was play fighting.

"Oh. Um..." He wasn't sure what to say to that. "But they were the ones to offer."

Dana crossed her arms on her chest and bit the inside of her cheek, regarding him slowly. "Look, Domenico told me himself that he doesn't know what to do about you. He saved you, and now he feels responsible, but frankly, you are not his responsibility."

Mark froze, fighting the wave of emotion flooding his body. Raj didn't want him, and of course, Dom or Seth wouldn't either. He pushed everyone too hard. He was too needy.

Mark settled for another swig of rum.

Dana sighed, seemingly frustrated with his silence. "You could really just go there by bus."

"I don't have money for the bus." It was a lame excuse, because he could have easily gathered it from the pocket money Dom gave him. Money he got for nothing, for just being there. Sure, he tried to be useful, did all the chores asked of him, but it wasn't like being paid for particular jobs.

Dana frowned at him but only shook her head. "I guess the bottom line is, I'm not enjoying the company downstairs, so I could give you a lift. This way, Domenico and Seth wouldn't have to bother with getting you there. They feel sorry for you, and the guilt wouldn't let them just give you bus money."

Mark swallowed. Maybe this would be for the best? The last thing he wanted was to repay them for their kindness by being even more of a burden than he already

was. He'd just rip off this band-aid and get it over with. "How do I know you won't just dump me in the swamp?"

Dana scowled. "Don't be ridiculous."

"Let me just get my stuff." Mark went into his room. It was ridiculous how little he had. He stuffed the new earphones and MP3 player into his backpack, and that was that. After a moment of consideration, he drank one more gulp of rum for courage and left the bottle on the floor. He wrote a note on the back of the cardboard packaging from his earphones and left Dom and Seth two Snickers bars. A pathetic excuse for a gift, but he didn't have anything else. He supposed the biggest thank you was actually leaving and being out of their hair. The last thing they needed now were his good-byes, when they were probably fucking and whispering to each other in Italian about things Mark would never have anyone say to him.

He was feeling better about this decision by the minute as the alcoholic buzz grew louder in his brain. What had he been thinking to force Domenico and Seth to help him so much? He'd attached himself to them like a leech.

He and Dana sneaked out the back door, and he couldn't help but glance at the window of the room where Domenico and Seth stayed.

Dana wasn't particularly warm or charming, but at least she provided company and distraction on the forty-minute drive to Fred's house. Mark knew exactly how to get there from the local supermarket, and so they found the store first and then followed the instructions.

When they got to Fred's farmhouse, Mark wished he'd drunk more rum, but this was what his life would be now. Staying with Fred. As he got out, Dana actually smiled at him and told him that Dom and Seth would surely appreciate his go-getter attitude tomorrow.

When she drove away, Mark followed the dark path to the house with his heart in his throat. The nearest lights

were quite far away, behind the field, and so he couldn't even change his mind now that Dana was gone.

Hey, I'm here early :) he texted, but didn't really smile.

Chapter 24 - Domenico

Domenico was feeling fresh after the long fuck in the shower he shared with Seth. While the Mark-made shower in the swamps did have some advantages, it wasn't nearly as good as the real thing, and Domenico loved the feeling of being thoroughly clean again. And speaking of Mark, it was high time to find the boy. He and Seth were already packed into the van they bought off the bikers, but at 11:00 am, Mark needed to get up, whether he liked it or not.

Domenico knocked on his door, lost in thought. He wasn't happy about what they were about to do, but there was no other way. At least he'd make sure the guy wasn't some abusive creep.

Dana waved at Dom from the other end of the corridor. "Morning. Ready to hit the road? I am so done with this stinking place."

Domenico rolled his eyes. "The kid's still asleep," he said and pushed the door. It opened without any trouble, and Domenico walked in, ready to scold Mark about leaving himself open to drunken bikers. But all he found

were two chocolate bars on the bed with a note that read: *Thank you for everything. Mark.*

"Oh, he's gone," Dana said from the door, and Dom found it hard to process.

He stared at her as his heart rate rose. "What?"

Dana took a step back. "You were with Seth. I didn't want to bother you, but he was so eager to go yesterday..."

Domenico looked between Dana and the bars, feeling his blood boil. How dare the little fucker just leave without a word after all they'd done for him? He probably didn't want any more lectures and was pretty happy about bartering his ass for a place to sleep, even when he had options. Domenico would be ready to work out those options if Mark were willing enough. He didn't know what he could have done yet, but it didn't matter now anyway. So typical. You give someone a finger, and they take the whole hand.

He grabbed Dana by the hair and pressed her against the wall, breathing hard.

"Hey! Why me? I didn't do anything!" she groaned but didn't fight him off.

Domenico hissed and threw her on the bed. He shook his head, shocked by her attitude. "And you did nothing, you bitch."

"I just did what he asked me to!" Dana hissed at him. "I don't know why I'm the bad guy here!"

"No? Did I tell you to let him go? I'm still your mentor, and you defy me, because you wanted us to go straight for the border, isn't that right?" He growled, pulling both her hands back far enough for it to hurt. The twitching in her muscles actually brought some relief.

"I had the time, so I took him! I just wanted to be nice."

Dana. Nice. Dom could laugh if he weren't so annoyed. He let her go and snagged one of the Snickers

bars. "You know what? Make yourself useful and come back with that fucker Jed."

Dana groaned and rushed out of his reach, massaging her wrists. She gave him a glare and left without a word. He could swear that sometimes she acted as if she were in some kind of fucked up no-sex relationship with him.

Domenico opened the Snickers and sank his teeth into it as he picked up the note. The sense of betrayal was spreading through his body like poison. He couldn't believe both his trainees double-crossed him like that. Mark clearly didn't even want to stay, but there would be a price to pay for Dana.

She came back with Jed who had dark circles under his eyes, and his long blond hair was in a mess. If Dom hadn't known better, he'd venture that Jed had a drunk fuck with someone, but he supposed Jed just drank too much and slept on the floor.

"Get in and close the door," Dom said, leaning back and watching them both. They were so different—Dana cold and calculating, and sensitive Jed who was afraid to sext—they would make one another so miserable.

"What is it?" asked Jed, massaging his eyeballs.

"You need a beard," said Domenico.

Jed looked up at him with a frown and touched his chin. "Huh? Since when are you my fashion advisor as well?"

"Since my cousin's staying with you," hissed Domenico, shooting Dana a cold glance. She drew in a sharp breath and met Jed's panicked gaze halfway.

"You can't do this!"

Domenico raised his eyebrows. Just seeing them so unhappy was making his anger a bit more bearable. "No? And you want to train under me?"

"How is being his beard helping me with anything? Or even you for that matter?" Dana asked in frustration, and Jed slowly raised his hand.

"Shut up," said Domenico, swallowing the chocolate and pushing straight into the bubble of Jed's personal space. "Or we'll talk about that video again."

Jed exhaled and looked at his feet, letting his hand drop. Domenico squeezed his jaw tight and poked the biker's chest. "Your club is working with the Villanis. I want you to help Dana get intel about their deals. Understood?"

"Only about what doesn't hurt my club," Jed muttered, but he didn't pull out of Dom's grip. It felt like holding a mouse in a trap and watching it squirm.

Domenico snorted. "I don't care about your club. I want to know about my enemies. That's what I want, and the two of you will get it for me. Do you understand, or do I have to make myself even more clear?" he asked, looking between the two scowling faces.

Jed groaned. "Fine."

"How long am I supposed to stay here?" Dana asked and crossed her arms on her chest.

Domenico straightened and stared her down. "As long as I want you to. It might be shorter if you don't disappoint me again. Let's start with a month."

Dana shook her head slightly but didn't argue anymore, just looking Jed up and down, likely assessing his usefulness or lack of thereof.

A knock on the door had them all tensing, but when Seth looked in, Domenico's face brightened. Just seeing Seth could do the strangest things to him.

"Hey there. You ready to go?"

"I was gonna ask the same thing. Dana?" Seth smiled at her, but she barely managed to lift the corners of her lips in the worst fake smile attempt she'd ever given.

Domenico waved his hand. "She's staying. And they say hostage situations can't produce a match made in

heaven," said Domenico, grabbing the other Snickers bar from the bed. Even its sweetness couldn't dissolve the bitterness in his mouth.

Seth raised his eyebrows. "Oh. Okay..." was all he had. At least someone knew when not to ask too many questions. "Where's Mark then? I doubt *he* fell in love here."

Anger bubbled up in Domenico's chest again, and he pushed through Dana and Jed, walking out into the corridor. "No. He left for his new dick last night. Let's grab the bags and go."

Seth followed him. "I packed everything. It's not like we have much here. It would be best to stop by the swamp house and pick up our laundry. Dana? I'll leave your pants there, so pick them up yourself."

She pressed her lips together and looked away, and when that had her looking at Jed, she walked off to the only window. It was only fair to let her taste a bit of rejection. She would not give up on training with Domenico after being so clearly shown how much she had yet to learn.

Domenico smiled at Seth as he entered their room to pick up his bag, even though he didn't feel any joy. "We can do that."

Seth rubbed Dom's shoulder. "Do you want me to drive?"

Domenico exhaled, and some of the stiffness left his frame. "Sure," he muttered, holding Seth's gaze for a good few seconds before heading downstairs. They waved at Ripper, who sat in the lounge with a notebook and the map Domenico had drawn for him, but there were no tearful good-byes. Domenico really wanted to leave this whole episode behind him anyway.

Ryder was still sleeping on the sofa, and the whole lounge needed a good scrub, in Dom's opinion. Seth threw their bags into the back seat of the van and put on a pair of shades. He gave Dom a wide smile. "You wanna call Mark?"

Domenico's head exploded. "No. Fuck him. *He* didn't want to fucking say good-bye and just left us the chocolate he didn't want anymore. So fucking typical," growled Dom, slapping the dashboard. And to think that he'd been actually sorry for the little fucker.

Seth sighed and got into the car, but as Dom sat down as well, he couldn't let go of the topic. What kind of audacity did the kid have to do this to *Domenico Acerbi*? Just blow him off this way?

"Maybe he's bad at good-byes?" Seth suggested and started the car.

"That's not my problem, is it?" asked Domenico. He pulled a baseball cap out of the glove compartment and hid his hair underneath, just to be on the safe side. He was still technically a wanted man. Though *technically*, he'd been a wanted man for the last ten years.

"I know it's a bit shitty, but I suppose it's his choice at the end of the day. It's not like he stole our car or something."

Domenico closed his mouth, staring at the back of the van ahead of them. Seth was right, but the investment of time Domenico had put into Mark wasn't something to be just thanked for with a chocolate bar, as tasty as they were. He couldn't pinpoint why it bothered him so much if they wanted to leave the boy behind anyway, but each time he thought about it, it just pulled on the wrong strings in him. Mark had lost the money Domenico was thinking about leaving with him, just in case, and there would be no checking on Fred or good advice. *Suit yourself, Mark.*

"Whatever."

Seth drove down the well-known route to the swamp house. "He did leave a *thank you* note..."

"Wow. That's an achievement. He's gonna be sorry when it turns out Fred wants to piss on him," grumbled Domenico, remembering the night when he pushed Mark into understanding the error of his ways. He imagined it

had been quite cathartic for Mark, and that Dom had become a father figure of sorts for him, which was why the whole disappearance felt all the more like a slap in the face.

Seth groaned. "Jesus, Dom. You don't have to be crude. We saved him from Jed, gave him some quality time, and he decided that was it. He's a teenager, give him a break."

Domenico opened the window, really wanting some bird noises to fill his ears instead of Seth's self-righteous nagging. "When I was his age, I already killed men. I knew my place and my responsibilities."

Seth's knuckles went white as he gripped the wheel harder. "He's not you."

Domenico's mind stopped racing for a second, and for a few moments, it felt like *he* was the loneliest man in the world, not Jed. He put his hand on Seth's. "Nobody's like me."

"Don't you want to at least call him, so we can see if Fred isn't a cannibal lamp maker?" Seth turned into the forest road with a pout.

Domenico shrugged. "I told him we could. He said no, and then actually walked out on us. Clearly, that's not what he wants."

"And what would you have done if you found out about the guy being a creep, huh? Given him money to stay at a motel? He's sixteen, and not responsible like you were. Just the other day, he wanted to buy a pair of white sneakers, and we lived by the swamp."

Domenico gritted his teeth and hissed when the car shook on a bump. "I don't know. I didn't really think about it. He's probably fine," Dom said, even though thinking about an adult man coercing a teenager into sex appalled him no less than it did years ago, when he'd been the prey.

"It's not like he has a passport to stay with us for longer. And it wouldn't be safe for him anyway. No

stability. I don't even know where we will be in a month..."
Seth glanced Dom's way, then back to the road.

Domenico swallowed around the lump that
suddenly grew in his throat. "He's a good kid, but no one's
looking out for him."

"There's no way to leave him a contact to us, Dom.
It wouldn't be safe."

"I know. I know we can't really help him. Even if we
found him some kind of home, he'd still be alone after that.
He needs to fare on his own somehow," said Domenico as
he saw their damaged van on the side of the road. Seth only
managed to pass next to it after driving one wheel over the
wall of the gully. Dana could take care of it and claim the
vehicle as her own.

Once they got to the shack, Seth gave Dom a quick
kiss before leaving. Dom watched him pick up the laundry
and was happy to see Seth not limping all that badly. He
remembered how annoyed he'd been with Mark setting up
that laundry line. Back then, he told Mark that they
wouldn't be staying in the shack for long enough to use it,
but Mark insisted Seth would appreciate it. They had both
been right to some extent.

Domenico slid out of the car and slowly made his
way inside the little, shabby home. Mark had been all over
this place, cleaning the walls of spiders and dusting every
surface. It'd been fun to watch him so determined. When
Domenico pushed the curtain aside, a big cloud of dust flew
into his face, and he coughed, leaning down to gather his
things. There weren't that many, but he still took his time
packing them all and moving everything they could still use
to the back of the van.

Seth took their only pan, the gas stove, and any
non-perishable foods. Even the stupid knife set he'd bought
for cutting up an alligator. If Dom never saw another
alligator in his life, it would be too soon.

"I think we've got everything," Seth said half an hour later, lighting himself a cigarette next to the van.

"Yeah," said Domenico, looking at the shack with a hint of nostalgia. He hoped Dana had really buried the owner's body, as clearly she didn't always do what she was told when she thought she could get away with it. He let Seth light one for him too, and they took their time watching the place that had been their safe space for a few days. It still felt odd to leave. But leaving came with peace of mind, too. When he looked at Seth, feeling better, healthy, able to pull the stunt he did at the base, it made him feel that maybe the nightmares would be going away finally, leaving Dom to enjoy his lover without fear.

Five minutes later, they were on their way back to the asphalt road, with Domenico studying the map. They would go for the quickest way out of the state.

"So Dana's staying here? For how long?" Seth asked, and only now Dom noticed he had an alligator tooth pendant hanging down his chest.

He smiled and reached to the tooth. "Did you get that at the souvenir store?"

Seth hesitated with the answer, which only intrigued Dom more. "No, Mark made it for me. From the alligator you killed."

Domenico gently pulled on the tooth, squeezing it between his fingers. His heartbeat quickened. "He cut the thing up? Does he have one too?" Was this some kind of friendship necklace, or some shit like that? Though he did feel the thing suited Seth's rugged looks. Especially with the stubble back on Seth's face.

Seth snorted. "It was a thank you for saving him from the alligator. He had to fiddle around with its corpse, I suppose. No other way to pull out a tooth. I regretted that no one saved the body so that I could cook it, so at least there's this."

Domenico rubbed his eyes as they finally drove onto the asphalt road. "You do realize there's neither a fridge nor a freezer in that shack?"

"Spoilsport."

"That's me. Always spoiling everyone's fun," muttered Domenico. He opened the bag of sweets they'd retrieved from the house and helped himself to a toffee. Mark would have liked them.

Seth pushed him with his elbow. "Don't beat yourself up about it. Nobody's perfect."

"Maybe. I don't want to make any mistakes again." He pulled down the cap when a police car rushed past them, driving the other way. "I used to think there was always one correct solution, but that's not true." Whatever he'd have chosen today, it would have been a mistake in some way.

Seth took a deep breath and got more serious. "There are more ways to do something, but those ways require giving up on one or another principle. I've always found that... even when you do some things I don't agree with, there's integrity to them."

Domenico relaxed into the seat and looked at Seth, with a glimmer of hope flickering in his heart. "I didn't think you'd ever say that."

"I don't want you to get muddled up in thinking too much about 'what ifs.' I do enough of that for both of us. I like that you make a decision and stick to it."

Domenico smiled. It felt good to have this kind of support from someone he valued so much. From the one person who knew the real Domenico Acerbi, without any parts of him left in the dark. "I like that you understand."

Seth just smiled back, and they drove on in the most comfortable silence, commenting on some house from time to time, stopping for an alligator to pass the street and enjoying the sunshine. Despite his anger, Dom did hope that Mark was now somewhere safe, enjoying the

sun, and maybe even having a barbecue, as Fred was supposedly so fond of them.

The sound of Seth's guitar-based ringtone came as a surprise, but Domenico reached straight into Seth's front pocket anyway, taking his time to brush the cock tucked beneath the denim. His mind emptied when he saw Mark's name on the screen. Heat rose in Domenico's veins as it did in anticipation of a fight, and he put Mark on loudspeaker, already gnashing his teeth.

"Hey."

Seth raised his eyebrows. "Hey, Mark! We were just about to call you. How are you doing?"

The traitor spoke in a cheery voice. "Oh, it's great, fine. I wanted to call so you don't worry about me."

"Why would we worry?" asked Domenico, feeling his skin harden. "You were really eager to go."

"Um... yeah. I didn't want to bother you, and Dana offered the lift..."

Seth sighed. "So how's Fred? Is he okay? Is he the same guy from the photo and all that?"

"Yes, he's great. He's a lot like my dad, Seth. But in a sexy way, of course." Mark laughed.

Domenico scowled. As much as he hated Mark's behavior, he was somewhat relieved to hear the good news. "That's disgusting, but to each their own."

Seth groaned. "Um, okay. Anything else you want to tell us? Because I don't know when we will be within reach again."

"No, I gotta go. Just say thank you to Dana from me for the ride. The place was just forty minutes away, but I really appreciate it. Okay, bye!" Mark said quickly and disconnected.

Domenico took another toffee and put the phone in the basin-like space on the dashboard. "At least he had the decency to call."

All of a sudden, Seth pulled over on the side of the road. He took off his shades and looked at Dom. "Something's terribly wrong."

Domenico stared at him, surprised by the change of mood, but the serious expression on Seth's face made him stop himself from laughing. "What? Why?"

"Mark told me the other day that his parents weren't dead. That his father abused him, beat him, and forced him into prostitution. He's a drunk. In no way Mark saying that the guy is a lot like his dad is a good thing. I bet the bastard was listening, and he had to think of a way to tell us. He's in trouble, Dom." Seth ran his fingers through his hair, searching Dom's eyes for answers he didn't have.

Heat climbed up Domenico's neck, and he stared ahead, breathing hard as the new information sank in. Mark was asking them for help. "Fuck. Fuck. Fucking fuck!" he growled, smashing his hands against the dashboard. "I knew this was a fucking bad idea."

Seth slumped in the seat with a sneer. "It's still not that far away..."

Domenico leaned forward and hid his face in his hands. "Whatever we do, he'll still be stranded. He'll just find another Fred, and that's that," hissed Domenico as Mark's teary face in the woods came back to haunt him. And what about their own safety? Having an extra person around like Mark, a minor, could compromise their whole journey. Compromise Seth's safety.

"Couldn't we find a way to get him a fake passport somewhere?" Seth whispered.

"What?" Domenico peeked out from behind his fingers, hardly breathing. "We can't just take him. That's nuts..."

"You like him. He's got no one else in the world." Seth's words were sweet, but so naive it hurt to even hear them. They were to travel with a kid out of the country? And then what?

Domenico straightened his back and bit down on his hand. Of course, he liked Mark. That's why he got angry about him leaving in the first place. "You are the priority. I can't put you in danger. I promised," he whispered even as his stomach clenched with sadness.

"I'm sure you can think of something. Can't we leave him with Jed and Dana? Give him an allowance on a credit card? I don't know... There must be something we can do." Seth turned around and grabbed Dom's hand. "I'll be fine."

Domenico laughed, but there was no joy in it. Just like the girls at the base, Mark was a casualty of the life Domenico chose for himself and Seth. "Credit card? My resources aren't unlimited, you know. Let's go," he said, trying not to think about the boy he was leaving behind. Mark wouldn't be the first person Domenico had to forget about. There was a whole array of faces he needed to forget. Some blurry, some slightly more in focus. If he could kill his father for Seth, he could leave behind a boy he barely knew.

Seth grabbed Dom's face and forced Dom to look his way. "I'm not letting you do this. You would regret it for the rest of your life." His voice softened. "Wouldn't *you* have wanted someone to come for you when you were a kid? There was also a time when you didn't know any better and made stupid choices you paid for the hard way. If there had been someone who reached out, wouldn't that have changed *your* life?"

Domenico's heart drummed the rhythm of imminent execution as he sank into the depths of Seth's eyes and remembered the chocolate bar Tassa gave him when he was too thin for his clothes. No one saved him. Tassa only came for him when Domenico proved himself by getting away through the narrow tunnels, running from death like a rat. But Mark wasn't Domenico Acerbi. He couldn't save himself, and Dom knew that much.

He wanted to protest, but all that came out was a ragged breath, and he looked away. His heart was heavier by the second. How bad was Fred really if Mark decided to call them instead of just running away? What was going on there?

"Is he gonna die?"

Seth took a deep breath. "We don't know. If he had to lie about what's happening, it could be really bad. As far as this guy knows, Mark is alone, no one knows where he is, and no one will look for him. Mark made some bad choices, but his heart seems to be in the right place." Seth squeezed his hand over the tooth pendant.

Domenico bit his lip and slowly pressed his mouth to Seth's. A spark streamed down his body, and all of a sudden, his heart was quieting down, as if someone had drowned it in molasses. "Let's go."

"And then he can make his own choice about what to do next." Seth stroked Dom's hand, and it was hard to comprehend that this time he seemed to know Dom better than he did himself.

Domenico chuckled, feeling lighter than air. "Let's shoot the motherfucker," he said, looking into the glove compartment where he had stored his second handgun.

"Only if he deserves it," Seth added, but judging by his silly grin and the energy with which he turned the car around, he wasn't opposed to the idea.

"He does."

Chapter 25 - Seth

It was a pain in the ass to have to obey the speed limit, but the last thing Dom and Seth wanted right now was the police pulling them over. The heat around them was rising, and all Seth wanted was to leave the state, but they had to find Mark first and make sure he was safe. It was a risky move with all that they had on their plate, but it needed to be done. Seth could see in Domenico's eyes just how much the kid's fate affected him, even if Dom was the last person to play hero for no reason.

Greaseball met them at the gate, without the ever-present dressing on his head, but as soon as he realized who was coming, he quickly unblocked their way. Domenico checked his Beretta, put it back in the holster underneath his open shirt, and rushed out of the car as soon as Seth parked. It was good to see him move with such purpose—the same old Dom Seth met and fell in love with.

Seth would follow him like a lamb anywhere, so he was quick to go into the clubhouse right behind him. There was such a confidence in Dom's moves. All hesitation gone,

he knew exactly where he was going. Unfortunately, Dana didn't know she was the target just yet. She had her back turned to them and talked to Axe while sitting on the pool table.

Domenico grabbed her by the neck before the redheaded biker could even alert her of his arrival. She twisted her body, trying to kick and turn, but Domenico pulled her down, holding her limbs prisoner. It was fucking hot to see Domenico like this, and Seth was a little ashamed of thinking so.

"Where did you take Mark?" hissed Dom to the soundtrack of a few men getting to their feet.

Dana struggled in his grip and looked back, her eyes wide. "What are you doing here?"

Domenico must have done something hurtful, as she moaned and fell to the floor, but she stopped playing nice. In the most surreal moment ever, Dana opened her mouth and bit into Dom's leg like a young shark.

"Fuck me! She's feisty!" laughed a biker who didn't even bother getting off the couch.

"What the hell is this about?" Jed yelled, approaching the fight, but Axe moved first. His bull-like body charged at Domenico, only to be sent on its way down with a billiard cue that broke in two once it connected with his back. Domenico used one of the halves to strike Dana in the ribs.

She cried out, letting go of his leg, and she was on her back with Dom's foot pressing on her throat, without Seth being able to follow how exactly that had happened.

He gasped, but his awe didn't last long when he saw Axe approaching again, with his expression wild with fury. Seth ran up to him and pushed him on the pool table with all he had. He didn't quite expect the skull-jingling punch to the side of his head and fell to the floor, rolling over as the world around him made a turn.

Domenico looked at him, wide-eyed, and moved toward Axe, but Ryder grew between the two men like a solid wall. "The fuck is this about?"

Domenico ground his teeth so hard the sound had Seth squirming. "He punched my man!"

"And you punched my woman!" hissed Jed, picking up Dana at the periphery of Seth's vision.

Seth got up, holding the side of his head. "I'm fine. You're also *fine,* Dana, aren't you?"

She slowly got up as Dom let her go, but she couldn't help a snarl. "*Fine.*"

Ryder looked between them with a deep frown before settling his eyes on Jed. "Since when? You haven't told me!"

Dana pouted. "Today."

"Looks like we're family now," grumbled Domenico.

"Dana, where did you take Mark?" Seth asked, making sure no one was preparing to strike him.

"I can take you there if you're so desperate. I don't remember the address." Dana crossed her arms on her chest and stood next to Jed. Like she needed his protection. Ridiculous.

Axe's face twisted when he moved, but it seemed it was a matter of pride not to show just how badly Dom got him. "Stop beating up women on my turf."

Domenico frowned at him. "She's not a woman. She's my cousin. And we've been doing that since childhood. Isn't that right, Dana?"

She nodded. "Rough upbringing."

Seth ran his fingers through his hair. "Let's go. You'll show us where you took him."

Axe sneered. "Oh, so you can take her and beat her up elsewhere? She's not going anywhere. Right, Jed?"

Jed licked his lips, as all eyes were on him all of a sudden. It was sad to see him squirm. "I... Yeah. I'm going wherever she's going."

Seth raised his eyebrows. That was a good answer. Diplomatic.

"Fine," said Dom, looking straight at Ryder. "You can go if you want to watch me work my magic on someone who's hurting little boys." He nodded at Dana, and everyone's eyes turned to her in a sudden silence. Nothing enraged masculine straight men more than men molesting boys. "She took Mark to this shady guy behind my back."

"He asked me to!" cried Dana.

"He's a kid," Seth groaned. "He doesn't know any better. You should have asked."

Jed looked at the pool table, to the window, anywhere but at Domenico.

Axe frowned. "How do you know something's up with the guy?"

Domenico shrugged. "Mark called us to tell us that the fucker is just like his dad. And his dad beat him up and starved him. I'm gonna break this motherfucker's neck, and if you want to help me, be my guests. You might as well join in on the party."

"Do you know if it's just him there?" Jed asked Dana, and she shrugged.

"The house was big."

"He wouldn't keep a boy there if he has family," muttered Dom. "Let's just go."

Axe raised his hands. "I'm sure you can do just fine by yourself if it's just one guy."

Dom glared at him and pulled Dana by the arm. Seth followed with Jed, but Ryder was quick to catch up with them as well.

"Maybe you should stay?" Jed asked his brother.

Ryder sighed. "No, I'll come with you. Might as well offer my help in return."

Seth held back a grin. Now that was some appreciation.

Domenico looked back at him and gave a slow nod. "This kind of scum you don't want to have around anyway."

Domenico frowned at how normal the house was in the orange light of the slowly setting sun. It was almost five o'clock when they arrived, and it appeared that the guy was home, as the car was in the open garage. The place had a large barbecue in the back, but it also probably had an underground cell Fred kept his victims in.

They were all waiting for the door to open as Dana approached the house across a perfectly manicured lawn. There was no reason to overcomplicate things by lockpicking or forced entry. Dom assumed that the easiest way to put Fred's vigilance to sleep was to have a woman knock at his door. With her pretty face and girl-next-door look, Dana didn't seem threatening, even if she was actually deadlier than a cobra.

A minute after she rang the doorbell, a dark-haired man emerged from behind the door. Before he could say a word, Dana punched his face so hard they could hear the crackle all the way in the bushes. She threw all her weight at him, darting forward with her head low. As soon as her shoulder hit Fred's chest, they disappeared from sight, falling to the floor inside the house.

Ryder frowned. "I didn't expect *that*."

"As I told you, we've been at it since kindergarten," Domenico said with a small smirk. "Let's go."

They made their way to the back door, pulling on gloves on the way. And sure enough, it unlocked upon their approach. Dana was making progress, even if she wasn't anywhere near perfect yet. Then again, not everyone had the opportunity to be trained by Luigi Tassa himself.

Dana's blue eyes moved over their all-male group, as if she were assessing whether she should invite them inside, but in the end, she stepped back, letting them into a kitchen with surfaces so ridiculously clean that the room looked like a show house.

Fred was on the floor, gagged and with his hands cuffed behind his back.

"I'll go check if there's anyone else," Jed said and was quick to rush down the corridor with a gun in hand.

Seth started looking around. "Maybe I can find Mark's backpack or something like that."

Domenico groaned, searching for any clues about the kid's whereabouts, but found nothing at first glance. No piles of chocolate bars, and no curly brown hair in sight. There was something extremely odd about the house though. It was picture perfect, with white walls and bright wooden floors, but the lack of personality was hitting Dom in the face.

Ryder seemed to share his thoughts. "Did this fucker just move in, or something?"

Fred stirred on the floor, apparently coming back from his trip courtesy of Dana's fist, and Domenico rushed over, grabbing the thick chain between the cuffs.

"Hi, Freddie," he said, forcing him into a sitting position by yanking the pulled-back arms. It spurred a muffled cry.

"No one else in the house," Jed informed, as he came back, thumping his boots against the wooden floor. "I'll go look outside and see if there's any barn of horror or anything like that."

Ryder walked out with his brother, leaving Dana, Domenico, and Seth alone with the damn barbecue guy. For a terrible few seconds, Domenico wondered whether he wasn't one of those people who fantasized about roasting their lovers alive and then eating their flesh and crisp skin.

Fred looked up at Dom with a frown. As if he had any leverage here. It pissed Domenico off so much that he pulled on the bastard's arms again, dragging him toward what looked like the living room.

Fred screamed, trying to change position and pull his arms back, desperate to keep his joints from breaking apart, but physics was not merciful to him.

"The boy that got here last night, Freddie."

Seth followed, and Dana was kind enough to take the makeshift fabric gag out of Fred's mouth, wiping away some blood that streamed from his nostril.

"I don't know what you're talking about," he started babbling, his eyes bobbing to the sides, looking for ways out, for weapons he could make use of. "No one was here."

Domenico smirked. "Come on. He showed me your picture."

A glint of fear trembled in Fred's eyes, the same ones that smiled in the picture from above a succulent rack of ribs.

"I think you should think again," said Domenico, glancing at the empty walls. Even the furniture was extremely generic, and a strange idea was slowly curling in his mind. "It's not your house, is it?"

Fred hesitated. "I moved in just lately…" The way he said it was much too calm for a civilian who just got his face punched and his house invaded. As if it wasn't the first time something like this happened. As if Fred believed he would eventually free himself.

Domenico understood that very well. Whenever he got in trouble, that was the mindset that got him to make the best of the situation and win the game. As normal as Fred looked, he was a damn psycho, no doubt about that.

Domenico slowly kneeled down, preparing to fend off any attack, even if it turned out Freddie had lasers in his eyes. If the man couldn't get rid of Dana, he was not a

worthy opponent for Dom. Then again, Dana had the advantage of surprise.

"Where is he? I know he came here. She brought him over," Dom said, swaying his head toward Dana.

She nodded, crouching next to Dom. "I saw him walk down the driveway and stand at your door."

Fred swallowed. "I didn't want anyone to know about him. But he never came. I swear. He texted that he would be here early and never arrived. He must have gotten cold feet."

Domenico cast a glance at Dana, and she shook her head.

"He's lying."

Domenico shrugged and peeked into Fred's eyes, already feeling the pleasant buzz spreading underneath his skin. His gaze trailed up Fred's forehead, and the slight sheen of perspiration was unmistakable there. Dom could flay Fred bit by bit, were he to stubbornly refuse them information. "I believe her."

Fred took a deep breath and shook his head violently. "What the hell can she know about this? The boy's been messing with his arrival date for weeks. I don't know what happened to him. I mean, I'm terribly sorry if he got into trouble yesterday. I would love to help find him."

Domenico raised the fabric above his ankle and pulled out his small knife, making sure the blade caught the light. "Are you keeping the boys somewhere else, Fred?"

That was when Fred shut up with his bullshit. His eyes widened, and even his breath became a bit shallow. "I don't know what you're talking about. I had good intentions..." His voice became ragged and turned into a choked wail when Dom pushed the blade into the bare flesh of Fred's thigh, right where his shorts ended.

"Come on, Freddie. Try harder."

To Dom's surprise, Seth put down his gun and sat next to Fred. The sunlight coming through the window played with his black hair so beautifully, Dom was falling in love with him all over again. "This doesn't have to continue. Just take us to Mark, and we'll leave you alone. We don't want any trouble either."

Fred swallowed hard, staring at the metal handle sticking out of his flesh, shaking slightly as tremors ran through his body. "I…"

Domenico moved the knife inside, mindful of not cutting an artery. It was all just to shock and hurt. As much as Fred deserved to die, they couldn't have that happen yet.

"You?" he asked calmly. He loved the sensation of peace that overcame him at times like these. It would have been even better if he strapped Fred to something that would prevent him from moving, but this was not about Dom's satisfaction. The goal was to break Fred's morale and make him realize Domenico wasn't just a guy trying to find a lost friend. Dom meant business, and he would work on Fred as long as it took, and at this point, it seemed like he was slowly getting his point across.

Fred cried out, stiffening as he fought for each breath, wheezing with fear. "I did meet him," he uttered. "He didn't like me in person, so I drove him to town." Great. That was even more bullshit.

Seth shook his head. "I can promise you he won't kill you, but you need to be more honest with us than that."

Domenico bit his lip, looking at his lover with a warmth spreading throughout his chest. Months before, Seth would have never participated in a stunt like this, but clearly, his skin was slowly hardening. "Did you eat him, Freddie?" asked Domenico. He didn't really believe that was the case. No one waited so long for a beautiful boy only to dispose of him within the first day, but at the same time, just saying that out loud made Dom's stomach queasy.

"No! I'm nothing like that! I just wanted some company!" Fred cried out when the blade cut a little farther. Seth's 'good cop' act must have been working, because Fred turned to face him. "Please make him stop. I won't report this, I just want to live."

Domenico snorted and pulled out the knife, making blood slowly spill out of the cut. "I still have many techniques up my sleeve, Freddie," he said and pushed the knife under Fred's shirt, ripping it on him for easier access to flesh they could all see. "Where is Mark?"

"I don't know. Please don't do this. I would never want anything bad to happen to him," Fred whined, all red-faced, with a tear spilling down his cheek.

"We don't either. So we need to find him," Seth said, leaning a bit closer. "I'd love to just leave this house now, but this won't end until you tell us the truth."

Dom frowned as he noticed a few fresh scratches on Fred's shoulder, and a bruise on his arm. His blood boiled over, and he punched Fred right in the stomach. "Was that him, you fucker?" He grabbed Fred by the throat and hit his head against the floor. Not hard enough to knock him out, but certainly enough to rattle his brain and confuse him.

"Please, I can't..." Bloodied saliva dripped to the floor from Fred's mouth. Now they were getting somewhere.

"You can't?" Domenico gestured at Dana, and she dropped to her knees, helping him hold Fred down. "I tell you what you can't," Dom said, making a shallow stab into Fred's pec. "You can't fucking afford to lie."

The flesh stretched around the knife, and Fred gave a breathless cry, watching his skin move, as if there were a parasite underneath. He was lost between squealing and trying not to move at all.

"They'll kill me if I say. I was blackmailed into this."

If only Domenico got a dollar for every time he'd heard that...

"And if you *don't* tell me, I'll kill you. And believe me, Freddie, you don't want that," said Domenico, slightly more at ease now that he knew Mark was alive. He moved the knife gently below the surface of the skin, parting it from flesh, as if he were preparing meat for cooking. He didn't usually enjoy this, but this time, he was fucking ecstatic that he could make that piece of shit pay for what he'd done. Just like when he had tortured Vincente, this felt righteous and godly.

"Stop, please, stop, I'll tell you, just promise not to kill me," Fred cried, wheezing in Dana's grip and blinking back fat tears. Domenico watched him. Fred's eyes were glazing over, his skin shone with sweat, and the faint smell of urine teasing Dom's nostrils were all quite convincing. Fred couldn't take much more without fainting, and that would not help them find Mark.

Seth touched Fred's arm gently. "It will be fine as long as you tell us what happened."

"Just get on with it," hissed Dana, immobile like a statue. In the back, Dom could hear the door opening as Jed and Ryder entered the house again.

"Talk, Freddie, or I'll flay you. I'll wake you up every time you're gone and continue until I'm even done with the skin between your toes."

Fred wasn't wearing shoes or socks, so Dom could clearly see him curling his toes. Good.

"Jesus, fuck..." Jed hissed and covered his mouth, but to his credit, he didn't turn away.

"I sold him off. I know it's wrong. I know, I know," Fred whined. "I was so in debt, I had medical bills to pay, I didn't know what to do."

At this point, he'd probably say his whole family had cancer just to gain more sympathy.

Domenico smiled and cut a bit farther into the twitching body Dana held down. A dark patch grew on Fred's shorts as his bladder gave up, but Dom could take that. "I don't care. Where is he?"

"He's in this former military base, an hour away. It doesn't have an address. I can show you on the map, just please keep me out of it." Fred had to stop to breathe a few times, but when he finished talking, the atmosphere in the room became thicker than his blood.

Seth and Ryder looked at each other, but everyone knew what base Fred was talking about.

Domenico could swear his heart stopped for a few seconds. "The one in the woods?" he uttered, stiff and cold in the joints.

"Yes... the one where they have a cult... that's what they made everyone here believe..." Fred closed his eyes, but it wouldn't help with his pain.

Domenico slowly moved his knife out and looked at the red-stained blade. He couldn't believe this. "Dana, patch this fucker up," he said and sat back on his heels. Only now could he breathe deep.

Seth looked up at him with a frown. "What do we do?" he whispered.

Domenico shook his head and quickly walked to the sink to clean himself up. His eyes trailed to the grim faces of the brothers, to Seth, to the emotionless Dana. "We need to go in."

Ryder scowled. "We're not ready for this yet. Not everyone has arrived."

"And we can't go in there undercover again looking for a boy who just got snatched. It would be too suspicious," Seth said, inching away from a trail of blood heading his way on the floor.

Domenico shook water off the knife and then wiped the remaining wetness on his pants. His mind was racing at accelerated speed. Perverted fucks were cutting people's

arms off at that base. This couldn't just wait. "Freddie will help us," he said in the end, casting a glance at the wet, deathly pale face.

"Please, it was a mistake. I don't want anything to do with this anymore..." His eyes were wide with fear, but he wouldn't be getting off the hook so easily.

"Freddie? Are you familiar with the Sacrament of Penance and Reconciliation?" asked Domenico, putting the knife back into its sheath at his calf. "You confessed your sins, but you need to atone for them now."

Ryder hissed and pulled out his phone. "I'll talk to Ripper," he said, walking off to another room. At least someone was willing to move their ass.

Fred whined as Dana started patching him up without much gentleness. "I will help, but you have to promise not to kill me. I will make up for this, I swear."

Seth got up without a hint of expression to his face, and Domenico called him over with a gesture. "Only if you help. I will not hurt you after that," he said, not even caring whether he was lying or not. This rat was not worthy of Domenico Acerbi's word. There needed to be mutual respect for that, and the fucker kept lying through his teeth. Unlike Domenico, he was not a man of honor.

Seth walked up to Dom and put his head on his shoulder in silence.

"I'll help," Fred whispered and sobbed when Dana pushed a bandage against his skin.

Domenico turned his eyes away, not even willing to look at the sick fuck. How low could a man fall?

His eyes met Jed's as he hugged Seth tighter, absorbing his warmth. There was nothing more relaxing than holding Seth close.

Jed wrapped his arms around himself and looked away. "I'll help as well, of course..."

"You will?" asked Domenico slowly, not so sure about Jed's assertion after all the blackmail that he definitely deserved.

"It's not like I have much choice, do I?" Jed groaned. "But I don't want the guy raped and maimed by some sickos either."

Domenico's lips twitched despite the horror of the truth behind Jed's words. "That's penance and reconciliation right there. I'm proud of you," he said, feeling like a paternal figure to the lost gay man.

Jed rolled his eyes. "Jesus Christ. You don't have to make it weird."

Dom could feel Seth's smile against his cheek, and he got a tighter hug.

"He's always doing that. Get used to it," said Dana, who'd apparently listened despite seemingly being completely absorbed in her task.

"See? At least your woman's smart," said Dom with a wide grin.

Ryder walked back into the room. "Ripper's given it a green light. We're to come over to the club. More men are arriving in the next hours, and we can speed up the process." He walked over to Fred and kicked his ass. "It's showtime, motherfucker."

Domenico couldn't have said it better.

Chapter 26 - Domenico

Cold air rushed the scent of gunpowder, blood, and crushed bones straight into Domenico's face as he looked out of the helicopter, into the darkness lit up by outbreaks of bright orange and red among the trees. Even through the noise of the rotor above, he could hear the continuous gunfire, but a sudden burst from a bazooka made him laugh loudly. It had been a while since he'd seen something like this. Having mostly worked in undercover missions, he wasn't that familiar with full frontal assault, but after the fence of the base exploded on both sides of the vast enclosure and the Coffin Nails swarmed inside the base, it was a sight to behold from above. The club members carried all the heavy weaponry they could gather from the neighboring chapters and associated gangs and were making their way into the base like medieval cavalry after storming the walls of a castle. The fact that so many of them were on motorcycles only added to that impression as the bright lights moved through the darkness below.

At some point, Domenico did a double take, spotting the tank making its way across the rushed fence.

An actual freaking tank, like a giant in the ranks with human soldiers. It was one of the first vehicles to arrive, and its driver, Axe, shot at the tall fences, making them explode into pieces of flying concrete. The tank drove over the rubble and into the base, wreaking havoc in the ranks of security guards, who were ready to shoot, tackle, kill and maim, but not to fight a tank.

Dom needed to know the story behind the thing, and Dana would research that for him if she wanted to be on the inside of his operation again. Her obsession with Domenico was the one flaw in her robot-like personality, and he wouldn't be shy about using it. His skin tingled at the mere thought of getting contacts to people who smuggled this kind of heavy arms. It was big business, and even though he was retired, he couldn't help but think about a new venture that he could be a part of once he got his hands on the capital he kept safe in Colombia.

Dom had to admit that as crazy as the Coffin Nails were, their determination was admirable, and the assault plan, though simple, was an effective way of luring most of the manpower the traffickers had at their disposal away from the center of the base, where Fred told them they would find the human cargo.

Armed to the teeth, their small party flew past the chaos beneath their feet and straight for the buildings in the middle of the base, visible from above like fluorescent bubbles in the dark sea of trees. Ryder pressed an assault rifle to his chest, looking down like a hawk, ready for action if anyone endangered his precious steel baby.

Dom had been reluctant to leave the piloting to Dana, but if he had chosen to be in her place, he would not be able to follow Jed inside, so he made his choice, as hard as it was. It soon turned out Dana was just as good of a pilot as she claimed. Dom had scraps of information about her activities in South America, but clearly, she'd become very proficient at handling a helicopter during her time there.

Now that she was holding the cycling control with one hand and the collective with the other, a bright smile he rarely saw on her lips lit up her face, as if she were a kid gathering bounty at a toy store. Grease, who sat next to her, seemed enamored by her skill.

Seth and Jed sat opposite Domenico, their faces focused, but while Jed kept looking out the window to assess the situation, Seth seemed to only be interested in Dom. Dressed in an armor of Kevlar that made him look even bigger and meatier, he would be a scary sight to any man who dared confront them on the ground.

Domenico himself had chosen a light bulletproof vest to not restrict his movements, but even at Seth's insistence, he refused a helmet. If there was something he needed to use down there, it was his instinct and senses, and he would not block those abilities at the cost of extra protection. Seth caught Domenico's eyes and smiled, streaming all the warmth and confidence he needed.

"Check your weapons," said Domenico, casting a glance at Fred, who sat next to him, immobilized by handcuffs at the back and the tight-fitting safety belt.

Seth checked his weapon once more, but Dom also had a look at the three guns Seth got before they even went up into the air. He wouldn't take unnecessary risks, but trying to leave Seth at the club was not an option, and as much as it stressed Dom out, it was high time for Seth to test his combat abilities. At least if Seth knew he had a purpose in the action, Dom could control what he did more efficiently. They agreed that with Seth's armor comparable to riot gear, he would serve as backup, and not go into combat if there was no need for it. Telling him that he'd be Dom's second pair of eyes seemed to really make Seth understand his role, and Domenico hoped it would also make him be extra cautious, for both their sake.

A loud *staccato* of bullets tore through the air, and the helicopter made a rapid jerk as Dana pulled it up to

escape the assault fire. Ryder was the first to react. Eyes on the target, he answered with an even greater amount of firepower and effectively silenced the foe on the ground.

"Now's the time," he screamed toward the pilot seat, threads of his long hair floating in the moving air, and Dana responded with a gentle glide downward.

Ryder gathered the bundle of thick rope and looked out. A bright glow was teasing the edges of Dom's vision as Dana lowered the helicopter's position over the main building he and Seth had visited. Fred claimed that the flat roof was accessible, so they chose to use that as an asset, instead of approaching the structure on equal ground with their armed opponents, as there surely would be some men left to guard the prisoners and documents. Domenico was certain that in an event of a police raid, the instructions would be clear about burning of the analogue catalogs.

The moon was bright in the sky, and they were getting a lot of extra light from a fire that was blazing somewhere to their right, in a building close to the fence, further taking attention from Dom's stealthy operation.

Ryder whistled at Dana and pushed the rope down. "Jed, after me," he yelled and slid down, as if he'd been trained all his life to do just that.

Domenico hissed and looked into Fred's tense face, red from the stress and impending infection. "Don't try to act funny, or the guys down there will shoot you," he muttered, unbuckling the seat belt on him. He uncuffed one of the bastard's hands and prompted him toward the rope, right after Jed disappeared in the open door.

Fred shook his head but said nothing and pulled closer to the edge of the cabin. Now that he had only air under him, all cockiness was gone, as if it had spilled out through his wounds. Clearly, jumping off a hovering helicopter was not in his repertoire.

"What about a ladder?"

Domenico got to his knees and pointed his Beretta at Fred, nearing the end of his patience. "Go down or I will push you out."

Fred bit his lip, and as the moving air sent most of his hair into his face, he looked at his naked hands.

"No gloves. Get your ass down there," hissed Domenico, moving so close, so abruptly that Fred actually flinched back. True terror emerged on his face as he tipped back, and only the handle at the side of the door rescued him from falling to his death.

"Fucker," he wheezed through his teeth, but he seemed to finally get the memo. Even with the vision of imminent doom crawling into his pale eyes, he finally rushed down the rope.

Domenico exhaled in relief and looked at Seth before casting a glance down. Fred rolled to his back, holding his burning hands to his chest, but Jed was right there to cuff them back in place. Domenico smiled.

"Follow me," he said and rolled straight down. The heat of the friction created on the edge of the rope and glove was palpable, but the height was not great enough to tear through the leather. Domenico exhaled in relief when his feet hit the tiles of the roof, and he quickly stepped back, getting down like everyone else, just in case some crazy asshole wanted to shoot them from one of the other buildings.

Seth appeared over their heads first as an irregularity in the dark shape of the helicopter, but then he was speeding down, as efficiently as a soldier of the special forces. Domenico rushed to his side and pulled him to his knees before tugging at the rope three times. He smelled the Kevlar on Seth's chest, hardly stopping himself from trying to bite into it. Above their heads, Grease started pulling up the rope, and with a wheezing sound, the helicopter was off.

Dom had a phone on him to let Dana know when they needed her back and a pager that Axe had pulled out of his box of old equipment as backup. The buzz of adrenaline over leading everyone was slightly unexpected but so intense that it went right into Dom's bones. He was used to hunting as a lone wolf, but it turned out leading a pack could be in his nature just as much.

He was glad his man was here with him, as safe as he could be in the black Kevlar and helmet, holding a riot shield, yet able to be a part of the mission even despite the slight limp. Seth wanted to get the shield in the first place, and Domenico had been skeptical at best, but they agreed Seth would just leave it behind if things got too heated, and for once, he believed Seth would do as asked instead of making a brash and stupid decision. Seth had been affected by the evil he'd seen at this base, and he wanted be a part of its demise. Dom could understand that. And they were both here to find Mark. It wouldn't have been right to push him away from helping.

There was a concrete shaft looming at the edge of the roof, and as soon as they spotted a door in one of its walls, Domenico led the way. With Jed leading Fred by the neck and Ryder and Seth playing the roles of heavily armed shooters at the flanks, Domenico confidently rushed to the entrance and opened it, ready to shoot. There was no one there, and so he switched on the flashlight fastened to his shoulder and moved down the stairs made of raw concrete. It was clear this area wasn't used much, as no one had taken care to plaster the walls, and Dom only hoped leaving the shaft would not prove too difficult.

"Where to?" he asked Fred, taking every turn of the stairs with caution. They were narrow and spiraled around what had to be a ventilation shaft.

Fred took a deep breath. "Third door down. Then I'll lead you further along the corridor."

Domenico was ready to shoot the fucker if he pulled some trick on them, but he was the first one to rush down the stairs, and gestured for the other men to follow. Their group wasn't the stealthiest considering how they got here, but with the chaos raging inside the base, loud footsteps could belong to anyone, not just the invaders. On top of that, the constant gunfire outside was their best ally in infiltrating the building.

The staircase was unpleasantly hot, making Domenico sticky with sweat, but when he opened the right door and walked into an air-conditioned corridor, it didn't make him feel any better.

One of the lamps shining over the empty walkway that looked like any other office was blinking, and that alone was enough to put Dom on edge. The trembling light made everything more alive, as if even the pictures on the walls could twitch into life at any given moment. Fred led the way toward a turn into darkness, where the light had an oddly grayish quality, and as Domenico watched Seth's powerful, armored form follow, he grabbed Ryder's arm and turned him back.

Ryder stiffened and squeezed his hands tighter on the rifle, but raised his brows, waiting for whatever Domenico was going to say. And the damn light was still blinking, as if it were imitating the crazily irregular heartbeat in Dom's chest.

"I'm gonna be first in line," whispered Dom, keeping his voice steady. "If something happens, take care of Seth." He took a deep breath as he glanced at the rapidly growing distance between them and the rest of the group. "If there's a choice between helping me and him, leave me. I can handle my shit."

Ryder stared at Dom with a frown, but he nodded in silence. At least the man knew his debts and was willing to pay them. The two of them caught up with the others just before they could make the turn into darkness. Fred

made his way to the light switch, seemingly wanting to push on it with his shoulder, but Ryder stopped him in his tracks.

"We'll be better off without it. Fewer people will notice us from outside," he said, and Domenico nodded.

Fred hissed. "We need to take the stairs up. This place consists of two parts. They might look like one building, but they've been planned as separate structures with just one link."

Domenico frowned as they raced through the dark corridor, trying hard not to stomp too much, but some noise was inevitable, and each screech their soles made against the floor made Domenico cringe.

"Is there a password to access the cargo?"

Fred growled. "What do you think this is? NASA? Next you're gonna ask me about eyeball detection or fucking fingerpr—" Domenico struck Fred across the face, sending him into the wall.

"Shut up when I'm not asking."

Fred somehow kept himself on his feet and spat on the floor, but at least he didn't try to play the sassy villain anymore.

Jed took over again so Domenico could focus completely on detecting danger as they proceeded down the corridor. All of a sudden, his ears picked up a pounding noise, and at his sign, everyone froze. Guns were drawn, and as light flickered ahead, even Domenico felt the adrenaline rush melting his brain. The rapid footsteps were quicker and quicker in the bright spot ahead when their dark tunnel met a well-lit corridor. One person. Barefoot.

They all let out excess air as the naked figure of a bald man with a potbelly rushed in and out of their sight. A customer? Worthy of getting a bullet through his brain, no doubt, but it wasn't the time to alert anyone to their position.

Domenico exhaled. "Fine. Let's go."

368 | G u n s n ' B o y s B o o k 4

Fred slouched farther, but he did move again and instead of following the steps of the naked man, he took them into a short walkway branching out from the corridor toward a closed door in the corner.

"There."

Domenico caught Seth and Ryder's gazes in the darkness and gently pushed on the handle. The door gave a tiny squeak, so he pushed on the handle as hard as he could and opened the door in one swift move. It soon became clear that he shouldn't have worried, as he now faced a narrow, steep staircase with gray carpeting on the steps. A buzz of machinery grew stronger with every step, and Domenico tried to focus on the rhythmical noise of something that could be a power generator. At the end of the stairs was a landing and two doors, one of which clearly emitted the noise.

Fred pushed himself past Seth and joined Dom at the landing. His face was completely pale and sweaty, but his eyes seemed as lively as ever. With the lack of hands to use, he nodded at the other door and leaned against the wall as everyone else reached the landing.

Domenico opened the door.

From the inside, three men looked back at them but took only half a second to pull out their guns and shoot, no questions asked. The faint lights of monitors and consoles inside became a blur when Dom was hit by a bullet in the chest. The force behind it punched the air out of his lungs, and the tile inside the fabric burst with an explosion of heat, but he still rushed forward, crouched close to the floor, and aimed his gun upward. Dom shot one of the men in the head, and the brains exploded out his slack jaw.

He didn't have to see a gun pointed at the back of his head to sense its presence, but his pack followed inside, and as Dom shot the man above him, splattering bits of bone and meat at the wall, another body fell to the ground close by.

The last guard rolled over the desk and shot from behind it, missing Dom's hair by an inch. When Seth screamed, Dom's heart stopped, but it flooded with warm blood once again as soon as Seth yelled that he was fine.

Only then, when immediate danger was out of the way, did Dom rapidly yank the vest off his burning skin. He was gasping by the time he touched the spot of impact, which radiated pain all over his chest. But there was no wetness other than sweat. Thank fuck for bulletproof technology. Domenico searched for Seth, and he was relieved to see a small smile on the handsome face across the room.

There was a noise behind the consoles, and Dom shot at the desk next to it, hoping to at least give the guard some splinters in the face, and judging by the scream that followed, he'd been successful. The smell of blood filled Dom's nose, but instead of disgusting him, it spurred him on into action. Only the indistinguishable bits of body parts in his hair bothered him. For once, he was happy that he had it tied back.

He shot at the desk again, but Ryder ran past him, jumped on, and sent a round of bullets from his machine gun, silencing any movement of the last guard.

Domenico turned around to look behind him, just in time to see Seth push Fred to the ground with his crazy shield that now had a small crack on the right top edge.

"Fucker tried to run," Seth said from behind his helmet and kicked Fred's foot with the steel tip of his boot.

Something creaked, and then a masculine voice came from a speaker at the console. "Max? Can you send backup?" The edge of panic and the trembling quality of the sound dawned on Domenico. This was some kind of control room. And when he looked up at the monitors, the outskirts of the base were visible, including an image of the damaged fence that now looked like a big lump of rubble, with a dead man lying on the right side of the screen.

Domenico pulled in a lungful of cool air and glanced at Fred, who stared at him from beneath Seth like a wounded wild cat under the boot of its captor. If he could, he'd claw Seth's eyes out. The fucker had led them into a trap, so it was only fair he got a taste of his own medicine.

Ryder picked up the mic and spoke into it through his hand. "Copy. Sending now. It's fucking mayhem."

"They're getting through. Send someone to get rid of the papers, for fuck's sake!"

Domenico exhaled and looked toward Jed, who was back at the door, ready to shoot anyone willing to bust in here. "You two, stay here. Don't let anyone through, or we'll be fucked," he said on his way to Seth. He picked him up and yanked on Fred's hair.

"That's what you wanted? I can do this all fucking day until there's no one left here. Including you."

Fred looked up at him with those lying eyes of his, pupils wide with fear. "I made a mistake! But the door to get lower is just through this room. That's why we're here. I was sure they'd be gone by now!"

Domenico smirked. "Sure you were." He looked at Seth and touched his face, just because it was the only naked part of his body. "Are you okay?" he whispered, holding on to Fred's hair as if his head were cut off from the body already.

"Shield came in handy." Seth grinned and gestured to it with his head.

Ryder groaned. "There's no time for this." Yet he looked over toward the door and took two steps closer to Jed.

"Just spread chaos," said Dom as he pulled Fred to his feet. It was time to go. "You can speak to your own men at the same time and tell them all about those fuckers' soft underbelly."

Ryder's nostrils flared, but he nodded nevertheless. Domenico knew it was difficult for the man to listen to a

stranger's orders, but without even thinking about it, Dom had become the leader of their small party. It felt right.

"Let's go. No tricks this time," said Dom, pushing Fred forward.

"I swear," Fred mewled. "My mind got clouded. I'm so scared..."

Even Seth wasn't buying that shit, and he shook his head at Dom before pulling the clear shield over his eyes.

"You're like a futuristic soldier," whispered Domenico as soon as they were out the door on the other side of the room. Stepping over the body of the fallen guard posed no problem for Seth after witnessing the atrocities that had happened in the base. Domenico felt proud of him manning up.

Seth gave him a smug smile and pushed Fred with the tip of his gun. "I'm still finding my own brand."

The red light of the lamp above reflected off his eye guard, and for a moment Dom almost felt like he was in a science-fiction-themed sex hotel. He waved off the silly thought and kissed Seth's lips before prompting a very resigned Fred to lead. Clearly, the man would go for his best bet immediately, and now he had no choice but to do what was asked of him.

They passed an elevator Dom and Seth recognized and eventually reached the equally familiar staircase, but this time, Fred took them behind the stairs in the first floor, where another door was hidden in the shadows. A full two stories underground, they finally reached a heavy door.

Domenico jumped down the last few stairs and touched the damp wall, smirking at the sight of an electric lock by the handle. He pushed on it anyway, and the heavy steel didn't budge. "Did you say no codes?" he asked, grabbing Fred's hand and pushing him at the door. Fred hit his head with a dull thud and slid down to his knees, breathing hard.

Domenico squeezed his fist, hardly stopping himself from beating the life out of the fucker.

Fred coughed and rolled to his ass, blinking up at Dom. "I didn't know... I'm just an... associate. New to this whole thing. This was my first time..."

Domenico laughed into his face. "Right. But you knew where this place is. Like fuck you're just an associate."

"You said that there's no codes, but somehow you led us to a door you knew damn well needed one for access," Seth said in a cold voice Dom rarely got to hear, and at the back of his brain he knew he wanted to. Sometimes. "I'm not buying that you don't know how to get in there."

Fred gritted his teeth and opened his mouth to speak again, but Dom kicked him right in the fresh wound on his chest, and he went down with a searing scream.

"So, what's the code?" asked Domenico calmly, touching the metal keyboard.

Fred wept on the ground, curling up into a ball. "Nine-three-two-five."

Seth snorted. "Knew it."

Domenico put in the code, and a second later, the screen above the handle flashed them a green light. Domenico kicked Fred aside and opened the door.

A gust of wind that smelled of sweaty bodies hit Domenico's face, and as he stepped into complete darkness, his hand searched for a switch. His fingers finally traced a plastic box with a rubbery membrane stretched over a piece of plastic that Domenico pressed on. A hum of electricity echoed all around, and moments later, weak white lights flickered over a short tunnel with a rounded ceiling and thick ropes of cables glued to the gray walls.

Domenico took a deep breath, noticing several openings in the wall on both sides, flinching slightly at the thud of the closing door behind him. All were separated

with thick metal bars, and as Domenico moved forward, a high-pitched gasping sound triggered goose bumps to grow all over his body. He looked back at Seth, to make sure he had Fred, and then slowly moved forward with his gun ready to shoot. For once, the familiar steel felt heavy and unnecessary.

The smell of excrement made him scowl, but he moved along until he stood between the first two cells. In one breathless heartbeat, he looked into ten pairs of eyes staring at him from the shadows at the back wall of the small cell. There were thin futons lining the floor with faded blankets on top. He stepped forward, and each time he moved closer, the crowd of girls pressed into a tighter mass.

No. He needed to search for boys.

Domenico looked across the hallway and then ran over to the other set of cells. It was all women. "Where are they?" hissed Domenico, spinning around to look at Fred.

The man didn't dare look up at Dom, and for a moment, Domenico froze, wondering if this meant that Mark was already dead and Fred only led them to the base hoping to get away. But no. Fred spoke.

"These here are for transport. He was to stay. New arrivals are at the end." His voice was raspy and his lips deservedly covered in blood.

Seth frowned, looking at Dom over Fred's shoulder. "We were told this place *is* just for transport. Who do they keep?"

"There are clients with particular tastes," Fred whispered, looking as if he wanted to disappear, with his head down and his shoulders slouched.

Domenico could hardly breathe and yanked Fred forward by his shirt. The image of Jo's broken body, of her stump, came to his mind in a rapid wave. "You're making people into toys? Training them?" he uttered, looking

around, at all the cells in this corridor. There were probably more of those, and each one held several people.

"Not me!" Fred moaned. "Not me! I was only here once. I was so, so desperate. It's the fucking sadists who come here. It's their fault. There's people who want to do some crazy shit. Cut others up... just anything. I broke under the pressure of it all, I wanted to quit, but they threatened my family, held me by the balls."

"Right. In your fake house," roared Domenico and punched Fred in the stomach. The fucker was lying all the damn time, even though he clearly knew the operation well enough to memorize the code to the most important door in the whole base.

Domenico kicked Fred right in the ass. "Get up, you trash."

Fred wailed and only listened when Seth pulled on his arm. Dom went forward, passing dozens of cells. The women must have listened in on the conversation, because they approached the cell doors, reaching their arms out and crying. Their pleas for help melted into one, but even when Dom heard one scream that Fred had been here before, and that she'd seen him, he didn't stop.

Every step he made was quicker. He turned a corner, followed the damp gray tunnel faster and faster, realizing just how desperate he was to find the stupid boy who dared to believe that someone would take care of him.

He tried not to look at the cages around him as he sped up without looking back anymore. Seth would be fine, and there was no one dangerous here.

After getting into a dead end, he ran along a whole array of cells holding people in bandages and casts. He didn't pay any attention to the details, letting them turn into a grayish mass as he ran for the open doorway at the end of the corridor. It was dark there, and so Dom's gaze searched for the light switch. His chest was burning as voices rose in front of him in the pitch black of a room that

made them echo. Frustrated, he stepped down the few stairs that led him out of the safety of the faint light and into the unknown. Only at the edge of the illumination behind him did Dom switch on his flashlight.

In the ghastly glow, he saw a floor dotted with grated sewer covers, or maybe ventilation shafts, and it reminded him of the disgusting pockets in flesh where toads kept their young. But as he stepped closer, movement made his blood turn into ice. There were hands reaching from between the bars of the covers, grabbing the metal and clawing at air.

So many hands.

Chapter 27 – Domenico

Domenico's breath shook as he stepped inside the room. From the way noise echoed from its walls, Domenico assumed there was a high ceiling above him, but the floor itself was the size of a basketball field, with well-like cells organized into rows, with enough space to walk between them. Domenico swallowed hard, already knowing he couldn't just let all those people out. There was a tank and bazookas out there. He couldn't risk them all running ahead like suicidal ducks, straight underneath the wheels. What he needed was Mark, but with his voice trapped in his throat, he shone down one of the wells instead.

From the shadow of the bars, a squarish face emerged covered with so many bruises Dom couldn't recognize the person's gender. Wide-eyed, with strained muscles, the person, the young man inside yelled for help.

Domenico opened his mouth, but all mercy had to wait when a bullet ricocheted off the floor in front of Dom. Its speed tickled Domenico's hair, but he moved instinctively and spun back so fast he started falling to the floor. But even as his back stiffened and his shoulders set,

Domenico pulled the trigger three times. A choked roar rushed through the air at the impact of Domenico falling to the floor, but a second later, something heavy thudded against the grating in the corner

Domenico grabbed his flashlight with a trembling hand and pointed the ray of light across the room at the twisted remains of a man in a black jumpsuit. As Domenico sat up hearing Seth's voice coming from behind a thick fog, the grating under the guard shook with gunfire. A flash of light and a heart-searing shriek told Dom there was yet another casualty. Inside the well.

"Fuck," he uttered, pointing the light around to see if there were any more guards hidden. Wails and cries were so many he had to ignore them, even as he watched hands clutching at the bars.

Seth's clear loud voice cut through easily. "Dom! Are you all right? You should have kept the fucking vest on!"

"Seth? Domenico?" a high-pitched cry came from the side, and Domenico's heart stopped when he recognized the voice.

He looked that way, just in time to pull his hand away from being grabbed by an anonymous set of fingers. He was back on his feet within a split second. "Mark? Where are you?" asked Dom, shining his flashlight around and moving along the row of holes. His chest was so tight he didn't feel like he could take more than one gulp of air. He couldn't even pinpoint why it affected him so much. His nerves had been made of steel for a long time now, darkness didn't bother him, and despite the scale of this underground prison, he'd seen other horrendous things in his life that had made him numb. Yet something about that choked voice calling out to him was pulling him to a time when his heart wasn't stone cold just yet.

He too had been afraid, looking at a round opening above his head, and unable to reach it. And no one had come to his aid back then.

"Mark!" yelled Domenico, trying to sieve the familiar voice out from dozens of others coming both from the holes and the cells down the corridor. His head was spinning, and the wet, earthy taste in his mouth came with a darkness he didn't want to think about.

When a slim hand caught his ankle, he'd almost shaken it off in frustration, but when he pointed the flashlight down, there it was. Mark's tearful face, with a bruise covering his eye and cheek and snot running down his mouth, as he was struggling for each breath.

"I'm here," he uttered so quietly it was barely audible.

Domenico fell to his knees and grabbed Mark's fingers over the thick bars. "I'm gonna get you," he whispered, unable to tear his gaze away from the terrified eyes. "It'll be okay," he promised, even as he glanced at a fat padlock that kept the grate shut. Domenico pulled at it, but it was locked, and there was no way he could open it without equipment. "Does that guard have keys?"

Seth had stayed back before, probably not to drag Fred into the dark room, but now he had to get inside. "I'll check," he said and carefully walked between the holes, not to step on anyone's hand.

Mark grabbed Dom's fingers as hard as he could through the bars. "Please don't leave me here..."

Domenico shook his head. "Are you fucking kidding? We came by helicopter." He slowly looked back, without taking his hands off Mark's skin. As illogical as it was, he couldn't shake off the feeling that if he let go, some unknown force would pull Mark away, and they'd never see him again.

"For me?" Mark's breath hitched, and Domenico wasn't even going to tell him not to cry like a girl.

"I've got them!" Seth said and rushed over.

Domenico shook his head and reached inside, pushing his forearm between the two steel bars. His fingers slid into Mark's matted mane, and with his thumb, he drew a small cross on the sweaty forehead. "You asked," muttered Domenico.

Seth fiddled around with the keys until he found the right ones and pulled the grate open, only for the screams for help around them to intensify, but Domenico could only focus on one person

"I was so scared," Mark held his arms up to him. "The people around here... Some of them were tortured so horribly... I didn't want to listen. I thought I was all alone."

Domenico leaned down, reaching into the concrete well only broad enough for a person to curl up in a sitting position. His heart trembled as he held Mark underneath his armpits and pulled. The tiny prison smelled nothing like Domenico's former place of captivity. This one stunk much worse, small enough to drive a person insane, and the only water provided was in a bottle on the floor. It was like being permanently stuck in the narrow tunnel between the well and the Villani mansion. The same one that gave even grown-up Domenico the chills.

As soon as Mark was out, he clung to Dom like a frightened child much younger than he was. "They made me call you. I tried to put a message in there. I hoped Seth would understand," he whispered into Dom's chest.

Domenico pulled him close and rested his chin on the cushion of wavy hair. Mark felt so solid in Dom's arms, and he wasn't going anywhere. "You're safe. No one's going to hurt you now that we're here," he said, looking up at Seth, who smiled and just gave a nod.

Not only had they managed to save Mark, but they'd also come in time for the boy not to be hurt like Jo had been. He could have been raped and cut up into pieces

within hours, yet he seemed whole, even had his clothes on. Something most of the captives didn't have.

"I tried to think of a better way, maybe to stay with Raj, but it didn't work out. And Dana said I was trouble to you already. I didn't know what else to do but go to Fred." Mark gasped for air every few words. "I'm not useless. All I need is a bit of help..."

Domenico had to bite his tongue not to explode. "Dana's a lying bitch. And she's staying with her new fucking boyfriend for much more than a month," he growled, dragging Mark to his feet. "Are you good to walk?" he asked, ignoring the loud pleas coming from other cells. Bikers and the police would take care of them later.

"I am. They didn't get to me." Mark looked up at Dom and unglued himself to rub away the snot and tears with his T-shirt. "You were my only hope." His big brown eyes bore into Dom with so much hunger for affection that it was hard not to rub his shoulder.

Domenico bit his lip, not knowing what to say. Instead, he glanced at Seth, who seemed so collected and impressive in his riot gear.

"Where's the bastard?" asked Domenico, and the moment he thought of Fred, flames of fury started licking at his throat again.

Seth looked toward the exit. "Fuck. He's gone. Come on. The entry's locked, so he couldn't have gone far." He was the first to rush forward, and Domenico prayed to God for the stitches in his calf not to give.

Domenico pulled Mark closer, just in case he fainted or got scared, and followed Seth. "He's not going anywhere. There's no way he can open that door without using hands. Too heavy."

"Seth?" Mark yelled, but held on to the back of Dom's T-shirt, hidden under Domenico's arm. "Thank you!"

Seth glanced over his shoulder, then turned the corner, and grinned. "Just no more Cheetos for alligators!"

Domenico chuckled. No amount of ammo and rabid guards could worsen his mood now. He patted Mark on the back and followed Seth, the man mountain with a riot shield. Who would have thought he'd ever be comfortable doing this? Though Dom was still sure Seth would rather go bungee jumping or surfing with medusas for the adrenaline kick than witness what he had seen here.

Domenico felt light and warm. Even despite the horror of this place, coming here had not been a waste. What he'd done tonight really mattered. He'd saved a young man on the brink of adulthood, and he would get to shape his life into something better.

They got to the alley of cells by the door, and as they progressed down the hall, Mark clung to Domenico a bit harder. They both watched Seth look around the empty corridor with a scowl.

"Wh—"

"There, there, he's in the empty cell!" screamed a vicious-sounding female voice, though nobody could blame her for her need of revenge.

Seth nodded at her and pushed open the door of the cell, pointing his gun at the single person inside. "Out." And as Fred crawled out on his knees, the woman started laughing in high-pitched shrieks, leaning against the bars with her whole body.

Domenico kicked him all the way to the floor, without letting go of Mark. "Get up," he uttered right after Fred managed to roll back to his knees. There was a fair amount of pleasure in taunting a piece of shit like him, but time was precious, and Domenico opened the latch and then the electronic lock, pulling the heavy door open. "Out."

Feminine voices erupted around them again, but he didn't want to talk and followed Fred, dragging Mark with him. This would end very soon.

Seth closed the door behind them, and Mark looked around nervously, but then his eyes settled on Fred,

crouched in the corner by the stairs, and his body pressed even tighter against Dom.

"J-just leave. I won't tell anyone," whispered Fred, hiding his face behind the sweaty hair, as if he hoped Mark somehow wouldn't recognize the rat who sold him into being raped and tortured.

Domenico raised his leg, and just as he pulled up the denim, Fred curled into a tighter ball. Ignoring him, Domenico took out his knife and untangled himself from Mark's arms, weighing both the blade and his Beretta in his hands.

Mark took a deep breath but finally choked up some words. "So you can... do this to others? You sick... fuck!" he whimpered, staring at Fred's hunched form.

Fred flinched. "I was desperate... I—"

"Shut the fuck up!" Domenico kicked him so hard Fred fell over again, weakened by all the violence of the day. Served him right.

Domenico's eyes slowly turned toward Mark. He hadn't spoken about this to Seth, but if they were to save this lonely boy again, they couldn't just leave him behind. Mark already knew far too much, but were they to take care of his future, he needed to prove himself, show them what his heart was made of. Was he a lion or a rabbit on the inside?

Dom extended his hands, one with the Beretta, one with the knife. "He's yours," he said quietly, drilling his gaze into Mark, searching for the answers he so desperately needed. If Mark chose to stay a civilian, they couldn't take him in. They would have to work something out for him in the next month, but he wouldn't be able to go across the border, start a life he wouldn't truly want.

Mark's lips parted, and he watched the weapons in Domenico's hands, back pressed against the wall. Dom half expected Seth to say something in protest. To say that they could leave Fred to the bikers, or to the police, or that Mark

shouldn't be doing this, but nothing came from where Seth stood in a shadowy corner of the staircase.

"Kid," Fred rasped. "You don't need to do anything. You don't understand my situatio—"

Mark's face hardened, and all of a sudden, his pretty eyes weren't frightened anymore. "You knew mine."

"Yes, but..." Even Fred couldn't think of anything more to back his lies on the spot.

Mark looked into Dom's eyes before reaching for the gun.

Domenico smiled. A gun. Not cruel. Efficient. "Have you used one before?" he asked, noticing how uncertainly Mark was holding the grip, his hands trembling slightly.

Mark shook his head, accustoming himself to the weight of the weapon. Even Fred shut up, staring at the barrel with his eyes wide as saucers.

Domenico stood behind Mark and put his hands over his cool fingers, steadying them. He had a look at Fred's curled-up form and whispered, guiding Mark to ready the gun for a clear shot. The heart or the head were the best bets to ensure the fucker died. Mark's fingers weren't perfectly steady, but he was nodding in acknowledgement, all the way until Domenico let him go and stepped back. This initiation was something Mark needed to go through on his own, as Dom had so many years ago. Only the man Domenico had killed was a stranger. He had owed money to the Villanis and tried to flee. He had never hurt Domenico and hadn't even tried to protect himself once he saw the gun pointed at him. This was different.

Domenico's eyes briefly met Seth's, and he wondered if Seth was remembering Angelo, the man he was forced to kill for betrayal of the family. Back then, Domenico had promised Seth that he wouldn't have to kill again, but he wasn't sure anymore if that would be the case. He quickly focused back on the villain and his

innocent victim, who was about to avenge himself and countless others. And though he'd lose his innocence in the process, it was just. He'd become a man.

Mark swallowed loudly, and just as Fred opened his mouth to plead for his life, Mark shot him twice, in the shoulder and the head. The impact sent him two steps back, and he gasped for air.

Domenico swallowed hard as the weight of the moment dawned in his chest. Mark got made. No longer an innocent, he could stay with them. "Good. Now put on the safety," Domenico said in a cool voice.

Mark nodded and followed Dom's instruction, even though he shivered so hard it showed in the faint light. There was tension to his shoulders, and Domenico couldn't help but imagine Mark in a few years, grown tall and strong. Mark didn't shy away from looking back at what he'd done either.

"He deserved it, right?" he whispered.

Domenico nodded and took his weapon. "Yes. You did the right thing, Mark. He will never hurt any other boy or girl again," he said, squeezing Mark's shoulder. A smile bloomed on his lips, and he pulled him close for a tight hug.

Mark clung to him again, but not with the same desperation as in the cells. He even stopped shivering, and only his heart drumming madly against Dom's chest told Domenico that Mark wasn't calming down just yet.

Domenico pulled away and looked into Mark's eyes. "You're a man now, and I will regard you as such."

Mark didn't even blink, nodding, even though Dom was sure he didn't yet truly comprehend the weight of his choice.

Now Mark really was their responsibility. Dom would make a man out of him. Show him the ropes.

Domenico reached out to Seth and squeezed his hand. "Come here."

Seth came closer, fiddling with something beneath the armor on his chest. He pulled out something Dom least expected, a Snickers bar. "I thought you might be hungry when we get to you. Sorry, it's a bit squished." He handed the chocolate to Mark, who slowly smiled, despite the ugly bruises on his face.

Domenico pulled Seth close and kissed the plastic guard over his eyes, touched by the gesture. This was the man he fell in love with. No matter how tough he was when necessary, his heart always kept the warmth Dom craved. "You've been amazing."

Seth smiled and knocked on the plastic shield. "It gave me a level-up."

Domenico grinned and rustled Mark's hair, watching the kid eat, strategically turned away from the fresh body.

"I guess that seals the deal between the three of us."

Mark looked up at Dom with those hopeful eyes. "Can I come with you? I'll go wherever. I don't mind. I can live in the swamp, or in the desert. I can be useful. I... I don't want to meet another Fred."

Domenico felt a twitch in his stomach at the thought of his very own older "friend," still alive and well, still preying on some young man. He patted Mark on the shoulder. "You need to know we are not civilians. It might not always be safe. Are you up for this kind of life?"

Mark took a deep breath. "I don't care about the danger. My life isn't safe anyway. I want to be more... like you. I want to be a confident badass. I want to be a part of *something*."

Domenico exhaled, holding on to Seth as hard as he could. "We're on the run from the mafia."

Seth cleared his throat. "Not special forces. Not witness protection."

386 | G u n s n ' B o y s B o o k 4

Mark hardly blinked, looking between the two of them intensely as he finished his chocolate. "I want to come with you."

Relief flooded Domenico's heart as he looked into the big eyes that were so ready to drink up anything he was willing to give. "You will go with us to Colombia. You will learn the language and train under me, so that you can deal with whatever shit the world throws at us, understood?"

Mark made a gesture that Dom suspected was meant as a salute. He didn't have the heart to point out how bad it was. "Do I get a gun?"

Domenico laughed and leaned against the sturdiness of Seth's body. "You will have to learn how to use it first."

Chapter 28 - Seth

Seth was sitting at the desk and cutting up fruit for the trip for all three of them. Domenico would most probably prefer chocolate, but he ate that all the time, so Seth needed to make sure Dom was getting his vitamins as well. Were they in Italy, it would have been much easier to shop around on the way, but here, they couldn't really predict whether they'd find a place with healthy food options or some fucking deep-fried hot dogs.

Just next to him, Dom had been shouting at Dana for the past quarter of an hour, so Seth spaced out at some point, but he got back to listening when he heard a mention of tanks. He'd also been curious about the heavy artillery the club seemed to own. Not to mention the helicopter. That was pretty cool.

Apparently, Dana had told Mark that he was a burden to them, and she was the one who talked him into leaving in secret, not just given him a ride because he asked, as she had claimed before. When Dom heard that from Mark, he went mental over the extent of her insubordination.

"You will stay here not for a month. You are gonna sit on your ass for a year and gather all the fucking intel on both the Villanis and the people who armed those morons in fucking tanks and bazookas. Can you do that, or will it be too difficult for you?" hissed Domenico, looking down at Dana, who sat in a chair like a scolded teenager.

Her mouth twisted. "What about my training?"

Domenico snorted. "Training? If you ever want to train under me, you will find out good stuff for me, is that clear?"

Seth was slightly dubious about butting in, but he couldn't help himself. "This is a bit like acting training, right? A mission to test your abilities?"

Dana sent him a deathly glare but said nothing. Domenico shook his head at her and glanced through the window at Mark, who sat at the back of their new van, rummaging through their bags. "The Villanis might be after you. Have you ever thought about a face job?"

Dana took a long breath. "Have you?"

Domenico shook his head. "No chance. But you could use one if you're to infiltrate the Villanis after you turned your back on them."

Seth looked up at her. "It might be a good moment for it, if you're going to spend a year here. You could move around them, and they'd never know. You'd be a snake in the grass." He wiggled his eyebrows, but the vision he created for her only had her sneer.

"I could do *something*, I guess." For a fraction of a second, her face seemed softer. "But you *will* keep in touch? You won't disappear?" she asked Dom and even got up and took a step closer to him. If Seth wasn't so certain of Dom's sexuality, he'd tell her to back off. Dana clearly had a weird kind of hero worship going on.

Domenico brightened and pulled her into the briefest hug that she seemed to drink up and absorb to the very last split second. "Absolutely. I will be calling your cell

phone, and if you want to get in touch, use that Internet forum the way we discussed. I *need* you to be here, Dana."

She took a deep breath. "I'll get the intel. I'll find my way to the higher-ups."

"Thank you. We can get back together once we know all about what's going on here. I hope that's enough of a challenge for you."

Dana nodded, and after a few more words, she said her good-byes. She even took the fruit salad Seth had prepared for her.

"Can't get the staff these days, right?" Seth laughed to Dom and got up as he closed the plastic boxes. "At least you've got good catering."

Domenico chuckled and sat in Seth's lap, pulling him into a kiss. Domenico's skin was smooth and fragrant, and the smooch seemed to last forever as they both leaned into one another. Domenico eventually pulled Seth to his feet.

"Enough rest. We've got to go."

"Getting Mark new documents? That's going to be an adventure." Seth put on a pair of sunglasses as they walked out of the room.

"And a stretch on my wallet," sighed Domenico as they walked out of the room and straight outside. Dana was still walking toward the main building of the Coffin Nails compound as Seth and Domenico approached the van.

Seth nudged Dom's shoulder with his nose. "How bad is it? Will I have to get a job?" He couldn't help the little smile.

Domenico laughed again, completely relaxed. "No, you're good as my house husband."

"Trophy husband." Seth couldn't help another kiss, which ended abruptly when Mark honked at them from the van. At least wherever they'd end up, Seth knew Domenico was his one true purpose.

End of book 4
Domenico and Seth's journey continues in book 5

(psst, don't miss the post-credits scene!)

If you're interested in the Loneliest
Man in the World...

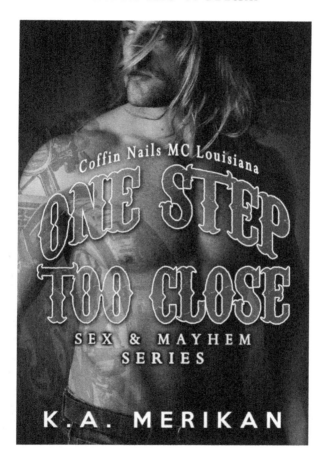

Coffin Nails MC Louisiana

ONE STEP
TOO CLOSE

SEX & MAYHEM
SERIES

K.A. MERIKAN

One Step Too Close (Sex & Mayhem #6)
K.A. Merikan

--- One love. One motorcycle club. Two stepbrothers. ---

Ryder. Controlling. Ambitious. Protective.
Jed. Self-destructive. Trapped. Lonely.
Their love? Forbidden. Taboo. All-consuming.

For Jed, the Coffin Nails Motorcycle Club is family. With them, he learned how to think, what to enjoy, and how to fight, but there is one thing he knows his friends can't find about. They would never accept him as gay, and so his life is a constant struggle with desires that fill him with despair. Only there is a much darker secret lurking in Jed's heart. His feelings for his stepbrother, Ryder, go far beyond brotherly. Trapped with a yearning that can never be fulfilled, Jed spirals out of control and unwillingly puts the love of his life in danger.

Ryder is climbing up the ranks. Recently promoted to Sergeant-at-arms, he has it all: drive, respect, and the love of his biker family. When his stepbrother gets into trouble with the law, Ryder decides to take the blame and save him from a long sentence. Deep inside, he knows there is nothing he wouldn't do for Jed, but through a desperate attempt to suppress his own hidden desires, he might irreversibly break the man he secretly loves.

But finding out what they feel for each other might only put them on a path to destruction.

POSSIBLE SPOILERS:

Themes: Outlaw motorcycle club, criminal activity, forbidden love, stepbrothers, blackmail, homophobia

Genre: M/M erotic romance, suspense, drama

Length: standalone novel

WARNING: Adult content that might be considered taboo. Explicit gay sex, strong language, violence. Reader discretion   advised.

Newsletter

If you're interested in our upcoming releases, exclusive deals, extra content, freebies and the like, sign up for our full newsletter.

http://kamerikan.com/newsletter

We promise not to spam you, and when you sign up, you get any one of our books for $3.99 or under for FREE. Win-Win!

At the same address you can also tick a box for the "Guns n' Boys" mailing list for coupons, news, freebies and extra content.

PATREON

Would you like more "Guns n' Boys"?
Look no further! We now have a PATREON account.
https://www.patreon.com/kamerikan

As a patron, you will have access to flash fiction with the "Guns n' Boys" characters and those from other books, plus you can get a special treat - the beginning of "Guns n' Boys: He is Poison" as seen by Domenico Acerbi. 15,000 words rewritten in his point of view and containing extra storylines. NOT digital, but printed and sent to you!

If you love the series, we will appreciate support on Patreon to keep it going. These books are niche, and with each new book in a series, a part of the readership disappears. Some readers choose to not read a series until it's finished, some even pirate the books, killing the possibility of writing this series more than once a year. With your help, we will be able to publish "Guns n' Boys" much more frequently, and you get lots of perks and fun content.
Win-win!

About the author

K.A. Merikan are a team of writers who try not to suck at adulting, with some success. Always eager to explore the murky waters of the weird and wonderful, K.A. Merikan don't follow fixed formulas and want each of their books to be a surprise for those who choose to hop on for the ride.

K.A. Merikan have a few sweeter M/M romances as well, but they specialize in the dark, dirty, and dangerous side of M/M, full of bikers, bad boys, mafiosi, and scorching hot romance.

FUN FACTS!
- We're Polish
- We're neither sisters nor a couple
- Kat's fingers are two times longer than Agnes's.

e-mail: kamerikan@gmail.com

Post-Credit Scene (Miguel)

Miguel glanced at the lid of the coffin that would be left on the other side of their tunnel. It seemed that some people didn't understand that just because the tunnel had been out of use for a while, it wasn't fair game. Soon enough, Miguel would revive the trade route with the USA. For now, the coffin should serve as enough of a warning that it was *Los Sepultureros* territory.

Miguel took a deep breath, caressing the grip of the gun at his belt. But there would be no need for bullets tonight. While efficient in a fight, blades were so much more effective at breeding terror.

He turned around to face the man kneeling between two of Miguel's own. His mouth had been beaten into steaks, but Miguel could still see there was a natural grace to the now swollen lips.

He picked up the sharpened machete from a bench nearby and walked up to the man, trying not to admire the Colombian's thick biceps, or the way his pecs bulged because his arms were tied back. In his line of work, none of that mattered.

Miguel used the tip of the blade to force the man's chin up. "Do you know who this tunnel belongs to?"

The swollen lips moved but didn't utter a sound. The man's eyes, dark and expressive, rose to meet Miguel's, surprisingly making his heart skip a beat. "It looked deserted," he said and spat out some blood. What game would he play now? Did he hope Miguel would let him go?

Miguel's gaze slipped to the caiman tail peeking out from under the man's belt above his hip. "Pull down his pants," he said to one of his men, and placed the machete against the captive's throat as soon as he started to struggle. "I can make it take days. Or I can make it quick," he whispered.

The man's lips quivered, and for the first time Miguel managed to make his facade crack. "I can pass a message from you."

So he wanted to live after all. "This is a mark of the Moreno cartel, is it not?" Miguel asked and pointed to the caiman tattoo on the man's bared thigh. The beast's head reached almost to the knee. "We don't negotiate with the Morenos."

He slit the man's throat in one quick move to spare the poor bastard agony. No matter how handsome he was, or how thick and muscular his thighs were, he would not escape his fate.

His head would pass the message.

Hop on the bitch seat and go for a dangerous ride

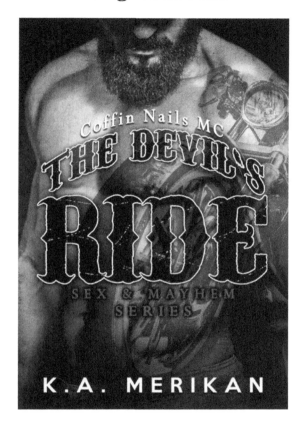

The Devil's Ride
K. A. Merikan

— You don't fuck with the club president's son. —

Tooth. Vice President of the Coffin Nails Motorcycle Club. On a neverending quest for vengeance. The last thing he needs is becoming a permanent babysitter for a male hooker.
Lucifer. Fallen. Lost. Alone.

After a childhood filled with neglect and abuse, followed by his mother's suicide, Lucifer set out into the world alone. There was nothing for him out there other than taking it one day at a time. As the bastard son of the Coffin Nails club president, Lucifer never got much fatherly love. So when the Nails show up at the strip joint Lucifer works in, the last thing he expects is to be put in the custody of Tooth, the Nails Vice President famous for his gruesome interrogation techniques. The man proves to be the sexiest beast Lucifer has ever met. He's also older, straight, and an itch Luci can't ever scratch.

Tooth's life came to a halt twelve years ago. His lover got brutally murdered, police never found the perpetrators, and all leads were dead ends. To find peace and his own justice, Tooth joined the Coffin Nails, but years on, he's gotten nowhere with the case, yet still lives on with the burning fire for revenge.
Babysitting a deeply scarred teenager with a talent for disappearing is the last thing on his bucket list. He promised himself to never get attached to someone like him again. To make sure the openly gay boy is safe in the clubhouse, Tooth is stuck keeping an eye on him. The big, blue, attention seeking gaze is drawing Tooth in, but

fucking the president's son is a complete no-go, even when both their feelings go beyond lust.

What Tooth doesn't know is that Lucifer might hold the key to the closure Tooth so desperately needs.

WARNING Contains adult content: a gritty storyline, sex, explicit language, violence and abuse. Inappropriate use of dental tools and milk.

POSSIBLE SPOILERS:

Themes: Prostitution, Outlaw Motorcycle Club, organized crime, homophobia, family issues, coming out, discipline/punishment, organ snatching, hurt-comfort, age gap

Genre: contemporary gay erotic dark romance

Length: ~ 125,000 words (Standalone novel, no cliffhanger.)

Made in the USA
Las Vegas, NV
07 June 2021

24315064R10223